Ama Ata Aidoo, one of Africa's leading feminist writers, was born and educated in Ghana. She has taught at universities in Ghana, Tanzania and Kenya and was Minister of Education in Ghana. Her concerns as a writer, a woman and a teacher of literature have encouraged her to travel and lecture extensively in Africa, Europe and North America.

Her first novel *Our Sister Killjoy,* a collection of short stories, *No Sweetness Here* and her plays *The Dilemma of a Ghost* and *Anowa* are all published in the LONGMAN AFRICAN WRITERS series.

NO SWEETNESS HERE

Ama Ata Aidoo

Longman

Everything Counts was first published in 'Zuka', *In the Cutting of a Drink* in 'Flamingo', *The Message in Writing Today in Africa* (an anthology, Penguin), *Certain Winds from the South* and *No Sweetness Here* in 'Black Orpheus', *A Gift from Somewhere* in 'Journal of the New African Literature', *The Late Bud* in 'Okyeame', *Other Versions* in 'The New African'. *Two Sisters* was first recorded as a short radio play by the The Transcription Centre, London.

Longman Group Limited,
Longman House, Burnt Mill, Harlow,
Essex CM20 2JE, England
and Associated Companies throughout the world.

First published 1970
First published as Longman African Classic 1988
First published as Longman African Writers 1994

Printed in China
PPC/01

ISBN 0 582 26456.1

Contents

For those without whom living would have
been almost impossible

Everything Counts

She used to look at their serious faces and laugh silently to herself. They meant what they were saying. The only thing was that loving them all as sister, lover and mother, she also knew them. She knew them as intimately as the hems of her dresses. That it was so much easier for them to talk about the beauty of being oneself. Not to struggle to look like white girls. Not straightening one's hair. And above all, not to wear the wig.

The wig. Ah, the wig. They say it is made of artificial fibre. Others swear that if it is not gipsy hair, then it is Chinese. Extremists are sure they are made from the hairs of dead white folk – this one gave her nightmares, for she had read somewhere, a long time ago, about Germans making lampshades out of Jewish people's skins. And she would shiver for all the world to see. At other times, when her world was sweet like when she and Fiifi were together, the pictures that came into her mind were not so terrible. She would just think of the words of that crazy *highlife* song and laugh. The one about the people at home scrambling to pay exorbitant prices for second-hand clothes from America . . . and then as a student of economics, she would also try to remember some other truths she knew about Africa. Second-rate experts giving first-class dangerous advice. Or expressing uselessly fifth-rate opinions. Second-hand machinery from someone else's junkyard.

Snow-ploughs for tropical farms.

Outmoded tractors.

Discarded aeroplanes.

And now, wigs – made from other people's unwanted hair.

At this point, tough though she was, tears would come into her eyes. Perhaps her people had really missed the boat of original thinking after all? And if Fiifi asked her what was wrong, she explained, telling the same story every time. He always shook his head and laughed at her, which meant that in the end, she would laugh with him.

At the beginning, she used to argue with them, earnestly. 'But what has wearing wigs got to do with the revolution?' 'A lot sister,' they would say. 'How?' she would ask, struggling not to understand.

'Because it means that we have no confidence in ourselves.' Of course, she understood what they meant.

'But this is funny. Listen, my brothers, if we honestly tackled the problems facing us, we wouldn't have the time to worry about such trifles as wigs.'

She made them angry. Not with the mild displeasure of brothers, but with the hatred of wounded lovers. They looked terrible, their eyes changing, turning red and warning her that if she wasn't careful, they would destroy her. Ah, they frightened her a lot, quite often too. Especially when she thought of what filled them with that kind of hatred.

This was something else. She had always known that in her society men and women had had more important things to do than fight each other in the mind. It was not in school that she had learnt this. Because you know, one did not really go to school to learn about Africa. . . . As for this, what did the experts call it? War of the sexes? Yes, as for this war of the sexes, if there had been any at all in the old days among her people, they could not possibly have been on such a scale. These days, any little 'No' one says to a boy's 'Yes' means one is asking for a battle. O, there just are too many problems.

As for imitating white women, mm, what else can one

do, seeing how some of our brothers behave? The things one has seen with one's own eyes. The stories one has heard. About African politicians and diplomats abroad. But then, one has enough troubles already without treading on big toes.

After a time, she gave up arguing with them, her brothers. She just stated clearly that the wig was an easy way out as far as she was concerned. She could not afford to waste that much time on her hair. The wig was, after all, only a hat. A turban. Would they please leave her alone? What was more, if they really wanted to see a revolution, why didn't they work constructively in other ways for it?

She shut them up. For they knew their own weaknesses too, that they themselves were neither prepared nor ready to face the realities and give up those aspects of their personal dream which stood between them and the meaningful actions they ought to take. Above all, she was really beautiful and intelligent. They loved and respected her.

She didn't work that hard and she didn't do brilliantly in the examinations. But she passed and got the new degree. Three months later, she and Fiifi agreed that it would be better for them to get married among a foreign people. Weddings at home were too full of misguided foolishness. She flew home, a month after the wedding, with two suitcases. The rest of their luggage was following them in a ship. Fiifi would not be starting work for about three months so he had branched off to visit some one or two African countries.

Really, she had found it difficult to believe her eyes. How could she? From the air-stewardesses to the grade-three typists in the offices, every girl simply wore a wig. Not cut discreetly short and disguised to look like her own hair as she had tried to do with hers. But blatantly, aggressively, crudely. Most of them actually had masses of flowing curls falling on their shoulders. Or huge affairs piled on top of their heads.

Even that was not the whole story. Suddenly, it seemed as if all the girls and women she knew and remembered as having smooth black skins had turned light-skinned. Not uniformly. Lord, people looked as though a terrible plague was sweeping through the land. A plague that made funny patchworks of faces and necks.

She couldn't understand it so she told herself she was dreaming. Maybe there was a simple explanation. Perhaps a new god had been born while she was away, for whom there was a new festival. And when the celebrations were over, they would remove the masks from their faces and those horrid-looking things off their heads.

A week went by and the masks were still on. More than once, she thought of asking one of the girls she had been to school with, what it was all about. But she restrained herself. She did not want to look more of a stranger than she already felt – seeing she was also the one *black* girl in the whole city. . . .

Then the long vacation was over and the students of the national university returned to the campus. O . . . she was full of enthusiasm, as she prepared her lectures for the first few weeks. She was going to tell them what was what. That as students of economics, their role in nation-building was going to be crucial. Much more than big-mouthed, big-living politicians, they could do vital work to save the continent from the grip of its enemies. If only for a little while: and blah, blah, blah.

Meanwhile, she was wearing her own hair. Just lightly touched to make it easier to comb. In fact, she had been doing that since the day they got married. The result of some hard bargaining. The final agreement was that any day of the year, she would be around with her own hair. But she could still keep that thing by for emergencies. Anyhow, the first morning in her life as a lecturer arrived. She met the students at eleven. They numbered between fifteen and twenty. About a third of them were girls. She had not seen them walk in and so could not tell whether they had beautiful bodies or not. But lord, were their faces pretty? So she wondered as she stared, open-mouthed at them, how she would have felt if she had been a young male. She smiled momentarily at herself for the silliness of the idea. It was a mistake to stop the smile. She should just have gone on and developed it into a laugh. For close at its heels was a jealousy so big, she did not know what to do with it. Who were these girls? Where had they come from to confront her with their youth? The fact that she wasn't really that much older than any of them did not matter. Nor even that she recognised one or two who had come as first years, when she was in her fifth year. She remembered them quite clearly. Little skinny greenhorns scuttling timidly away to do her bidding as the house-prefect. Little frightened lost creatures from villages and developing slums who had come to this citadel of an alien culture to be turned into ladies. . . .

And yet she was there as a lecturer. Talking about one thing or another. Perhaps it was on automation as the newest weapon from the industrially developed countries against the wretched ones of the earth. Or something of the sort. Perhaps since it was her first hour with them, she was only giving them general ideas on what the course was about.

Anyhow, her mind was not there with them. Look at that one, Grace Mensah. Poor thing. She had cried and cried when she was being taught to use knives and forks. And now look at her.

It was then she noticed the wigs. All the girls were wearing them. The biggest ones she had seen so far. She felt very hot and she who hardly ever sweated, realised that not only were her hands wet, but also streams of water were pouring from the nape of her neck down her spine. Her brassière felt too tight. Later, she was thankful that black women have not yet learnt to faint away in moments of extreme agitation.

But what frightened her was that she could not stop the voice of one of the boys as it came from across the sea, from the foreign land, where she had once been with them.

'But Sissie, look here, we see what you mean. Except that

it is not the real point we are getting at. Traditionally, women from your area might have worn their hair long. However, you've still got to admit that there is an element in this wig-wearing that is totally foreign. Unhealthy.'

Eventually, that first horrid lecture was over. The girls came to greet her. They might have wondered what was wrong with this new lecturer. And so probably did the boys. She was not going to allow that to worry her. There always is something wrong with lecturers. Besides, she was going to have lots of opportunities to correct what bad impressions she had created. . . .

The next few weeks came and went without changing anything. Indeed, things got worse and worse. When she went home to see her relatives, the questions they asked her were so painful she could not find answers for them.

'What car are you bringing home, Sissie? We hope it is not one of those little coconut shells with two doors, heh? . . . And oh, we hope you brought a refrigerator. Because you simply cannot find one here these days. And if you do, it costs so much. . . .' How could she tell them that cars and fridges are ropes with which we are hanging ourselves? She looked at their faces and wondered if they were the same ones she had longed to see with such pain, when she was away. Hmm, she began to think she was in another country. Perhaps she had come down from the plane at the wrong airport? Too soon? Too late? Fiifi had not arrived in the country yet. That might have had something to do with the sudden interest she developed in the beauty contest. It wasn't really a part of her. But there it was. Now she was eagerly buying the morning papers to look out for the photos of the winners from the regions. Of course, the winner on the national level was going to enter for the Miss Earth title.

She knew all along that she would go to the stadium. And she did not find it difficult to get a good seat.

She should have known that it would turn out like that. She had not thought any of the girls beautiful. But her opinions were not really asked for, were they? She just recalled, later, that all the contestants had worn wigs except one. The winner. The most light-skinned of them all. No, she didn't wear a wig. Her hair, a mulatto's, quite simply, quite naturally, fell in a luxuriant mane on her shoulders. . . .

She hurried home and into the bathroom where she vomited – and cried and cried and vomited for what seemed to her to be days. And all this time, she was thinking of how right the boys had been. She would have liked to run to where they were to tell them so. To ask them to forgive her for having dared to contradict them. They had been so very right. Her brothers, lovers and husbands. But nearly all of them were still abroad. In Europe, America or some place else. They used to tell her that they found the thought of returning home frightening. They would be frustrated. . . .

Others were still studying for one or two more degrees. A Master's here. A Doctorate there. . . . That was the other thing about the revolution.

For Whom Things Did Not Change

Knock . . . knock . . . knock . . .

'A-ha?'

'Massa, Massa, Massa . . .'

'A-ha? A-ha? A-ha?'

'You say make I com' wake you. Make I com' wake you for eight. Eight o'clock 'e reach.'

'Okay, thank you.'

Knock . . . knock . . . knock . . .

'A-ha?'

'Massa, Massa, Massa.'

'A-ha? A-ha? A-ha?'

'You say make I com' wake you. Make I com' wake you for eight. Eight o'clock reach long time.'

'Okay, thank you, Zirigu.'

. . . . .

'I think this is a strange one. This young master. You can see he is very tired. But he insists that he should be woken up at eight o'clock. And I wonder what he thinks he can do in a place like this from that hour. He must be one of these people who don't know how to rest. Even when they are scholars.'

'Zirigu my husband, sometimes you talk as though it is not yourself speaking but some child. Do you think people are all the same because they all went to school and are big masters?'

'Setu, you know I do not think anything like that. But you must agree that after all these years, I can say something about the type of human beings who come here. This young one seems different.'

'And what is the difference?'

'Ah-ah. He does not drink at all. He has never asked me to serve him with anything strong or buy him any from the town.'

'Maybe he is a Believer?'

'No-no. He is from the coast. And I have not met many big men from those areas who are Moslems. But that is not what I mean really. Most of the Believers from your area who are big men are not different from the others. Yes, they do not drink – some do even that – but then, that is all. They are all like the others.'

'As for me, what I have just noticed is that he did not bring a woman with him.'

'*Eh-heh!* Ah Setu, so you know what I mean?'

'What do I know?'

'That this one is different?'

'Maybe. He certainly did not bring one of those nasty pieces with their heads swollen outside and inside like the meat and feathers of overfed turkeys. Ah, Allah!'

'What is it, Setu?'

'Zirigu, I am thinking of those girls.'

'My wife, it is because you have nothing to do. Are you not making kaffa to take to the market today?'

'No. I have no meal left. And I thought my ears were aching too much last night. Allah knows I have debts like everyone else. But since they will not come and kill me if I do not pay them this morning, I think I shall rest today from carrying agidi; and maybe go and see the doctor. After all, how much does one make?'

'Hm, hm! And so this is why you have got all this time and mouth to talk about those girls?'

'Yes. And I think they are a pain. Oh you do not think so,

B

my husband? Do not shake your head with that glint in your eyes as though I a.n mad for talking like this. Do they not come from homes? Have they not got fathers and mothers?'

'What are you saying, Setu?'

'I'm saying, Zirigu, that there must be something wrong when young girls who have seen their blood not many moons gone, go sleeping with men who are old enough to be their fathers, and sometimes their grandfathers. And no one is saying anything. Look, look, ho, ho, look. Everyone sees them on the land, and no one says anything.'

'But the men are big men. They have the money. They have all the nice things, like big cars and the false hair which come from the white man's land. And the little girls sleep with them because they like these things.'

'But what do the mothers of these little girls say?'

'What can they say? Some of them do not even know that their children are like this. They live in the villages and when their daughters take good things home, they think it is because they are ladies and have got them all with the pay from their work. Some clans learn from the wayside how their daughters are living in the cities. But they are afraid to say anything.'

'But why should anyone fear her own daughter?'

'Because she has got a big mouth from what she has seen.'

'Allah!'

'But my wife, that is not all. Sometimes they are not afraid of the daughter herself but the big man. Because he has big power and he can ruin them if they do not give him what he wants – their daughter. And Setu my wife, such things have been known to happen.'

'O Allah, what times we live in. What rulers we have. How can men behave in this way who are our lords?'

'Mm. Was it different in the old days, Setu my wife? Did not the lords take the little girls they liked among the women?'

'Zirigu, I do not know. I'm sure you are right. But Allah has made it so. All women are slaves of our lords. These new masters are not Believers. It is not Allah's will. And they are shameful acts.'

'But my wife, what are you saying? When a man is your lord, he is your lord. And he behaves like your lord. How else should he behave? And how are we to say that new lords must not do what old ones did? When the white men were here, did they not do the same? Sleep with very little girls, oh, such little girls?'

'I do not know, Zirigu, I do not know, my husband. . . . Yes, I saw some of these things, when those people were here. But listen, my husband. If one day when you are not looking, a man comes and takes your farmhouse or your kraal, and he begins doing all the things a good man should not do; sells all the yams in your barns without leaving any for planting; boils your eggs as soon as they have been laid and does not spare one for a single hen to hatch; gives great feasts to all his family and all his friends, with your lambs and calves; and generally carries on in such a way that your heart hurts as though it is falling into your bowels every time you look on; and yet you are not able to do anything for many many years, but then one day, thanks to Allah, you get your farmhouse or your kraal back, what then do you do, my husband? So, from the first day, you too begin to kill or sell what is left of your old and miserable cows, sheep and chickens? And if an egg is just laid, you boil it right away, and generally continue the destruction of your property which that robber had started?

'I do not know, Zirigu, but it is certainly good that all my children are boys. It is good I never had a daughter. Because if I had had a daughter, and I knew a big man was doing unholy things with her, then with a matchet in my own hand, I would have cut that big man to pieces myself!'

'Oh, Jesu preserve my soul. O Jesu! Setu, what kind of talk is this? You must pray more than everybody else on Friday for these foul words.'

'Yes, my husband. Let us thank Allah for what he gives. As I say, it is good I have no daughter.'

'Maybe it is better that all mothers are not like you. Otherwise the land would be flowing with the blood of all the big men.'

'And who shall lament to see the blood of evil men flow?'

'But since the masters of the land are always bad, or they have been bad for a long, long time, do you not know that people would not like to see the new ones die? They, like the daughters, also come from homes. Homes where people eat well because they know the big men. Do you think that everybody in the land is like you and me? No, my wife. There are people who will lament to see a big man killed. Because knowing a big man means having someone in the town who has a huge house. It means . . . but it is enough, my wife. The big men we saw yesterday were bad. These we see today are worse. And be sure that those of tomorrow will be like those of yesterday and today put together.'

'Stop, stop. Stop, Zirigu. You make me feel cold all of a sudden.'

'Women! Were you not the same Setu who, a while ago, was all ready to cut someone down with a matchet?'

'But what does one do?'

'How do I know? I serve them the drinks they ask, cook their meals if they want me to, make their beds, sweep their rooms, and more. And if they bring their women, look after them too. You know, my wife, as well as I, that that has been my life. As for the families of those things – as you call the little girls – that, my wife, I do not know.'

'Yes, Zirigu, now that you say it, I remember that not all of them, I mean their mothers, even disapprove.'

'Ah . . .'

'Look at that Munatu, girl.'

'Ah . . .'

'Do you know how those uncles of hers could have found the money to build that mansion?'

'Ah . . .'

'Twelve rooms, they say it has. Twelve rooms. And many pipes for government water in the house. And those who have been inside and peeped into some of the rooms, say that one must see them with one's own eyes to believe that there are women and men who have such rooms to sleep in.'

'Ah . . .'

'And so people try to profit by their daughters by giving them to the big men? And they sometimes even encourage them . . .?'

'Ah . . .'

'And if they are like that Munatu's mother, they come to the market-place telling everybody what and what my lord master is doing and saying . . .?'

'Ah . . .'

'When you know that the man will leave your daughter when he's tired of her or he sees another girl who is more beautiful?'

'Ah . . .'

'I spit upon such big men! I spit upon such mothers! I spit upon such daughters!'

'My wife, now that you are feeling better inside, I will leave you and go to wake up my young master.'

'And I am getting ready to go and see the doctor about my ears.'

. . . . .

Knock, knock, knock.

'Massa, Massa, Massa . . .'

'Y-e-s?'

'Massa, Massa, Massa.'

'Y-e-s?'

'You say: "Zirigu, wake me for eight." At eight, I com', you no wake. At 'a pas' eight, I com', you no wake. Now, you go wake because 'e be nine o'clock.'

'But Zirigu, the door was not locked. You could have come and dragged me out!'

13

'Ah, Massa, you make me laugh. Me, Zirigu, com' where yourself sleep com' pull you?'

'Why not?'

'I no fit.'

'Okay, we shall not argue further about it. Thank you for managing to get me up at last.'

'But weyting you think you fit do for this place so you wake up early so?'

'Nothing really. You are right. But I just want to keep on waking up early. It will be bad for me to get used to sleeping late. I should try to get up much earlier than this anyway, but I feel very tired so I am going slow.'

'But why? For Massa, you fit sleep late. Weyting you go do for office? Like me, I wake early, yes. But you, no!'

'Zirigu, not all educated people work in offices.'

'No?'

'No. And one of these days, I think I'm going to tell you why I don't want to get used to sleeping late.'

Christ I can feel it coming.

'I don' make you coffee for long time. Maybe now, 'e be cold. I go stand am for stove.'

'Take your time, man. I'll wash myself and then come and fetch it. Please Zirigu, I've said that you shouldn't wait on me hand and foot.'

'Massa!'

'Well, I don't see why you should. You are old enough to be my father.'

'My white Massa!'

'And I am not a white man.'

'Massa!'

'Listen, the kitchen is your territory and I shall not come and mess around there. Besides, I am a guest here so there are things I know I should not do. But I'll be damned if you are going to get me to behave as though I were some accursed invalid or something.'

'Lord, lord, Massa, such talk no fit for your mout'. I like

yourself so you fit do weyting you like. The sun don' com' up long time. I wan' go get good meat for you so I must hurry to market before twelve. Tell me what you sabe for breakfast make I do. Omelette? Poached eggs. Fried egg on toast. Eggs and bacon. Orange juice . . .'

'Stop, Zirigu!'

'Why, Massa?'

'I'm not having any breakfast. Have you got fresh oranges?'

'No? . . . Yes, in my wife's kitchen. I go bring am for you.'

'I will pay for it.'

'No fear. When I go for market, I go buy you better. Plenty Massas only drink orange juice for the bottle.'

'I'm mad but I think I'm sane enough not to drink pressed, homogenised, dehydrated, re-crystallised, thawed, diluted and heaven-knows-what-else orange juice, imported from countries where oranges do not grow, when I can eat oranges.'

'What you say, Massa?'

'Never mind, Zirigu.'

. . . . .

'If you ask them, why ten years after independence, some of us still have to be slaves, they say you are nuts to ask questions like that.'

'You are getting your definitions wrong. By what stretch of imagination does a steward-boy or a housemaid become a slave?'

'Was it not enough that whole sections of us were bred so that all they could do was to minister to the needs of white men and women? Doing soul-killing jobs? Do they have to do them for us too?'

'What are you talking about? It partially solves the unemployment problem. Or minimises it, at least. Can you imagine what would happen if all the house-boys and housemaids were not doing what they are doing?'

'How about the pay?'

'How about it?'

'And anyway, most of them, especially the house-girls, are people's relatives . . .'

'Problems are solved only when you tackle them in all seriousness.'

'Eh – captain, another beer, please.'

.   .   .   .   .

'Massa, I must go to market now. I say I wan' get good meat. What you go chop?'

'I'll eat anything you cook.'

'Massa, you tink you go like fried fillet of calf? Or a braised lamb liver? Yes, here a good one. An escalope of veal with onions and fried potatoes.'

'Zirigu, whom did you say you were going to cook for?'

'Yourself, Massa.'

'But that is not the food I eat.'

'But 'e be white man chop.'

'Zirigu, I no be white man. And that is the second time this morning I've told you that. And if you do it again, I'll pack up and leave.'

Jesus, isn't there anywhere on this bloody land one can have some blinking peace? Jesus . . . Lord I am sweating . . . God . . . see how I'm sweating. Jesus see how I'm sweating.

'Massa, why you sweat so?'

'It gets hot here early.'

'Yes, make I open them windows.'

Jesus!

'Massa, I beg. Don't make so. I no wan' vex you. This here chop, 'e be white man's chop. 'E be the chop I cook for all massas, for fifteen years. The Ministars, the party people who stay for here, the big men from the Ministries, the Unifartisy people, the big offisars from the army and police. . . . 'E be same chop, they chop, this white man chop.'

'Zirigu, can't you cook any food of the land? Don't they sell things in that market with which you could make the food of this land?'

'Yes. But I no fit cook your kind food. No, I no fit cook food of your area.'

'How about the food of your area? Your food?'

'I no fit cook that.'

'Jesus. And you've been a cook steward here for all these years?'

'Yes. But Massa. I know my job. Massa, don't com' make trouble for me. O, look, my hair don' gone white. I no fit find another job. Who go look for my pickin'? I know how to cook, Massa, white man's chop.'

'That's the problem. Listen. God forbid you should even think I'll make trouble for you. In fact, that is not what I am talking about. But I'm just about beginning to understand. Gradually. You went into training, qualified and have been gaining experience all these years as a cook for white people. You do not know how to cook the food of the land because it is your food. And you are a man. And a man normally does not cook. But you cook the white man's chop because that is white man's chop, your job, not food. Or . . .'

'Massa, God knows I know my job.'

'Of course! As a man of the land and your wife's husband you are a man and therefore you do not cook. As a black man facing a white man, his servant, you are a black, not a man, therefore you can cook.'

'Massa, Massa. You call me woman? I swear, by God, Massa, this na tough. I no be woman. God forbid!'

'Ah, Zirigu. I am only thinking something out. Ah . . . God is above, I no call you woman. Soon I go talk all for you.'

'But Massa, you no know. Don't call me woman.'

'No, I will not.'

. . . . .

When a black man is with his wife who cooks and chores for him, he is a man. When he is with white folk for whom he cooks and chores, he is a woman. Dear Lord, what then is a black man who cooks and chores for black men?

. . . . .

'Listen Zirigu, does the Mother your wife know how to cook the food of the land?'

'Yes. But not of your area.'

'No. Of your area.'

'Yes!'

'Okay, can you charge me the normal rate for supper and ask the Mother to count my mouth in for the supper this evening?'

'W-h-a-t? What you say Massa? What?'

'I say, Zirigu, can the Mother count my stomach in for the evening's meal?'

'Massa. I no wan' play?'

'I am not playing.'

'Heh? God. You mean you go eat *tuo*?'

'Why not? At home I eat *banku*. Isn't it the same? One of rice, the other of corn? Aren't they all farina? Semolina? Whatever?'

'Massa, I no wan' trouble.'

'What kind of trouble do you think you are going to get? Perhaps you think I'm a child?'

'I mean your tommy.'

'What about my tummy? Do you get tummy trouble when you eat your wife's food? What are you saying, man? And anyway, I can look after myself in that kind of way. I am a medical doctor, you know.'

'I know, young Massa. I say, this man look small but him too, 'e be big man. . . . But you go chop, *tuo*?'

'Yes.'

'As for you self!'

. . . . . .

'S-e-t-u! S-e-t-u! S-e-t-u-e-e-e! Where is that woman? S-e-t-u!'

'What is it, Zirigu? I was in the bath. Did I not tell you I was getting ready to go and see the doctor?'

'Listen, my wife. I never heard a story like this before.'

'Well, I haven't either. But how can I know for sure when you are not telling it?'

'Hmm . . . S-e-t-u . . . how shall I begin?'

'Perhaps we better wait until this evening, since I have no time to . . ."

'No . . . no . . . no! Hmm Setu, the young Master says he does not want to eat this evening.'

'And is that a story?'

'But that is not all.'

'Well, just tell me the rest.'

'He says he will eat some of your food this evening!'

'*H-e-e-eh!* Allah. Zirigu, it is not true.'

'He is in there, sitting by the table eating his orange. Go and ask him.'

'*E-e-e* Allah. Zirigu, do you think this boy is right in his head? '

'Setu, I am not sure. Setu, really, I am not sure. But his eyes do not rove so even if he is ill, it is not serious yet. He talks funny sometimes though. But I don't know. Yes, he says he will eat *tuo* and that I can charge it to his general bill. Lord, in all the twenty or so years I've been general keeper and cook for this Rest House, I have not encountered a thing like this, eh Setu, have we?'

'No, my husband. But times do change.'

'Yes, you are right, my wife. So after you've been to see the doctor, go straight to the market, buy some very good vegetables, fresh greens, okro . . .'

'Zirigu, now you better shut up your mouth before you annoy me. Since when did you start teaching me how to do my marketing? This is my job. A woman's job.'

'Yes, Setu.'

. . . . .

'Massa . . .'

'Zirigu, how often should I tell you not to call me that?'

'But you are my massa!'

19

'I am nothing of the sort. I was born not six years when you were going away to fight. How can I be your massa? And this is a Government Rest House, not mine, I am not even your employer. So how can I be your Master?'

'But all the other Massas, they don't say make I no call them so?'

'Hell they don't. That is their business. Not mine. My name is Kobina, not Master.'

'Kob-i-n-a . . . K-o . . . Massa, I beg, I no fit call you that. I simple no fit.'

'Too bad. That means I'll have to leave here too, earlier than I had hoped.'

'I dey go for town buy eggs, soap and some more yama-yama for the house. Make I buy you something?'

'Oranges, more fruit.'

'No drink?'

'Christ, no. Ah, yes, perhaps *pito*?'

'As for you, Massa self! You wan' drink *pito*?'

'I want to taste it. I understand one can get it real fresh around here. And I want to taste it. Haven't drunk any before. Is it good? Does it make one drunk?'

'Yes. Very good. No, 'e no make one drunk. Not too mus.'

. . . . .

There should be something said for open spaces. And yet what? Nothing. It should be possible that if one can see several miles out in front, into the distance, one should also be able to see into time. All this breeze. These clear skies. Fresh breezes should blow the nonsense from our souls, the stupidities from our minds and lift the veils off our eyes. But it's not like that. It's never been like that. There are as many cramped souls around here as there are among the dwellers down there. In the thick woods and on the beaches. Like everyone else, those poets were wrong. They lied. But Zirigu is alright. And so is his wife, the Mother. They are alright, like all of us. Alright, I only hope that one day, they will learn that we are all the same.

One day, when I was tiny and I went to spend the holidays with Nanaa I pattered behind her to the farms. I can hear her now. 'Now, my young scholar, do not follow me: the farm is for seasoned ones like me. Hmm, how can I answer if anything goes wrong?' . . . And on and on and on. But I went all the same. All I remember is that everything just smelt like it had never done before – or since. Good. Good. Good. It was not just the smell of green leaves. Green leaves and wet earth, fire spilling from a gun and fresh-spilt human blood smell different, to be sure. At Nanaa's farm, things smelt good. All the vegetables were there. Anyway, we had been hardly an hour there when I began to holler for food. Nanaa muttered something about obviously that day on the farm going to be devoted to eating. And then she dashed behind some bush and came out with this huge yam. I mean it was big. A giant. Of course when you are young, even little things have a way of gaining size in your eyes, but this yam was big. She removed the little kerosene tin pot – they used to sell them for fourpence and sixpence in the market – from its hiding place and poured some water into it. At the sight of the yam my throat had begun doing what throats do. She had said she would cut just a little bit of the tip and cook it for me because she herself was not hungry, and anyway, yam is no good cold. All this sounded fine to me. It just meant that when she came to cook hers, I would have more yam to eat. I already knew that when yam is good it is white or whitish-yellow or something. But when Nanaa cut the piece it was brown. And she said something about that piece being no good. She cut another. It was the same. She cut another piece, it was not different. And she cut another and yet another. They were all the same. Somewhere at the middle, Nanaa looked at the yam and said, 'Yam, you really are wicked. Why didn't you leave a piece of yourself good when you were going bad, so I could have cooked you for my little master?' But I told her to cut on, for I still hoped that all was not lost. So she turned the remaining piece round and cut out the head. It was brown and soft. I threw myself into the sand and dust of the farm and screamed. She cooked me a fresh piece from the barn, but I refused to eat it. It was only later when she boiled some for herself and by which time I was too hungry to refuse anyway, that I ate. And I have never forgotten about that yam. What was it that ate it up so completely? And yet, here I go again, old yam has to rot in order that new yam can grow. Where is the earth? Who is going to do the planting? Certainly not us – too full with drink, eyes clouded in smoke, and heads full of women . . . and our hearts desiring only nonsensical articles from someone else's factory. . . .

There was an air of festivity at the Rest House because I had said I was going to eat what Zirigu and his wife ate. The woman came to let me know, with the few words of my language she knew, that I should have given her adequate warning so she could have feasted me properly. I said that was okay because there was another day coming. Zirigu laid the table and when I told him that he should not give me a fork and a knife because I was going to eat with hands and that I only needed a spoon to scoop down the soup, he opened his mouth wide. When I was eating, both of them came to watch me. The food was alright. Of course, it tasted strange like anything else you are not used to. I could detect a not-too-familiar seasoning here, a foreign spice there. But on the whole there was nothing in the strangeness of it that I thought one could not get used to. I have eaten stranger meals. Zirigu let me know of just one anxiety he had. That my bowels would run in the night. Later, he brought the *pito*. I asked him to sit down and drink with me. He attempted to protest. One doesn't drink with the master, you know. I assured him it was alright. The wine was good. It has a sweetness in it. As we drank, we talked. I told him more about myself. He seemed to understand and sympathise. When we were through with my bottle, he said that he was going to bring one of his own.

He did. Gradually the main part of the talking switched to him.

. . . . .

'My young Master, forgive me for still addressing you like this. But then, is there anything else I can do? At my age, it is too late for me to start being too familiar with my betters. No, no, don't say any more. You are a good, young man. I like you. But really, how can I call you this Kobina? Yes, in years you are a baby. You don't have to tell me that. Can I not see that for myself? I can see that for myself. But now, age alone does not mean much, not much. It is a long time since age lost weight. In the old days, when a person was one day older than you, you had to defer to him or the whole clan would let you know your actual self, an insignificant miserable worm! But when your age does not prevent you from washing the underclothes of a white woman whom you know to be much much younger than yourself, what then is age? Thank God, I stopped doing that a long time ago. As for the black men who became the new masters when the white men went, well, they do not seem to think much of age either. I will tell you something soon. But even in the old times, people said that just to be old in itself was nothing. One could be old wise or old foolish. They used to say that to travel then was the thing. Well, my young master, I, Zirigu, I have travelled some. As I told you, I am an Ex-Serviceman. Went to Burma – or some place like that. Seen the front. But now you tell me you know what it is to be a soldier because you went to the Congo with our boys. Then I shall not tell you about the front. But it was there I learnt about white people. Oh, my young Master, when they are hungry, they can fight for food, and cheat each other like anybody else. . . . Sometimes you put food there for some people who were away. And their friends would eat it. When those people came back and there was nothing, they beat you. Yes, maybe, they would argue with their own brothers, but it was us they beat up. Hah, what man has seen!

'Of course, some of us fought. That's how people died. Or lost legs and arms. And to this day that I am talking to you, my Master, I don't know whom we were there fighting and why.

'You know book, my young Master, so to be sure, you've read all about the ex-Servicemen and the promises and how nothing was done. A few months after we came back and found ourselves demobilised many of us started going to pieces. I was afraid of not having anything to do for my living. With my friend – he was Setu's brother – I left the Gold Coast. Where have I not been in West Africa? Togoland? Nigeria? Sa'Lo? But everywhere it was the same, there were always too many ex-Servicemen already without jobs. I tried peddling, bicycle repairing, carpentering. . . . It was the same; emptiness behind and emptiness before. We came back. But one thing I forgot to tell you. Before I went to the war I was selling yam in the big market in Takoradi. It was a good trade. And when I was just about to leave, I gave the little money I had saved to my own brother. My father's child. My mother's child. I said to him: "Buda, keep this for me. If they do not kill me and I come back, I will still trade in yam. And maybe we will do it together because it is a good trade." My Master, I will not talk too long. Buda is my own brother. He came after me one year and a half from the same womb. When I returned home from the wars, he had eaten the money. Married a wife with some of it, and the two of them had eaten the rest of my money. You people over there think that all of us over here are thieves and murderers or something. But listen, when I didn't take a knife and cut my brother down, I know I can never kill anybody else in cold blood as long as they call me Zirigu. In fact, that was one reason why I left this land with Setu's brother. And we came back after six years, with nothing. At that time, both of us thought we were already getting too old. We heard there was a place somewhere in the big city where other ex-Servicemen were training to be cooks, steward-boys and garden-boys. I talked it over with Setu's brother. He said, "Chah! Allah, I will not do it. You know, Zirigu, I have a hot heart in my chest. How can I serve another man? Cook? Steward-boy? Garden-boy? Chah. It all means that some fool who is big only because he is white or because he can read book will make me a dog. I will beat him or kill him and go to prison before I am awake." He went to prison later because they say he did other things. But I don't know. I think he was a good man. He said to me: "You, you are a cool one. It would be better for you to do that than wandering. Go and train." I did. I worked in white men's homes for about two years. Setu's brother was not finding things easy. One day he said, "Zirigu, you are a sober man. You must think of marrying. You are already too old." I said, "Yes. Maybe I will go home next Christmas and marry." He said, "You know my sister, Setu?" "Yes," I said. "Her husband died. She has one child, a son. You are not a Believer and my father's ghost will curse me for what I'm going to ask you to do. But you are a good man and she is a good woman. Marry Setu and look after her for me." My young Master, I met and married Setu. Her brother was right. She is a good woman. Like most of our women, she always believes in a woman having her own little money, so that she does not have to go to her husband for everything. On the coast, she mostly sold roasted plantains and groundnuts. Here, she makes *kaffa*.

'And how did I come here, you are asking me, my young Master? I will tell you. The last white master I served on the coast liked me very much. When he was going to go away for good, he told me not go too far away from the bungalow. In fact, that I should stay in the boys' quarters for the first two months after he was gone. That in the third month, a new master would come from their country. My old master was going to leave a recommendation with me for the new master so that he would employ me. I said, "Yes, Master." But just a few days before he left, he let me know that there was a Government Rest House attached to his office in this area. That the keeper of it was going away for some reason of his own. My master knew it had a better salary. He had recommended me for it. That's how I came here.

'Yes, my Master, that is more than ten years ago. At first, it was only white people who came here. Then a few black men began coming too. Now, *they* don't come any more – I mean the white men. How can I be sorry? Do I sound sorry? Between me and you, I can say that I don't know whether it has made much difference for me or not. Sometimes I am really glad when I think that our own people have done so well. About two years after the white people left, I stopped wearing the uniform. No one seemed to notice. Now I can feel the type of person a visitor is and then I may or may not even wait at table. But that is all, I am still Zirigu. I thank God that my little sons here seem to be doing well at school. I don't think I will have money to send them to college. But I will not grieve about that. Setu is a good wife. For the rest, I don't know. I have lived here for many years. It is the only home the children know. I hope that by the time I am too old to be the keeper here, the children too will be old enough to look after themselves.

'Master, I'm sure it is very late. After all that *tuo* and now the *pito*, I'm sure you need a long night's sleep. I only hope you will not have to get up to look after running bowels.

'Sleep well, my young Master.'

'No, neither of us is going to bed yet. No, not until you have told me the rest of the story you promised.'

'Weyting?'

'You said you were going to tell me something else soon.'

'Hah, I don't know. But listen, my young Master, this place was not like this when I first came here. There was only one block to this main house with two rooms, A and B. With this front room here where we are sitting now. It was later, the first year or two after we had the freedom that they built C and D, and the other kitchen. It has never been used – I mean the other kitchen. If it had been built in the days of the white people, someone might have brought his own cook here with him some time to use it. But our people do not care about that kind of thing. And there has always been me. When they decided to build the other block, they gave notice that for about six months, people should not come and stay. At the same time, they decided the boys' quarters looked too bad and that it should be renovated. So Setu and I thought that we would go home for a while, leaving the children to stay here with some sisters of Setu's. We did not want their schooling to be interrupted. Yes, they said they were going to make the boys' quarters new. The place has always been sufficient for me. Not only because there is an extra room for the children to sleep in, but there is also that land with it. Every year, I have cultivated the plots and harvested good cassava, millet, okra and even yams. My young Master, much of the time, the four of us live on what we earn from this earth. And then we keep what Setu and I make from other work for more important things. Like buying the children's books, their uniforms and paying their fees. In the years the children were going to school free, we put by the money from those things for other necessary expenses. Because, my Master, for people like us, money is never, never idle. Sometimes Setu and I wonder how God created the other people who have so much money that they can put some in a bank. And yet, we also know that even we are better off than so many of our friends and relatives. But I should not burden you with the troubles of my whole clan. What I was saying is that this place seemed sufficient for us. But still, when they said they were going to do something about it I hoped they would put in a good lavatory, like the water-closet, and give us good lights. Electric lights. Yes, my Master, the lavatory in the boys' quarters is the old pail and have you not noticed we use kerosene lamps? So I thought, "Zirigu, now you can really become something. When the white people were here, and they were our masters, it was only understandable that they should have electric lights and water-closets and give us, the boys, latrine pails and kerosene lamps. But now we are independent they are going to make this house new. My own people will give me a closet and an electric light." I did not tell my thoughts to Setu because I was afraid she would say that I wanted to have the same things as my betters. And this is not good since Allah wants us to be satisfied with our lot. She is a Moslem but I am not a Moslem. You people think all of us from the north are Moslems. It is because you do not know anything about the north. Later, I knew from Setu herself that in spite of Allah's wishes, she too had hoped for a water-closet and electric lights. But she had been afraid to discuss it with me because she thought I would have laughed at her. I asked the man who first told me about the work whether we could have a water-closet and electric lights. He said he was in charge of buying supplies and finding the people to come and do the work. "Yes," he said, "that should not be difficult." He didn't think it would add much to the cost of the work, especially as they had already counted in the boys' quarters. But he would have to discuss it with the real big men under whom he was working. He was sure they would consider it a small matter and even scold him for not going ahead with it without asking them before. But still . . . And when we came, what did we find? They had put fresh paint on the walls. They had repaired the steps leading to the rooms and they had made us a little verandah. But there were no electric lights and in the lavatory, no water-closet. I discovered they had taken away the old pail and given me a new one. Ah, my Master, I did not know I wanted these things so much until I knew I was not going to get them. They had taken the old pail and given me a new one. My own people who are big men do not think I should use these good things they use. Something went out of me then which has not returned since. I do not understand why I was so pained and angry, but I was. Setu told me that we deserved it for wanting to be like our betters. Allah had punished us. But I do not agree with her. I do want not to be like them . . . or like you. For over ten years, I had kept this place well. I know I had, otherwise why did they still keep me here? Being a keeper, cook-steward here is not a bad job. It is a good job, the type of small job which some big man would want to take and give to a poor and distant relative. And neither Setu nor I know any big men. So they have let us stay all these years because we kept the place well. I serve them well too. I do what they want. My hair is going grey. Is one or two electric bulbs too much to expect? At least, that would have meant not spending sixpences and shillings on kerosene. I have thought and thought and thought about it. I have never understood why. For a long time, I was drinking. I wanted to go away. I wanted to kill somebody. Any time I went to the office in town to get my pay and give my reports about the place, I felt like spitting into their eyes. Those scholars. But Setu talked to me. She said I was behaving like a child. That it is nothing. We should never forget who we are, that's all. Now the anger is gone, and I stay here. My young Master, what does "Independence" mean?'

In the Cutting of a Drink

I say, my uncles, if you are going to Accra and anyone tells you that the best place for you to drop down is at the Circle, then he has done you good, but . . . Hm . . . I even do not know how to describe it. . . .

'Are all these beings that are passing this way and that way human? Did men buy all these cars with money . . .?'

But my elders, I do not want to waste your time. I looked round and did not find my bag. I just fixed my eyes on the ground and walked on. . . . Do not ask me why. Each time I tried to raise my eyes, I was dizzy from the number of cars which were passing. And I could not stand still. If I did, I felt as if the whole world was made up of cars in motion. There is something somewhere, my uncles. Not desiring to deafen you with too long a story . . .

I stopped walking just before I stepped into the Circle itself. I stood there for a long time. Then a lorry came along and I beckoned to the driver to stop. Not that it really stopped.

'Where are you going?' he asked me.

'I am going to Mamprobi,' I replied. 'Jump in,' he said, and he started to drive away. Hm . . . I nearly fell down climbing in. As we went round the thing which was like a big bowl on a very huge stump of wood, I had it in mind to have a good look at it, and later Duayaw told me that it shoots water in the air . . . but the driver was talking to me, so I could not look at it properly. He told me he himself was not going to Ma-

mprobi but he was going to the station where I could take a
lorry which would be going there. . . .

Yes, my uncle, he did not deceive me. Immediately we
arrived at the station I found the driver of a lorry shouting
'Mamprobi, Mamprobi'. Finally when the clock struck about
two-thirty, I was knocking on the door of Duayaw. I did not
knock for long when the door opened. Ah, I say, he was fast
asleep, fast asleep I say, on a Saturday afternoon.

'How can folks find time to sleep on Saturday afternoons?'
I asked myself. We hailed each other heartily. My uncles,
Duayaw has done well for himself. His mother Nsedua is a
very lucky woman.

How is it some people are lucky with school and others are
not? Did not Mansa go to school with Duayaw here in this
very school which I can see for myself? What have we done
that Mansa should have wanted to stop going to school?

But I must continue with my tale. . . . Yes, Duayaw has
done well for himself. His room has fine furniture. Only it is
too small. I asked him why and he told me he was even lucky
to have got that narrow place that looks like a box. It is very
hard to find a place to sleep in the city. . . .

He asked me about the purpose of my journey. I told him
everything. How, as he himself knew, my sister Mansa had
refused to go to school after 'Klase Tri' and how my mother
had tried to persuade her to go . . .

My mother, do not interrupt me, everyone present here
knows you tried to do what you could by your daughter.

Yes, I told him how, after she had refused to go, we finally
took her to this woman who promised to teach her to keep
house and to work with the sewing machine . . . and how she
came home the first Christmas after the woman took her but
has never been home again, these twelve years.

Duayaw asked me whether it was my intention then to look
for my sister in the city. I told him yes. He laughed saying,
'You are funny. Do you think you can find a woman in this
place? You do not know where she is staying. You do not even

know whether she is married or not. Where can we find her
if someone big has married her and she is now living in one
of those big bungalows which are some ten miles from the
city?'

Do you cry 'My Lord', mother? You are surprised about
what I said about the marriage? Do not be. I was surprised
too, when he talked that way. I too cried 'My Lord' . . . Yes, I
too did, mother. But you and I have forgotten that Mansa
was born a girl and girls do not take much time to grow. We
are thinking of her as we last saw her when she was ten years
old. But mother, that is twelve years ago. . . .

Yes, Duayaw told me that she is by now old enough to
marry and to do something more than merely marry. I asked
him whether he knew where she was and if he knew whether
she had any children – 'Children?' he cried, and he started
laughing, a certain laugh. . . .

I was looking at him all the time he was talking. He told
me he was not just discouraging me but he wanted me to see
how big and difficult it was, what I proposed to do. I replied
that it did not matter. What was necessary was that even if
Mansa was dead, her ghost would know that we had not forgotten her entirely. That we had not let her wander in other
people's towns and that we had tried to bring her home. . . .

These are useless tears you have started to weep, my
mother. Have I said anything to show that she was dead?

Duayaw and I decided on the little things we would do the
following day as the beginning of our search. Then he gave me
water for my bath and brought me food. He sat by me while I
ate and asked me for news of home. I told him that his father
has married another woman and of how last year the *akatse*
spoiled all our cocoa. We know about that already. When I
finished eating, Duayaw asked me to stretch out my bones on
the bed and I did. I think I slept fine because when I opened
my eyes it was dark. He had switched on his light and there
was a woman in the room. He showed me her as a friend but I
think she is the girl he wants to marry against the wishes of

his people. She is as beautiful as sunrise, but she does not come from our parts. . . .

When Duayaw saw that I was properly awake, he told me it had struck eight o'clock in the evening and his friend had brought some food. The three of us ate together.

Do not say 'Ei', uncle, it seems as if people do this thing in the city. A woman prepares a meal for a man and eats it with him. Yes, they do so often.

My mouth could not manage the food. It was prepared from cassava and corn dough, but it was strange food all the same. I tried to do my best. After the meal, Duayaw told me we were going for a night out. It was then I remembered my bag. I told him that as matters stood, I could not change my cloth and I could not go out with them. He would not hear of it. 'It would certainly be a crime to come to this city and not go out on a Saturday night.' He warned me though that there might not be many people, or anybody at all, where we were going who would also be in cloth but I should not worry about that.

Cut me a drink, for my throat is very dry, my uncle. . . .

When we were on the street, I could not believe my eyes. The whole place was as clear as the sky. Some of these lights are very beautiful indeed. Everyone should see them . . . and there are so many of them! 'Who is paying for all these lights? I asked myself. I could not say that aloud for fear Duayaw would laugh.

We walked through many streets until we came to a big building where a band was playing. Duayaw went to buy tickets for the three of us.

You all know that I had not been to anywhere like that before. You must allow me to say that I was amazed. 'Ei, are all these people children of human beings? And where are they going? And what do they want?'

Before I went in, I thought the building was big, but when I went in, I realised the crowd in it was bigger. Some were in front of a counter buying drinks, others were dancing . . .

33

Yes, that was the case, uncle, we had gone to a place where they had given a dance, but I did not know.

Some people were sitting on iron chairs around iron tables. Duayaw told some people to bring us a table and chairs and they did. As soon as we sat down, Duayaw asked us what we would drink. As for me, I told him *lamlale* but his woman asked for 'Beer' . . .

Do not be surprised, uncles.

Yes, I remember very well, she asked for beer. It was not long before Duayaw brought them. I was too surprised to drink mine. I sat with my mouth open and watched the daughter of a woman cut beer like a man. The band had stopped playing for some time and soon they started again. Duayaw and his woman went to dance. I sat there and drank my *lamlale*. I cannot describe how they danced.

After some time, the band stopped playing and Duayaw and his woman came to sit down. I was feeling cold and I told Duayaw. He said, 'And this is no wonder, have you not been drinking this women's drink all the time?'

'Does it make one cold?' I asked him.

'Yes,' he replied. 'Did you not know that? You must drink beer.'

'Yes,' I replied. So he bought me beer. When I was drinking the beer, he told me I would be warm if I danced.

'You know I cannot dance the way you people dance,' I told him.

'And how do we dance?' he asked me.

'I think you all dance like white men and as I do not know how that is done, people would laugh at me,' I said. Duayaw started laughing. He could not contain himself. He laughed so much his woman asked him what it was all about. He said something in the white man's language and they started laughing again. Duayaw then told me that if people were dancing, they would be so busy that they would not have time to watch others dance. And also, in the city, no one cares if you dance well or not . . .

Yes, I danced too, my uncles. I did not know anyone, that is true. My uncle, do not say that instead of concerning myself with the business for which I had gone to the city, I went dancing. Oh, if you only knew what happened at this place, you would not be saying this. I would not like to stop somewhere and tell you the end . . . I would rather like to put a rod under the story, as it were, clear off every little creeper in the bush . . .

But as we were talking about the dancing, something made Duayaw turn to look behind him where four women were sitting by the table. . . . Oh! he turned his eyes quickly, screwed his face into something queer which I could not understand and told me that if I wanted to dance, I could ask one of those women to dance with me.

My uncles, I too was very surprised when I heard that. I asked Duayaw if people who did not know me would dance with me' He said 'Yes.' I lifted my eyes, my uncles, and looked at those four young women sitting round a table alone. They were sitting all alone, I say. I got up.

I hope I am making myself clear, my uncles, but I was trembling like water in a brass bowl.

Immediately one of them saw me, she jumped up and said something in that kind of white man's language which everyone, even those who have not gone to school, speak in the city. I shook my head. She said something else in the language of the people of the place. I shook my head again. Then I heard her ask me in Fante whether I wanted to dance with her. I replied 'Yes.'

Ei! my little sister, are you asking me a question? Oh! you want to know whether I found Mansa? I do not know. . . . Our uncles have asked me to tell everything that happened there, and you too! I am cooking the whole meal for you, why do you want to lick the ladle now?

Yes, I went to dance with her. I kept looking at her so much I think I was all the time stepping on her feet. I say, she was as black as you and I, but her hair was very long and fell on her shoulders like that of a white woman. I did not touch it but I saw it was very soft. Her lips with that red paint looked like a fresh wound. There was no space between her skin and her dress. Yes, I danced with her. When the music ended, I went back to where I was sitting. I do not know what she told her companions about me, but I heard them laugh.

It was this time that something made me realise that they were all bad women of the city. Duayaw had told me I would feel warm if I danced, yet after I had danced, I was colder than before. You would think someone had poured water on me. I was unhappy thinking about these women. 'Have they no homes?' I asked myself. 'Do not their mothers like them? God, we are all toiling for our threepence to buy something to eat . . . but oh! God! this is no work.'

When I thought of my own sister, who was lost, I became a little happy because I felt that although I had not found her, she was nevertheless married to a big man and all was well with her.

When they started to play the band again, I went to the women's table to ask the one with whom I had danced to dance again. But someone had gone with her already. I got one of the two who were still sitting there. She went with me. When we were dancing she asked me whether it was true that I was a Fante. I replied 'Yes.' We did not speak again. When the band stopped playing, she told me to take her to where they sold things to buy her beer and cigarettes. I was wondering whether I had the money. When we were where the lights were shining brightly, something told me to look at her face. Something pulled at my heart.

'Young woman, is this the work you do?' I asked her.

'Young man, what work do you mean?' she too asked me. I laughed.

'Do you not know what work?' I asked again.

'And who are you to ask me such questions? I say, who are you? Let me tell you that any kind of work is work. You villager, you villager, who are you?' she screamed.

I was afraid. People around were looking at us. I laid my hands on her shoulders to calm her down and she hit them away.

'Mansa, Mansa,' I said. 'Do you not know me?' She looked at me for a long time and started laughing. She laughed, laughed as if the laughter did not come from her stomach. Yes, as if she was hungry.

'I think you are my brother,' she said. 'Hm.'

Oh, my mother and my aunt, oh, little sister, are you all weeping? As for you women!

What is there to weep about? I was sent to find a lost child. I found her a woman.

Cut me a drink . . .

Any kind of work is work. . . . This is what Mansa told me with a mouth that looked like clotted blood. Any kind of work is work . . . so do not weep. She will come home this Christmas.

My brother, cut me another drink. Any form of work is work . . . is work . . . is work!

The Message

'Look here my sister, it should not be said but they say they opened her up.'

'They opened her up?'

'Yes, opened her up.'

'And the baby removed?'

'Yes, the baby removed.'

'Yes, the baby removed.'

'I say . . .'

'They do not say, my sister.'

'Have you heard it?'

'What?'

'This and this and that . . .'

'A-a-ah! that is it . . .'

'*Meewuo!*'

'They don't say *meewuo* . . .'

'And how is she?'

'Am I not here with you? Do I know the highway which leads to Cape Coast?'

'Hmmm . . .'

'And anyway how can she live? What is it like even giving birth with a stomach which is whole . . . eh? . . . I am asking you. And if you are always standing on the brink of death who go to war with a stomach that is whole, then how would she do whose stomach is open to the winds?'

'Oh, *poo*, pity . . .'

'I say . . .'

My little bundle, come. You and I are going to Cape Coast today.

I am taking one of her own cloths with me, just in case. These people on the coast do not know how to do a thing and I am not going to have anybody mishandling my child's body. I hope they give it to me. Horrible things I have heard done to people's bodies. Cutting them up and using them for instructions. Whereas even murderers still have decent burials.

I see Mensima coming. . . . And there is Nkama too . . . and Adwoa Meenu. . . . Now they are coming to . . . '*poo* pity' me. Witches, witches, witches . . . they have picked mine up while theirs prosper around them, children, grandchildren and great-grandchildren – theirs shoot up like mushrooms.

'Esi, we have heard of your misfortune . . .'

'That our little lady's womb has been opened up . . .'

'And her baby removed . . .'

Thank you very much.

'Has she lived through it?'

I do not know.

'Esi, bring her here, back home whatever happens.'

Yoo, thank you. If the government's people allow it, I shall bring her home.

'And have you got ready your things?'

Yes. . . . No.

I cannot even think well.

It feels so noisy in my head. . . . Oh my little child. . . . I am wasting time. . . . And so I am going . . .

Yes, to Cape Coast.

No, I do not know anyone there now but do you think no one would show me the way to this big hospital . . . if I asked around?

Hmmm . . . it's me has ended up like this. I was thinking that everything was alright now. . . . *Yoo*. And thank you too. Shut the door for me when you are leaving. You may stay too long outside if you wait for me, so go home and be about your business. I will let you know when I bring her in.

'Maami Amfoa, where are you going?'

My daughter, I am going to Cape Coast.

'And what is our old mother going to do with such swift steps? Is it serious?'

My daughter, it is very serious.

'Mother, may God go with you.'

Yoo, my daughter.

'Eno, and what calls at this hour of the day?'

They want me in Cape Coast.

'Does my friend want to go and see how much the city has changed since we went there to meet the new Wesleyan Chairman, twenty years ago?'

My sister, do you think I have knees to go parading on the streets of Cape Coast?

'Is it heavy?'

Yes, very heavy indeed. They have opened up my grandchild at the hospital, *hi, hi, hi.* . . .

'Eno *due, due, due*... I did not know. May God go with you....'

Thank you. *Yaa.*

'O, the world!'

'It's her grandchild. The only daughter of her only son. Do you remember Kojo Amisa who went to sodja and fell in the great war, overseas?'

'Yes, it's his daughter. . . .'

. . . O, *poo*, pity.

'Kobina, run to the street, tell Draba Anan to wait for Nana Amfoa.'

'. . . Draba Anan, Draba, my mother says I must come and tell you to wait for Nana Amfoa.'

'And where is she?'

'There she comes.'

'Just look at how she hops like a bird . . . does she think we are going to be here all day? And anyway we are full already . . .'

O, you drivers!

'What have drivers done?'

'And do you think it shows respect when you speak in this way? It is only that things have not gone right; but she could, at least have been your mother. . . .'

'But what have I said? I have not insulted her. I just think that only Youth must be permitted to see Cape Coast, the town of the Dear and Expensive. . . .'

'And do you think she is going on a peaceful journey? The only daughter of her only son has been opened up and her baby removed from her womb.'

O . . . God.

O

O

O

Poo, pity.

'Me . . . *poo* – pity, I am right about our modern wives I always say they are useless as compared with our mothers.

'You drivers!'

'Now what have your modern wives done?'

'Am I not right what I always say about them?'

'You go and watch them in the big towns. All so thin and dry as sticks – you can literally blow them away with your breath. No decent flesh anywhere. Wooden chairs groan when they meet with their hard exteriors.'

'O you drivers. . . .'

'But of course all drivers . . .'

'What have I done? Don't all my male passengers agree with me? These modern girls. . . . Now here is one who cannot even have a baby in a decent way. But must have the baby removed from her stomach. *Tchiaa!*'

'What . . .'

'Here is the old woman.'

'Whose grandchild . . .?'

'Yes.'

'Nana, I hear you are coming to Cape Coast with us.'

C

Yes my master.

'We nearly left you behind but we heard it was you and that it is a heavy journey you are making.'

Yes my master . . . thank you my master.

'Push up please . . . push up. Won't you push up? Why do you all sit looking at me with such eyes as if I was a block of wood?'

'It is not that there is nowhere to push up to. Five fat women should go on that seat, but look at you!

'And our own grandmother here is none too plump herself. . . . Nana, if they won't push, come to the front seat with me.'

'. . . *Hei*, scholar, go to the back. . . .

'. . . And do not scowl on me. I know your sort too well. Something tells me you do not have any job at all. As for that suit you are wearing and looking so grand in, you hired or borrowed it. . . .'

'Oh you drivers!'

Oh you drivers . . .

The scholar who read this tengram thing, said it was made about three days ago. My lady's husband sent it. . . . Three days. . . . God – that is too long ago. Have they buried her . . . where? Or did they cut her up. . . . I should not think about it . . . or something will happen to me. Eleven or twelve . . . Efua Panyin, Okuma, Kwame Gyasi and who else? But they should not have left me here. Sometimes . . . ah, I hate this nausea. But it is this smell of petrol. Now I have remembered I never could travel in a lorry. I always was so sick. But now I hope at least that will not happen. These young people will think it is because I am old and they will laugh. At least if I knew the child of my child was alive, it would have been good. And the little things she sent me. . . . Sometimes some people like Mensima and Nkansa make me feel as if I had been a barren woman instead of only one with whom infant-mortality pledged friendship . . .

I will give her that set of earrings, bracelet and chain which Odwumfo Ata made for me. It is the most beautiful and the most expensive thing I have. . . . It does not hurt me to think that I am going to die very soon and have them and their children gloating over my things. After all what did they swallow my children for? It does not hurt me at all. If I had been someone else, I would have given them all away before I died. But it does not matter. They can share their own curse. Now, that is the end of me and my roots. . . . Eternal death has worked like a warrior rat, with diabolical sense of duty, to gnaw my bottom. Everything is finished now. The vacant lot is swept and the scraps of old sugar-cane pulp, dry sticks and bunches of hair burnt . . . how it reeks, the smoke!

'O, Nana do not weep . . .'

'Is the old woman weeping?'

'If the only child of your only child died, won't you weep?'

'Why do you ask me? Did I know her grandchild is dead?'

'Where have you been, not in this lorry? Where were your ears when we were discussing it?'

'I do not go putting my mouth in other people's affairs . . .'

'So what?'

'So go and die.'

'*Hei*, *hei*, it is prohibited to quarrel in my lorry.'

'Draba, here is me, sitting quiet and this lady of muscles and bones being cheeky to me.'

'Look, I can beat you.'

'Beat me . . . beat me . . . let's see.'

'*Hei*, you are not civilised, eh?'

'Keep quiet and let us think, both of you, or I will put you down.'

'Nana, do not weep. There is God above.'

Thank you my master.

'But we are in Cape Coast already.'

Meewuo! My God, hold me tight or something will happen to me.

My master, I will come down here.

'O Nana, I thought you said you were going to the hospital. . . . We are not there yet.'

I am saying maybe I will get down here and ask my way around.

'Nana, you do not know these people, eh? They are very impudent here. They have no use for old age. So they do not respect it. Sit down, I will take you there.'

Are you going there, my master?

'No, but I will take you there.'

Ah, my master, your old mother thanks you. Do not shed a tear when you hear of my death . . . my master, your old mother thanks you.

I hear there is somewhere where they keep corpses until their owners claim them . . . if she has been buried, then I must find her husband . . . Esi Amfoa, what did I come to do under this sky? I have buried all my children and now I am going to bury my only grandchild!

'Nana we are there.'

Is this the hospital?

'Yes, Nana. What is your child's name?'

Esi Amfoa. Her father named her after me.

'Do you know her European name?'

No, my master.

'What shall we do?'

'. . . *Ei* lady, Lady Nurse, we are looking for somebody.'

'You are looking for somebody and can you read? If you cannot, you must ask someone what the rules in the hospital are. You can only come and visit people at three o'clock.'

Lady, please. She was my only grandchild . . .

'Who? And anyway, it is none of our business.'

'Nana, you must be patient . . . and not cry . . .'

'Old woman, why are you crying, it is not allowed here. No one must make any noise . . .'

My lady, I am sorry but she was all I had.

'Who? Oh, are you the old woman who is looking for somebody?'

Yes.

'Who is he?'

She was my granddaughter – the only child of my only son.

'I mean, what was her name?'

Esi Amfoa.

'Esi Amfoa . . . Esi Amfoa. I am sorry, we do not have anyone whom they call like that here.'

Is that it?

'Nana, I told you they may know only her European name here.'

My master, what shall we do then?

'What is she ill with?'

She came here to have a child . . .

'. . . And they say, they opened her stomach and removed the baby.'

'Oh . . . oh, I see.'

My Lord, hold me tight so that nothing will happen to me now.

'I see. It is the Caesarean case.'

'Nurse, you know her?'

And when I take her back, Anona Ebusuafo will say that I did not wait for them to come with me . . .

'Yes. Are you her brother?'

'No. I am only the driver who brought the old woman.'

'Did she bring all her clan?'

'No. She came alone.'

'Strange thing for a villager to do.'

I hope they have not cut her up already.

'Did she bring a whole bag full of cassava and plantain and kenkey?'

'No. She has only her little bundle.'

'Follow me. But you must not make any noise. This is not the hour for coming here . . .'

My master, does she know her?

'Yes.'

I hear it is very cold where they put them . . .

. . . . .

It was feeding time for new babies. When old Esi Amfoa saw young Esi Amfoa, the latter was all neat and nice. White sheets and all. She did not see the beautiful stitches under the sheets. 'This woman is a tough bundle,' Dr. Gyamfi had declared after the identical twins had been removed, the last stitches had been threaded off and Mary Koomson, alias Esi Amfoa, had come to.

The old woman somersaulted into the room and lay groaning, not screaming, by the bed. For was not her last pot broken? So they lay them in state even in hospitals and not always cut them up for instruction?

The Nursing Sister was furious. Young Esi Amfoa spoke. And this time old Esi Amfoa wept loud and hard – wept all her tears.

Scrappy nurse-under-training, Jessy Treeson, second-generation-Cape-Coaster-her-grandmother-still-remembered-at-Egyaa No. 7 said, 'As for these villagers,' and giggled.

Draba Anan looked hard at Jessy Treeson, looked hard at her, all of her: her starched uniform, apron and cap . . . and then dismissed them all. . . . 'Such a cassava stick . . . but maybe I will break my toe if I kicked at her buttocks,' he thought.

And by the bed the old woman was trying hard to rise and look at the only pot which had refused to get broken.

Certain Winds from the South

M'ma Asana eyed the wretched pile of cola-nuts, spat, and picked up the reed-bowl. Then she put down the bowl, picked up one of the nuts, bit at it, threw it back, spat again, and stood up. First, a sharp little ache, just a sharp little one, shot up from somewhere under her left ear. Then her eyes became misty.

'I must check on those logs,' she thought, thinking this misting of her eyes was due to the chill in the air. She stooped over the nuts.

'You never know what evil eyes are prowling this dusk over these grasslands – I must pick them up quickly.'

On the way back to the kraal, her eyes fell on the especially patchy circles that marked where the old pits had been. At this time, in the old days, they would have been full to bursting and as one scratched out the remains of the out-going season, one felt a near-sexual thrill of pleasure looking at these pits, just as one imagines a man might feel who looks upon his wife in the ninth month of pregnancy.

Pregnancy and birth and death and pain; and death again. . . . When there are no more pregnancies, there are no more births and therefore, no more deaths. But there is only one death and only one pain . . .

Show me a fresh corpse my sister, so I can weep you old tears.

The pit of her belly went cold, then her womb moved and she had to lean by the doorway. In twenty years, Fuseni's has been the only pregnancy and the only birth . . . twenty years, and the first child and a male! In the old days, there would have been bucks and you got scolded for serving a woman in maternity a duicker. But these days, those mean poachers on the government reserves sneak away their miserable duickers, such wretched hinds! Yes, they sneak away even the duickers to the houses of those sweet-toothed southerners.

In the old days, how time goes, and how quickly age comes. But then does one expect to grow younger when one starts getting grandchildren? Allah be praised for a grandson.

The fire was still strong when she returned to the room. . . . M'ma Asana put the nuts down. She craned her neck into the corner. At least those logs should take them to the following week. For the rest of the evening, she set about preparing for the morrow's marketing.

The evening prayers were done. The money was in the bag. The grassland was still, Hawa was sleeping and so was Fuseni. M'ma came out to the main gate, first to check up if all was well outside and then to draw the door across. It was not the figure, but rather the soft rustle of light footsteps trying to move still more lightly over the grass that caught her attention.

'If only it could be my husband.'

But of course it was not her husband!

'Who comes?'

'It is me, M'ma.'

'You Issa, my son?'

'Yes, M'ma.'

'They are asleep.'

'I thought so. That is why I am coming now.'

There was a long pause in the conversation as they both hesitated about whether the son-in-law should go in to see Hawa and the baby or not. Nothing was said about this struggle but then one does not say everything.

M'ma Asana did not see but she felt him win the battle. She crossed the threshold outside and drew the door behind her. Issa led the way. They did not walk far, however. They just turned into a corner between two of the projecting pillars in the wall of the kraal. It was Issa who stood with his back to the wall. And this was as it should have been, for it was he who needed the comforting coolness of it for his backbone.

'M'ma, is Fuseni well?'

'Yes.'

'M'ma, is Hawa well?'

'Yes.'

'M'ma please tell me, is Fuseni very well?'

'A-ah, my son. For what are you troubling yourself so much?' 'Fuseni is a new baby who was born not more than ten days. How can I tell you he is very well? When a grown-up goes to live in other people's village . . .'

'M'ma.'

'What is it?'

'No. Please it is nothing.'

'My son, I cannot understand you this evening. Yes, if you, a grown-up person, goes to live in another village, will you say after the first few days that you are perfectly well?'

'No.'

'Shall you not get yourself used to their food? Shall you not find first where you can get water for yourself and your sheep?'

'Yes, M'ma.'

'Then how is it you ask me if Fuseni is very well? The navel is healing very fast . . . and how would it not? Not a single navel of all that I have cut here got infected. Shall I now cut my grandson's and then sit and see it rot? But it is his male that I can't say. Mallam did it neat and proper and it must be alright. Your family is not noted for males that rot, is it now?'

'No, M'ma.'

'Then let your heart lie quiet in your breast. Fuseni is well but we cannot say how well yet.'

'I have heard you, M'ma . . . M'ma . . .'

'Yes, my son.'

'M'ma, I am going South.'

'Where did you say?'

'South.'

'How far?'

'As far as the sea. M'ma I thought you would understand.'

'Have I spoken yet?'

'No, you have not.'

'Then why did you say that?'

'That was not well said.'

'And what are you going to do there?'

'Find some work .'

'What work?'

'I do not know.'

'Yes, you know, you are going to cut grass.'

'Perhaps.'

'But my son, why must you travel that far just to cut grass? Is there not enough of it all round here? Around this kraal, your father's and all the others in the village? Why do you not cut these?'

'M'ma, you know it is not the same. If I did that here people will think I am mad. But over there, I have heard that not only do they like it but the government pays you to do it.'

'Even still, our men do not go South to cut grass. This is for those further north. They of the wilderness, it is they who go South to cut grass. This is not for our men.'

'Please M'ma, already time is going. Hawa is a new mother and Fuseni my first child.'

'And yet you are leaving them to go South and cut grass.'

'But M'ma, what will be the use in my staying here and watching them starve? You yourself know that all the cola went bad, and even if they had not, with trade as it is, how much money do you think I would have got from them? And that is why I am going. Trade is broken and since we do not know when things will be good again, I think it will be better for me to go away.'

'Does Hawa know?'

'No, she does not.'

'Are you coming to wake her up at this late hour to tell her?'

'No.'

'You are wise.'

'M'ma, I have left everything in the hands of Amadu. He will come and see Hawa tomorrow.'

'Good. When shall we expect you back?'

'. . .'

'Issa . . .'

'M'ma.'

'When shall we expect you back?'

'M'ma, I do not know. Perhaps next Ramaddan.'

'Good.'

'So I go now.'

'Allah go with you.'

'And may His prophet look after you all.'

M'ma went straight back to bed, but not to sleep. And how could she sleep? At dawn, her eyes were still wide-open.

'Is his family noted for males that rot? No, certainly not. It is us who are noted for our unlucky females. There must be something wrong with them. . . . Or how is it we cannot hold our men? Allah, how is it?

Twenty years ago. Twenty years, perhaps more than twenty years . . . perhaps more than twenty years and Allah please, give me strength to tell Hawa.

Or shall I go to the market now and then tell her when I come back? No. Hawa, Hawa, now look at how you are stretched down there like a log! Does a mother sleep like this? Hawa, H-a-a-w-a! Oh, I shall not leave you alone. . . . And how can you hear your baby when it cries in the night since you die when you sleep?

. . . Listen to her asking me questions! Yes, it is broad daylight. I thought you really were dead. If it is cold, draw your blanket round you and listen to me for I have something to tell you.

Hawa, Issa has gone South.

And why do you stare at me with such shining eyes? I am telling you that Issa is gone south.

And what question do you think you are asking me? How could he take you along when you have a baby whose navel wound has not even healed yet?

He went away last night.

Don't ask me why I did not come to wake you up. What should I have woken you up for?

Listen, Issa said he could not stay here and just watch you and Fuseni starve.

He is going South to find work and . . . Hawa, where do you think you are getting up to go to? Issa is not at the door waiting for you. The whole neighbourhood is not up yet, so do not let me shout . . . and why are you behaving like a baby? Now you are a mother and you must decide to grow up . . . where are you getting up to go? Listen to me telling you this. Issa is gone. He went last night because he wants to catch the government bus that leaves Tamale very early in the morning. So . . .

Hawa, ah-ah, are you crying? Why are you crying? That your husband has left you to go and work? Go on weeping, for he will bring the money to look after me and not you. . . . I do not understand, you say? May be I do not. . . . See, now you have woken up Fuseni. Sit down and feed him and listen to me . . .

Listen to me and I will tell you of another man who left his newborn child and went away.

Did he come back? No, he did not come back. But do not ask me any more questions for I will tell you all.

He used to go and come, then one day he went away and never came back. Not that he had had to go like the rest of them . . .

Oh, they were soldiers. I am talking of a soldier. He need

not have gone to be a soldier. After all, his father was one of the richest men of this land. He was not the eldest son, that is true, but still, there were so many things he could have done to look after himself and his wife when he came to marry. But he would not listen to anybody. How could he sit by and have other boys out-do him in smartness?

Their clothes that shone and shone with pressing. . . . I say, you could have looked into any of them and put khole under your eyes. And their shoes, how they roared! You know soldiers for yourself. Oh, the stir on the land when they came in from the South! Mothers spoke hard and long to daughters about the excellencies of proper marriages, while fathers hurried through with betrothals. Most of them were afraid of getting a case like that of Memunat on their hands. Her father had taken the cattle and everything and then Memunat goes and plays with a soldier. Oh, the scandal she caused herself then!

Who was this Memunat? No, she is not your friend's mother. No, this Memunat in the end ran away South herself. We hear she became a bad woman in the city and made a lot of money. No, we do not hear of her now – she is not dead either, for we hear such women usually go to their homes to die, and she has not come back here yet.

But us, we were different. I had not been betrothed.

Do you ask me why I say we? Because this man was your father. . . . Ah-ah, you open your mouth and eyes wide? Yes my child, it is of your father I am speaking.

No, I was not lying when I told you that he died. But keep quiet and listen. . . .

He was going South to get himself a house for married soldiers.

No, it was not that time he did not come back. He came here, but not to fetch me.

He asked us if we had heard of the war.

Had we not heard of the war? Was it not difficult to get things like tinned fish, kerosene and cloth?

Yes, we said, but we thought it was only because the traders were not bringing them in.

Well yes, he said, but the traders do not get them even in the South.

And why, we asked.

O you people, have you not heard of the German-people? He had no patience with us. He told us that in the South they were singing dirty songs with their name.

But when are we going, I asked him.

What he told me was that that was why he had come. He could not take me along with him. You see, he said, since we were under the Anglis-people's rule and they were fighting with the German-people . . .

Ask me, my child, for that was exactly what I asked him, what has all that got to do with you and me? Why can I not come South with you?

Because I have to travel to the lands beyond the sea and fight...

In other people's war? My child, it is as if you were there. That is what I asked him.

But it is not as simple as that, he said.

We could not understand him. You shall not go, said his father. You shall not go, for it is not us fighting with the Grunshies or the Gonjas. . . . I know about the Anglis-people but not about any German-people, but anyway they are in their land.

Of course his father was playing, and so was I.

A soldier must obey at all time, he said.

I wanted to give him so many things to take with him but he said he could only take cola.

Then the news came. It did not enter my head, for there all was empty. Everything went into my womb. You were just three days old.

The news was like fire which settled in the pit of my belly. And from time to time, some would shoot up, searing my womb, singeing my intestines and burning up and up and up until I screamed with madness when it got into my head.

I had told myself when you were born that it did not matter you were a girl, all gifts from Allah are good and anyway he was coming back and we were going to have many more children, lots of sons.

But Hawa, you had a lot of strength, for how you managed to live I do not know. Three days you were and suddenly like a rivulet that is hit by an early harmattan, my breasts went dry. . . . Hawa, you have a lot of strength.

Later, they told me that if I could go South and prove to the government's people that I was his wife, I would get a lot of money.

But I did not go. It was him I wanted, not his body turned into gold.

I never saw the South.

Do you say oh? My child I am always telling you that the world was created a long while ago and it is old-age one has not seen but not youth. So do not say oh.

Those people, the government's people, who come and go, tell us trade is bad now, and once again there is no tinned fish and no cloth. But this time they say, this is because our children are going to get them in abundance one day.

Issa has gone South now because he cannot afford even goat flesh for his wife in maternity. This has to be, so that Fuseni can stay with his wife and eat cow-meat with her? Hmm. And he will come back alive . . . perhaps not next Ramaddan but the next. Now, my daughter, you know of another man who went to fight. And he went to fight in other people's war and he never came back.

I am going to the market now. Get up early to wash Fuseni. I hope to get something for those miserable colas. There is enough rice to make *tuo*, is there not? Good. Today even if it takes all the money, I hope to get us some smoked fish, the biggest I can find, to make us a real good sauce. . . .'

No Sweetness Here

He was beautiful, but that was not important. Beauty does not play such a vital role in a man's life as it does in a woman's, or so people think. If a man's beauty is so ill-mannered as to be noticeable, people discreetly ignore its existence. Only an immodest girl like me would dare comment on a boy's beauty. 'Kwesi is so handsome,' I was always telling his mother. 'If ever I am transferred from this place, I will kidnap him.' I enjoyed teasing the dear woman and she enjoyed being teased about him. She would look scandalised, pleased and alarmed all in one fleeting moment.

'Ei, Chicha. You should not say such things. The boy is not very handsome really.' But she knew she was lying. 'Besides, Chicha, who cares whether a boy is handsome or not?' Again she knew that at least she cared, for, after all, didn't the boy's wonderful personality throw a warm light on the mother's lively though already waning beauty? Then gingerly, but in a remarkably matter-of-fact tone, she would voice out her gnawing fear. 'Please Chicha, I always know you are just making fun of me, but please, promise me you won't take Kwesi away with you.' Almost at once her tiny mouth would quiver and she would hide her eyes in her cloth as if ashamed of her great love and her fears. But I understood. 'O, Maami, don't cry, you know I don't mean it.'

'Chicha I am sorry, and I trust you. Only I can't help fearing, can I? What will I do, Chicha, what would I do, should something happen to my child?' She would raise her pretty eyes, glistening with unshed tears.

'Nothing will happen to him,' I would assure her. 'He is a good boy. He does not fight and therefore there is no chance of anyone beating him. He is not dull, at least not too dull, which means he does not get more cane-lashes than the rest of his mates. . . .'

'Chicha, I shall willingly submit to your canes if he gets his sums wrong,' she would hastily intervene.

'Don't be funny. A little warming-up on a cold morning wouldn't do him any harm. But if you say so, I won't object to hitting that soft flesh of yours.' At this, the tension would break and both of us begin laughing. Yet I always went away with the image of her quivering mouth and unshed tears in my mind.

Maami Ama loved her son; and this is a silly statement, as silly as saying Maami Ama is a woman. Which mother would not? At the time of this story, he had just turned ten years old. He was in Primary Class Four and quite tall for his age. His skin was as smooth as shea-butter and as dark as charcoal. His black hair was as soft as his mother's. His eyes were of the kind that always remind one of a long dream on a hot afternoon. It is indecent to dwell on a boy's physical appearance, but then Kwesi's beauty was indecent.

The evening was not yet come. My watch read 4.15 p.m., that ambiguous time of the day which these people, despite their great ancient astronomic knowledge, have always failed to identify. For the very young and very old, it is certainly evening, for they've stayed at home all day and they begin to persuade themselves that the day is ending. Bored with their own company, they sprawl in the market-place or by their own walls. The children begin to whimper for their mothers, for they are tired with playing 'house'. Fancying themselves starving, they go back to what was left of their lunch, but really they only pray that mother will come home from the farm soon. The very old certainly do not go back on lunch remains but they do bite back at old conversational topics which were fresh at ten o'clock.

'I say, Kwame, as I was saying this morning, my first wife was a most beautiful woman,' old Kofi would say.

'Oh! yes, yes, she was an unusually beautiful girl. I remember her.' Old Kwame would nod his head but the truth was he was tired of the story and he was sleepy. 'It's high time the young people came back from the farm.'

But I was a teacher, and I went the white man's way. School was over. Maami Ama's hut was at one end of the village and the school was at the other. Nevertheless it was not a long walk from the school to her place because Bamso is not really a big village. I had left my books to little Grace Ason to take home for me; so I had only my little clock in my hand and I was walking in a leisurely way. As I passed the old people, they shouted their greetings. It was always the Fanticised form of the English.

'Kudiimin-o, Chicha.' Then I would answer, 'Kudiimin, Nana.' When I greeted first, the response was 'Tanchiw'.

'Chicha, how are you?'

'Nana, I am well.'

'And how are the children?'

'Nana, they are well.'

'*Yoo*, that is good.' When an old man felt inclined to be talkative, especially if he had more than me for audience, he would compliment me on the work I was doing. Then he would go on to the assets of education, especially female education, ending up with quoting Dr. Aggrey.

So this evening too, I was delayed: but it was as well, for when I arrived at the hut, Maami Ama had just arrived from the farm. The door opened, facing the village, and so I could see her. Oh, that picture is still vivid in my mind. She was sitting on a low stool with her load before her. Like all the loads the other women would bring from the farms into their homes, it was colourful with miscellaneous articles. At the very bottom of the wide wooden tray were the cassava and yam tubers, rich muddy brown, the colour of the earth. Next were the plantain, of the green colour of the woods from which they came. Then there were the gay vegetables, the scarlet pepper, garden eggs, golden pawpaw and crimson tomatoes. Over this riot of colours the little woman's eyes were fixed, absorbed, while the tiny hands delicately picked the pepper. I made a scratchy noise at the door. She looked up and smiled. Her smile was a wonderful flashing whiteness.

'Oh Chicha, I have just arrived.'

'So I see. *Ayekoo.*'

'*Yaa*, my own. And how are you, my child?'

'Very well, Mother. And you?'

'Tanchiw. Do sit down, there's a stool in that corner. Sit down. Mmmm. . . . Life is a battle. What can we do? We are just trying, my daughter.'

'Why were you longer at the farm today?'

'After weeding that plot I told you about last week, I thought I would go for one or two yams.'

'Ah!' I cried.

'You know tomorrow is Ahobaa. Even if one does not feel happy, one must have some yam for old Ahor.'

'Yes. So I understand. The old saviour deserves it. After all it is not often that a man offers himself as a sacrifice to the gods to save his people from a pestilence.'

'No, Chicha, we were so lucky.'

'But Maami Ama, why do you look so sad? After all, the yams are quite big.' She gave me a small grin, looking at the yams she had now packed at the corner.

'Do you think so? Well, they are the best of the lot. My daughter, when life fails you, it fails you totally. One's yams reflect the total sum of one's life. And mine look wretched enough.'

'O, Maami, why are you always speaking in this way? Look at Kwesi, how many mothers can boast of such a son? Even though he is only one, consider those who have none at all. Perhaps some woman is sitting at some corner envying you '

She chuckled. 'What an unhappy woman she must be who would envy Ama! But thank you, I should be grateful for Kwesi.'

After that we were quiet for a while. I always loved to see her moving quietly about her work. Having finished unpacking, she knocked the dirt out of the tray and started making fire to prepare the evening meal. She started humming a religious lyric. She was a Methodist.

We are fighting
We are fighting
We are fighting for Canaan, the Heavenly Kingdom above.

I watched her and my eyes became misty, she looked so much like my own mother. Presently, the fire began to smoke. She turned round. 'Chicha.'

'Maami Ama.'

'Do you know that tomorrow I am going to have a formal divorce?'

'Oh!' And I could not help the dismay in my voice.

I had heard, soon after my arrival in the village, that the parents of that most beautiful boy were as good as divorced. I had hoped they would come to a respectful understanding for the boy's sake. Later on when I got to know his mother, I had wished for this, for her own sweet self's sake too. But as time went on I had realised this could not be or was not even desirable. Kodjo Fi was a selfish and bullying man, whom no decent woman ought to have married. He got on marvellously with his two other wives but they were three of a feather. Yet I was sorry to hear Maami was going to have a final breach with him.

'Yes, I am,' she went on. 'I should. What am I going on like this for? What is man struggling after? Seven years is a long time to bear ill-usage from a man coupled with contempt and insults from his wives. What have I done to deserve the abuse of his sisters? And his mother!'

'Does she insult you too?' I exclaimed.

'Why not? Don't you think she would? Considering that I don't buy her the most expensive cloths on the market and I don't give her the best fish from my soup, like her daughters-in-law do.'

I laughed. 'The mean old witch!'

'Chicha, don't laugh. I am quite sure she wanted to eat Kwesi but I baptised him and she couldn't.'

'Oh, don't say that, Maami. I am quite sure they all like you, only you don't know.'

'My child, they don't. They hate me.'

But what happened?' I asked the question I had wanted to ask for so long.

'You would ask, Chicha! I don't know. They suddenly began hating me when Kwesi was barely two. Kodjo Fi reduced my housekeeping money and sometimes he refused to give me anything at all. He wouldn't eat my food. At first, I used to ask him why. He always replied, "It is nothing." If I had not been such an unlucky woman, his mother and sisters might have taken my side, but for me there was no one. That planting time, although I was his first wife, he allotted to me the smallest, thorniest plot.'

'Ei, what did you say about it?'

'What could I say? At that time my mother was alive, though my father was already dead. When I complained to her about the treatment I was getting from my husband, she told me that in marriage, a woman must sometimes be a fool. But I have been a fool for far too long a time.'

'Oh!' I frowned.

'Mother has died and left me and I was an only child too. My aunts are very busy looking after the affairs of their own daughters. I've told my uncles several times but they never take me seriously. They feel I am only a discontented woman.'

'You?' I asked in surprise.

'Perhaps you would not think so. But there are several who do feel like that in this village.'

She paused for a while, while she stared at the floor.

'You don't know, but I've been the topic of gossip for many years. Now, I only want to live on my own looking after my child. I don't think I will ever get any more children. Chicha, our people say a bad marriage kills the soul. Mine is fit for burial.'

'Maami, don't grieve.'

'My daughter, my mother and father who brought me to this world have left me alone and I've stopped grieving for them. When death summoned them, they were glad to lay down their tools and go to their parents. Yes, they loved me all right but even they had to leave me. Why should I make myself unhappy about a man for whom I ceased to exist a long time ago?'

She went to the big basket, took out some cassava and plantain, and sitting down began peeling them. Remembering she had forgotten the wooden bowl into which she would put the food, she got up to go for it.

'In this case,' I continued the conversation, 'what will happen to Kwesi?'

'What will happen to him?' she asked in surprise. 'This is no problem. They may tell me to give him to his father.'

'And would you?'

'No, I wouldn't.'

'And would you succeed in keeping him if his father insisted?'

'Well, I would struggle, for my son is his father's child but he belongs to my family.'

I sat there listening to these references to the age-old customs of which I had been ignorant. I was surprised. She washed the food, now cut into lumps, and arranged it in the cooking-pot. She added water and put it on the fire. She blew at it and it burst into flames.

'Maami Ama, has not your husband got a right to take Kwesi from you?' I asked her.

'He has, I suppose, but not entirely. Anyway, if the elders

who would make the divorce settlement ask me to let him go and stay with his father, I wouldn't refuse.'

'You are a brave woman.'

'Life has taught me to be brave,' she said, looking at me and smiling, 'By the way, what is the time?'

I told her, 'It is six minutes to six o'clock.'

'And Kwesi has not yet come home?' she exclaimed.

'Mama, here I am,' a piping voice announced.

'My husband, my brother, my father, my all-in-all, where are you?' And there he was. All at once, for the care-worn village woman, the sun might well have been rising from the east instead of setting behind the coconut palms. Her eyes shone. Kwesi saluted me and then his mother. He was a little shy of me and he ran away to the inner chamber. There was a thud which meant he had thrown his books down.

'Kwesi,' his mother called out to him. 'I have always told you to put your books down gently. I did not buy them with sand, and you ought to be careful with them.'

He returned to where we were. I looked at him. He was very dirty. There was sand in his hair, ears and eyes. His uniform was smeared with mud, crayon and berry-juice. His braces were hanging down on one side. His mother gave an affectionate frown. 'Kwesi, you are very dirty, just look at yourself. You are a disgrace to me. Anyone would think your mother does not look after you well.' I was very much amused, for I knew she meant this for my ears. Kwesi just stood there, without a care in the world.

'Can't you play without putting sand in your hair?' his mother persisted.

'I am hungry,' he announced. I laughed.

'Shame, shame, and your chicha is here. Chicha, you see? He does not fetch me water. He does not fetch me firewood. He does not weed my farm on Saturdays as other schoolboys do for their mothers. He only eats and eats.' I looked at him; he fled again into the inner chamber for shame. We both started laughing at him. After a time I got up to go.

'Chicha, I would have liked you to eat before you went away; that's why I am hurrying up with the food.' Maami tried to detain me.

'Oh, it does not matter. You know I eat here when I come, but today I must go away. I have the children's books to mark.'

'Then I must not keep you away from your work.'

'Tomorrow I will come to see you,' I promised.

'*Yoo*, thank you.'

'Sleep well, Maami.'

'Sleep well, my daughter.' I stepped into the open air. The sun was far receding. I walked slowly away. Just before I was out of earshot, Maami shouted after me, 'And remember, if Kwesi gets his sums wrong, I will come to school to receive his lashes, if only you would tell me.'

'*Yoo*,' I shouted back. Then I went away.

The next day was Ahobaada. It was a day of rejoicing for everyone. In the morning, old family quarrels were being patched up. In Maami Ama's family all became peaceful. Her aunts had – or thought they had – reconciled themselves to the fact that, when Maami Ama's mother was dying, she had instructed her sisters, much to their chagrin, to give all her jewels to her only child. This had been one of the reasons why the aunts and cousins had left Ama so much to her own devices. After all, she has her mother's goods, what else does she need?' they were often saying. However, today, aunts, cousins and nieces have come to a better understanding. Ahobaa is a season of goodwill! Nevertheless, Ama is going to have a formal divorce today. . . .

It had not been laid down anywhere in the Education Ordinance that schoolchildren were to be given holidays during local festivals. And so no matter how much I sympathised with the kids, I could not give them a holiday, although Ahobaa was such an important occasion for them; they naturally felt it a grievance to be forced to go to school while their friends at home were eating so much yam and meat. But they had their revenge on me. They fidgeted the whole day. What was worse, the schoolroom was actually just one big shed. When I left the Class One chicks to look at the older ones, they chattered; when I turned to them, Class Two and Class Three began shouting. Oh, it was a fine situation. In the afternoon, after having gone home to taste some of the festival dishes, they nearly drove me mad. So I was relieved when it was three o'clock. Feeling no sense of guilt, I turned them all out to play. They rushed out to the field. I packed my books on the table for little Grace to take home. My intention was to go and see the divorce proceedings which had begun at one o'clock and then come back at four to dismiss them. These divorce cases took hours to settle, and I hoped I would hear some of it.

As I walked down between the rows of desks, I hit my leg against one. The books on it tumbled down. As I picked them up I saw they belonged to Kwesi. It was the desk he shared with a little girl. I began thinking about him and the unhappy connection he had with what was going on at that moment down in the village. I remembered every word of the conversation I had had with his mother the previous evening. I became sad at the prospect of a possible separation from the mother who loved him so much and whom he loved. From his infancy they had known only each other, a lonely mother and a lonely son. Through the hot sun, she had carried him on her back as she weeded her cornfield. How could she dare to put him down under a tree in the shade when there was no one to look after him? Other women had their own younger sisters or those of their husbands to help with the baby; but she had had no one. The only face the little one had known was his mother's. And now . . .

'But,' I told myself, 'I am sure it will be all right with him.'
'Will it?' I asked myself.
'Why not? He is a happy child.'
'Does that solve the problem?'
'Not altogether, but . . .'

'No buts; one should think of the house into which he would be taken now. He may not be a favourite there.'

But my other voice told me that a child need not be a favourite to be happy.

I had to bring the one-man argument to an end. I had to hurry. Passing by the field, I saw some of the boys playing football. At the goal at the further end was a headful of hair shining in the afternoon sun. I knew the body to which it belonged. A goalkeeper is a dubious character in infant soccer. He is either a good goalkeeper and that is why he is at the goal, which is usually difficult to know in a child, or he is a bad player. If he is a bad player, he might as well be in the goal as anywhere else. Kwesi loved football, that was certain, and he was always the goalkeeper. Whether he was good or not I had never been able to see. Just as I passed, he caught a ball and his team clapped. I heard him give the little squeaky noise that passed for his laugh. No doubt he was a happy child.

Now I really ran into the village. I immediately made my way to Nana Kum's house, for the case was going on there. There was a great crowd in front of the house. Why were there so many people about? Then I remembered that it being a holiday, everyone was at home. And of course, after the eating and the drinking of palm-wine in the morning and midday, divorce proceedings certainly provide an agreeable diversion, especially when other people are involved and not ourselves.

The courtyard was a long one and as I jostled to where Maami Ama was sitting, pieces of comments floated into my ears. 'The elders certainly have settled the case fairly,' someone was saying. 'But it seemed as if Kodjo Fi had no strong proofs for his arguments,' another was saying. 'Well, they both have been sensible. If one feels one can't live with a woman, one might as well divorce her. And I hate a woman who cringes to a man,' a third said. Finally I reached her side. Around her were her family, her two aunts, Esi and Ama, her two cousins and the two uncles. To the right were the elders who were judging the case; opposite were Kodjo Fi and his family.

'I have come, Maami Ama,' I announced myself.

She looked at me. 'You ought to have been here earlier, the case has been settled already.'

'And how are things?' I inquired.

'I am a divorced woman.'

'What were his grounds for wanting to divorce you?'

'He said I had done nothing, he only wanted to . . .'

'Eh! Only the two of you know what went wrong,' the younger aunt cried out, reproachfully. 'If after his saying that, you had refused to be divorced, he would have had to pay the Ejecting Fee, but now he has got the better of you.'

'But aunt,' Maami protested, 'how could I refuse to be divorced?'

'It's up to you. I know it's your own affair, only I wouldn't like your mother's ghost to think that we haven't looked after you well.'

'I agree with you,' the elder aunt said.

'Maami Ama, what was your debt?' I asked her.

'It is quite a big sum.'

'I hope you too had something to reckon against him?'

'I did. He reckoned the dowry, the ten cloths he gave me, the Knocking Fee. . . .'

All this had been heard by Kodjo Fi and his family and soon they made us aware of it.

'Kodjo,' his youngest sister burst out, 'you forgot to reckon the Knife Fee.'

'No. *Yaa*, I did not forget,' Kodjo Fi told her. 'She had no brothers to whom I would give the fee.'

'It's all right then,' his second sister added.

But the rest of his womenfolk took this to be a signal for more free comments.

'She is a bad woman and I think you are well rid of her,' one aunt screamed.

'I think she is a witch,' the youngest sister said.

'Oh, that she is. Anyway, only witches have no brothers or sisters. They eat them in the mother's womb long before they are born.'

Ama's aunts and cousins had said nothing so far. They were inclined to believe Ama was a witch too. But Maami sat still. When the comments had gone down a bit, she resumed the conversation with me.

'As I was saying, Chicha, he also reckoned the price of the trunk he had given me and all the cost of the medicine he gave me to make me have more children. There was only the Cooking Cost for me to reckon against his.'

'Have you got money to pay the debt?' I asked her.

'No, but I am not going to pay it. My uncles will pay it out of the family fund and put the debt down against my name.'

'Oh!'

'But you are a fool,' Maami Ama's eldest aunt shouted at her.

'I say you are a fool,' she insisted.

'But aunt . . .' Maami Ama began to protest.

'Yes! And I hope you are not going to answer back. I was born before your mother and now that she is dead, I'm your mother! Besides, when she was alive I could scold her when she went wrong, and now I say you are a fool. For seven years you have struggled to look after a child. Whether he ate or not was your affair alone. Whether he had any cloth or not did not concern any other person. When Kwesi was a child he had no father. When he nearly died of measles, no grandmother looked in. As for aunts, he began getting them when he started going to school. And now you are allowing them to take him away from you. Now that he is grown enough to be counted among the living, a father knows he has got a son.'

'So, so!' Kodjo Fi's mother sneered at her. 'What did you think? That Kodjo would give his son as a present to you, eh? The boy belongs to his family, but he must be of some service to his father too.'

'Have I called your name?' Ama's aunt asked the old woman.

'You have not called her name but you were speaking against her son.' This again was from Kodjo Fi's youngest sister.

'And who are you to answer my mother back?' Ama's two cousins demanded of her.

'Go away. But who are you people?'

'Go away, too, you greedy lot.'

'It is you who are greedy, witches.'

'You are always calling other people witches. Only a witch can know a witch.'

Soon everyone was shouting at everyone else. The people who had come started going home, and only the most curious ones stood by to listen. Maami Ama was murmuring something under her breath which I could not hear. I persuaded her to come with me. All that time no word had passed between her and her ex-husband. As we turned to go, Kodjo Fi's mother shouted at her, 'You are hurt. But that is what you deserve. We will get the child. We will! What did you want to do with him?'

Maami Ama turned round to look at her. 'What are you putting yourself to so much trouble for? When Nana Kum said the boy ought to go and stay with his father, did I make any objection? He is at the school. Go and fetch him. To-morrow, you can send your carriers to come and fetch his belongings from my hut.' These words were said quietly.

Then I remembered suddenly that I had to hurry to school to dismiss the children. I told Maami Ama to go home but that I would try to see her before night.

This time I did not go by the main street. I took the back door through back streets and lanes. It was past four already. As I hurried along, I heard a loud roaring sound which I took to be echoes of the quarrel, so I went my way. When I reached the school, I did not like what I saw. There was not a single childish soul anywhere. But everyone's books were there. The shed was as untidy as ever. Little Grace had left my books too.

Of course I was more than puzzled. 'How naughty these children are. How did they dare to disobey me when I had told them to wait here until I came to dismiss them?' It was no use looking around the place. They were not there. 'They need discipline,' I threatened to the empty shed. I picked up my books and clock. Then I noticed that Kwesi's desk was clean of all his books. Nothing need be queer about this; he had probably taken his home. As I was descending the hill the second time that afternoon, I saw that the whole school was at the other end of the main street. What were the children doing so near Maami Ama's place? I ran towards them.

I was not prepared for what I saw. As if intentionally, the children had formed a circle. When some of them saw me, they all began to tell me what had happened. But I did not hear a word. In the middle of the circle, Kwesi was lying flat on his back. His shirt was off. His right arm was swollen to the size of his head. I simply stood there with my mouth open. From the back yard, Maami Ama screamed, 'I am drowning, people of Bamso, come and save me!' Soon the whole village was there.

What is the matter? What has happened? Kwesi has been bitten by a snake. Where? Where? At school. He was playing football. Where? What has happened? Bitten by a snake, a snake, a snake.

Questions and answers were tossed from mouth to mouth in the shocked evening air. Meanwhile, those who knew about snake-bites were giving the names of different cures. Kwesi's father was looking anxiously at his son. That strong powerful man was almost stupid with shock and alarm. Dose upon dose was forced down the reluctant throat but nothing seemed to have any effect. Women paced up and down around the hut, totally oblivious of the fact that they had left their festival meals half prepared. Each one was trying to imagine how she would have felt if Kwesi had been her child, and in imagination they suffered more than the suffering mother. 'The gods and spirits of our fathers protect us from calamity!'

After what seemed an unbearably long time, the messenger who had been earlier sent to Surdo, the village next to Bamso, to summon the chief medicine man arrived, followed by the eminent doctor himself. He was renowned for his cure of snake-bites. When he appeared, everyone gave a sigh of relief. They all remembered someone, perhaps a father, brother or husband, he had snatched from the jaws of death. When he gave his potion to the boy, he would be violently sick, and then of course, he would be out of danger. The potion was given. Thirty minutes; an hour; two hours; three, four hours. He had not retched. Before midnight, he was dead. No grown-up in Bamso village slept that night. Kwesi was the first boy to have died since the school was inaugurated some six years previously. 'And he was his mother's only child. She has no one now. We do not understand it. Life is not sweet!' Thus ran the verdict.

The morning was very beautiful. It seemed as if every natural object in and around the village had kept vigil too. So they too were tired. I was tired too. I had gone to bed at about five o'clock in the morning and since it was a Saturday I could have a long sleep. At ten o'clock, I was suddenly roused from sleep by shouting. I opened my window but I could not see the speakers. Presently Kweku Sam, one of the young men in the village, came past my window. 'Good morning, Chicha.' He shouted his greeting to me.

'Good morning, Kweku,' I responded. 'What is the shouting about?'

'They are quarrelling.'

'And what are they quarrelling about now?'

'Each is accusing the other of having been responsible for the boy's death.'

'How?'

'Chicha, I don't know. Only women make too much trouble for themselves. It seems as if they are never content to sit quiet but they must always hurl abuse at each other. What has happened is too serious to be a subject for quarrels. Perhaps

71

the village has displeased the gods in some unknown way and that is why they have taken away this boy.' He sighed. I could not say anything to that. I could not explain it myself, and if the villagers believed there was something more in Kwesi's death than the ordinary human mind could explain, who was I to argue?

'Is Maami Ama herself there?'

'No, I have not seen her there.'

He was quiet and I was quiet.

'Chicha, I think I should go away now. I have just heard that my sister has given birth to a girl.'

'So,' I smiled to myself. 'Give her my congratulations and tell her I will come to see her tomorrow.'

'*Yoo.*'

He walked away to greet his new niece. I stood for a long time at the window staring at nothing, while I heard snatches of words and phrases from the quarrel. And these were mingled with weeping. Then I turned from the window. Looking into the little mirror on the wall, I was not surprised to see my whole face bathed in unconscious tears. I did not feel like going to bed. I did not feel like doing anything at all. I toyed with the idea of going to see Maami Ama and then finally decided against it. I could not bear to face her; at least, not yet. So I sat down thinking about him. I went over the most presumptuous daydreams I had indulged in on his account. 'I would have taken him away with me in spite of his mother's protests.' She was just being absurd. 'The child is a boy, and sooner or later, she must learn to live without him. The highest class here is Primary Six and when I am going away, I will take him. I will give him a grammar education. Perhaps, who knows, one day he may win a scholarship to the university.' In my daydreams, I had never determined what career he would have followed, but he would be famous, that was certain. Devastatingly handsome, he would be the idol of women and the envy of every man. He would visit Britain, America and all those countries we have heard so much about. He would see all the seven wonders of the world. 'Maami shall be happy in the end,' I had told myself. 'People will flock to see the mother of such an illustrious man. Although she has not had many children, she will be surrounded by her grandchildren. Of course, away from the village.' In all these reveries his father never had a place, but there was I, and there was Maami Ama, and there was his father, and he, that bone of contention, was lost to all three. I saw the highest castles I had built for him come tumbling down, noiselessly and swiftly.

He was buried at four o'clock. I had taken the schoolchildren to where he lay in state. When his different relatives saw the little uniformed figure they all forgot their differences and burst into loud lamentations. 'Chicha, O Chicha, what shall I do now that Kwesi is dead?' His grandmother addressed me. 'Kwesi, my Beauty, Kwesi my Master, Kwesi-my-own-Kwesi,' one aunt was chanting, 'Father Death has done me an ill turn.'

'Chicha,' the grandmother continued, 'my washing days are over, for who will give me water? My eating days are over, for who will give me food?' I stood there, saying nothing. I had let the children sing 'Saviour Blessed Saviour'. And we had gone to the cemetery with him.

After the funeral, I went to the House of Mourning as one should do after a burial. No one was supposed to weep again for the rest of the day. I sat there listening to visitors who had come from the neighbouring villages.

'This is certainly sad, and it is most strange. School has become like business; those who found it earlier for their children are eating more than the children themselves. To have a schoolboy snatched away like this is unbearable indeed,' one woman said.

'Ah, do not speak,' his father's youngest sister broke in. 'We have lost a treasure.'

'My daughter,' said the grandmother again, 'Kwesi is gone, gone for ever to our forefathers. And what can we do?'

'What can we do indeed? When flour is scattered in the

D

73

sand, who can sift it? But this is the saddest I've heard, that he was his mother's only one.'

'Is that so?' another visitor cried. 'I always thought she had other children. What does one do, when one's only water-pot breaks?' she whispered. The question was left hanging in the air. No one dared say anything more.

I went out. I never knew how I got there, but I saw myself approaching Maami Ama's hut. As usual, the door was open. I entered the outer room. She was not there. Only sheep and goats from the village were busy munching at the cassava and the yams. I looked into the inner chamber. She was there. Still clad in the cloth she had worn to the divorce proceedings, she was not sitting, standing or lying down. She was kneeling, and like one drowning who catches at a straw, she was clutching Kwesi's books and school uniform to her breast. 'Maami Ama, Maami Ama,' I called out to her. She did not move. I left her alone. Having driven the sheep and goats away, I went out, shutting the door behind me. 'I must go home now,' I spoke to myself once more. The sun was sinking behind the coconut palm. I looked at my watch. It was six o'clock; but this time, I did not run.

A Gift from Somewhere

The Mallam had been to the village once. A long time ago. A long time ago, he had come to do these parts with Ahmadu. That had been his first time. He did not remember what had actually happened except that Ahmadu had died one night during the trip. Allah, the things that can happen to us in our exile and wanderings!

Now the village was quiet. But these people. How can they leave their villages so empty every day like this? Any time you come to a village in these parts in the afternoon, you only find the too young, the too old, the maimed and the dying, or else goats and chickens, never men and women. They don't have any cause for alarm. There is no fighting here, no marauding.

He entered several compounds which were completely deserted. Then he came to this one and saw the woman. Pointing to her stomach, he said, 'Mami Fanti, there is something there.' The woman started shivering. He was embarrassed.

Something told him that there was nothing wrong with the woman herself. Perhaps there was a baby? Oh Allah, one always has to make such violent guesses. He looked round for a stool. When he saw one lying by the wall, he ran to pick it up. He returned with it to where the woman was sitting, placed it right opposite her, and sat down.

Then he said, 'Mami, by Allah, by his holy prophet Mohamet, let your heart rest quiet in your breast. This little one, this child, he will live . . .'

And she lifted her head which until then was so bent her chin touched her breasts, and raised her eyes to the face of the Mallam for the first time, and asked 'Papa Kramo, is that true?'

'Ah Mami Fanti,' the Mallam rejoined. 'Mm . . . mm,' shaking awhile the forefinger of his right hand. This movement accompanied simultaneously as it was by his turbanned head and face, made him look very knowing indeed.

'Mm . . . mm, and why must you yourself be asking me if it is true? Have I myself lied to you before, eh Mami Fanti?'

'Hmmmm. . . .' sighed she of the anxious heart. 'It is just that I cannot find it possible to believe that he will live. That is why I asked you that.'

His eyes glittered with the pleasure of his first victory and her heart did a little somersault.

'Mami Fanti, I myself, me, I am telling you. The little one, he will live. Now today he may not look good, perhaps not today. Perhaps even after eight days he will not be good but I tell you, Mami, one moon, he will be good . . . good . . . good,' and he drew up his arms, bent them, contracted his shoulders and shook up the upper part of his body to indicate how well and strong he thought the child would be. It was a beautiful sight and for an instant a smile passed over her face. But the smile was not able to stay. It was chased away by the anxiety that seemed to have come to occupy her face forever.

'Papa Kramo, if you say that, I believe you. But you will give me something to protect him from the witches?'

'Mami Fanti, you yourself you are in too much hurry, and why? Have I got up to go?'

She shook her head and said 'No' with a voice that quaked with fear.

'Aha . . . so you yourself you must be patient. I myself will do everything . . . everything. . . . Allah is present and Mohamet his holy prophet is here too. I will do everything for you. You hear?'

She breathed deeply and loudly in reply.

'Now bring to me the child.' She stood up, and unwound the other cloth with which she had so far covered up her bruised soul and tied it around her waist. She turned in her step and knocked over the stool. The clanging noise did not attract her attention in the least. Slowly, she walked towards the door. The Mallam's eyes followed her while his left hand groped through the folds of his boubou in search of his last piece of cola. Then he remembered that his sack was still on his shoulder. He removed it, placed it on the floor and now with both his hands free, he fished out the cola. He popped it into his mouth and his tongue received the bitter piece of fruit with the eagerness of a lover.

The stillness of the afternoon was yet to be broken. In the hearth, a piece of coal yielded its tiny ash to the naughty breeze, blinked with its last spark and folded itself up in death. Above, a lonely cloud passed over the Mallam's turban, on its way to join camp in the south. And as if the Mallam had felt the motion of the cloud, he looked up and scanned the sky.

Perhaps it shall rain tonight? I must hurry up with this woman so that I can reach the next village before nightfall.

'Papa Kramo-e-e –!'

This single cry pierced through the dark interior of the room in which the child was lying, hit the aluminium utensils in the outer room, gathered itself together, cut through the silence of that noon, and echoed in the several corners of the village. The Mallam sprang up. 'What is it, Mami Fanti?' And the two collided at the door to her rooms. But neither of them saw how she managed to throw the baby on him and how he came to himself sufficiently to catch it. But the world is a wonderful place and such things happen in it daily. The Mallam caught the baby before it fell.

'Look, look, Papa Kramo, look! Look and see if this baby is not dead. See if this baby too is not dead. Just look – o – o Papa Kramo, look!' And she started running up and down, jumping, wringing her hands and undoing the threads in her hair. Was she immediately mad? Perhaps. The only way to tell that a possessed woman of this kind is not completely out of her senses is that she does not uncloth herself to nakedness. The Mallam was bewildered.

'Mami Fanti, *hei*, Mami Fanti,' he called unheeded. Then he looked down at the child in his arms.

Allah, tch, tch, tch. Now, O holy Allah. Now only you can rescue me from this trouble, since my steps found this house guided by the Prophet, but Allah, this baby is dead.

And he looked down again at it to confirm his suspicion.

Allah, the child is breathing but what kind of breath is this? I must hurry up and leave. Ah . . . what a bad day this is. But I will surely not want the baby to grow still in my arms! At all . . . for that will be bad luck, big bad luck. . . . And now where is its mother? This is not good. I am so hungry now. I thought at least I was going to earn some four pennies so I could eat. I do not like to go without food when it is not Ramaddan. Now look – And I can almost count its ribs! One, two, three, four, five. . . . And Ah . . . llah, it is pale. I could swear this is a Fulani child only its face does not show that it is. If this is the pallor of sickness . . . O Mohamet! Now I must think up something quickly to comfort the mother with.

'*Hei* Mami Fanti, Mami Fanti!'

'Papaa!'

"Come.'

She danced in from the doorway still wringing her hands and sucking in the air through her mouth like one who had swallowed a mouthful of scalding-hot porridge.

'It is dead, is it not?' she asked with the courtesy of the insane.

'Mami, sit down.'

She sat.

'Mami, what is it yourself you are doing? Yourself you make plenty noise. It is not good. Eh, what is it for yourself you do that?'

Not knowing how to answer the questions, she kept quiet. 'Yourself, look well.' She craned her neck as though she were looking for an object in a distance. She saw his breath flutter.

'Yourself you see he is not dead?'

'Yes,' she replied without conviction. It was too faint a breath to build any hopes on, but she did not say this to the Mallam.

'Now listen Mami,' he said, and he proceeded to spit on the child: once on his forehead and then on his navel. Then he spat into his right palm and with this spittle started massaging the child very hard on his joints, the neck, shoulder blades, ankles and wrists. You could see he was straining himself very hard. You would have thought the child's skin would peel off any time. And the woman could not bear to look on.

If the child had any life in him, surely, he could have yelled at least once more? She sank her chin deeper into her breast.

'Now Mami, I myself say, you yourself, you must listen.'

'Papa, I am listening.'

'Mami, I myself say, this child will live. Now himself he is too small. Yourself you must not eat meat. You must not eat fish from the sea, Friday, Sunday. You hear?' She nodded in reply. 'He himself, if he is about ten years,' and he counted ten by flicking the five fingers of his left hand twice over, 'if he is about ten, tell him he must not eat meat and fish from the sea, Friday, Sunday. If he himself he does not eat, you Mami Fanti, you can eat. You hear?'

She nodded again.

'Now, the child he will live, yourself you must stop weeping. If you do that it is not good. Now you have the blue dye for washing?'

'Yes,' she murmured.

'And a piece of white cloth?'

'Yes, but it is not big. Just about a yard and a quarter.'

'That does not matter. Yourself, find those things for me and I will do something and your child he shall be good.'

She did not say anything.

'Did you yourself hear me, Mami Fanti?'

'Yes.'

'Now take the child, put him in the room. Come back, go and find all the things.'

She took the thing which might once have been a human child but now was certainly looking like something else and went back with it to the room.

And she was thinking.

Who does the Mallam think he is deceiving? This is the third child to die. The others never looked half this sick. No! In fact the last one was fat. . . . I had been playing with it. After the evening meal I had laid him down on the mat to go and take a quick bath. Nothing strange in that. When I returned to the house later, I powdered myself and finished up the last bits of my toilet. . . . When I eventually went in to pick up my baby, he was dead.

. . . O my Lord, my Mighty God, who does the Mallam think he is deceiving?

And he was thinking.

Ah . . . llah just look, I cannot remain here. It will be bad of me to ask the woman for so much as a penny when I know this child will die. Ah . . . llah, look, the day has come a long way and I have still not eaten.

He rose up, picked up his bag from the ground and with a quietness and swiftness of which only a nomad is capable, he vanished from the house. When the woman had laid the child down, she returned to the courtyard.

'Papa Kramo, Papa Kramo,' she called. A goat who had been lying nearby chewing the cud got up and went out quietly too.

'Kramo, Kramo,' only her own voice echoed in her brain. She sat down again on the stool. If she was surprised at all, it was only at the neatness of his escape. So he too had seen death.

Should any of my friends hear me moaning, they will say

I am behaving like one who has not lost a baby before, like a fresh bride who sees her first baby dying. Now all I must do is to try and prepare myself for another pregnancy, for it seems this is the reason why I was created . . . to be pregnant for nine of the twelve months of every year. . . . Or is there a way out of it at all? And where does this road lie? I shall have to get used to it. . . . It is the pattern set for my life. For the moment, I must be quiet until the mothers come back in the evening to bury him.

Then rewrapping the other cloth around her shoulders, she put her chin in her breast and she sat, as though the Mallam had never been there.

· · · · ·

But do you know, this child did not die. It is wonderful but this child did not die. Mmm. . . . This strange world always has something to surprise us with . . . Kweku Nyamekye. Somehow, he did not die. To his day name Kweku, I have added Nyamekye. Kweku Nyamekye. For, was he not a gift from God through the Mallam of the Bound Mouth? And he, the Mallam of the Bound Mouth, had not taken from me a penny, not a single penny that ever bore a hole. And the way he had vanished! Or it was perhaps the god who yielded me to my mother who came to my aid at last? As he had promised her he would? I remember Maame telling me that when I was only a baby, the god of Mbemu from whom I came, had promised never to desert me and that he would come to me once in my life when I needed him most. And was it not him who had come in the person of the Mallam? . . . But was it not strange, the way he disappeared without asking for a penny? He had not even waited for me to buy the things he had prescribed. He was going to make a charm. It is good that he did not, for how can a scholar go through life wearing something like that? Looking at the others of the Bound Mouth, sometimes you can spot familiar faces, but my Mallam has never been here again.

Nyamekye, hmm, and after him I have not lost any more children. Let me touch wood. In this world, it is true, there is always something somewhere, covered with leaves. Nyamekye lived. I thought his breathing would have stopped, by the time the old women returned in the evening. But it did not. Towards nightfall his colour changed completely. He did not feel so hot. His breathing improved and from then, he grew stronger every day. But if ever I come upon the Mallam, I will just fall down before him, wipe his tired feet with a silk kente, and then spread it before him and ask him to walk on it. If I do not do that then no one should call me Abena Gyaawa again.

When he started recovering, I took up the taboo as the Mallam had instructed. He is now going to be eleven years old I think. Eleven years, and I have never, since I took it up, missed observing it any Friday or Sunday. Not once. Sometimes I wonder why he chose these two days and not others. If my eyes had not been scattered about me that afternoon, I would have asked him to explain the reason behind this choice to me. And now I shall never know.

Yes, eleven years. But it has been difficult. Oh, it is true I do not think that I am one of these women with a sweet tooth for fish and meats. But if you say that you are going to eat soup, then it is soup you are going to eat. Perhaps no meat or fish may actually hit your teeth but how can you say any broth has soul when it does not contain anything at all? It is true that like everyone else, I liked kontomire. But like everyone else too, I ate it only when my throat ached for it or when I was on the farm. But since I took up the taboo, I have had to eat it at least twice two days of the week, Sunday and Friday. I have come to hate its deep-green look. My only relief came with the season of snails and mushrooms. But everyone knows that these days they are getting rarer because it does not rain as often as it used to. Then after about five years of this strict observance, someone who knew about these things advised me. He said that since the Mallam had mentioned the sea, at least I could eat freshwater fish or prawns and crabs. I did not like the idea of eating fish at all. Who can tell which minnow has paid a visit to the ocean? So I began eating freshwater prawns and crabs – but of course, only when I could get them. Normally, you do not get these things unless you have a grown-up son who would go trapping in the river for you.

But I do not mind these difficulties. If the Mallam came back to tell me that I must stop eating fish and meat altogether so that Nyamekye and the others would live, I would do it. I would. After all, he had told me that I could explain the taboo to Nyamekye when he was old enough to understand, so he could take it up himself. But I have not done it and I do not think I shall ever do it. How can a schoolboy, and who knows, one day he may become a real scholar, how can he go through life dragging this type of taboo along with him? I have never heard any scholar doing it, and my son is not going to be first to do it. No. I myself will go on observing it until I die. For, how could I have gone on living with my two empty hands? – I swear by everything, I do not understand people who complain that I am spoiling them, especially him. And anyway, is it any business of theirs? Even if I daily anointed them with shea-butter and placed them in the sun, whom would I hurt? Who else should be concerned apart from me?

But the person whose misunderstanding hurts me is their father. I do not know what to do. Something tells me it's his people and his wives who prevent him from having good thoughts about me and mine. I was his first wife and if you knew how at the outset of our lives, death haunted us, hmmm. Neither of us had a head to think in. And if things were what they should be, should he be behaving in this way? In fact, I swear by everything, he hates Nyamekye. Or how could what happened last week have happened?

It was a Friday and they had not gone to school. It was a holiday for them. I do not know what this one was for but it was one of those days they do not go. When the time came for us to leave for the farm, I showed him where food was and asked him to look after himself and his younger brother and sisters. Well my tongue was still moving when his father came in with his face shut down, the way it is when he is angry. He came up to us and asked '*Hei*, Nyamekye, are you not following your mother to the farm?' Oh, I was hurt. Is this the way to talk to a ten-year-old child? If he had been any other father, he would have said, 'Nyamekye, since you are not going to school today, pick up your knife and come with me to the farm.'

Would that not have been beautiful?

'Nyamekye, are you not following your mother to the farm?' As if I am the boy's only parent. But he is stuck with this habit, especially where I and my little ones are concerned.

'Gyaawa, your child is crying. . . . Gyaawa, your child is going to fall off the terrace if you do not pay more attention to him. . . . Gyaawa, your child this, and your child that!'

Anyway, that morning I was hurt and when I opened up my mouth, all the words which came to my lips were, 'I thought this boy was going to be a scholar and not a farm-goer. What was the use in sending him to school if I knew he was going to follow me to the farm?'

This had made him more angry. 'I did not know that if you go to school, your skin must not touch a leaf!'

I did not say anything. What had I to say? We went to the farm leaving Nyamekye with the children. I returned home earlier than his father did. Nyamekye was not in the house. I asked his brother and sisters if they knew where he had gone. But they had not seen him since they finished eating earlier in the afternoon. When he had not come home by five o'clock, I started getting worried. Then his father too returned from the farm. He learned immediately that he was missing. He clouded up. After he had had his bath, he went to sit in his chair, dark as a rainy sky. Then he got up to go by the chicken coop. I did not know that he was going to fetch a cane. Just as he was sitting in the chair again, Nyamekye appeared.

'*Hei*, Kweku Nyamekye, come here.'

Nyamekye was holding the little bucket and I knew where he had been to. He moved slowly up to his father.

'Papa, I went to the river to visit my trap, because today is Friday.'

'Have I asked you for anything? And your traps! Is that what you go to school to learn?'

And then he pulled out the cane and fell on the child. The bucket dropped and a few little prawns fell out. Something tells me it was the sight of those prawns which finished his father. He poured those blows on him as though he were made of wood. I had made up my mind never to interfere in any manner he chose to punish the children, for after all, they are his too. But this time I thought he was going too far. I rushed out to rescue Nyamekye and then it came, wham! The sharpest blow I have ever received in my life caught me on the inside of my arm. Blood gushed out. When he saw what had happened, he was ashamed. He went away into his room. That evening he did not eat the fufu I served him.

Slowly, I picked up the bucket and the prawns. Nyamekye followed me to my room where I wept.

The scar healed quickly but the scar is of the type which rises so anyone can see it. Nyamekye's father's attitude has changed towards us. He is worse. He is angry all the time. He is angry with shame.

But I do not even care. I have my little ones. And I am sure someone is wishing she were me. I have Nyamekye. And for this, I do not even know whom to thank.

'Do I thank you, O Mallam of the Bound Mouth?

Or you, Nana Mbemu, since I think you came in the person of the Mallam?

Or Mighty Jehovah-after-whom-there-is-none-other, to you alone should I give my thanks?

But why should I let this worry me? I thank you all. Oh, I thank you all. And you, our ancestral spirits, if you are looking after me, then look after the Mallam too. Remember him at meals, for he is a kinsman.

And as for this scar, I am glad it is not on Nyamekye. Any time I see it I only recall one afternoon when I sat with my chin in my breast before a Mallam came in, and after a Mallam went out.

Two Sisters

As she shakes out the typewriter cloak and covers the machine with it, the thought of the bus she has to hurry to catch goes through her like a pain. It is her luck, she thinks. Everything is just her luck. Why, if she had one of those graduates for a boy-friend, wouldn't he come and take her home every evening? And she knows that a girl does not herself have to be a graduate to get one of those boys. Certainly, Joe is dying to do exactly that – with his taxi. And he is as handsome as anything, and a good man, but you know . . . Besides there are cars and there are cars. As for the possibility of the other actually coming to fetch her – oh well. She has to admit it will take some time before she can bring herself to make demands of that sort on *him*. She has also to admit that the temptation is extremely strong. Would it really be so dangerously indiscreet? Doesn't one government car look like another? The hugeness of it? Its shaded glass? The uniformed chauffeur? She can already see herself stepping out to greet the dead-with-envy glances of the other girls. To begin with, she will insist on a little discretion. The driver can drop her under the neem trees in the morning and pick her up from there in the evening . . . anyway, she will have to wait a little while for that and it is all her luck.

There are other ways, surely. One of these, for some reason, she has sworn to have nothing of. Her boss has a car and does not look bad. In fact the man is alright. But she keeps telling herself that she does not fancy having some old and dried-out housewife walking into the office one afternoon to tear her hair out and make a row. . . . Mm, so for the meantime, it is going to continue to be the municipal bus with its grimy seats, its common passengers and impudent conductors. . . . Jesus! She doesn't wish herself dead or anything as stupidly final as that. Oh no. She just wishes she could sleep deep and only wake up on the morning of her glory.

The new pair of black shoes are more realistic than their owner, though. As she walks down the corridor, they sing:

> *Count, Mercy, count your blessings*
> *Count, Mercy, count your blessings*
> *Count, count, count your blessings.*

They sing along the corridor, into the avenue, across the road and into the bus. And they resume their song along the gravel path, as she opens the front gate and crosses the cemented courtyard to the door.

'Sissie!' she called.

'*Hei* Mercy,' and the door opened to show the face of Connie, big sister, six years or more older and now heavy with her second child. Mercy collapsed into the nearest chair.

'Welcome home. How was the office today?'

'Sister, don't ask. Look at my hands. My fingers are dead with typing. Oh God, I don't know what to do.'

'Why, what is wrong?'

'You tell me what is right. Why should I be a typist?'

'What else would you be?'

'What a strange question. Is typing the only thing one can do in this world? You are a teacher, are you not?'

'But . . . but . . .'

'But what? Or you want me to know that if I had done better in the exams, I could have trained to be a teacher too, eh, sister? Or even a proper secretary?'

'Mercy, what is the matter? What have I done? What have I done? Why have you come home so angry?'

Mercy broke into tears.

'Oh I am sorry. I am sorry, Sissie. It's just that I am sick of everything. The office, living with you and your husband. I want a husband of my own, children. I want . . . I want . . .'

'But you are so beautiful.'

'Thank you. But so are you.'

'You are young and beautiful. As for marriage, it's you who are postponing it. Look at all these people who are running after you.'

'Sissie, I don't like what you are doing. So stop it.'

'Okay, okay, okay.'

And there was a silence.

'Which of them could I marry? Joe is – mm, fine – but, but I just don't like him.'

'You mean . . .'

'Oh, Sissie!'

'Little sister, you and I can be truthful with one another.'
'Oh yes.'

'What I would like to say is that I am not that old or wise. But still I could advise you a little. Joe drives someone's car now. Well, you never know. Lots of taxi drivers come to own their taxis, sometimes fleets of cars.'

'Of course. But it's a pity you are married already. Or I could be a go-between for you and Joe!'

And the two of them burst out laughing. It was when she rose to go to the bedroom that Connie noticed the new shoes.

'*Ei*, those are beautiful shoes. Are they new?'

From the other room, Mercy's voice came interrupted by the motions of her body as she undressed and then dressed again. However, the uncertainty in it was due to something entirely different.

'Oh, I forgot to tell you about them. In fact, I was going to show them to you. I think it was on Tuesday I bought them. Or was it Wednesday? When I came home from the office, you and James had taken Akosua out. And later, I forgot all about them.'

'I see. But they are very pretty. Were they expensive?'

'No, not really.' This reply was too hurriedly said.

And she said only last week that she didn't have a penny on her. And I believed her because I know what they pay her is just not enough to last anyone through any month, even minus rent. . . . I have been thinking she manages very well. But these shoes. And she is not the type who would borrow money just to buy a pair of shoes, when she could have gone on wearing her old pairs until things get better. Oh I wish I knew what to do. I mean I am not her mother. And I wonder how James will see these problems.

'Sissie, you look worried.'

'Hmm, when don't I? With the baby due in a couple of months and the government's new ruling on salaries and all. On top of everything, I have reliable information that James is running after a new girl.'

Mercy laughed.

'Oh Sissie. You always get reliable information on these things.'

'But yes. And I don't know why.'

'Sissie, men are like that.'

'They are selfish.'

'No, it's just that women allow them to behave the way they do instead of seizing some freedom themselves.'

'But I am sure that even if we were free to carry on in the same way, I wouldn't make use of it.'

'But why not?'

'Because I love James. I love James and I am not interested in any other man.' Her voice was full of tears. But Mercy was amused.

'O God. Now listen to that. It's women like you who keep all of us down.'

'Well, I am sorry but it's how the good God created me.'

'Mm. I am sure that I can love several men at the same time.'

'Mercy!'

They burst out laughing again. And yet they are sad. But laughter is always best.

Mercy complained of hunger and so they went to the kitchen to heat up some food and eat. The two sisters alone. It is no use waiting for James. And this evening, a friend of Connie's has come to take out the baby girl, Akosua, and had threatened to keep her until her bedtime.

'Sissie, I am going to see a film.' This from Mercy.

'Where?'

'The Globe.'

'Are you going with Joe?'

'No.'

'Are you going alone?'

'No.'

Careful Connie.

'Whom are you going with?'

Careful Connie, please. Little sister's nostrils are widening dangerously. Look at the sudden creasing-up of her mouth and between her brows. Connie, a sister is a good thing. Even a younger sister. Especially when you have no mother or father.

'Mercy, whom are you going out with?'

'Well, I had food in my mouth! And I had to swallow it down before I could answer you, no?'

'I am sorry.' How softly said.

'And anyway, do I have to tell you everything?'

'Oh no. It's just that I didn't think it was a question I should not have asked.'

There was more silence. Then Mercy sucked her teeth with irritation and Connie cleared her throat with fear.

'I am going out with Mensar-Arthur.'

As Connie asked the next question, she wondered if the words were leaving her lips.

'Mensar-Arthur?'

'Yes.'

'Which one?'

'How many do you know?'

Her fingers were too numb to pick up the food. She put the plate down. Something jumped in her chest and she wondered what it was. Perhaps it was the baby.

'Do you mean that member of Parliament?'

'Yes.'

'But Mercy . . .'

Little sister only sits and chews her food.

'But Mercy . . .'

Chew, chew, chew.

'But Mercy . . .'

'What?'

She startled Connie.

'He is so old.'

Chew, chew, chew.

'Perhaps, I mean, perhaps that really doesn't matter, does it? Not very much anyway. But they say he has so many wives and girl-friends.'

Please little sister. I am not trying to interfere in your private life. You said yourself a little while ago that you wanted a man of your own. That man belongs to so many women already. . . .

That silence again. Then there was only Mercy's footsteps as she went to put her plate in the kitchen sink, running water as she washed her plate and her hands. She drank some water and coughed. Then as tears streamed down her sister's averted face, there was the sound of her footsteps as she left the kitchen. At the end of it all, she banged a door. Connie only said something like, 'O Lord, O Lord,' and continued sitting in the kitchen. She had hardly eaten anything at all. Very soon Mercy went to have a bath. Then Connie heard her getting ready to leave the house. The shoes. Then she was gone. She needn't have carried on like that, eh? Because Connie had not meant to probe or bring on a quarrel. What use is there in this old world for a sister, if you can't have a chat with her? What's more, things like this never happen to people like Mercy. Their parents were good Presbyterians. They feared God. Mama had not managed to give them all the rules of life before she died. But Connie knows that running around with an old and depraved public man would have been considered an abomination by the parents.

A big car with a super-smooth engine purred into the drive. It actually purrs: this huge machine from the white man's land. Indeed, its well-mannered protest as the tyres slid on to the gravel seemed like a lullaby compared to the loud thumping of the girl's stiletto shoes. When Mensar-Arthur saw Mercy, he stretched his arm and opened the door to the passenger seat. She sat down and the door closed with a civilised thud. The engine hummed into motion and the car sailed away.

After a distance of a mile or so from the house, the man started conversation.

'And how is my darling today?'

'I am well,' and only the words did not imply tragedy.

'You look solemn today, why?'

She remained silent and still.

'My dear, what is the matter?'

'Nothing.'

'Oh . . .' he cleared his throat again. 'Eh, and how were the shoes?'

'Very nice. In fact, I am wearing them now. They pinch a little but then all new shoes are like that.'

'And the handbag?'

'I like it very much too. . . . My sister noticed them. I mean the shoes.' The tragedy was announced.

'Did she ask you where you got them from?'

'No.'

He cleared his throat again.

'Where did we agree to go tonight?'

'The Globe, but I don't want to see a film.'

'Is that so? Mm, I am glad because people always notice things.'

'But they won't be too surprised.'

'What are you saying, my dear?'

'Nothing.'

'Okay, so what shall we do?'

'I don't know.'

'Shall I drive to the Seaway?'

'Oh yes.'

He drove to the Seaway. To a section of the beach they knew very well. She loves it here. This wide expanse of sand and the old sea. She has often wished she could do what she fancied: one thing she fancies. Which is to drive very near to the end of the sands until the tyres of the car touched the water. Of course it is a very foolish idea as he pointed out sharply to her the first time she thought aloud about it. It was in his occasional I-am-more-than-old-enough-to-be-your-father tone. There are always disadvantages. Things could be different. Like if one had a younger lover. Handsome, maybe not rich like this man here, but well-off, sufficiently well-off to be able to afford a sports car. A little something very much like those in the films driven by the white racing drivers. With tyres that can do everything . . . and they would drive exactly where the sea and the sand meet.

'We are here.'

'Don't let's get out. Let's just sit inside and talk.'

'Talk?'

'Yes.'

'Okay. But what is it, my darling?'

'I have told my sister about you.'

'Good God. Why?'

'But I had to. I couldn't keep it to myself any longer.'

'Childish. It was not necessary at all. She is not your mother.'

'No. But she is all I have. And she has been very good to me.'

'Well, it was her duty.'

'Then it is my duty to tell her about something like this. I may get into trouble.'

'Don't be silly,' he said, 'I normally take good care of my girl-friends.'

'I see,' she said and for the first time in the one month since she agreed to be this man's lover, the tears which suddenly rose into her eyes were not forced.

'And you promised you wouldn't tell her.' It was father's voice now.

'Don't be angry. After all, people talk so much, as you said a little while ago. She was bound to hear it one day.'

'My darling, you are too wise. What did she say?'

'She was pained.'

'Don't worry. Find out something she wants very much but cannot get in this country because of the import restrictions.'

'I know for sure she wants an electric motor for her sewing machine.'

'Is that all?'

'That's what I know of.'

'Mm. I am going to London next week on some delegation, so if you bring me the details on the make of the machine, I shall get her the motor.'

'Thank you.'

'What else is worrying my Black Beauty?'

'Nothing.'

'And by the way, let me know as soon as you want to leave your sister's place. I have got you one of the government estate houses.'

'Oh . . . oh,' she said, pleased, contented for the first time since this typically ghastly day had begun, at half-past six in the morning.

Dear little child came back from the playground with her toe bruised. Shall we just blow cold air from our mouth on it or put on a salve? Nothing matters really. Just see that she does not feel unattended. And the old sea roars on. This is a calm sea, generally. Too calm in fact, this Gulf of Guinea. The natives sacrifice to him on Tuesdays and once a year celebrate him. They might save their chickens, their eggs and their yams. And as for the feast once a year, he doesn't pay much attention to it either. They are always celebrating one thing or another and they surely don't need him for an excuse to celebrate one day more. He has seen things happen along these beaches. Different things. Contradictory things. Or just repetitions of old patterns. He never interferes in their affairs. Why should he? Except in places like Keta where he eats houses away because they leave him no choice. Otherwise he never allows them to see his passions. People are worms, and even the God who created them is immensely bored with their antics. Here is a fifty-year-old 'big man' who thinks he is somebody. And a twenty-three-year-old child who chooses a silly way to conquer unconquerable problems. Well, what did one expect of human beings? And so as those two settled on the back seat of the car to play with each other's bodies, he, the Gulf of Guinea, shut his eyes with boredom. It is right. He could sleep, no? He spread himself and moved further ashore. But the car was parked at a very safe distance and the rising tides could not wet its tyres.

James has come home late. But then he has been coming back late for the past few weeks. Connie is crying and he knows it as soon as he enters the bedroom. He hates tears, for like so many men, he knows it is one of the most potent weapons in women's bitchy and inexhaustible arsenal. She speaks first.

'James.'

'Oh, you are still awake?' He always tries to deal with these nightly funeral parlour doings by pretending not to know what they are about.

'I couldn't sleep.'

'What is wrong?'

'Nothing.'

So he moves quickly and sits beside her.

'Connie, what is the matter? You have been crying again.'

'You are very late again.'

'Is that why you are crying? Or is there something else?'

'Yes.'

'Yes to what?'

'James, where were you?'

'Connie, I have warned you about what I shall do if you don't stop examining me, as though I were your prisoner, every time I am a little late.'

She sat up.

'A little late! It is nearly two o'clock.'

'Anyway, you won't believe me if I told you the truth, so why do you want me to waste my breath?'

'Oh well.' She lies down again and turns her face to the wall. He stands up but does not walk away. He looks down at her. So she remembers every night: they have agreed, after many arguments, that she should sleep like this. During her first pregnancy, he kept saying after the third month or so that the sight of her tummy the last thing before he slept always gave him nightmares. Now he regrets all this. The bed creaks as he throws himself down by her.

'James.'

'Yes.'

'There is something much more serious.'

'You have heard about my newest affair?'

'Yes, but that is not what I am referring to.'

'Jesus, is it possible that there is anything more important than that?'

And as they laugh they know that something has happened. One of those things which, with luck, will keep them together for some time to come.

'He teases me on top of everything.'

'What else can one do to you but tease when you are in this state?'

'James! How profane!'

'It is your dirty mind which gave my statement its shocking meaning.'

'Okay! But what shall I do?'

'About what?'

'Mercy. Listen, she is having an affair with Mensar-Arthur.'

'Wonderful.'

She sits up and he sits up.

'James, we must do something about it. It is very serious.'

'Is that why you were crying?'

'Of course.'

'Why shouldn't she?'

'But it is wrong. And she is ruining herself.'

'Since every other girl she knows has ruined herself prosperously, why shouldn't she? Just forget for once that you are a teacher. Or at least, remember she is not your pupil.'

'I don't like your answers.'

'What would you like me to say? Every morning her friends who don't earn any more than she does wear new dresses, shoes, wigs and what-have-you to work. What would you have her do?'

'The fact that other girls do it does not mean that Mercy should do it too.'

'You are being very silly. If I were Mercy, I am sure that's exactly what I would do. And you know I mean it too.'

James is cruel. He is terrible and mean. Connie breaks into fresh tears and James comforts her. There is one point he must drive home though.

'In fact, encourage her. He may be able to intercede with the Ministry for you so that after the baby is born they will not transfer you from here for some time.'

'James, you want me to use my sister!'

'She is using herself, remember.'

'James, you are wicked.'

'And maybe he would even agree to get us a new car from abroad. I shall pay for everything. That would be better than paying a fortune for that old thing I was thinking of buying. Think of that.'

'You will ride in it alone.'

'Well . . .'

That was a few months before the *coup*. Mensar-Arthur did go to London for a conference and bought something for all his wives and girl-friends, including Mercy. He even remembered the motor for Connie's machine. When Mercy took it to her she was quite confused. She had wanted this thing for a long time, and it would make everything so much easier, like the clothes for the new baby. And yet one side of her said that accepting it was a betrayal. Of what, she wasn't even sure. She and Mercy could never bring the whole business into the open and discuss it. And there was always James supporting Mercy, to Connie's bewilderment. She took the motor with thanks and sold even her right to dissent. In a short while, Mercy left the house to go and live in the estate house Mensar-Arthur had procured for her. Then, a couple of weeks later, the *coup*. Mercy left her new place before anyone could evict her. James never got his car. Connie's new baby was born. Of the three, the one who greeted the new order with undisguised relief was Connie. She is not really a demonstrative person but it was obvious from her eyes that she was happy. As far as she was concerned, the old order as symbolised by Mensar-Arthur was a threat to her sister and therefore to her own peace of mind. With it gone, things could return to normal. Mercy would move back to the house, perhaps start to date someone more – ordinary, let's say. Eventually, she would get married and then the nightmare of those past weeks would be forgotten. God being so good, he brought the *coup* early before the news of the affair could spread and brand her sister. . . .

The arrival of the new baby has magically waved away the difficulties between James and Connie. He is that kind of man, and she that kind of woman. Mercy has not been seen for many days. Connie is beginning to get worried. . . .

James heard the baby yelling – a familiar noise, by now – the moment he opened the front gate. He ran in, clutching to his chest the few things he had bought on his way home.

'We are in here.'

'I certainly could hear you. If there is anything people of this country have, it is a big mouth.'

'Don't I agree? But on the whole, we are well. He is eating normally and everything. You?'

'Nothing new. Same routine. More stories about the overthrown politicians.'

'What do you mean, nothing new? Look at the excellent job the soldiers have done, cleaning up the country of all that dirt. I feel free already and I am dying to get out and enjoy it.'

James laughed mirthlessly.

'All I know is that Mensar-Arthur is in jail. No use. And I am not getting my car. Rough deal.'

'I never took you seriously on that car business.'

'Honestly, if this were in the ancient days, I could brand you a witch. You don't want me, your husband, to prosper?'

'Not out of my sister's ruin.'

'Ruin, ruin, ruin! Christ! See Connie, the funny thing is that I am sure you are the only person who thought it was a disaster to have a sister who was the girl-friend of a big man.'

'Okay; now all is over, and don't let's quarrel.'

'I bet the *coup* could have succeeded on your prayers alone.'

And Connie wondered why he said that with so much bitterness. She wondered if . . .

'Has Mercy been here?'

'Not yet, later, maybe. Mm. I had hoped she would move back here and start all over again.'

'I am not surprised she hasn't. In fact, if I were her, I wouldn't come back here either. Not to your nagging, no thank you, big sister.'

And as the argument progressed, as always, each was forced into a more aggressive defensive stand.

'Well, just say what pleases you, I am very glad about the soldiers. Mercy is my only sister, brother; everything. I can't sit and see her life going wrong without feeling it. I am grateful to whatever forces there are which put a stop to that.

What pains me now is that she should be so vague about where she is living at the moment. She makes mention of a girl-friend but I am not sure that I know her.'

'If I were you, I would stop worrying because it seems Mercy can look after herself quite well.'

'Hmm,' was all she tried to say.

Who heard something like the sound of a car pulling into the drive? Ah, but the footsteps are unmistakably Mercy's. Are those shoes the old pair which were new a couple of months ago? Or are they the newest pair? And here she is herself, the pretty one. A gay Mercy.

'Hello, hello, my clan!' and she makes a lot of her nephew.

'Dow-dah-dee-day! And how is my dear young man to-day? My lord, grow up fast and come to take care of Auntie Mercy.'

Both Connie and James cannot take their eyes off her. Connie says, 'He says to Auntie Mercy he is fine.'

Still they watch her, horrified, fascinated and wondering what it's all about. Because they both know it is about something.'

'Listen people, I brought a friend to meet you. A man.'

'Where is he?' from James.

'Bring him in,' from Connie.

'You know, Sissie, you are a new mother. I thought I'd come and ask you if it's all right.'

'Of course,' say James and Connie, and for some reason they are both very nervous.

'He is Captain Ashey.'

'Which one?'

'*How many do you know?*'

James still thinks it is impossible. 'Eh . . . do you mean the officer who has been appointed the . . . the . . .'

'Yes.'

'Wasn't there a picture in *The Crystal* over the week-end about his daughter's wedding? And another one of him with his wife and children and grandchildren?'

'Yes.'

'And he is heading a commission to investigate something or other?'

'Yes.'

Connie just sits there with her mouth open that wide. . . .

The Late Bud

'The good child who willingly goes on errands eats the food of peace.' This was a favourite saying in the house. Maami, Aunt Efua, Aunt Araba . . . oh, they all said it, especially when they had prepared something delicious like cocoyam porridge and seasoned beef. You know how it is.

First, as they stirred it with the ladle, its scent rose from the pot and became a little cloud hanging over the hearth. Gradually, it spread through the courtyard and entered the inner and outer rooms of the women's apartments. This was the first scent that greeted the afternoon sleeper. She stretched herself luxuriously, inhaled a large quantity of the sweet scent, cried 'Mm' and either fell back again to sleep or got up to be about her business. The aroma did not stay. It rolled into the next house and the next, until it filled the whole neighbourhood. And Yaaba would sniff it.

As usual, she would be playing with her friends by the Big Trunk. She would suddenly throw down her pebbles even if it was her turn, jump up, shake her cloth free of sand and announce, 'I am going home.'

'Why?'

'Yaaba, why?'

But the questions of her amazed companions would reach her faintly like whispers. She was flying home. Having crossed the threshold, she then slunk by the wall. But there would be none for her.

Yaaba never stayed at home to go on an errand. Even when she was around, she never would fetch water to save a dying soul. How could she then eat the food of peace? Oh, if it was a formal meal, like in the morning or evening, that was a different matter. Of that, even Yaaba got her lawful share. . . . But not this sweet-sweet porridge. 'Nsia, Antobam, Naa-banyin, Adwoa, come for some porridge.' And the other children trooped in with their little plates and bowls. But not the figure by the wall. They chattered as they came and the mother teased as she dished out their titbits.

'Is yours alright, Adwoa? . . . and yours, Tawia? . . . yours is certainly sufficient, Antobam. . . . But my child, this is only a titbit for us, the deserving. Other people,' and she would squint at Yaaba, 'who have not worked will not get the tiniest bit.' She then started eating hers. If Yaaba felt that the joke was being carried too far, she coughed. 'Oh,' the mother would cry out, 'people should be careful about their throats. Even if they coughed until they spat blood none of this porridge would touch their mouths.'

But it was not things and incidents like these which worried Yaaba. For inevitably, a mother's womb cried out for a lonely figure by a wall and she would be given some porridge. Even when her mother could be bile-bellied enough to look at her and dish out all the porridge, Yaaba could run into the doorway and ambush some child and rob him of the greater part of his share. No, it was not such things that worried her. Every mother might call her a bad girl. She enjoyed playing by the Big Trunk, for instance. Since to be a good girl, one had to stay by the hearth and not by the Big Trunk throwing pebbles, but with one's hands folded quietly on one's lap, waiting to be sent everywhere by all the mothers, Yaaba let people like Adwoa who wanted to be called 'good' be good. Thank you, she was not interested.

But there was something which disturbed Yaaba. No one knew it did, but it did. She used to wonder why, every time Maami called Adwoa, she called her 'My child Adwoa', while she was always merely called 'Yaaba'.

'My child Adwoa, pick me the drinking can. . . . My child you have done well. . . .'

Oh, it is so always. Am I not my mother's child?

'Yaaba, come for your food.' She always wished in her heart that she could ask somebody about it. . . . Paapa . . . Maami . . . Nana, am I not Maami's daughter? Who was my mother?

But you see, one does not go round asking elders such questions. Take the day Antobam asked her grandmother where her own mother was. The grandmother also asked Antobam whether she was not being looked after well, and then started weeping and saying things. Other mothers joined in the weeping. Then some more women came over from the neighbourhood and her aunts and uncles came too and there was more weeping and there was also drinking and libation-pouring. At the end of it all, they gave Antobam a stiff talking-to.

No, one does not go round asking one's elders such questions.

But Adwoa, my child, bring me the knife. . . . Yaaba . . . Yaaba, your cloth is dirty. Yaaba, Yaaba . . .

It was the afternoon of the Saturday before Christmas Sunday. Yaaba had just come from the playgrounds to gobble down her afternoon meal. It was kenkey and a little fish stewed in palm oil. She had eaten in such a hurry that a bone had got stuck in her throat. She had drunk a lot of water but still the bone was sticking there. She did not want to tell Maami about it. She knew she would get a scolding or even a knock on the head. It was while she was in the outer room looking for a bit of kenkey to push down the troublesome bone that she heard Maami talking in the inner room.

'Ah, and what shall I do now? But I thought there was a whole big lump left. . . . O . . . O! Things like this irritate me so. How can I spend Christmas without varnishing my floor?'

Yaaba discovered a piece of kenkey which was left from the week before, hidden in its huge wrappings. She pounced upon it and without breaking away the mildew, swallowed it.

E

She choked, stretched her neck and the bone was gone. She drank some water and with her cloth, wiped away the tears which had started gathering in her eyes. She was about to bounce away to the playgrounds when she remembered that she had heard Maami speaking to herself.

Although one must not stand by to listen to elders if they are not addressing one, yet one can hide and listen. And anyway, it would be interesting to hear the sort of things our elders say to themselves. 'And how can I celebrate Christmas on a hardened, whitened floor?' Maami's voice went on. 'If I could only get a piece of red earth. But I cannot go round my friends begging, "Give me a piece of red earth." No. O . . . O! And it is growing dark already. If only my child Adwoa was here. I am sure she could have run to the red-earth pit and fetched me just a hoeful. Then I could varnish the floor before the church bells ring tomorrow.' Yaaba was thinking she had heard enough.

After all, our elders do not say anything interesting to themselves. It is their usual complaints about how difficult life is. If it is not the price of cloth or fish, then it is the scarcity of water. It is all very uninteresting. I will always play with my children when they grow up. I will not grumble about anything. . . .

It was quite dark. The children could hardly see their own hands as they threw up the pebbles. But Yaaba insisted that they go on. There were only three left of the eight girls who were playing *soso-mba*. From time to time mothers, fathers or elder sisters had come and called to the others to go home. The two still with Yaaba were Panyin and Kakra. Their mother had travelled and that was why they were still there. No one came any longer to call Yaaba. Up till the year before, Maami always came to yell for her when it was sundown. When she could not come, she sent Adwoa. But of course, Yaaba never listened to them.

What is the point in breaking a game to go home? She stayed out and played even by herself until it was dark and she was satisfied. And now, at the age of ten, no one came to call her.

The pebble hit Kakra on the head.

'*Ajii.*'

'What is it?'

'The pebble has hit me.'

'I am sorry. It was not intentional.' Panyin said, 'But it is dark Kakra, let us go home.' So they stood up.

'Panyin, will you go to church tomorrow?'

'No.'

'Why? You have no new cloths?'

'We have new cloths but we will not get gold chains or earrings. Our mother is not at home. She has gone to some place and will only return in the afternoon. Kakra, remember we will get up very early tomorrow morning.'

'Why?'

'Have you forgotten what mother told us before she went away? Did she not tell us to go and get some red earth from the pit? Yaaba, we are going away.'

'*Yoo.*'

And the twins turned towards home.

Red earth! The pit! Probably, Maami will be the only woman in the village who will not have red earth to varnish her floor. *Oo*!

'Panyin! Kakra! Panyin!'

'Who is calling us?'

'It is me, Yaaba. Wait for me.'

She ran in the darkness and almost collided with someone who was carrying food to her husband's house.

'Panyin, do you say you will go to the pit tomorrow morning?'

'Yes, what is it?'

'I want to go with you.'

'Why?'

'Because I want to get some red earth for my mother.'

'But tomorrow you will go to church.'

'Yes, but I will try to get it done in time to go to church as well.'

'See, you cannot. Do you not know the pit? It is very far away. Everyone will already be at church by the time we get back home.'

Yaaba stood quietly digging her right toe into the hard ground beneath her. 'It doesn't matter, I will go.'

'Do you not want to wear your gold things? Kakra and I are very sorry that we cannot wear ours because our mother is not here.'

'It does not matter. Come and wake me up.'

'Where do you sleep?'

'Under my mother's window. I will wake up if you hit the window with a small pebble.'

'*Yoo*. . . . We will come to call you.'

'Do not forget your *apampa* and your hoe.'

'*Yoo*.'

When Yaaba arrived home, they had already finished eating the evening meal. Adwoa had arrived from an errand it seemed. In fact she had gone on several others. Yaaba was slinking like a cat to take her food which she knew would be under the wooden bowl, when Maami saw her. 'Yes, go and take it. You are hungry, are you not? And very soon you will be swallowing all that huge lump of fufu as quickly as a hen would swallow corn.' Yaaba stood still.

'*Aa*. My Father God, who inflicted on me such a child? Look here, Yaaba. You are growing, so be careful how you live your life. When you are ten years old you are not a child any more. And a woman that lives on the playground is not a woman. If you were a boy, it would be bad enough, but for a girl, it is a curse. The house cannot hold you. *Tchia*.'

Yaaba crept into the outer room. She saw the wooden bowl. She turned it over and as she had known all the time, her food was there. She swallowed it more quickly than a hen would have swallowed corn. When she finished eating, she went into the inner room, she picked her mat, spread it on the floor, threw herself down and was soon asleep. Long afterwards, Maami came in from the conversation with the other mothers.

When she saw the figure of Yaaba, her heart did a somersault. Pooh, went her fists on the figure in the corner. Pooh, 'You lazy lazy thing.' Pooh, pooh! 'You good-for-nothing, empty-corn husk of a daughter . . .' She pulled her ears, and Yaaba screamed. Still sleepy-eyed, she sat up on the mat.

'If you like, you scream, and watch what I will do to you. If I do not pull your mouth until it is as long as a pestle, then my name is not Benyiwa.'

But Yaaba was now wide awake and tearless. Who said she was screaming, anyway? She stared at Maami with shining tearless eyes. Maami was angry at this too.

'I spit in your eyes, witch! Stare at me and tell me if I am going to die tomorrow. At your age . . .' and the blows came pooh, pooh, pooh. 'You do not know that you wash yourself before your skin touches the mat. And after a long day in the sand, the dust and filth by the Big Trunk. *Hoo! Pooh!* You moth-bitten grain. *Pooh!*'

The clock in the chief's house struck twelve o'clock midnight. Yaaba never cried. She only tried, without success, to ward off the blows. Perhaps Maami was tired herself, perhaps she was satisfied. Or perhaps she was afraid she was putting herself in the position of Kweku Ananse tempting the spirits to carry their kindness as far as to come and help her beat her daughter. Of course, this would kill Yaaba. Anyway, she stopped beating her and lay down by Kofi, Kwame and Adwoa. Yaaba saw the figure of Adwoa lying peacefully there. It was then her eyes misted. The tears flowed from her eyes. Every time, she wiped them with her cloth but more came. They did not make any noise for Maami to hear. Soon the cloth was wet. When the clock struck one, she heard Maami snoring. She herself could not sleep even when she lay down.

Is this woman my mother?

Perhaps I should not go and fetch her some red earth. But the twins will come. . . .

Yaaba rose and went into the outer room. There was no door between the inner and outer rooms to creak and wake

anybody. She wanted the *apampa* and a hoe. At ten years of
age, she should have had her own of both, but of course, she
had not. Adwoa's hoe, she knew, was in the corner left of the
door. She groped and found it. She also knew Adwoa's
apampa was on the bamboo shelf. It was when she turned and
was groping towards the bamboo shelf that she stumbled
over the large water-bowl. Her chest hit the edge of the tray.
The tray tilted and the water poured on the floor. She could
not rise up. When Maami heard the noise her fall made, she
screamed 'Thief! Thief! Thief! Everybody, come, there is a
thief in my room.'

She gave the thief a chance to run away since he might
attack her before the men of the village came. But no thief
rushed through the door and there were no running footsteps
in the courtyard. In fact, all was too quiet.

She picked up the lantern, pushed the wick up to blazing
point and went gingerly to the outer room. There was Yaaba,
sprawled like a freshly-killed overgrown cock on the tray. She
screamed again.

'Ah Yaaba, why do you frighten me like this? What were
you looking for? That is why I always say you are a witch.
What do you want at this time of the night that you should fall
on a water-bowl? And look at the floor. But of course, you
were playing when someone lent me a piece of red earth to
polish it, eh?' The figure in the tray just lay there. Maami
bent down to help her up and then she saw the hoe. She stood
up again.

'A hoe! I swear by all that be that I do not understand this.'
She lifted her up and was carrying her to the inner room
when Yaaba's lips parted as if to say something. She closed
the lips again, her eyelids fluttered down and the neck sagged.
'My Saviour!' There was nothing strange in the fact that the
cry was heard in the north and south of the village. Was it not
past midnight?

People had heard Maami's first cry of 'Thief' and by the
time she cried out again, the first men were coming from all

directions. Soon the courtyard was full. Questions and answers went round. Some said Yaaba was trying to catch a thief, others that she was running from her mother's beating. But the first thing was to wake her up.

'Pour anowata into her nose!' – and the mothers ran into their husbands' chambers to bring their giant-sized bottles of the sweetest scents. 'Touch her feet with a little fire.' . . . 'Squeeze a little ginger juice into her nose.'

The latter was done and before she could suffer further ordeals, Yaaba's eyelids fluttered up.

'*Aa*. . . . *Oo* . . . we thank God. She is awake, she is awake.' Everyone said it. Some were too far away and saw her neither in the faint nor awake. But they said it as they trooped back to piece together their broken sleep. Egya Yaw, the village medicine-man, examined her and told the now-mad Maami that she should not worry. 'The impact was violent but I do not think anything has happened to the breast-bone. I will bind her up in beaten herbs and she should be all right in a few days.' 'Thank you, Egya,' said Maami, Paapa, her grandmother, the other mothers and all her relatives. The medicine-man went to his house and came back. Yaaba's brawniest uncles beat up the herbs. Soon, Yaaba was bound up. The cock had crowed once, when they laid her down. Her relatives then left for their own homes. Only Maami, Paapa and the other mothers were left. 'And how is she?' one of the women asked.

'But what really happened?'

'Only Benyiwa can answer you.'

'Benyiwa, what happened?'

'But I am surprised myself. After she had eaten her kenkey this afternoon, I heard her movements in the outer room but I did not mind her. Then she went away and came back when it was dark to eat her food. After our talk, I went to sleep. And there she was lying. As usual, she had not had a wash, so I just held her . . .'

'You held her what? Had she met with death you would

have been the one that pushed her into it – beating a child in the night!'

'But Yaaba is too troublesome!'

'And so you think every child will be good? But how did she come to fall in the tray?'

'That is what I cannot tell. My eyes were just playing me tricks when I heard some noise in the outer room.'

'Is that why you cried "Thief"?'

'Yes. When I went to see what it was, I saw her lying in the tray, clutching a hoe.'

'A hoe?'

'Yes, Adwoa's hoe.'

'Perhaps there was a thief after all? She can tell us the truth . . . but . . .'

So they went on through the early morning. Yaaba slept. The second cock-crow came. The church bell soon did its Christmas reveille. In the distance, they heard the songs of the dawn procession. Quite near in the doorway, the regular pat, pat of the twins' footsteps drew nearer towards the elderly group by the hearth. Both parties were surprised at the encounter.

'Children, what do you want at dawn?'

'Where is Yaaba?'

'Yaaba is asleep.'

'May we go and wake her, she asked us to.'

'Why?'

'She said she will go with us to the red-earth pit.'

'O . . . O!' The group around the hearth was amazed but they did not show it before the children.

'*Yoo*. You go today. She may come with you next time.'

'*Yoo*, Mother.'

'Walk well, my children. When she wakes up, we shall tell her you came.'

'We cannot understand it. Yaaba? What affected her head?'

'My sister, the world is a strange place. That is all.'

'And my sister, the child that will not do anything is better than a sheep.'

'Benyiwa, we will go and lie down a little.'

'Good morning.'

'Good morning.'

'Good morning.'

'*Yoo*. I thank you all.'

So Maami went into the apartment and closed the door. She knelt by the sleeping Yaaba and put her left hand on her bound chest. 'My child, I say thank you. You were getting ready to go and fetch me red earth? Is that why you were holding the hoe? My child, my child, I thank you.'

And the tears streamed down her face. Yaaba heard 'My child' from very far away. She opened her eyes. Maami was weeping and still calling her 'My child' and saying things which she did not understand.

Is Maami really calling me that? May the twins come. Am I Maami's own child?

'My child Yaaba . . .'

But how will I get red earth?

But why can I not speak . . .?

'I wish the twins would come . . .'

I want to wear the gold earrings . . .

I want to know whether Maami called me her child. Does it mean I am her child like Adwoa is? But one does not ask our elders such questions. And anyway, there is too much pain. And there are barriers where my chest is.

Probably tomorrow . . . but now Maami called me 'My child!' . . .

And she fell asleep again.

Something to Talk About on the Way to the Funeral

. . . Adwoa my sister, when did you come back?

'Last night.'

Did you come specially for Auntie Araba?

'What else, my sister? I just rushed into my room to pick up my *akatado* when I heard the news. How could I remain another hour in Tarkwa after getting such news? I arrived in the night.'

And your husband?

'He could not come. You know government-work. You must give notice several days ahead if you want to go away for half of one day. O, and so many other problems. But he will see to all that before next *Akwanbo*. Then we may both be present for the festival and the libation ceremony if her family plans it for a day around that time.'

Did you hear the Bosoë dance group practising the bread song?

'Yes. I hear they are going to make it the chief song at the funeral this afternoon. It is most fitting that they should do that. After all, when the group was formed, Auntie Araba's bread song was the first one they turned into a Bosoë song and danced to.'

Yes, it was a familiar song in those days. Indeed it had been heard around here for over twenty years. First in Auntie Araba's own voice with its delicate thin sweetness that clung like asawa berry on the tongue: which later, much later, had roughened a little. Then all of a sudden, it changed again, completely. Yes, it still was a woman's voice. But it was deeper and this time, like good honey, was rough and heavy, its sweetness within itself.

'Are you talking of when Mansa took over the hawking of the bread?'

Yes. That is how, in fact, that whole little quarter came to be known as *Bosohwe*. Very often, Auntie Araba did not have to carry the bread. The moment the aroma burst out of the oven, children began tugging at their parents' clothes for pennies and threepences. Certainly, the first batch was nearly always in those penny rows. Dozens of them. Of course, the children always caught the aroma before their mothers did.

'Were we not among them?'

We were, my sister. We remember that on market days and other holidays, Auntie Araba's ovenside became a little market-place all by itself. And then there was Auntie Araba herself. She always was a beautiful woman. Even three months ago when they were saying that all her life was gone, I thought she looked better than some of us who claim to be in our prime. If she was a young woman at this time when they are selling beauty to our big men in the towns, she would have made something for herself.

'Though it is a crying shame that young girls should be doing that. As for our big men! Hmm, let me shut my trouble-seeking mouth up. But our big men are something else too. You know, indeed, these our educated big men have never been up to much good.'

Like you know, my sister. After all, was it not a lawyer-or-a-doctor-or-something-like-that who was at the bottom of all Auntie Araba's troubles?

I did not know that, my sister.

Yes, my sister. One speaks of it only in whispers. Let me turn my head and look behind me. . . . And don't go standing in the river telling people. Or if you do, you better not say that you heard it from me.

'How could I do that? Am I a baby?'

Yes, Auntie Araba was always a beauty. My mother says she really was a come-and-have-a-look type, when she was a girl. Her plaits hung at the back of her neck like the branches of a giant tree, while the skin of her arms shone like charcoal from good wood. And since her family is one of these families with always some members abroad, when Auntie Araba was just about getting ready for her puberty, they sent her to go and stay at A— with some lady relative. That's where she learnt to mess around with flour so well. But after less than four years, they found she was in trouble.

'*Eh-eh?*'

Eh-eh, my sister. And now bring your ear nearer.

. . . .

'That lawyer-or-doctor-or-something-like-that who was the lady's husband?'

Yes.

'And what did they do about it?'

They did not want to spoil their marriage so they hushed up everything and sent her home quietly. Very quietly. That girl was our own Auntie Araba. And that child is Ato, the big scholar we hear of.

'*Ei*, there are plenty of things in the world's old box to pick up and talk about, my sister.'

You have said it. But be quiet and listen. I have not finished the story. If anything like that had happened to me, my life would have been ruined. Not that there is much to it now. But when Auntie Araba returned home to her mother, she was looking like a ram from the north. Big, beautiful and strong. And her mother did not behave as childishly as some would in a case like this. No, she did not tear herself apart as if the world had fallen down. . . .

'Look at how Mother Kuma treated her daughter. Rained insults on her head daily, refused to give her food and then drove her out of their house. Ah, and look at what the father of Mansa did to her too. . . .'

But isn't this what I am coming to? This is what I am coming to.

'Ah-h-h . . .'

Anyway, Auntie Araba's mother took her daughter in and treated her like an egg until the baby was born. And then did Auntie Araba tighten her girdle and get ready to work? Lord, there is no type of dough of flour they say she has not mixed and fried or baked. *Epitsi? Tatare? Atwemo? Bofrot? Boodo? Boodoo-ngo? Sweetbad? Hei*, she went there and dashed here. But they say that somehow, she was not getting much from these efforts. Some people even say that they landed her in debts.

'But I think someone should have told her that these things are good to eat but they suit more the tastes of the town-dwellers. I myself cannot see any man or woman who spends his living days on the farm, wasting his pennies on any of these sweeties which only satisfy the tongue but do not fill the stomach. Our people in the villages might buy *tatare* and *epitsi*, yes, but not the others.'

Like you know, my sister. This is what Auntie Araba discovered, but only after some time. I don't know who advised her to drop all those fancy foods. But she did, and finally started baking bread, ordinary bread. That turned out better for her.

'And how did she come to marry Egya Nyaako?'

They say that she grew in beauty and in strength after her baby was weaned. Good men and rich from all the villages of the state wanted to marry her.

'*Ei*, so soon? Were they prepared to take her with her baby?'

tartare – plantain pancake
epitsi – plantain cake
boodoo – sweet, unleavened corn bread
atwemo – plain sugared pastry drawn out in strips and fried in hot oil

boodoo-ngo – bread of unleavened corn meal mixed with palm oil and baked
bofrot – doughnuts
sweetbad – a hard coconut pastry baked or fried

117

Yes.

'Hmm, a good woman does not rot.'

That is what our fathers said.

'And she chose Egya Nyaako?'

Yes. But then, we should remember that he was a good man himself.

'Yes, he was. I used to be one of those he hired regularly during the cocoa harvests. He never insisted that we press down the cocoa as most of these farmers do. No, he never tried to cheat us out of our fair pay.'

Which is not what I can say of his heir!

'Not from what we've heard about him. A real mean one they say he is.'

So Auntie agreed to marry Egya Nyaako and she and her son came to live here. The boy, this big scholar we now know of, went with the other youngsters to the school the first day they started it here. In the old Wesleyan chapel. They say she used to say that if she never could sleep her fill, it was because she wanted to give her son a good education.

'*Poo*, pity. And that must have been true. She mixed and rolled her dough far into the night, and with the first cock-crow, got up from bed to light her fires. Except on Sundays.'

She certainly went to church twice every Sunday. She was a good Christian. And yet, look at how the boy turned out and what he did to her.

'Yes? You know I have been away much of the time. And I have never heard much of him to respect. Besides, I only know very little.'

That is the story I am telling you. I am taking you to bird-town so I can't understand why you insist on searching for eggs from the suburb!

'I will not interrupt you again, my sister.'

Maybe, it was because she never had any more children and therefore, Ato became an only child. They say she spoilt him. Though I am not sure I would not have done the same if I had been in her position. But they say that before he was six years old, he was fighting her. And he continued to fight her until he became a big scholar. And then his father came to acknowledge him as his son, and it seems that ruined him completely.

'Do you mean that lawyer-or-doctor-or-something-like-that man?'

Himself. They say he and his lady wife never had a male child so when he was finishing Stan' 7 or so, he came to father him.

'*Poo*, scholars!'

It is a shame, my sister. Just when all the big troubles were over.

'If I had been Auntie Araba, eh, I would have charged him about a thousand pounds for neglect.'

But Auntie Araba was not you. They say she was very happy that at last the boy was going to know his real father. She even hoped that that would settle his wild spirits. No, she did not want to make trouble. So this big man from the city came one day with his friends or relatives and met Auntie Araba and her relatives. It was one Sunday afternoon. In two big cars. They say some of her sisters and relatives had sharpened their mouths ready to give him what he deserved. But when they saw all the big men and their big cars, they kept quiet. They murmured among themselves, and that was all. He told them, I mean this new father, that he was going to send Ato to college.

'And did he?'

Yes he did. And he spoilt him even more than his mother had done. He gave him lots of money. I don't know what college he sent him to since I don't know about colleges. But he used to come here to spend some of his holidays. And every time, he left his mother with big debts to pay from his high living. Though I must add that she did not seem to mind.

'You know how mothers are, even when they have got several children.'

119

But, my sister, she really had a big blow when he put Mansa into trouble. Mansa's father nearly killed her.

'I hear Mansa's father is a proud man who believes that there is nothing which any man from his age group can do which he cannot do better.'

So you know. When school education came here, all his children were too old to go to school except Mansa. And he used to boast that he was only going to feel he had done his best by her when she reached the biggest college in the white man's land.

'And did he have the money?'

Don't ask me. As if I was in his pocket! Whether he had the money or not, he was certainly saying these things. But then people also knew him to add on these occasions, 'let us say it will be good, so it shall be good'. Don't laugh, my sister. Now, you can imagine how he felt when Ato did this to his daughter Mansa. I remember they reported him as saying that he was going to sue Ato for heavy damages. But luckily, Ato just stopped coming here in the holidays. But of course, his mother Auntie Araba was here. And she got something from Mansa's father. And under his very nose was Mansa's own mother. He used to go up and down ranting about some women who had no sense to advise their sons to keep their manhoods between their thighs, until they could afford the consequences of letting them loose, and other mothers who had not the courage to tie their daughters to their mats.

'O Lord.'

Yes, my sister.

'Hmm, I never knew any of these things.'

This is because you have been away in *the Mines* all the time. But me, I have been here. I am one of those who sit in that village waiting for the travellers. But also in connection with this story, I have had the chance to know so much because my husband's family house is in that quarter. I say, Mansa's father never let anyone sleep. And so about the sixth month of Mansa's pregnancy, her mother and Auntie Araba

decided to do something about the situation. Auntie Araba
would take Mansa in, see her through until the baby was born
and then later, they would think about what to do. So Mansa
went to live with her. And from that moment, people did not
even know how to describe the relationship between the two.
Some people said they were like mother and daughter. Others
that they were like sisters. Still more others even said they
were like friends. When the baby was born, Auntie Araba took
one or two of her relatives with her to Mansa's parents. Their
purpose was simple. Mansa had returned from the battlefield
safe. The baby looked strong and sound. If Mansa's father
wanted her to go back to school . . .

'Yes, some girls do this.'

But Mansa's father had lost interest in Mansa's education.

'I can understand him.'

I too. So Auntie Araba said that in that case, there was no
problem. Mansa was a good girl. Not like one of these *yetse-
yetse* things who think putting a toe in a classroom turns
them into goddesses. The child and mother should go on
living with her until Ato finished his education. Then they
could marry properly.

'Our Auntie Araba is going to heaven.'

If there is any heaven and God is not like man, my sister.

'What did Mansa's parents say?'

What else could they say? Her mother was very happy. She
knew that if Mansa came back to live with them she would
always remind her father of everything and then there would
never be peace for anybody in the house. They say that from
that time, the baking business grew and grew and grew.
Mansa's hands pulled in money like a good hunter's gun does
with game. Auntie Araba herself became young again. She
used to say that if all mothers knew they would get daughters-
in-law like Mansa, birth pains would be easier to bear. When
her husband Egya Nyaako died, would she not have gone
mad if Mansa was not with her? She was afraid of the time
when her son would finish college, come and marry Mansa

121

properly and take her away. Three years later, Ato finished college. He is a teacher, as you know, my sister. The government was sending him to teach somewhere far away from here. Then about two weeks or so before Christmas, they got a letter from him that he was coming home.

'Ah, I am sure Mansa was very glad.'

Don't say it loudly, my sister. The news spread very fast. We teased her. 'These days some women go round with a smile playing round their lips all the time. Maybe there is a bird on the neem tree behind their back door which is giving them special good news,' we said. Auntie Araba told her friends that her day of doom was coming upon her. What was she going to do on her own? But her friends knew that she was also very glad. So far, she had looked after her charges very well. But if you boil anything for too long, it burns. Her real glory would come only when her son came to take away his bride and his child.

'And the boy-child was a very handsome somebody too.'

And clever, my sister. Before he was two, he was delighting us all by imitating his grandmother and his mother singing the bread-hawking song. A week before the Saturday Ato was expected, Mansa moved back to her parents' house.

'That was a good thing to do.'

She could not have been better advised. That Saturday, people saw her at her bath quite early. My little girl had caught a fever and I myself had not gone to the farm. When eleven o'clock struck, I met Mansa in the market-place, looking like a festive dish. I asked her if what we had heard was true, that our lord and master was coming on the market-day lorry that afternoon. She said I had heard right.

'Maybe she was very eager to see him and could not wait in the house.'

Could you have waited quietly if you had been her?

'Oh, women. We are to be pitied.'

Tell me, my sister. I had wanted to put a stick under the story and clear it all for you. But we are already in town.

'Yes, look at that crowd. Is Auntie Araba's family house near the mouth of this road?'

Oh yes. Until the town grew to the big thing it is, the Twidan Abusia house was right on the road but now it is behind about four or so other houses. Why?

'I think I can hear singing.'

Yes, you are right.

'She is going to get a good funeral.'

That, my sister, is an answer to a question no one will ask.

'So finish me the story.'

Hmm, kinsman, when the market lorry arrived, there was no Scholar-Teacher-Ato on it.

'No?'

No.

'What did Auntie Araba and Mansa do?'

What could they do? Everyone said that the road always has stories to tell. Perhaps he had only missed the lorry. Perhaps he had fallen ill just on that day or a day or so before. They would wait for a while. Perhaps he would arrive that evening if he thought he could get another lorry, it being a market day. But he did not come any time that Saturday or the next morning. And no one saw him on Monday or Tuesday.

'Ohhh . . .'

They don't say, ohhh. . . . We heard about the middle of the next week – I have forgotten now whether it was the Wednesday or Thursday – that he had come.

'*Eheh?*'

Nyo. But he brought some news with him. He could not marry Mansa.

'Oh, why? After spoiling her . . .'

If you don't shut up, I will stop.

'Forgive me and go on, my sister.'

Let us stand in this alley here – that is the funeral parlour over there. I don't want anyone to overhear us.

'You are right.'

Chicha Ato said he could not marry Mansa because he had got another girl into trouble.

'*Whopei!*'

She had been in the college too. Her mother is a big lady and her father is a big man. They said if he did not marry their daughter, they would finish him. . . .

'*Whopei!*'

His lawyer-father thought it advisable for him to wed that girl soon because they were afraid of what the girl's father would do.

'*Whopei!*'

So he could not marry our Mansa.

'*Whopei!*'

They don't say, *Whopei*, my sister.

'So what did they do?'

Who?

'Everybody. Mansa? Auntie Araba?'

What could they do?

'*Whopei!*'

That was just before you came back to have your third baby, I think.

'About three years ago?'

Yes.

'It was my fourth. I had the third in Aboso but it died.'

Then it was your fourth. Yes, it was just before you came.

'I thought Auntie Araba was not looking like herself. But I had enough troubles of my own and had no eyes to go prying into other people's affairs. . . . So that was that. . . .'

Yes. From then on, Auntie Araba was just lost.

'And Mansa-ah?'

She really is like Auntie herself. She has all of her character. She too is a good woman. If she had stayed here, I am sure someone else would have married her. But she left.

'And the child?'

She left him with her mother. Haven't you seen him since you came?

'No. Because it will not occur to anybody to point him out to me until I ask. And I cannot recognise him from my mind. I do not know him at all.'

He is around, with the other schoolchildren.

'So what does Mansa do?'

When she left, everyone said she would become a whore in the city.

'*Whopei*. People are bad.'

Yes. But perhaps they would have been right if Mansa had not been the Mansa we all know. We hear Auntie Araba sent her to a friend and she found her a job with some people. They bake hundreds of loaves of bread an hour with machines.

'A good person does not rot.'

No. She sent money and other things home.

'May God bless her. And Auntie Araba herself?'

As I was telling you. After this affair, she never became herself again. She stopped baking. Immediately. She told her friends that she felt old age was coming on her. Then a few months later, they say she started getting some very bad stomach aches. She tried here, she tried there. Hospitals first, then our own doctors and their herbs. Nothing did any good.

'O our end! Couldn't the hospital doctors cut her up and find out?'

My sister, they say they don't work like that. They have to find out what is wrong before they cut people up.

'And they could not find out what was wrong with Auntie Araba?'

No. She spent whatever she had on this stomach. Egya Nyaako, as you know, had already died. So, about three months ago, she packed up all she had and came here, to squat by her ancestral hearth.

'And yesterday afternoon she died?'

Yes, and yesterday afternoon she died.

'Her spirit was gone.'

Certainly it was her son who drove it away. And then Mansa left with her soul.

'Have you ever seen Chicha Ato's lady-wife?'

No. We hear they had a church wedding. But Auntie Araba did not put her feet there. And he never brought her to Ofuntumase.

'Maybe the two of them may come here today?'

I don't see how he can fail to come. But she, I don't know. Some of these ladies will not set foot in a place like this for fear of getting dirty.

'Hmmm . . . it is their own cassava! But do you think Mansa will come and wail for Auntie Araba?'

My sister, if you have come, do you think Mansa will not?

Other Versions

The whole thing had started after the school certificate exams. Instead of going straight home, I had stayed in town to work. This was going to be my first proper meeting with the town and when I sent the letter home announcing my intentions, I felt a little strange. Bekoe and I were going to stay in a small room in his uncle's house. The room was like a coffin but who cared? We found a job as sorting hands in the Post Office. I've forgotten how much they were paying us. Really it's strange . . . but I have. Anyway, it was something like twelve pounds. Either it started at fourteen pounds and then with the deductions leaned out to twelve-'n'-something or it was twelve with no taxes. But I remember twelve. Bekoe told me that his uncle was not expecting us to pay anything for the room and that he had even instructed his wife to give us three meals a day for free. I say, this was very kind of him. Because you know what? Some people would have insisted on our paying. They would have said it would help us get experienced at budgeting in the future. And in fact we later discovered that the wife didn't have it in mind to feed us free like that. After the first week, she hinted it would be nice if we considered contributing something. She was not charging us for the meals. No, she was just asking us to contribute some- thing. We agreed on three pounds each. We also thought Bekoe shouldn't tell his uncle this. Not that Bekoe would have told on her anyway. He knew nephews and nieces have been able to break up marriages. *Ei*, he didn't want any trouble. Besides his mother would have killed him for it. His mother is a fierce trader and I know her. She could easily have slapped him and later boasted it around the market how she had beaten up her son who was finishing five years in college!

Anyhow, that was three pounds off the pay. Then there was this business of the blazer. I mean the school blazer I wanted to buy. It cost ten pounds and Father had made it quite clear that he considered his duty by me done when he paid my fees for the last term. How could I go to him with a blazer case? So I thought I would keep four pounds by every month towards that. We were going to work for three months. That was the only time we could have in the long vacation. You see, we both wanted to go to the sixth form. Well, if I was able to set by this four pounds every month, I would have two pounds over after I had bought it. And I could use this to look after myself until our pocket money from the government came.

Then I remembered what Mother had told me. I remembered her telling me one day that any time I got my first pay, I was to take something home. Part of this would be used to buy gin to pour libation to the spirits of our forefathers so they would come and bless me with prosperity. That was why the first Saturday after pay-day, I went to the lorry park and took *The Tailless Animal*. As for that lorry, *eh!* I was not surprised to read in Araba's letter the other day that Anan, its owner and driver, has bought a bus. Anyone would, after the two of them had for years literally owned what was to their right and to their left in the way of passengers.

Of course, I had always thought this money would go to Mother. And so see, how do you think I felt when, in a private discussion with her the afternoon I arrived, she told me it would be better if I gave it to Father? I had decided on four pounds here, too, reserving the last pound for regular spending. Anyway, the moment the money fell into her hand she burst into tears.

'*Ao*, I too am coming to something in this world. Who would have thought it? I never slept to dream that I shall live to see a day like this. . . . Now I too have got my own man who will take care of me. . . .' You know how women carry on when they mean to? She even knelt down to say a prayer of thanks to God and at that point I left the room. Yes, and after all this business she didn't take the silly money.

'Hand it over to your father. He will certainly buy a bottle of gin and pour some to the ancestors. Then I will ask him to give me about ten shillings to buy some yam and eggs for Sunday. . . .'

'That should leave at least three clear pounds,' I thought aloud.

'Listen my master, does it matter if your father has three pounds of your pay? It does not matter, I am telling you. Because then they shall not be able to say you have not given him anything since you started working.'

'But Mother, I am not starting work permanently.'

'And what do you mean?'

'Mother, I have done an examination. If I pass very well, I shall go to school again.'

'Ah, and were you not the one who made me understand that you would finish after five years?'

'Yes, but the government asks those who do very well to continue.'

'And does the government pay their fees too?'

'Yes.'

'Then that is good because I do not think your father would like to pay any more fees for you. Anyway, it does not matter about the money. You give it to him. His people do not know all these things about the government asking you to continue. What they know is that you are working.'

God!

I hadn't thought of giving anything of that sort. Certainly not that soon. . . . However, Sunday came and I ate the *oto* mother prepared with the yam and palm oil. I ate it with some of the eggs to congratulate my soul. Then I went to say good-bye to people, and Mother took me up to the mouth of the road. Being a Sunday, we thought it would be useless to wait for *The Tailless Animal* to wander in. Because it simply wouldn't. It did that only on the weekdays.

And I was to realise that I hadn't heard the last of the money business. Mother thought it would be good if I continued to give that 'little something' to Father as long as I worked.

'*Ho*, Father?'

'Yes. You know he has done very well. Taking you through college. Now, giving him something would not only show your gratitude but also go towards your sisters' fees.'

Ei, I say, have you heard a story like this before? I tell you, *eh*, I caught a fever in the raw. But Mother was still talking.

'I had thought of a nice dignified something like five pounds. But you brought four this time and maybe it will be better to maintain just that.'

'And how much do I give you?'

'Me?' She sounded quite shocked – 'why should you bring me anything? I do not need your money. All I want is for you to be happy and you shall not be if they say you are bad. And do you think I am an old fool to ask you for money? If you give that to your father, you will be doing a lot. Say you will do it, Kofi.'

'I shall do it, Mother,' I parroted.

I had a dazed feeling for the rest of the journey and the whole day. I just could not figure it out. To begin with, whose child was I? Why should I have to pay my father for sending me to school? And calling that 'college' did not help me either. Besides he only paid half the fees, since the Cocoa Brokers' Union, of which he is a member, had given me a scholarship to cover the other half. And anyway, Father. He is the kind of parent who checks out lists so thoroughly you would think his life depends upon them. And he doesn't mind which kind either. Textbook lists? '*Hei*, didn't I buy you a dictionary last year?' The lists of provisions you needed to survive the near-starvation diet in a boarding school? 'And whom are you going to feed with a dozen Heinz baked beans?'

Well, you know them. In fact from talking to people you learn that most fathers are like that and that's the only nice thing about it. Anyway Father is surely like that. It was a battle he and I fought at the beginning of every term. Once when Mother didn't know I was within earshot I heard her telling my little aunt that Father always feels through his coins for the ones which have gone soft to give away! Don't laugh. It's not very funny when you are his son. So you see why I got so mad to have Mother talk to me in that way? And the main thing was, it wasn't the money I was giving away which hurt me. It was the idea of Father getting it. I had always thought of making a small allowance for Mother from the moment I started working. I was the third child. My two older brothers were all working but married and couldn't care much about the rest of us. There were two girls after me, then one other boy. Father pays the fees and complains all the time. Mother gets us clothes and feeds us too because the three pounds he gives for our chop-money is a nice joke. Mother peddles cloth but I know she is not the fat rich market type – say, like Bekoe's mother. In the villages you always have to settle for instalments and money comes in in such miserable bits someone like Mother with four children just spends every penny of her profit as it comes. It is her favourite saying that she sells cloth for the fish-and-cassava women. There is always a threat of her eating into her capital. And naturally, it was of her I had thought in terms of any money-giving I was going to do.

But I obeyed her. I sent four pounds to Father at the end of the remaining months and each time just about burst up. 'Why not Mother? Why not Mother?' I kept asking myself. It drove me wild.

Well, we went to the sixth form. And of course Father realised I was still in school. He was quite proud of me too. He always managed to let slip into conversations with other men how Kofi was planning to go to the Unifartisy. Oh, it was fine as long as he was not paying. . . .

I passed higher and with lots of distinctions. I stopped working at my holiday jobs to get ready to go to our national University. And then I met Mr. Buntyne, who had been our chemistry teacher. He asked me if I would be interested in a scholarship for an American University. He knew a business syndicate. They were looking out for especially bright young people to help. They had not had an African yet. But he was sure they would be interested. Of course I applied. There were endless forms to fill out but I got the scholarship. And I came here.

Somehow I never forgot the money for Mother. I told myself that I would do something about that the first thing after graduation. Perhaps it is the way she genuinely thinks she does not need my earnings that much which makes me want to do something for her. I've even thought of finding a vacation job here to do so I can send some of my pay home with express instructions that it is for her. But that I know will distress her no end. Better still, I planned to save as much money as I could so I could take her about forty pounds or even four hundred to do something with. Like building a house 'for you children' as she always put it. . . .

And then somehow this thing happened. It was the very first month I came. I was invited by Mr. Merrows to go and have dinner with him and his family. He is either the chairman of this syndicate which brought me here or certainly one of its top men. They came to pick me up from the campus to their house. Oh, to be sure, it was a high and mighty hut. Everything was perfect. There were other guests besides the Merrows family. The food was gorgeous but the main course for the evening was me. What did I think of America? How did I plan to use this unique opportunity in the service of Africa? How many wives did my father have? etc., etc., etc.

I had assumed that everyone in the household was there at the dinner table. Mrs. Merrows kept popping in and out of the kitchen serving the food. And as I've said before, the food was really very good. Everyone complimented her on it and she smiled and gave the wives the recipes for this and that.

A couple of hours after the meal, Mr. Merrows proposed to take me back to the campus because it was getting late. I agreed. I said my thanks and good-nights and followed Mr. Merrows to the door. I waited for him while he pulled out the car from the garage. He asked me to jump in and I did. But then he left his seat, leaving the engine running and returned some five or ten minutes later followed by someone. It turned out to be a black woman. You know what sometimes your heart does? Mine did that just then. Kind of turned itself round in a funny way. Mr. Merrows opened the back seat for her and said,

'Kofi, Mrs. Hye helps us with the cooking sometimes and since I am taking you back anyway, I thought I could take her at least half her way. Mrs. Hye, Kofi is from Africa.'

In the car she and I smiled nervously at each other. . . . I tried not to feel agitated.

But then was it the next evening or two? I don't even remember.

I was returning again to the campus from visiting a boy I knew back at home and whom I had met the first few days I arrived. I took the subway. When the train pulled up at the station, I got into the car nearest to me. It looked empty. I sat down. Then I raised my eyes and realised there was someone else in it. There was a black woman sitting to the left end of the opposite seat.

Another black woman.

Now I can't tell whether she really was old or just middle-aged. She certainly was not young. I realised I had to be careful or I would be staring. She was just normal black with a buttony mouth, pretty deep-set eyes and an old black hand-bag. Somehow I noticed the bag. She was wearing the lined raincoat affair which everyone wears around here in the autumn. Except that I felt hers was too thin for that time of night.

That time of night.

I got to thinking of what a woman her age would be wanting in a subway car that time of night. I don't know why but immediately I remembered the other one who had been in the Merrows' kitchen while they ate and I ate. Then I started getting confused. I can swear the woman knew I was trying not to stare. She most probably knew too that I was thinking about her. Anyway, I don't know what made me. But I drew out my wallet. I had received money from my scholarship. So I took some dollar bills, crumpled them in my hand and jumped like one goaded with a firebrand.

'Eh . . . eh . . . I come from Africa and you remind me of my mother. Please would you take this from me?'

And all the time, I was trying hard not to stare.

'Sit down,' she said.

I'm not sure I really heard these words above the din. But I know she patted the space by her. The train was pulling up at a station.

'You say you come from Africa?' she said.

'Yes,' I said.

'What are you doing here, son?' she asked.

'A student,' I replied shortly.

'Son, keep them dollars. I sure know you need them more than I do,' she said. Of course, she was Mother. And so there was no need to see. But now I could openly look at her beautiful face. I got out at the stop. She waved to me and smiled. I stood there on the platform until the engine had wheezed and raged out of sight. I looked at the money which was still in my hand. I felt like opening them out; I did. There was one ten-dollar bill and two single ones. Twelve dollars. Then it occurred to me that that was as near to four pounds as you could get. It was not a constriction in the throat. Rather, the dazed feeling I had had that Sunday afternoon on the high road to town came back. And as I stumbled through the exit, and up the stairs, I heard myself mutter, 'O Mother.'

Also in Longman African Writers

The Dilemma of a Ghost and Anowa

Ama Ata Aidoo

These two witty and perceptive social dramas are sympathetic and honest explorations of the conflicts between the individualism of westernised culture and the social traditions of Africa. Both plays have been performed to audiences throughout the world and reinforce Ama Ata Aidoo's position as one of the leading creative voices in Africa today.

Dilemma of a Ghost
When Ato returns to Ghana from his studies in North America he brings with him a sophisticated black American wife. But their hopes of a happy marriage and of combining the 'sweetest and loveliest things in Africa and America' are soon shown to have been built on an unstable foundation.

Anowa
Based on an old Ghanaian legend, *Anowa* is the story of a young woman who decides, against her parents' wishes, to marry the man she loves. After many trials and tribulations the couple amass a fortune — but Anowa realises that something, somewhere is wrong.

Ama Ata Aidoo has a gift for the sparse economical language of sadness and despair and for the gaiety, rollicking boisterousness and acid wit of comedy, satire, irony and parady:
African Literature Today

ISBN 0 582 00244 3

Our Sister Killjoy

Ama Ata Aidoo

'I write about people, about what strikes me and interests me. It seems the most natural thing in the world for women to write with women as central characters; making women the centre of my universe was spontaneous.'

Ama Ata Aidoo in The Chronicle, Bulawayo

Out of Africa with her degree and her all-seeing eyes comes Sissie. She comes to Europe, to a land of towering mountains and low grey skies and tries to make sense of it all. What is she doing here? why aren't the natives friendly? and what will she do when she goes back home?

Ama Ata Aidoo's brilliantly conceived prose poem is by turns bitter and gentle, and is a highly personal exploration of the conflicts between Africa and Europe, between men and women and between a complacent acceptance of the status quo and a passionate desire to reform a rotten world.

'A profound vesion on the theme of self-discovery in strange lands. Modest, lyrical, reflective and intelligent, she sometimes breaks into poetic form ... it deserves as wide an audience as it can get..'

Angela Carter In The Guardian

ISBN 0 582 00391 1

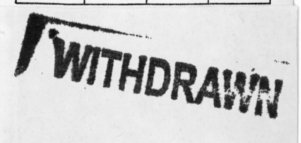

OPEN FAMILY LIVING

Books by Dr. McGinnis

OPEN FAMILY LIVING
OPEN FAMILY AND MARRIAGE: A GUIDE TO PERSONAL GROWTH
A GIRL'S GUIDE TO DATING AND GOING STEADY
YOUR FIRST YEAR OF MARRIAGE

Dear Reader—

This book represents a new approach which is designed to enable individuals, marital partners and
families to improve significantly the quality of their
lives. I encourage you to share your experiences in reading and applying this system of *Open Family Living* by
writing to me, c/o the Counseling and Psychotherapy
Center, P.A., 0–100 Twenty-seventh Street, Fair Lawn,
New Jersey, 07410. Your responses will contribute to
the refinement of the principles, guidelines and techniques of this approach so that it can be made more
useful in the lives of others.

Thank you,

Tom McGinnis

Tom McGinnis

OPEN FAMILY LIVING

A NEW APPROACH
FOR ENRICHING
YOUR LIFE TOGETHER

Dr. Thomas C. McGinnis
and John U. Ayres

DOUBLEDAY & COMPANY, INC., GARDEN CITY, NEW YORK 1976

Library of Congress Cataloging in Publication Data
McGinnis, Thomas C
Open family living.
Bibliography: p. 356
Includes index.
1. Marriage. 2. Family. 3. Parent and child.
I. Ayres, John U., joint author. II. Title.
HQ734.M18489   301.42
ISBN 0-385-02980-2
Library of Congress Catalog Card Number 75–17406
Printed in the United States of America
First Edition

ACKNOWLEDGMENTS

Behind an author lie many hidden authors whose thoughts, feelings and experiences contribute to a book's evolution. I feel especially grateful to the following:

To my dear friend and co-author, John U. Ayres, who personally went through the process of moving from a closed to a more open family living style. His unique stamp is on the book; and through our collaboration the book has an individual quality as of one author speaking, yet it speaks for us both.

To my wife, Mary Yorke, without whose love, patience and understanding the book could not have been written. Besides spending long hours in the preparation of the manuscript, she handled a great number of details at much sacrifice to her own personal needs and family responsibilities.

To my daughter, Karen, and my son Dick, who read and commented on the rough drafts and gave much help in making sure that the thoughts and feelings of young people are clearly and fairly presented. My son Tom, Jr., who now works with me as a professional colleague, made special contributions by reviewing the literature underpinning many of the concepts presented. Most importantly, I wish to express my very deep gratitude to each member of my family for his or her own contribution to our own movement away from a semi-closed family unit to one of considerable openness.

To John's wife, Alice, who became interested and involved as the book progressed and whose criticisms and suggestions helped to reflect the viewpoint of the emerging modern woman. Her personal enthusiasm and vitality did much to keep the project alive and moving. Other members of John's family were also supportive and made suggestions about what makes a healthy family.

To my students, patients and their families who have taught me much about family living by allowing me to share intimately in the joys and heartaches of their search for meaning in their families. Many made valuable suggestions after reading segments of the manuscript that related to them.

To innumerable friends and colleagues who have known of my interest in strengthening marriage and family life and have given much support and encouragement. Many have participated in and made important contributions to my efforts to conceptualize and teach my therapeutic approach for marital and family therapy. Special mention

is due to my former colleagues at New York University, particularly
Dr. Marian Hamburg, who made it possible for me to gain years of in-
valuable experience in teaching human sexuality, marriage and family
life with an open approach. I also want to mention my longtime close
associates of the staff of the Counseling and Psychotherapy Center,
P.A. of Fair Lawn, New Jersey. They include: Marilyn Nusbaum,
Elaine Schiffman, Dr. Victor Solomon, Dr. Joel Becker, Dr. Emanuel
Winocur, Tom McGinnis, Jr., and our capable secretaries, Joan Cottrell
and Joan Gerhold.

To my Doubleday editors, Ferris Mack and Karen Van Westering,
for their interest, encouragement, endless patience and friendship in
the challenge, excitement and hard work of getting this book published.

I appreciate the help of these many people and sincerely thank
them for their belief in and support of me and my concept of Open
Family Living.

THOMAS C. McGINNIS

CONTENTS

OPEN FAMILY LIVING

OPEN FAMILY LIVING is a flexible approach
for living together in a family. It is guided
by a "family code" which says, *"I can be
me. You can be you.* Together, *we* can be *us*
in a balanced blend of living for my sake,
your sake, our sake and the sake of others."
It is not an approach based on conformity to
rigid rules, values and expectations.

INTRODUCTION

People commonly treat each other in ways originally learned in their families when they were children. Individuals who have gentle and considerate parents may find it natural to behave with gentleness and consideration. The children of angry, violent parents often feel more at home with anger and violence. Children of indifferent, neglectful parents may tend to become alienated; they often have trouble in establishing any kind of intimate human relationships.

This is "old stuff" to people with any degree of psychological sophistication. But the implications to be drawn from it—implications for family life, for child raising, for educational and public policies—have scarcely begun to be thought out, much less acted upon. As individuals and as an organized society, we repeatedly think and behave as if none of this knowledge existed.

It is quite possible for us individually to enjoy more fulfilling relationships between the sexes and between persons of the same sex. We can build sounder and more satisfying marriages. We can develop a family life that contributes to the unfoldment of the human potential of all its members, young and old, and that produces caring human beings of all ages. Families can serve as anchors of strength and security in an uncertain, turbulent, unsafe world. People can develop family life with this kind of quality, provided they, as individuals and families, learn to apply existing knowledge of what circumstances of living (intellectual, emotional and behavioral) promote personal, marital and family health.

Consider a family life where the members, both children and adults, see each other as *persons*, not as objects; listen to each other, and are listened to; respect each other's feelings; care about each other; care also about people outside and about the community and the natural world of which the family is a part. Visualize, too, the opposite: a family where the members habitually ignore or hassle each other; manipulate or use each other; rarely listen to each other; rarely respect each other's feelings; and care little about people generally or the community or the natural world. It is easy to predict the kinds of individuals each of these types of families would tend to produce.

There is a universal yearning that, somehow, someday, a more stable, more peaceful, more *human* society may develop. If and when it does, the builders of it will almost certainly come out of families like the first. And if civilization falls prey to a tidal wave of wars, crimes, terrorism, repression, the pursuit of power and other dehumanizing forces, the perpetrators will probably be people who come out of families like the second. The family, when it fulfills the potential inherent within it, can serve a unique social and nurturing function which no other agency can serve so well. Where else but in the family, or an equivalent social arrangement, can a child or adult learn to understand and respect himself, to appreciate his uniqueness, to be sensitive and aware, to come alive, to reach out toward others, to love, to grow into a whole human being?

But the family, as it now functions, frequently does not rise to this challenge. World-wide, it is weakening and deteriorating while, at the same time, the growth of knowledge and psychological competence offers unprecedented opportunities for the enrichment of life. People living today, in my view, have the greatest opportunity in all history to develop a fulfilling personal life, build a strong marriage equally rewarding to both partners, and achieve a healthy family life capable of producing human beings of the highest caliber. But to do it we must be prepared to change many of our old ways of thinking, feeling and behaving.

This book searches the question of how and why human relationships, which frequently start out with promise and hope, so often deteriorate and turn destructive. It traces much of this destructive interaction to the struggle against an authoritarian, restrictive, role-centered pattern of living derived from the past, which I call the "closed" family style. This style worked reasonably well under conditions of male domination, female passivity, cultural homogeneity and relatively slow social change. As the conditions for its successful functioning are now rapidly passing away, it is becoming an obsolescent style of living—incapable of meeting the human needs of today.

As the closed style crumbles, people finding themselves unable to make it work are falling into a confused, unsettled style with few guidelines which I call the "directionless" family style. It is this style that so often leads to the excesses of permissiveness, confused family goals and the wandering, disattached youths who haunt our society (and many other societies) now.

But some individuals, couples and families, having partially freed themselves from the restrictiveness of the closed style yet finding the directionless style frustrating and unsatisfying, are groping for something better. Many are beginning to see the possibilities of a more human, more rewarding way of living in which marital partners and family members contribute to each other's growth instead of limiting each other, help meet each other's emotional needs, draw strength and encouragement from each other and enrich each other's lives. This is the style which I call "Open Family Living."

The first requirement of any move toward making a more human and compassionate world society, a healthier family life, and more functional and stable marriage is to learn to treat people *as people* instead of as objects or players of roles. People need to experience each other's uniqueness, not lump everybody into categories such as men, women, parents, children, whites, blacks, etc. The broad principles underlying human relationships are independent of sex, color, age, nationality, economic status or role. Since nearly everything said in the book applies equally to men and women, *the pronouns he, him and his refer to a person of either sex unless the context indicates otherwise*.

The thoughts and feelings expressed in this book have evolved out of my experiences and study during more than twenty years of practice as a psychotherapist and as a marriage and family counselor. They also reflect what I have learned from students in teaching human sexuality, marriage and family-life education at

New York University. In developing my therapeutic system,* I found, over and over again, that the basic need of the people I was trying to help was to become freed from restrictive, suppressive patterns of living that were preventing them from realizing their potential as full human beings. In the terms of this book, I was trying to help them to be less *closed* and more *open*. The book, then, translates the approach I take in my work into a set of guidelines for attaining a more open and more healthy type of personal, marital and family living.

Potentially, the human relationships in a family can be the most growth-enhancing of all experiences. But qualitative relationships need to be built and worked at; they do not come into being by themselves.† In a real sense, the future of mankind hinges on raising the quality of family life everywhere.

---

* The theoretical substructure of this book and a description of my therapeutic system may be found in the textbook: *Open Family and Marriage: A Guide to Personal Growth,* by Thomas C. McGinnis and Dana G. Finnegan; C. V. Mosby Co., 1976. It is expected that the present book and this textbook will be used jointly in training courses in Open Family Living to be made available by The Counseling and Psychotherapy Center, P.A. (Division of Human Services Center for Education and Research), Fair Lawn, New Jersey, as well as in various colleges and universities throughout the country.

† **Interaction Experiences** (IE). For those readers who wish to work more personally with the concepts and issues covered in this book, I have included a number of suggested Interaction Experiences. They are identified in the text by a flag and a number such as ►3 and described in detail at the ends of appropriate chapters. A complete list of them is given at the end of the book. You can, of course, skip these if you wish, but I would hope you do not. It is very easy to read about a different way of interacting with yourself and others and to say, "That's interesting, maybe I'll try it some day." And then you forget about it. The interaction experience challenges you to *try it now*.

ONE

THE FAMILY—
WHAT IS HAPPENING
TO IT?

The End of the Family? Or a New Beginning?

The family is moving into a new phase in its long history. The resistance is great and the passage is rough. Yet the healthier state of mind and feelings toward which the pioneers in this transition are moving may raise the quality of human relationships, creativity and self-realization to new levels. If that process can become general, society might be transformed. People might be kinder to themselves and to each other. The arts and crafts might flourish. Child raising might become a joy to parents instead of a corroding anxiety. Young people might experience their families as nurturing and caring communities and have much less need for struggling to break free from their parents. The alienations, suspicions and antagonisms that plague so many human associations might be softened and reduced.

These favorable opportunities all hinge on whether the potential of what I call *Open Family Living* can be developed. In individual cases there is no question but that it can. The potential is there. It seems to be innate in the human being. I have experienced much of its unfolding in my clinical practice of individual and group psychotherapy, marital counseling and family therapy as well as in my own family life. I know, too, that the principles and techniques that make this unfolding possible can be taught since I have taught them in psychotherapy sessions, in encounter groups and in my classes in human sexuality, marriage and family-life education at New York University.

But there are great obstacles to be overcome. The necessary alterations in ways of thinking, feeling and behaving seem strange to

many people and run counter to their old ways. People do not easily abandon long-established habits. They cling to the familiar.
The style they are accustomed to may make them acutely unhappy, yet they still cling to it, just as a person trying to take off
weight tends to go back to overeating and a cigarette smoker
trying to cut the habit often returns to it.

I once watched a family of two parents and four children, ages
about six to twelve, enter a restaurant. The entire family seemed
quietly happy. Parents and children alike had a relaxed quality,
almost of serenity, yet also of alert liveliness, that marked them off
from the other people in the room. The restaurant was one of
those where you give your order as you enter, and when it is ready
someone calls your number. When the family's number was called,
the father said quietly, "I'll need a little help." The children
jumped up, flocked after him and helped him carry the trays. One
small child, without being asked, took two trips. There was no
teasing, punching, complaining or jostling. With obvious enjoyment, they all pitched in and ate their meal. The father assisted
the youngest with spreading the butter and syrup on his pancakes.

I was interested in this family because, during the twenty
minutes I watched them, there was never a sharp word, an irritated exclamation, an attempt by any child to draw undue attention to himself, or any sign of boredom. This was not a result of
suppression (what people commonly call "discipline") because a
suppressive style produces a tightness, a tension that is easily dis-
cernible. It was evident to me that these children behaved considerately because their parents habitually treated them and each
other considerately. These six people were having fun simply being
together.

It is not difficult to identify the basic patterns of a family's life
when the members are interacting unself-consciously. A child who
is frequently put down, scolded and punished will nearly always
reveal this fact in his facial expressions, gestures and spoken
words. It is easy, too, to spot a child whose parents are so preoccupied with their own affairs that they ignore him much of the
time. Such a child advertises his frustrations by hitting, whining,
crying, teasing, showing off and by other tricks to get attention. So
common is this type of behavior that many people assume that is

simply the "way children are." But this is *not* the way children are. This is symptomatic behavior that suggests that certain of the child's emotional needs are not being met.

For a number of years I have been working with individuals, couples and families helping them to develop exactly the kind of free, open, accepting, caring relationship that was demonstrated in the restaurant. Those parents enjoyed and loved their kids—a fact clearly evident in every facial expression and gesture they made. And the kids, without question, enjoyed and loved their parents.

The restaurant family was almost certainly one of those that had negotiated the passage, at least part way, into the style of interaction that I call Open Family Living. The family members, no doubt, still have unhappy moments; what family does not? Even a well-established open living style is not immune to human mistakes, misunderstandings, disputes, hurt feelings, or flashes of anger or passion. But in the open style of living, these difficulties are resolved; they do not produce piled-up resentments, and they do not form a predominating, repetitive pattern. They are short-lived deviations, quickly corrected like the adjustments one makes in the steering of a car. There is less of the rigidity, anxiety, repression, punitiveness, tightness or boredom that so often characterize families that, because they have not learned to live in the open style, are being ground up in the gears of our rapidly changing society.

What Is This "Open Family Living"?

Open Family Living is a way of living together that offers new hope to families dissatisfied with the failures and limitations of the older styles. It is more flexible than the living styles of the past. It puts much stronger emphasis on respecting the uniqueness of each person, recognizing his feelings and needs, and encouraging the development of personal, marital and family potentials. It is *not* an approach based on conformity to rigid rules and fixed positions.

In this style of living, *people and their needs and feelings are put first.* ("You seem discouraged. Are you OK?") Family members experience each other primarily as human and unique; the roles they assume and the jobs they do are secondary. Thus, if a child is feeling neglected, attention is paid to him; he is a person. If a parent is feeling worried, irritated or hard-pressed, the family, including the children, takes account of the parent's need. Everybody treats everybody else with consideration and respect. Nobody puts down another or wounds him by sarcasm or ridicule. Nobody makes another feel small, unloved or "bad." No one dominates or rules another's life or smothers him by excessive directing, prodding or clinging. Each gives the others as much freedom as is consistent with orderly family life. There is no invasion of privacy. There is no nagging or scolding or use of words as weapons. *The objective of Open Family Living is the development of the fullest potential and self-realization of all its members —both parents and children—and a healthy interaction among them all.*

Openness and its opposite, closedness, are both learned through moment-to-moment human interaction. Neither is an innate trait. Either one can be deliberately and successfully taught. Most of us have been taught to be closed; but it is within our power to change this, to move toward openness. We never get there completely; openness is a relative, not an absolute, condition. Moving toward it involves risks and can produce new stresses and strains in a marriage or a family. But openness also fosters development of the personal competence of marital partners and family members to work effectively with these stresses and strains.

In its healthiest form, Open Family Living grows out of awareness, sensitivity and skillful communication. In its unhealthy form, it is applied indiscriminately and compulsively and represents a special kind of closedness. Open family relationships are not obsessed with the question of who gets, does or pays the most. Distribution of responsibilities and tasks is arrived at through fair negotiations that consider the feelings and needs of each family member, of the family as a unit and of people outside the family. The members are guided by a family code that says, "*I* can be *me*. *You* can be *you*. Together, *we* can be *us* in a balanced blend of living for my sake, your sake, our sake and the sake of others."

This is a large order expressed in both practical and idealistic terms. Set forth in such an uncompromising fashion, these ideals throw much light on what is unhealthy in prevailing family living styles. They can also chart our course as we strive to develop practical guidelines for healthier family living in the future.

A Confusion of Family Living Styles

In contrast to the open style, which is in an early stage of development, two broad family living styles are now common throughout the world. One I designate as "closed" for reasons that will soon be evident. The other I call "directionless" because it is a style of families that have abandoned the closed family pattern, finding it unworkable, but have not yet found a satisfactory pattern to replace it.

The **closed family style** is so-called because it centers around fixed, rigid concepts of what constitute "right" thinking, "right" feeling and "right" living. These concepts are not open to either discussion or change and are therefore "closed." They include ideas and feelings about manners, roles, duties, morals, appearances and beliefs. A typical belief of the closed family style is that children must strictly conform to the parents' views on acceptable behavior, must be obedient, must not argue, and must be punished for any deviation.

A parent in the closed style assumes (if he thinks about it at all) that an authoritarian family structure is best for children and young people and that they will ultimately benefit from it. When he punishes, he generally believes he is doing what is necessary to insure that his child develops in the "right" direction. He is usually not open to considering alternative approaches.

There are several major weaknesses to this system. The first is that under modern conditions it often simply does not work. Instead of producing obedient and conforming children, it frequently produces rebels who repudiate many of the parental teachings. The result can be a nearly unbridgeable generation gap. There are reasons for this outcome that are inherent in the kind of society we have built, and we shall examine them shortly.

A second weakness of the closed style is that it does not prepare children and young people to deal effectively with the enormous and accelerating changes that are taking place in the world. It is much too rigid and restricted. It looks too often at the past rather than at the present or future. Or it looks to some tight system of thought (like a church doctrine, the writings of Karl Marx, or the opinions of your grandfather) to provide answers, instead of trusting the healthy functioning of free, creative, unfettered minds. Thus, the closed style unfits its members for a dynamic, rapidly changing society. No past or present system of thought can, in its entirety, be trusted to solve *all* the ever-multiplying problems of an unbelievably complex world. Yet, even as he may admit this, a person who lives in the closed style is often unwilling to let go of even a part of the teachings, systems and rules that, for him, have served as a raft to float him through the rapids of the changing times, and he clings to the raft even though it is clearly headed for a smashup.

A third weakness of the closed style is the way in which it lends itself to foggy rationalizations and self-deception. The closed style is based much more on appearances than on reality. We find, for example, that parents in this style frequently deceive themselves about what their true objectives in child raising are. They may believe that making children conform to their own ideas of "right" thinking, "right" feeling and "right" behavior will bring about the optimum development of their children's potential. But they may be quite mistaken. An action that the parent thinks is necessary for the good of the child may actually serve a different purpose, such as preserving the family's reputation, enhancing the parent's status, satisfying his ego, "looking right" to the neighbors (or to Aunt Sally), insuring the perpetuation of a belief or system, or something similar. These unacknowledged purposes may have little to do with the unfolding of a child's potential. They may, in fact, have the opposite effect. They may suppress and limit a child's growth, hedge him around with restrictions, interfere with the free functioning of his mind and feelings.

For example, some years ago when boys first began to grow long hair and beards, great numbers of parents were outraged and tried to force their kids to get shaves and haircuts. The kids resented this interference. A protracted struggle between the generations ensued (which the older generation ultimately lost), and the whole episode illuminated a state of mind that had for a long time been driving the generations apart. Parents did not seem to be as aware as their kids were of what the dispute really meant. Actually, for the kids long hair symbolized a certain kind of freedom (freedom to grow?) which the young people were demanding. The parents, fearing what that freedom might bring, were determined not to yield.

Long hair exemplified differentness, which came across to many parents as freakiness. So the parents worried about the opinions of their neighbors and bosses. ("Did you see? Frank's Johnny has long hair! If he were my son . . .") Now that we can look back at this with some perspective, we can speculate that the whole struggle over hair was a struggle between two styles of life; one trying to emerge and the other trying to block its emergence. And what was the new style that was trying to be born? A new kind of relationship between parents and their children: a relationship of respect for individuality in place of enforced conformity to adult-approved customs. When parents refused to grant that respect, many of them lost their kids—permanently. Young people by the tens of thousands withdrew from their families, emotionally if not physically, and communication between many parents and their young faded out. An enormous opportunity for understanding between the generations was lost.

How would family living in the open style have dealt with this situation? Under Open Family Living, the problem would not have arisen—at least, not in this form. The struggle itself was a product of the closed family system. In the open style, human relationship and the freedom to be one's self and to grow (even hair!) are highly regarded. A young person already enjoying this freedom would have little need to perform a defiant symbolic act of proclaiming it. And the parent, dedicated to granting all the freedom a young person is mature enough to handle, would have no reason to oppose such a symbolic act. The open style places a lower value on conformity to neighbors' expectations, so the "freakiness" would matter less. If the boy chooses to wear his hair long, it is his business, not his neighbors'.

I can hear cries that the open style sets no "standards," that it does not inculcate fixed rules of conduct and morals. These objections arise from a fear of granting freedom. There is a strong current of belief, shared by many people, that only strict supervision, repression, discipline and punishment of infractions can keep children and young people from engaging in wrong, immoral or unsocial conduct. This is a very old conception, deeply embedded in religious and ethical teachings, and this idea was one of the forces that originally produced the closed living style. We will have to meet it head-on.

If modern psychological studies have taught us anything about human beings, it is that *a repressive, closed, punitive approach that puts the enforcement of rules ahead of human needs and feelings does a very poor job of producing kind, considerate, loving, creative and honest people.* If the closed style had been successful in producing such people, we would have a fairer, gentler and more just society because, until very recent times, the closed pattern has predominated. Yet it is obvious from a mere glance at history that the system of teaching conduct by rigid rules, unrealistic expectations and threats of punishment has worked poorly—so much so that mankind's attachment to it is a remarkable monument to his irrationality and resistance to change. For those who fear that if teaching is not based on rigid rules, morality will deteriorate, I can only reply that the evidence does not support their position. Nor, it seems to me, do the more profound religious teachings. In the Christian tradition, it is worth reflecting that whenever Jesus had to choose between meeting a human need and observing a rule, the Gospel accounts show him as invariably serving the human need. Jesus' own way of life might be described as the "open style" of his time.

The closed family style is in great difficulty today, and its increasing breakdown is producing a third family living style, which I call the **directionless style.** This style is characterized by a lack of clear guidelines and objectives. Parents are often frustrated, upset, irritable, weary, dissatisfied, unhappy, unable to control their children, not certain from one day to the next what is going to happen. Treatment of children is erratic and inconsistent, sometimes harsh, at other times overpermissive. A family of this sort tends to break apart, the children going one way and the parents another, and often each of the parents goes a different way. A family in this state may be not much more than a collection of individuals temporarily living in the same household with little common interest in their joint future. This kind of family needs a new vision of its unrealized potentialities. It has broken through some of the limitations imposed by the closed living pattern, yet it has not found its way to a more satisfying mode of life. It does not know how to take the next step. And it may not even want to take it. It may "want out," having "had it" with family life.

The closed and directionless styles are both ill-adapted to the conditions of a rapidly changing society. They yield far too little in human satisfactions. Their costs in human misery and deprivation are incalculable. They are not likely, therefore, to persist very long. But if they collapse and the open-living style does not take their place, there is danger that family life may ultimately vanish altogether to be replaced by some form of state-managed child-raising institution. That would, in all probability, usher in a "social engineering" approach to managing human affairs by which people would be rendered compliant by scientific behavior modification techniques and moved around by super-planners like pawns on a chessboard—a "1984" scenario. But family life does not have to collapse. There are alternatives which we shall explore.

What Are the Real Differences Among the Several Styles?

A living style is much more than a pattern of how one lives. It is, rather, a pattern of how one thinks, feels and acts. When we use the term life-style, many people assume we are referring to such things as—

What kind of house do you live in?
What kind of work do you do?
What kind of clothes do you wear?
What kind of car do you drive?
How much money do you make?
How many children do you have?
How do you manage your time?
What is your favorite recreation?
What time do you have dinner?

These, of course, are a part of what life-style ordinarily means. But I am using the term in a different sense. By the **life-style** of a person, I mean how that person habitually *responds* in thoughts, feelings and behavior to the ever-changing patterns of events, both inside and outside of himself, that affect his life. What he *thinks* about these events, how he *feels* about them, and what he *does* about them constitute his life-style.

This means that the house you live in, the work you do, the money you make, etc. do not determine your life-style in my meaning of the term. I look at it the other way around: your life-style determines the kind of house and work you choose and all the other patterns that go with that choice. You had certain thoughts and feelings first. The key thought might have been something like, "Mother and Dad struggled hard all their lives, and look how little they got out of it!" And the key feeling might have been, "I don't want to live like that!" So you saw to it that you got a better-paying job and could have your own place and acquire some nice furnishings and a new car. Your life-style embodies your idea of priorities—of what you put first.

We will quickly see that the differences between the closed, directionless and open styles are not found in the kind of house or car the family owns, nor even necessarily in the kind of work its members do. While it would probably not be possible to tell from looking at your house or your car whether your life-style is open or closed, your style might be very evident from the way you respond to situations and to people—especially to the members of your own family—for it is in these areas that the major differences lie.

Figure 1 on the following double-page spread will help give the "feel" of the three styles. And certainly their feel is as different as three family styles could possibly be. Are these styles dissimilar because the people in them are different? Yes and no. The people in the three styles are, of course, unlike in a number of specific ways: they differ in their handling of emotions, they have a different outlook on life, they perceive differently, and their values and goals are different. Yet, they are people; any of them might, under different circumstances, be living in any one of the three styles. Few adults today are lucky enough to have been born in an open style.

Yet a fair number have, at least partially, achieved such a style. And the next generation may contain enough individuals raised in that style to accelerate the movement toward Open Family Living.

The closed style, because it exists in a variety of forms, may not always display its closed characteristics clearly, even to those caught in it. Perhaps its commonest form is what I call the **suppressed** or tight-lipped **mode.** The people in such a family may not say much, but if thoughts and emotions could kill, all the family members would probably be dead. Such a family is likely to produce equally closed children, except that the children may stand the family system of values on its head. Thus, very closed religious parents may produce children who reject religion altogether; politically conservative parents may produce radical or revolutionary youth, etc. When the children of closed parents reject their parents' opinions and beliefs, they are apt to do so with the same judgmental intolerance that the parents showed in rejecting theirs. They embrace the same closed pattern exactly, with the colors reversed. Thus, children do imitate their parents' life-styles.

Another familiar form of the closed style might be called the **turbulent mode.** In its most extreme form, it could be typified by the fanatic, either religious or political, of either the "left" or the "right." The Nazis were examples of this mode. So are extremists of every variety. While this mode may not, at first glance, seem directly relevant to most people's family life, it is actually a pervasive tendency in many families. Its characteristics may be recognized in the dictatorial husband or father, the paranoid family member with a tendency to violence, the child abuser, the person who murders his spouse, and many others. And these are simply the extremes of the type. Great numbers of families harbor these same tendencies in less obvious form. The mode can be recognized by its attitude toward differences of opinion, values or feelings. The suppressed mode wants to shut out such differences and give no heed to them. The turbulent mode interprets differences of opinions, feelings and values as enemy opposition and sets out to destroy the opponents ("Shoot the bastards!").

Another common closed mode, which could be called the **es-cape mode,** makes a still different response to uncomfortable pres-

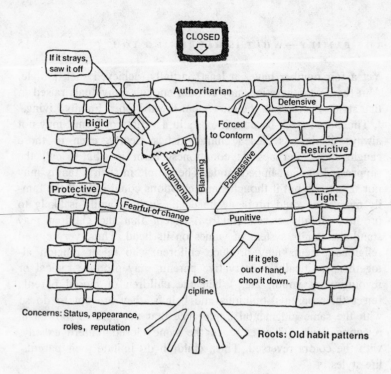

CLOSED

If it strays, saw it off

Authoritarian

Rigid

Defensive

Forced to Conform

Restrictive

Blaming

Judgmental

Possessive

Protective

Tight

Fearful of change

Punitive

If it gets out of hand, chop it down.

Dis- cipline

Concerns: Status, appearance, roles, reputation

Roots: Old habit patterns

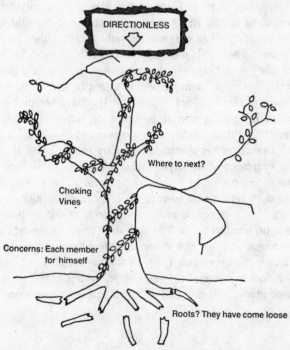

DIRECTIONLESS

Where to next?

Choking Vines

Concerns: Each member for himself

Roots? They have come loose

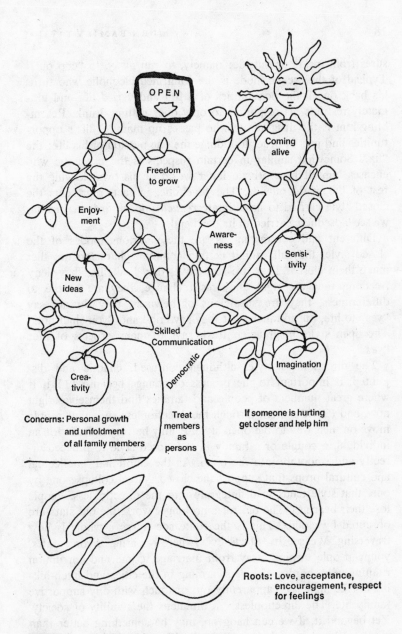

FIGURE 1. The Three Styles of Family Living

sures from inside or outside: namely, to run away, to "cop out." Typical of the escape mode is the confirmed alcoholic who turns his back on all the possibilities of a full and varied life and ultimately restricts his responses to only one: getting drunk. Resembling him is the drug addict who passes up many of life's opportunities and joys in order to indulge the one passion of his life: the "fix." Somewhat similar in certain respects is the psychotic who encases himself in a private inner world of his own, leaving the rest of the world outside. The psychotic, in fact, represents the closed style carried to its ultimate *reductio ad absurdum*. In him, we see closedness carried to its dead end.

Different and contrasting as are these various modes of the closed style, they all exhibit certain common characteristics that make them closed. They are restrictive, they limit life, they deny freedom, they are rigid, they resist change, they are hostile to differentness, they are suspicious of newness, they do not say "yes" to life, but to much of it they say "no" and "you shall not." The open style, in great contrast, says to many aspects of life: "yes."

The directionless style, although confused, chaotic and disjointed, is important to the process of change because (1) it is where great numbers of people and families find themselves right now, and (2) it is often through the directionless style that people move on their way to the open style. It may be very difficult for an individual, a couple or a family in the closed style to proceed directly and smoothly into the open. As the emotional, intellectual and cultural props that support the closed system collapse one by one, that style tends to disintegrate into the directionless. People lose their bearings. The old rules no longer work, the old stars are obscured by clouds. This is the route society as a whole is now traversing. We see its effects everywhere—soaring divorce rates, young people turning away from marriage, crime and corruption running wild, hordes of kids swarming in the cities and hitch-hiking on the highways, apparently out of touch with any supportive family life. The directionless era threatens the stability of society. Yet beyond it, if we can hang on, may be something better than mankind has known before: a family life reborn in freedom that can nourish, instead of impoverish, human beings.

How Open or Closed Is Your Family Style?

The movement toward a more open style is not likely to be uniformly in one direction. Change rarely is. People will probably shift back and forth between the several modes of closed, between the closed and the directionless, between the directionless and the open, and between the closed and the open. The directionless style may seem, for some, a welcome escape from the stifling restrictions of the closed. But it can bring great confusion, anxiety and disturbance; the person experiencing it may be unable to bear it and may flee back into the closed. Yet the closed style does not work well, either. The people who return to it may find themselves thrown once again into the directionless. Only when people decide to design their personal and family life and cease following unrewarding styles will they begin to work on the inner and outer changes necessary to guide them into the open style where all family members can grow unhampered like the tall tree in Figure 1.

This dynamic shifting process between the family styles of living can be illustrated as follows:

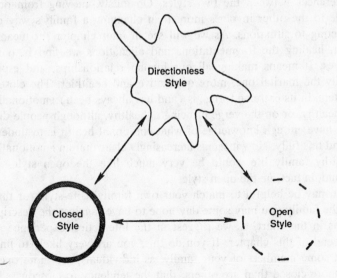

The arrows in the illustration show the potential back-and-forth interactions between the different family styles. The closed style is boldly drawn to reflect its tight, rigid characteristics. The directionless style is drawn to suggest that its boundaries are irregular and shifting like those of an amoeba. The open style is drawn to suggest that it has few boundaries, since we do not know the ultimate limits of the human spirit.

What are the main distinctions between the closed and open styles? Summing them up, let's omit the directionless style. That style, although numerically important, is featureless and transitory; it does not know where it is going. The closed style, at an earlier stage in history, knew where it was going, and even though it may not know now, its characteristics derive from a time when it did. And, of course, the open style has specific guidelines and goals: the nurturing of human beings, the enhancement of their personal growth and the enrichment of family life.

The contrast between the closed and open styles affects virtually every aspect of family life. Chart I, which follows, compares the two styles in ten vital areas of family functioning. Looking at this chart, it seems almost unbelievable how pervasive are the differences between the two styles. Obviously, moving from one style to the other involves more than changing a family's way of reacting to situations. As we will see in later chapters, it means, first, healing the fragmentations and alienations we find in ourselves. It means making all our human relationships, and especially the marital one, more qualitative and healthier. The closed system, in its extreme forms, is (and has always been) emotionally unhealthy, or on the verge of being unhealthy, although people did not have enough knowledge of what emotional health is to understand this fully. Now it seems increasingly clear that an emotionally healthy family life would be very much like the open style. It would, in fact, *be* the open style.

It may be helpful to match your own family's life-style (or that of the family you may some day hope to have) against the descriptions in the chart, as we suggest in the interaction experience at the end of this chapter. If you do this, you are very likely to find that some members of your family, as individuals, are more open or more closed than are others; that the tendency to closedness is

CHART I   Family Living Styles: Closed vs. Open

Areas of Functioning	Closed Style	Open Style
1. Basic family system	Authoritarian, suppressive, static. Requires conformity and obedience to rigid rules, values and expectations. Punishes "wrongdoing." Concerned with status, appearance, roles, reputation, etc.	Democratic, flexible, nurturing, freedom granting. Treats family members as persons, recognizes their feelings and needs, encourages their growth as whole human beings. Deliberately uses skillful communication to develop appropriate guidelines for living instead of rigid rules. Non-punitive.
2. Emotional atmosphere of family	Tense, tight, defensive and often negative. Insensitive to feelings. Often critical, blaming, judgmental, guilt producing, possessive, dull boring. Members tend to be emotionally starved, repressed.	Comfortable, warm, trusting and loving. Sensitive to feelings, empathetic, spontaneous, good-humored, affectionate, caring, non-possessive. Express feelings freely. Enjoy life.
3. Thoughts, beliefs and values of the family	Ideas and values rigidly held, defended. Contrary views are unacceptable. Narrow range of interests. "Untouchable" areas, such as sex, religion or politics.	Free, wide-ranging discussions; no "untouchable" areas. Willingness to listen to a variety of views and to respect differences and uniqueness. Willing to alter basic positions where appropriate.
4. Family behavior patterns	Automatic ("programmed"), repetitive, restrictive, limiting.	Aimed at enhancing the growth of family members, the marriage and the family as a unit.
5. Family communication patterns	Often limited, distorted and ineffective. Poor listening skills, inadequate checking out. Communication often cut off by critical or judgmental remarks, withdrawal, etc. Often unable or unwilling to share "deeper" feelings.	Generally open, clear and effective. Much sharing of moment-to-moment "deeper" feelings. Highly developed listening skills; careful checking out. Communication not cut off; people are heard out.

CHART I (*continued*)

Areas of Functioning	Closed Style	Open Style
6. Family decision-making patterns	One member overrides wishes or preferences of others; or there is unsatisfying compromise.	Free, open negotiation. Varying needs and preferences are listened to and considered.
7. Roles in the family	Stereotyped, unequal, resistant to change ("man's role," "woman's role," "child's role," etc.). Often unfair division of work and responsibility.	Flexible roles; negotiable as circumstances or feelings require. Fair division of work and responsibility.
8. Parent-child relationships:		
a. Aims of child training	Indoctrination. Child taught what to think and believe, how to feel, how to live. Strong emphasis on "shoulds" and "should nots" and on what's "right" and what's "wrong."	Development of human potentials. Child encouraged to develop his own capacities, to question, think, express and work with his feelings, become sensitive, aware and responsible.
b. Parent-small child relationship	Parent's role is to dictate, discipline and punish for wrongdoing. Child's role is to obey, be good, conform, have neat appearance, and respect his elders. Child typically treated as a possession and an object; his feelings ignored. Frequent reprimands and punishments, or else neglect. Love is often conditional on behavior.	Parent's role is to control when necessary but more often to help, guide and give affection. Child treated as a person in his own right, not as a possession or an object. His feelings listened to and respected.
c. Parent-teenager relationship	Parent continues to be authoritative but can rarely make it work. Mutual insensitivity, poor communication. Often a wide generation gap. Resentment.	Relationship continues to be warm, relaxed, trusting, mutually respecting, non-possessive, realistically supportive and understanding. Privacy is respected.

CHART I   (*continued*)

Areas of Functioning	Closed Style	Open Style
9. Attitudes toward people and society	People typically viewed in terms of status, roles, sex, race, politics, etc., but not primarily as individual human beings. Suspicious of outside relationships. Society seen as separate, "out there."	People viewed primarily as human beings. Status, roles, etc. are secondary. Outside relationships encouraged as part of personal growth. Family feels itself part of community and society.
10. Attitudes toward change and growth	Fearful of change; clinging to *status quo*. Resistant to personal growth. Emotional commitments and promises often felt to be unalterable. If family style does change even slightly, strong pressure is exerted to restore it to its former state.	Growth, change and new experiences welcomed as opportunities for meeting new challenges. Emotional commitments and promises are alterable as circumstances and people change.

much stronger in some areas (such as, for example, politics, religion or sex) than in other areas; and that your family life is more closed at certain times (such as when the grandparents are visiting) than at other times (such as when on vacation).

The chart depicts the closed and open styles sharply as if these characterizations were absolutes. But, of course, they are not; they are relative tendencies. Yet, in every individual, marriage and family, there are patterns that tend to take shape and can be identified. The question to ask yourself is not "Am I [or, "Are we"] open or closed?" There is no answer to this question. The question should be, rather, "How open or closed am I [or, "are we"] and in what areas?" And then: "What can I [or, "we"] do about it?"

The Accumulating Pressures Against the Closed Family Style

The story has been told many times of how the family once functioned as an integral part of a community in which it had its roots;

of how the *extended* family (meaning several generations and branches of the family living together or near one another) has been broken up by occupational mobility and other features of industrial and technological change; of the removal of productive work from the family, depriving it of one of its main reasons for existence; of the increasing isolation, rootlessness and helplessness of the *nuclear* family (meaning parents and children alone) which became the prevalent form after the break-up of the extended family. All this is familiar history. Except in small communities, there are not many extended families left in this country that can function effectively as unified bodies able to provide a significant sense of belonging. And the weakness of the nuclear family is evident in the statistics of separation and divorce. So unsatisfying has this form of family life become that many young people have no wish to marry; and some, if they have children, are attempting to raise them outside the formal framework of marriage.

The disintegration of the old-style family is world-wide. There is hardly a country on earth that is not experiencing family breakup and the rebellion of its youth. Student riots have broken out on every continent. In such diverse countries as France, Japan, Egypt and South Africa, the traditionally authoritarian universities have been subjected to demands by students to modify their policies. This constitutes a fracture of the closed political and social systems of those countries, for in a closed educational system, as in the closed family, the young are expected to be directed and guided by their elders. The idea of parents and university authorities having to listen to demands from the young has hitherto been unthinkable. But the unthinkable is being thought today, just as the unspeakable is being spoken and the "undoable" is being done.

How does it happen that the young have become so brash—and not only brash but, in some cases, defiant enough to face bullets and bayonets? One reason is because the closed systems are being torn apart by forces let loose by a technologically oriented culture. Consider the old-time family that now seems so quaint and so much a monument of the past. That family functioned within a virtually closed social system. This system included, in addition to the family, the local community of neighbors, the schools and the church. Few disruptive influences from outside were permitted to enter. Not many strangers (particularly those of widely different cultural or religious backgrounds) succeeded in breaking through the protective walls. The few who did were regarded with suspicion and closely watched. Ideas that penetrated the system from outside were strained through the filter of local minds (teachers and carefully selected textbooks). Even tradition and folklore were edited so that their impact would not disturb too much the structure of teachings, concepts, beliefs, morals, proprieties and life-styles that had been so painstakingly erected over the centuries.

Both elementary and higher education, until around the turn of the century, functioned as an integral part of this closed system, including sectarian as well as public schools. The Quakers used to call their form of schooling a "sheltered" education. Catholic schools, Jewish schools, and schools set up by other religious bodies were much the same. In fact, the educational purposes of any closed system are, essentially, *to produce a person who fits a predetermined mold—in emotions, in conduct, in manners, in morals, in thought, in belief and in the notions of propriety*. Training in conformity is important for the perpetuation of any closed system, either religious or political, and we still have many manifestations of it in the United States, such as the recurring controversies over "subversive" or non-conforming textbooks, sex education and similar matters.

Closed systems, including the closed family, can work effectively as long as the "input" to the system is fairly well controlled. When such a system loses control of the input, however, there is no way to insure that the old ways and beliefs will be perpetuated, for they constantly have to face competition with new influences. In this country we have taken pride in our ability to pioneer, to innovate, to conquer new territory, to "go West," to face the strange and the new. Our conquests were made primarily with plows, axes, hammers, ships and guns. Yet through all this, our patterns of thought, our basic beliefs and our ways of expressing emotions were not, until recent years, disturbed very much; they continued as a closed system. And it is this closed system of internal and interpersonal functioning that is now threatened.

One of the factors forcing open this formerly closed style of functioning in the family is the impact of influences from outside the system which stir the emotions, upset fixed opinions, undermine teachings, question established beliefs and, under present life-styles, often set family members against each other. Such inputs from outside come through television, radio, movies, plays, art, music, dancing, newspapers, magazines, books, advertising, travel, increased education, and, most important of all, human relationships with people of widely different cultural backgrounds. The American melting pot of heterogeneous peoples, races, religious faiths and cultures is producing, in spots, some fairly explosive mixtures. But all these variegated peoples in the pot have one thing in common: *originally, practically all of them were brought up in closed family systems.* Each ethnic or religious group, each racial group, each group that possesses a historic common background finds itself struggling against great odds to preserve some degree of separate identity and integrity. The Jews, who defended their unique way of life through centuries of oppression and the denial of nationhood, are a compelling example. The closed orthodox Jewish life-style is threatened today as never before by the uncontrolled input of thoughts and feelings from outside that conflict with the traditional teachings. This input has far more disruptive effect on a closed system than persecution; for persecution can draw together and solidify a people, whereas uncontrolled input does its work almost unnoticed until it has succeeded in splintering a formerly close-knit community.

A family that wishes to preserve its traditional way of life today has few options left. One, of course, is to try to cut off the input. That is the route taken by the Old Order Amish, for example, who try to protect their members from exposure to undermining influences from outside, often keep radios and TVs out of their homes, try as best they can to keep their communities intact and undefiled, even discourage higher education because of its tendency to subvert their faith, and follow a rigorous physical life-style that allows little time or surplus energy for diversions. Thus, the Amish communities are enclaves that try to remain, as far as possible, walled off from the world around them. They have been astonishingly successful in this, and their children are models of good behavior and peaceful devotion to a life of serving their families and communities.

But will the Amish be able to maintain this insulated existence indefinitely in the face of the overwhelming pressures building up against it? It does not seem possible. Internal strains already are becoming evident and are certain to increase. Closed systems have a rigidity that, when they finally break, often causes them to shatter disastrously. In this manner, many customs and beliefs of the past that were valuable and worth saving have been lost, such as the stand of the early Pennsylvania Quakers for fair and peaceful dealings with the native Indians.

Another route that a closed system may take to meet the threat is to attempt to alter, modify or edit the input and so render it harmless. To be effective, this probably requires action on a national, or even an international scale. The Soviets are trying to do it by censoring literature, regulating news media and jamming foreign broadcasts. But, even for them, with their leaders holding virtually total authority and power, it will probably be a losing battle. They have attempted to control rigidly the products of their authors and artists; yet some of the ablest ones, like Solzhenitsyn, refuse to bow to bureaucratic edicts. Censorship in one form or another has been tried repeatedly in nation after nation with very spotty results.

Individual families are in a position where it is virtually impossible to control input. You might forbid your children to watch television programs of which you disapprove, but for every program you succeed in shutting off they will probably see two or three that you were not on hand to catch or did not know about. If you refuse to allow a TV in your home, your children will find a set to watch somewhere else. And so it is with other media. A family in my neighborhood disapproves strongly of *Playboy* magazine; yet from time to time a copy (to the parents' dismay) finds its way into their house. Supervising the input of a family living in an urban or suburban area is almost as hopeless a task as trying to plug the leaks in a sinking boat with chewing gum.

Over and over, then, parents unable to carry on in the closed style in which they themselves were brought up fall back gradually and reluctantly upon the directionless style. In despair, they shut their eyes to what is happening. They try to make do from day to day and hope for the best. This is tragic, for there are constructive alternatives to this retreat. But, to find them, it is necessary to let go of many basic assumptions and restrictions of the closed style.

The collapse of autocratic parental authority has produced incredible confusion. Parents brought up in the authoritarian tradition and accustomed to thinking in these terms are at a loss what to do. Some of them keep trying to restore the authoritarian pattern; but their attempts, instead of producing obedient, conforming children, are driving great numbers of young people out of the family system altogether. Children of total abstainers are reacting by getting drunk. Children of parents raised in a military "spit-and-polish" tradition are becoming "dropouts" or pacifists. All sorts of crosscurrents are taking place that frustrate and enrage parents who have placed their reliance on maintaining a strong authoritarian position.

The fact is that *autocratic authority in a multicultural social order is not an effective way to handle young people*. It was not very successful even in its heyday. The methods we shall propose, had it been possible to employ them in past eras, might have resulted (as I suggested before) in a more humane and life-enhancing society than we have now. But we can credit the authoritarian system with producing a considerable degree of social conformity (which, in fact, was its true object). This was made possible by the fact that the dictates of parents were consistently backed up by the rules of the church, the schools and the community. The forces brought to bear on a child or young person were overwhelming—what could a kid do against them? The situation is far different today, as every struggling parent knows. It is a new era.

The decline of the autocratic parental style is not, in itself, a catastrophe, though to some parents it may seem so. It is catastrophic only for those families in which the parent tries to be an autocrat, cannot pull it off, and ends up alienating his young people; or in families where the parent succeeds so well that the children do not learn to think or feel for themselves. Authoritarianism in the family of former times was, in fact, a too-easy way to avoid difficulties. It took much less effort to lay down the law than to listen to and try to understand another struggling and erring human being. It was easier to punish than to love or forgive, easier to remain at arm's length than to develop intimacy, easier to be hard and inflexible than to be sensitive, easier to put down than to build up. The hoary adage, now fortunately out of style, that "children are to be seen and not heard," and the incredible maxim "spare the rod and spoil the child," summed up the position of some of our great grandparents. The world, including the family, was strictly for adults. Children were required to adapt themselves to that fact.

We know better now. We know now that childhood is a state of being all its own, much more than a temporary way station on the route to adulthood. The child is far more than the diminutive pre-adult our ancestors thought him. Artists, who portray very accurately how the people of their era feel about things, used to paint babies (in pre-Renaissance times) as small-sized adults. This is the way Jesus often was portrayed. People of that age could not conceive of the Son of God gurgling, spitting and wetting. Yet if He was human as well as divine, He must have been a baby once and have done just that.

We have learned a great deal about the complex emotional and mental life of little children, of how impressionable they are, of their extraordinary learning capacity and the depth of their feelings. In the closed family style, parents often treat little children as if they have no feelings worth considering—a most horrendous mistake. Every day one sees in the market place irritated parents dragging tiny children by one arm, snapping at them, slapping them when they cry, ignoring their pleas and their questions, scolding them for behavior that is natural for a child (such as picking up objects)—all because the parent is tired and irritable, and normal childlike behavior is inconvenient or embarrassing for the adult. Such unfeeling treatment of children seems to be increasing because our industrial society puts parents under continually greater tension. But, unhappily, this kind of treatment of children, if long continued, can produce young people who do not respect themselves or others and may lead to an unmanageable generation gap and, later, a disorderly society. It is a shame for parents to invest a large part of themselves in the raising of their children only to have much of it lost in the end. Parents would not do this if they knew a better way. A better way, of course, exists.

The better way begins with treating every individual in the family, regardless of age (and this includes a baby), as *a person in his own right,* fully entitled to respect and consideration. The authoritarian parent of an earlier generation did not feel it necessary to do this. But for the modern parent, it may be the only alternative to losing his kids. Parents now are in a position where they are required to move toward a different concept of parenthood—the concept of nurture, not dictation; encouragement, not repression; listening to their children, not telling them to "shut up"; guiding, not punishing; being kind, not hard; being flexible, not obdurate; building up, not putting down. A family life built on these lines can be a joy instead of a trial. The young person brought up in this way has feelings for his parents and siblings; he does not want to hurt them; he has self-respect; and he is much less likely than most young people to fall into destructive addictions or to exploit others.

Many people are incredulous that such results as these can be obtained without strict parental supervision and control and without the old pattern of parental edicts, scolding, repression and punishment. My position is that these results *can* be obtained and, moreover, that in the world that is now evolving, they probably can be achieved in no other way. The old pattern was based on teachings that did not have the benefit of a scientific knowledge of man. The open living mode is based on what many psychologists, sociologists, biologists, anthropologists, educators, psychotherapists and researchers have learned about man during the past seventy years. It is necessary that this knowledge be put to use in the family.

Impact of a Changing Society

Society is changing with incredible speed, as we witness daily, and many of these changes are ravaging the family. Rural and small-town life, where people knew each other, where the local businesses were run by neighbors and the town mayor was your old buddy, is fading away. Many of the local businesses now belong to chains owned by corporations whose executives you will probably never meet. Government is remote. Increasing numbers of people live in cities and suburbs where they have few friends and no roots. Friendships tend to be temporary and superficial. Work is impersonal and, to an increasing extent, dehumanizing and deadening. Much of it draws upon very little of a person's resources; yet it is—and perhaps for this reason—exhausting. Breadwinning work has lost much of the creativity it had in preindustrial days. Craftsmanship is declining. Skilled stone carvers, for example, such as those who built the medieval cathedrals, are becoming an extinct species. Entire crafts, such as that of the cabinetmakers who once made fine furniture by hand, are being lost to the machine. Work opportunities for the very young and the very old are limited; there is often little useful work for either of them to do. Family life in apartments, mobile homes or small houses does not offer much to absorb the time and energies of the dwellers, who often fall into sterile time-filling pursuits. We keep the youngsters in school long after they have ceased to be stimulated by the educational process, and we pack the aged off to retirement homes or communities. The effect on family life of all these changes has been near-catastrophic.

Traditional institutions, such as the church and the schools, also have been deeply shaken. One of the most historically stable and monolithic institutions in the world has been the Roman Catholic Church. Its teachings are grounded in traditions centuries old. Until recently its Mass was conducted in Latin, and everywhere in the world the Catholic services were similar. But a whirlwind has struck the Roman Catholic Church, typified by the demands for repudiation of the Church teachings on birth control, by the demands of some priests for the right to marry, and by pressures to admit women to the priesthood. There are rebel priests and nuns, defiant Cardinals, underground church services—all developments that would have been inconceivable as recently as a decade ago.

Another authoritarian institution, the nation's armed forces, has been faced with racial antagonism in ships at sea, peace demonstrators trying to block naval vessels in harbors, drug addiction of men stationed overseas, women demanding admission to the military and naval academies, and a reluctant relaxing of rules barring long hair and beards. Where is the old spit-and-polish? Rules were once made at the top for purposes conceived at the top. Now rules have to take into account the need to avoid disruptions at the bottom. To the devotees of authoritarianism, this is deplorable. But authoritarianism itself is cracking, just as its family counterpart, the closed family, is breaking up.

A physical parallel of these changes, with interesting symbolic overtones, is the recent rapid erosion of the stonework of old cathedrals and other public buildings that had stood undamaged for centuries. More erosion is said to have taken place in the past twenty or thirty years, due to air pollution, than in all the centuries up to then. This is both a fact and an allegory. It reminds us of the erosion of values on which we have depended. We are not always sure now whether the lost values were good ones or not. The changes in sex morality, for example—are these good or bad? There is less sexual repression, less covering up, less hypocrisy, less sexually based neurosis now. Good? There is a frightening rise in extramarital pregnancy, abortion and venereal disease. Bad! Where do we come out? Some people are uncertain. And so it is for many of the values being challenged today. Later in this book we will examine a number of these value shifts more closely because of their relationship to the problem of achieving better understanding between the young and their parents.

A value shift that could be far more destructive than the liberalization of views on sex is the growing cynicism about the reality of love. Mankind cannot do without love. The need for love begins in the womb. A baby cannot live without affectionate handling, hugging, being touched, loved, fed and cared for. Merely satisfying the baby's physical needs, such as for food and clothing, is not enough. Babies that are not touched and handled affectionately have been observed to sicken and die. So the need of children for love has been proved beyond question. But we may forget that the need for love persists throughout the entire lifetime of every human being. It is hidden in much adult life—people put up masks to conceal their need for love. But the yearning shows through in innumerable ways: in people's fondness for pets, in the way lonely people reach out to each other, in the vulnerability of the young to being hurt, in people's susceptibility to flattery, and in many other ways. Love is one of the strong motivations underlying human functioning. It is a healing force. And its absence results in twisted personalities and dehumanized goals. When love is missing in families, relationships lose their life-enhancing quality. Children starved for love may become desensitized and delinquent. They may grow up to be adults who care little for people, laugh at love and put their faith in punishment, hard-line positions, suppression and sometimes violence. This is tragedy, for their need from the beginning was love; it was denied them, and their destructiveness is the consequence.

The Inherent Strengths of Family Living

Despite all the accumulating pressures threatening to tear apart the family, I do not believe that family life is about to disappear. Even the closed family may survive, although troubled, as long as it can remain part of a like-minded community, motivated by a strong religious or ideological influence, which is able to operate its own system of education. But when the closed family is isolated, as in the big cities, cut off from the feeding roots of a related community, its doom seems inevitable. It may deteriorate and become stuck in the directionless phase; or as I hope, it may pull itself together as the members move through the directionless style into the open style.

My faith in the open-style family is based on the fact that *family life at its best fulfills a human need not fully met by any other arrangement or institution*. Babies and young children, for their optimum growth, require an environment of loving attention, acceptance, stability, security and interaction with other human beings. Where could they have such needs met except in a family of caring people? Children are often deeply shaken and hurt when a separation or divorce hits a family or when parents remain together but cannot get along. The children may recover from the hurt, but they are likely to need an extra amount of loving in the ensuing years to heal their scars.

Parents need their children perhaps as much as their children need them. Children can reawaken feelings long dormant in many adults—reacquaint them with the almost forgotten world of play, joy, wonder and excitement in which the adults themselves once lived. When parents grow old, their grown children can bring light and meaning to what otherwise might become lonely and barren lives. This, despite the annoyances and cares of raising a family, is a gift not to be carelessly thrown away.

Parents need each other—or, at least, each parent needs someone with whom he can share his thoughts, worries, feelings, dreams, hopes and disappointments. If parents cannot share in this fashion with each other, it is an unhappy condition. Extramarital affairs may in some cases, provide a substitute; but many such affairs are unsatisfying because they are temporary and clandestine and because they frequently only further undermine the marital relationship which otherwise might have been revitalized.

We are sometimes so engrossed with the forces that pull marital partners apart that we forget about the forces that hold them together. These forces can be powerful. Among the greatest ones are mutual care and need. No matter how irritable a person may get at times, he still may give his spouse more than he takes away. And no matter how preoccupied with work either one gets, the other is still likely to need him and want him. It takes an astonishing amount of frustration and bitterness to pry apart a couple who have lived together for a number of years and have had children by each other. People need family life. They keep turning back to it; there seem to be few fully satisfying alternatives to it.

There are, of course, quasi-families put together to satisfy the longings of people unable to find a meaningful relationship in a blood-related family. The commune is one example. The commune fills, at least for a time, a real void, for there is a vast amount of human wreckage from the storms that have torn apart nuclear families. Yet I cannot see the commune as the ultimate answer to the problem of the collapsing family. It is too unstable. Its members tend to come and go. The long-term stability and security which small children need may not be supplied. On the other hand, some communes offer a partially offsetting advantage in that there are more than one or two adults to whom a child can turn for help, comfort or instruction. In this respect, the commune may be seen as a kind of return to the extended family, and this could be one of its strengths. In such a case, it could function, temporarily at least, as a family.

The blood-related family remains, despite all its weaknesses, the most powerful influence in the lives of most children. Nothing else compares with it. It is from their own parents that most children learn their attitudes, values, ways of handling feelings, modes of communication, ways of relating to people, conceptions of roles, and basic life-styles. The mere fact that miserable, frustrated parents or messed-up parental relationships have a devastating effect on children simply underscores this fact of inescapable influence. For example, if parents are habitually critical of other people, the children are likely to develop a similar pattern. If parents generally hide their feelings, so, very probably, will the children. If parents relate warmly to each other and show affection openly, the children will be likely to develop similar characteristics. There are distinct patterns in families of how all these interactions occur, and the parents to a very large extent set these patterns.

It is doubtful that any organized, centrally directed institution can do for human beings what the family has the potential to do. At its best, the family is the breeding ground of love and caring, which we know are essential for optimum human growth and development. The family is where the most deeply human qualities have a chance to grow and unfold. If the family does not encourage that unfolding, it fails in the one function in which the family is superior to all other forms of human association. The family truly has the potential to be a human-being garden—a place where the finest human qualities can come to flower. Where else can this process occur? Not in the big institutional organizations where conformity is placed ahead of humanness. The schools, with the rarest exceptions, reward conformity more than originality, curiosity or even brilliance. So, unfortunately, do closed families. In so doing, such families are siding with the dehumanizing tendencies of the big institutions and missing the opportunity to contribute what only the family can contribute: encouragement to a young person to discover who he is and to develop his potential.

As we shall see later in this book, *the human being is endowed with qualities which, if he could learn to realize and develop them, could raise his life to a level of tremendous excitement, joy, creativity and self-fulfillment.* The open family style, I am convinced, is the most effective channel for releasing this potential. If family life does not rise to meet this challenge, untold human capacities will probably wither on the vine in the years to come; for most of the other institutions in our society exert subtle or direct pressures to inhibit their development. Corporations, as we know, prefer employees who exemplify the "corporate image." They like consumers who can be persuaded to buy their products. Big government wants citizens who will do as they are told and be loyal to the boss, not ones who ask embarrassing questions. The armed forces want obedient, non-troublemaking recruits. Who is interested in the original, creative, non-conforming, question-asking, provoking, individualistic, growing, changing, developing human being? Yet, if we discard him, where are we to get the new ideas, the original approach, the human touch, the caring for people, the concern for the future, the love of nature, the awe at the marvelous world in which we were born, the rediscovery of joy and play, the enrichment of the emotional life? These qualities probably only the family—and specifically the open family—can fully cultivate.

There is still great strength in the family system and in the people who comprise it. To draw upon that strength, family members need to recognize their untapped powers.

Revitalizing the Family

To revitalize the family, it is necessary to begin with the *individual*. Open Family Living means much more than an updating of techniques or a selection of new words to use in difficult situations. It is a redirection of the individual; a changed way of experiencing who he is and who those around him are; an altered conception of the nature of human relationships generally; a rededication to life. Many of us have been miseducated from childhood as to our true nature and our true work. This was nobody's fault. Almost the whole of human society shares this handicap. But we have knowledge today about the workings of the human mind, body and emotions which our ancestors did not have, and this knowledge arrives barely in time (we hope) to stave off disaster. This book is an attempt to show how this knowledge can be applied to increase the quality of family life everywhere. ►1

Suggested Interaction Experience

IE-1. APPRAISING YOUR OWN FAMILY LIVING STYLE (PP. 36–37)

On Chart I (pages 21–23) identify in what ways the descriptions fit your family life today or how your family's patterns in certain of these areas fall between the two styles. Try this also for the family in which you grew up (if it was different from your present family).

EVALUATION: Could you identify your family's patterns readily? What feelings did you have as you made these appraisals? Did you find significant differences between the two families? Or similarities? Is there anything you would like to change in your present family life? Who would have to change the most: you or other family members? Or would you all have to change together?

FOLLOW-UP: You may wish to ask one or more other family members to go through the same procedure. By comparing your perceptions with theirs, you might learn much about yourselves as individuals and as a family. What areas of functioning would other members of your family wish to modify or change?

HOW PEOPLE
AND FAMILIES
BREAK APART

Divided Man

Families are composed of individuals; and if family life is to be enriched and is to move toward openness, the work must begin with the individuals in it—with you and me.

We are divided within ourselves—here is the stubborn fact with which every movement toward human betterment has had to deal. It is the fatal flaw on which human hopes so often come to grief.

It is this fact of inner division that makes Man the restless, dissatisfied, tormented, destructive creature he frequently is—tearing apart his world, poisoning his environment and injuring his loved ones and himself. The disrupted family is a product of disrupted human beings.

This internal division is so pervasive that it affects us all. Looking at ourselves, we seem to be a mass of contradictions. Sometimes we are loving and kindly, but then we discover ourselves being cruel and vindictive. We are wise on occasion, but also frequently foolish. We are perceptive and aware beyond all other creatures, yet at times unbelievably blind and insensitive. We want to help people, but at the same time we find ourselves wishing to hurt. We long to be close to another human being, yet we cannot stand being close to anyone.

How can we understand ourselves? How can anyone understand us? The enigma of the warring opposites in man has fascinated poets, dramatists, philosophers and religious thinkers since recorded history began. For many centuries, the split in the human being was experienced as a struggle between good and evil

—between obedience to God (or the church) and the temptations of the Devil. People were taught to believe that their life was a battleground for contesting moral forces; that there could be no reconciliation between these forces; and that one (presumably, the "good") force, had to master and overthrow the other ("evil") force. According to this teaching, man had no choice but to wage a war of extermination within himself.

Such a division of the self, splitting each human being down the middle, has had far-reaching psychological consequences. Inner conflict cultivates the ground for outer conflict. How could it be otherwise? When we consider how split man has been throughout the ages (and still is), partly as a result—or as a reflection—of his own beliefs and teachings about himself, we need no other explanation for the religious persecutions and wars, the burning of heretics, the hunting down of witches, the thundering threats of hell-fire, and the almost hysterical attempts through the centuries to control children's thoughts, beliefs, feelings and behavior. The manifestations of inner division are as old as history and as new as tomorrow, and they are revealed today in both the closed and directionless family life-styles and in the more repressive features of the society in which we live. Yet, it is not necessary for man to live so tormented.

How Did We Become So Fragmented?

Science, which has revolutionized thought in the physical realm, is altering profoundly our conception of human beings as well. Thousands of observations and experiences by a great number of professional workers in many fields have constructed, bit by bit, a picture of how an individual human being comes to be the kind of person he is. We have a fairly good idea now of how he (or she —remember I am talking about both sexes) arrives at his divided, fragmented state. It is apparent that his development is not random, nor is it a mysterious process that cannot be understood. Although every person has his individual reactions and no two people are exactly alike, *there are broad principles regarding the ways in which human beings interact that can be learned and applied*. There is a vast amount of available information, for example, on what kind of natural equipment a baby is born with; on how the baby responds to his environment; on what his physcial, emotional and mental needs are; on how and what he learns; on how he interacts with his parents and other people around him; on what kinds of patterns this interaction makes; on how the interaction shapes the child's personality; and on how the patterns learned in childhood can dominate a person's life through adulthood and even in old age. Putting together all these kinds of information has been like assembling a jigsaw puzzle with thousands of pieces. The puzzle is far from complete and may never be; but the general outlines are nevertheless emerging.

Despite all this accumulating knowledge, there has not been until very recent years an adequate understanding of what happens when two or more individual human beings react to and respond to each other (as in a family). Psychology, biology and the medical and other sciences have opened up a vast amount of knowledge about man's inner functioning; and the social sciences have thrown valuable light on how masses of people behave in their political, social and economic relationships. But until the past two decades, surprisingly little attention was paid to developing the principles of *interpersonal dynamics*—the relation of individual to individual. One reason may have been that it was tacitly assumed that if enough could be learned about how individuals function, there would be no problem in explaining their interaction. Psychotherapists are finding, however, that people who have learned to understand themselves quite well are not automatically helped in their relationships with others. Interpersonal relationship brings in a different dimension that requires specific attention on its own. It often becomes necessary to supplement individual psychotherapy with some form of group therapy.

Because of the urgent need for the qualitative improvement of human interaction, there has been in recent years a proliferation of experimental work with interpersonal dynamics. This work has included the development of sensitivity training groups, encounter groups, marathon therapy groups and a variety of other approaches to intensive group interaction.

Some of the characteristics that emerge in the more successful of these group experiences are these:

Awareness: People in these groups are encouraged to interact in ways that increase their awareness of themselves and each other as unique individuals.

Emotional involvement: They learn to become emotionally involved with each other. They begin to care about each other as persons.

Communication: They learn to communicate and relate much more honestly and openly than people generally do in ordinary social or business relationships or in most family settings.

Three-sided interaction: They interact in three areas of human functioning—*intellectual* (e.g., talk, discussion); *emotional* (expression of feelings), and *behavioral* (role playing, bodily movements, touching, etc.)

Realization of potential: Through their interaction, participants begin to discover powers in themselves which most of them never knew they had and which had been lying dormant.

Aliveness: The experience is exciting to most of the participants; it is a liberating process; it moves people toward greater openness in their interpersonal relationships; and it can be (if the person allows it to be) long-lasting in its effects.

These group experiences suggest ways in which there could be enormous qualitative improvement in marriage and family life. In a successful group session, people emerge from their shells. They begin to appear to each other as real, alive and human. Differences of age, race, nationality, religion, social position, education, experience, politics, economic level, etc., which in ordinary life tend to keep people apart, melt away in the group experience until they become irrelevant. An entirely different set of qualities comes into focus as the basis of interaction: honesty, awareness, acceptance, empathy, caring and recognition of humanness. These same qualities can be put at the center of human relationships in a family; and the same kind of interaction that can make an all-night marathon a never-to-be-forgotten experience can also make marriage and family life exciting and rewarding.

What would happen if people gave the human relationships in their marriages and families a fraction of the concerned attention that participants give each other in the group experience? Would not the quality of family life be transformed? A considerable part of the problem with families is neglect: Family members become preoccupied with outside matters, cease paying much attention to each other, become indifferent to feelings and begin to take each other for granted. Thus, disintegrative forces are at work in many families that do not come into operation in the group sessions.

Sessions in group dynamics are popular because many people are starved for relationships having more meaning than they find in the weekly poker game, in pick-ups at the bar, or in a half-dead marriage or a closed family life. They feel alienated from themselves, from each other even in their own families and from the world around them. Much of the odd behavior that we see in people, including a variety of obsessions and addictions, is a product of these alienations. Individuals who seek group dynamics sessions are apt to be ones who have become sufficiently aware of their emotional starvation (a part of the alienation) to take action directly to alleviate it. But there are also other possible solutions, as we shall see.

The work in group dynamics has brought into focus one insight of overriding importance—not a new one, but one that tends to be widely forgotten, even in the helping professions: *People need each other. They are good for each other. When they are sufficiently real to each other, they heal each other.* Isolated and alone, people have the greatest difficulty in unfolding, realizing their potential or maintaining emotional health. The sick need healthy people to help them get well. The healthy need other healthy people around them to keep them well. Parents need their children to help keep them human, flexible and in touch with life. Children need their parents to help them achieve a sense of identity and to give them a feeling for their origins, their place, their function (as well as for the more obvious economic, educational and social reasons).

In the matter of emotional needs, the difference between an infant and an adult is much less than we have been taught to think. We know that a baby, in order to grow and develop, needs to be communicated with, recognized, played with, touched and loved.

The baby each of us once was still lives in us all, and those needs of the baby are still our needs. They will continue to be our needs as long as we live.

The poet Ned O'Gorman, who, for a time, worked with black children in a storefront child center in Harlem, wrote: "Our workers know that *children cure each other*. (Italics mine) Sylvia came in the door her first day in the storefront and cried with such intensity that I thought she'd swallowed a pin. Anthony Day went to her and held her hand. He is five. She is three. She stopped crying. Anthony went about his business. Every morning for a week Anthony held her hand and soon she didn't need to cry in the mornings. A teacher who didn't know would meddle, fuss, and tempt Sylvia to stop crying. (If I buy you an ice cream, will you stop?)"*

Why, we may ask, do children sometimes *not* cure each other but tear each other down? That happens also. Children can be corrupted by the adults around them, and it can happen at an early age: fear and ridicule of the strange or unusual, hatred of a different race or ethnic group, suspicion of neighbors, addiction to violence, desire for vengeance. Our society is full of alienations that act like corrosive acids eating away the natural goodness of young and old alike.

Alienations—The Sickness of Western Society ·

Man's inner division shows itself in his alienations. Alienation is not part of the natural heritage of man. It is taught. It is a product of ways of thinking, feeling and living that have come down out of the past. Let us consider the principal kinds of alienation that pervade our lives and, for many of us, make qualitative family life difficult if not impossible.

ALIENATION OF THE EMOTIONS

Most of us have been brought up in a head-oriented, emotion-disparaging culture. Men, in particular, have been trained in the

---

* From "Storefront," in *Columbia Forum,* Fall 1970 (Columbia University).

past to show little emotion, especially of the tender variety, and to have little respect for feelings. One evidence of this is the curious way we distrust leaders and professional people who visibly betray emotions. We have been taught to associate open expression of feeling with poor judgment. This is a very strange reaction, and it would make little sense to an observer from another planet (or from some parts of this one) because it suggests that we distrust an open person and trust a closed one. The sphinx, the stoneface, who wins our confidence might be robbing us blind; we would have no way of knowing because we cannot look behind his visage. But in a perverse way we believe in him, since he is so like us! One of our favorite cartoon heroes has been Superman who performs incredible feats with never a tear falling from his masculine eyes or a smile of happiness on his square-jawed face. Superman always has important business to attend to; he dares not let himself be seduced by anything so frivolous as a surge of pleasure or grief.

Our loss of touch with our emotions is a learned characteristic. The training begins in the playpen. Children learn very quickly to cover up and falsify their emotions.

"I hate you!" says an angry little girl to her mother.

"Sarah, you know you don't mean that," interposes the father sternly. "You must tell your mother you love her."

"I won't," says the little girl.

She gets spanked, verbally or physically. Thus, she is taught to hide her true feelings. Eventually she learns to hide them even from herself because they upset her as well as those around her. By the time she grows up, she may scarcely know what her true feelings are except as they occasionally reveal themselves in dreams or by unintended remarks or gestures in times of excitement or stress.

We are taught very early to suppress the so called "bad" feelings—anger, hatred, fear, jealousy, greed—which may explain some of the cruelty and acquisitiveness loose in the world, for suppressed feelings tend to show themselves in unguarded moments or to break loose in uncontrolled ways. But we also, for quite different reasons, suppress many of our "good" feelings. Affection is an example. We are uninhibited about showing affection for babies (fortunately for the babies). But as our children grow into teen-agers and then into adults, many of us shy away from overt affection (kissing and hugging); we feel self-conscious about it and perhaps even a little afraid or ashamed. (If you are a parent, ask yourself: When did I last hug and kiss my children? If you are a young person, ask yourself: When did I last hug and kiss my parents? If the answers are "not for a long time," you can be sure that the process of separation from your emotions has been going on.)

This alienation of the emotions acts like a poison in family life. A parent suffering from it has the greatest difficulty in satisfying the needs of his children and his spouse for affection. Women are somewhat less hampered than are men by the traditions that have discouraged the free expression of feelings. A male-dominated society has permitted girls to be emotional because it has not (in the past) expected serious or important work from them. (Men, interestingly enough, have not regarded homemaking and child raising as "serious" or "important" in anything like the degree that they have regarded their own work.) It is typical of the masculine attitude toward emotions (and toward women) that the supposed greater emotionality of women has been looked upon as proof of feminine "weakness." Yet the great heroes of ancient Greek legend expressed feeling in ways that in our culture, would be looked upon as effeminate. The godlike warrior, Achilles, is described as follows in the *Iliad* (when he received news that his beloved friend, Patroclus, had been killed in battle): "A dark cloud of grief fell upon Achilles as he listened. He filled both hands with dust from off the ground and poured it over his head, disfiguring his comely face and letting the refuse settle over his shirt so fair and new. He flung himself down . . . at full length and tore his hair with his hands. Then Achilles gave a loud cry . . ."

Our stoneface ideal of masculinity and our pretty cover girl concept of femininity are both cultural stereotypes of a very restricting kind, neither having anything to do with inborn masculine or feminine traits. Both are products of an alienation that disavows true, honest emotions. We are taught to be embarrassed by a deep feeling such as grief, as if it were somehow disgraceful. And that is true even within the family (where, of all places, real feeling ought to be accepted).

The gentler emotions such as affection, appreciation, compassion, kindliness, awe, reverence, thankfulness, wonder, concern, sadness, wistfulness, contentment, love of beauty—these are the ones generally most submerged in our society—are often unappreciated, unrewarded, even treated with scorn. There are many reasons for this. Emotions such as these do, at times, get in the way of enterprise. Our recent ancestors built a great nation; threaded it with railroads, canals and highways; dotted the land with cities, industries and farms; built banks and schools and governments. There was not much time or opportunity in all this activity for tender feelings. They were looked upon as a luxury. And for this oversight a penalty is now being paid. People have become separated from an essential part of themselves and, to this extent, have become a little bit less than fully human.

But an awakening is in progress. The vast physical plant, of which we were once so proud—the buildings and chimneys soaring into the sky, the ribbonlike highways, the endless streams of cars and trucks, the streets and houses stretching as far as the eye can see—suddenly begin to crowd in upon us and appear to loom over us like oppressive monsters. We feel diminished by them. And poverty and crime push upon us from all sides. We sense that we have become victims of some strange kind of deprivation. Ugliness, violence and empty meaninglessness pervade the lives of people all around us and threaten to destroy much of what our hard-working forebears built. We are slowly beginning to be aware of the price that is being exacted for our way of life. It is too high—vastly, unacceptably high. Each one of us as an individual, and each family as a group of individuals, now needs to begin the task of rediscovery of the self—of learning to feel feelings again, to explore the life of the tender emotions so long pushed down and neglected.

Some will remember a child's story by Munro Leaf called *Ferdinand the Bull*. Ferdinand was a fighting bull trained for the arena. He was supposed to rush at the matador, toss him if he could, and supply entertainment for the crowd. But Ferdinand preferred to smell flowers, and whenever there were flowers around he would amble over and smell them, paying no attention to the waving cape and the screaming fans. This reduced his popularity rating. But why, Ferdinand wondered, should he pursue the trail of glory and end up dead when there are sweet flowers to enjoy—alive?

A trail leading back to the rediscovery of the emotions is being blazed now by some of the younger generation. In some cases, entire families are emerging slowly from the closed-off condition, the husbands learning to express affection to their wives and children and to share in the housekeeping and child-raising chores. Both partners in these families are learning to deal with their own and each other's feelings honestly and non-destructively; and the children are being permitted to say how they feel without facing threats of punishment. Broadening interest in music and other arts is also providing channels for many people to cultivate their awareness of feelings. But all these movements still have far to go. ►2

ALIENATION FROM THE BODY

Until the human body came into view on the world's beaches, many people in our culture had curiously divided feelings about it. They had little respect for the body as such, and so commonly ignored their own bodies, carelessly allowing them to grow fat, flabby and shapeless. But past generations also feared the body, or, rather, the activities which the body signified, and so kept the body covered and hidden. Yet, at the same time, there was a surreptitious desire to look at the bodies of other people, and a great admiration of the exceptional bodies of movie stars and athletes—body worship at a distance. There was (and is) a good deal of self-deception in American attitudes toward the body. We Americans like, for example, to believe that we are a sports-loving people; but the sports many of us like best are the ones we watch on TV or from a seat in the stadium.

As little children, great numbers of us were taught to dislike our bodies. The eliminative functions were regarded as nasty and unpleasant. Sweat and other emissions had to be washed off quickly. The sexual organs were, in our grandparents' time, considered unmentionable. And the growing girl was led to think of her menstrual processes as "the curse," to be hidden and never talked about. These attitudes, fortunately, are disappearing. But the body has still to emerge into our general consciousness as a part of us to admire, respect, be proud of, care for, nurture and love. Many a person takes better care of his house and his automobile than he does of his body.

It is not surprising, therefore, with these early-formed attitudes, that people are careless about what they put into their bodies. Nutrition is a science that has a bearing on everybody's life; yet an individual who takes great care to feed his livestock or pets with the necessary balance of nutrients and vitamins often gives himself and his family a thoughtlessly assembled collection of snacks, sweets, convenience foods and soft drinks which, if fed to animals, would make them sick.

People who do not respect their bodies naturally give little thought to the consequences of using chemical preservatives, pesticides, drugs and poisons. How do we account for a person who gives himself a shot of some drug of uncertain purity and potency? He not only risks making himself ill, he may even kill himself. But what does it matter to him? All he risks is his body and his life, and he has been taught to look upon both with remarkable indifference. Smoking cigarettes is said to be a "hazard to your health"; but how many avoid smoking merely for that reason? What about the many other things we do that are hazardous to our health: our sedentary habits, infrequent exercise and habitual overeating? If the body protests, we can always take an antacid tablet or a glass of Alka-Seltzer. But eat sensibly? Who does?

Contempt for the body is deeply embedded in our culture and even has roots in religious teachings. In certain religious traditions, "spirit" and "flesh" (i.e., body) are seen as antagonistic principles. Since "spirit" is looked upon as superior to the body or "flesh," the psychological consequence is to denigrate the body. This may not have been the intention of the religious teachers who preached the duality of spirit and body (Jesus, after all, healed bodies as well as spirits), but it does seem to be one of the practical results of an attitude that places one aspect of the human being very much above the others. Alienation from the body has had profound consequences in the family as well as in the larger world, for a sluggish, poorly maintained body leads to sluggish thought and depressed emotional states if not to outright sickness.

In our attitudes toward the body, our culture emphasizes external appearance more than internal functioning. In this respect, it gives rise to a kind of cultural schizophrenia. On the one hand, it says that a woman should be slender and pretty. On the other, it teaches her contempt for her body or some parts of it. The best route to slenderness and beauty might be assumed to be a healthy internal functioning of the body, but since our culture works against this, the woman is induced to attempt injurious starvation diets and to use cosmetics with dubious ingredients to hide the effects of a lack of natural vitality.

There are not yet many convincing signs of a broad-based movement toward personal wholeness in which the body is a fully accepted element. But there are some. The campaign against cigarette smoking is one, although the continued heavy use of tobacco is discouraging to those concerned about what people are doing to their bodies. Another is the popularization of such recreations as skiing, water skiing, swimming, golf, tennis, handball, surfing, skating, square dancing, etc. Another is the interest in health foods which, whether scientifically based or not, shows a growing concern for what we put into our bodies. Still another is the broadening interest in physical-mental-spiritual disciplines such as yoga. Still another is the slow growth of healthier attitudes toward the sexual functioning of the body.

As often happens with changes in cultural attitudes, some people swing over to the opposite extreme and become obsessed with the body, excessively concerned with its care, its development, its sickness or health, its sexuality, its pains and pleasures. This only tilts the balance the other way. A person obsessed with the body can be as unbalanced and as fragmented as one who is alienated from it. ▶3

ALIENATION FROM PEOPLE

As our cities and suburbs become more and more congested, people living in them seem to grow more and more individually isolated. It is as if they feel the weight of people pressing in among them and, in self-defense, push them away. The concept of neigh-

borliness seems to be losing ground. The word "neighbor" refers
to a person living nearby with whom one has some sort of
relationship. You might expect to call upon a neighbor for help
in time of trouble. "Neighborly," according to my old dictionary,
means "kind, friendly, sociable, etc." Has this concept of neigh-
borliness vanished? Perhaps not totally, but it seems to be di-
minishing. Distrust, suspicion and fear have made many people
reluctant to let anyone past their front door.

But our alienation from people goes far deeper. Many may
recall a famous murder committed in Brooklyn, New York, several years ago in full view of dozens of apartment dwellers
watching from their windows, not one of whom bothered to call
the police. When onlookers were later asked why they did nothing, their reply was, "We didn't want to get involved." Doubtless
the scene they were watching in the street below closely resembled
hundreds of scenes of violence they had seen on TV. Did they
equate the real-life drama with entertainment? Is it possible that
habitual TV-watching conditions people to passivity, insensitivity
and non-involvement? Or is the TV habit a *product* of passivity,
insensitivity and non-involvement? Perhaps both are true. But
there can be little question that non-involvement (which is alienation) has deeply permeated our society.

Highways can be dangerous places today, not merely from the
familiar hazards of accidents, weather and drunken driving, but
also because, in the event of sudden illness or injury, it may be
difficult to get help. There have been cases of disabled travelers
waiting for hours while cars streamed heedlessly by.

Most of us, hearing or reading about these cases of indifference
to human need, disassociate ourselves from them. "I would never
do such a thing," we tell ourselves. And perhaps we would not.
Yet, alienation from people is a concomitant of modern life; we
are part of it whether we want to be or not. As the population
of our country becomes more and more homogenized and as the
ethnic neighborhoods in the cities and elsewhere—Italian, Greek,
Irish, Jewish, Swedish, etc—become scattered and lose their
identities, the bonds between people seem increasingly fragile and
easily fractured. Suspicion and fear of your next-door neighbor
replaces friendliness. You may be afraid to enter an elevator with

a stranger or even to open your apartment door without positive identification of the knocker. And perhaps justifiably so.

But distrust and separation are not only felt between so-called "strangers." Husband and wife are often strangers to each other. So, in many cases, are parents and children, parents and grandparents, children and grandparents. Alienation within the family is often so deep that marital partners virtually have nothing to say to each other beyond "please pass the salt." And parents and young people in some families might as well be speaking different languages, so unable are they to achieve a common understanding even of simple words.

Certain of the people who were utterly shocked by the behavior of the witnesses to the street murder are themselves unknowing victims of the same kind of alienation that produced the cry, "I don't want to be involved." There is such a thing as involvement in external matters to avoid involvement with the self.

I know a couple whose entire family life is centered around working for causes: world peace, civil rights, racial justice, fair treatment for the American Indian. These people live what seems to be a selfless life of total involvement. But so selfless is it that their communications have ceased to reflect them as persons. Their Christmas letter to their friends, for example, was an exhortation to "write your congressman to . . ." followed by their latest concern. It contained not a word about themselves, their personal lives, their feelings or how their children are. We wrote back and said, "Tell us about *yourselves*." They wrote: "If you have a specific question to ask about us, we'll be glad to answer it. But *do* be sure and write your congressman." This, too, is alienation —the same disease that helped produce the social conditions this family so deplores—but here it takes a disguised form: escape from the self, from the *person* one is. People cannot live by causes alone or by work alone or by bread alone. *People need each other,* not merely in the capacity of fellow workers or fellow zealots, but as human beings. This is the basic need, and when it is denied, the emptiness in the life of the family is never filled no matter what noble works are done.

Many people who feel lonely and isolated in the midst of their families yearn for a more meaningful relationship with those closest to them, but cannot seem to bring it about; and many have lost hope of ever attaining it. A discouraged mother becomes deeply depressed because she cannot communicate with either her husband or her children. He is too busy and the children are too young to understand. A lonely teen-ager drugs himself because he feels there is nobody he can really talk to who loves and understands him. A father buries himself in his work because he feels shut off from everyone; he enjoys neither intimate friends and companions nor a close relationship with his family. Old people often feel the most lonely and isolated of all. Many feel displaced, shelved, useless and unwanted, and their busy children pay them little attention.

Alienation in family life takes a thousand subtle forms generally unrecognized by those experiencing it but devastating in its cumulative effect. As human beings, we cannot long survive alienation and still remain emotionally or spiritually healthy. Alienation violates our deepest nature. It haunts us, robs us of joy, imprisons us in a cell of our own making, drains life of its meaning. Its ultimate consequences, sometimes requiring several generations to come to fruition, are the neglect, abandonment, or abuse of children by their parents—something so unnatural that not even ferocious beasts do it under the conditions of nature.

Alienation from people is still very deep almost everywhere, and there are few signs of an early reversal in society at large. As society grows more complex, more bureaucratic and more dependent on technology, work becomes ever more separated from human values, and social relationships ever more superficial. The outlook seems to be for increased dehumanization. Yet, as the physicists say, every action has an opposite and equal reaction. When man's humanness is denied, the desire to re-establish it can become a powerful force.

Signs of breakdown of the technological society, typified by the proliferation of clerical and computer errors, equipment failures, poor-quality merchandise, failure to acknowledge communications, and a thousand other examples of faulty performance, may very well reflect the individual workers' rejection of a system in which he feels less than human. And there are indications that significant numbers of people are consciously setting out to rediscover and reaffirm themselves as human beings. The growth of the human potential movement mentioned earlier (sensitivity training, encounter groups, marathon therapy groups) is one indication of this. Another is a significant change that has been taking place in the nature of programs at church conferences in a wide spectrum of faiths, denominations and professional groups. This change is toward the replacement of lectures and sermons by free interaction in small groups. The spread of the interactive approach, in its myriad forms, seems to me to be a movement of great significance. Among the pioneers in this work have been the Marriage Encounter Movement in the Catholic Church, the marriage enrichment programs of David and Vera Mace and the Association of Couples for Marriage Enrichment (ACME), and the work of the Laymen's Movement with headquarters at Wainwright House in Rye, New York. ▶4

ALIENATION FROM THE COMMUNITY

Closely related to alienation from people is alienation from the community. This is steadily increasing as people become more and more rootless. Individuals alienated in this way think of the community (or nation) as a provider of services, but they do not experience themselves as part of it. They feel no responsibility for it. They attend few public meetings. They often do not bother to vote. They live as if the community were a sort of vending machine. You put in a dime and a job or a check drops out.

It is people with this form of alienation who dump garbage, trash and discarded appliances on the roadside; throw beer cans out of car windows; give little thought to teaching their children moral behavior. They feel little or no responsibility for the future of society or for mankind's survival on planet Earth. To them, society is something "out there" to which they feel no allegiance and in which they have minimal interest.

To lack a sense of community is to be adrift in a kind of emotional statelessness. Patriotism is the sense of community elevated to a national level. While it is subject to its own kind of distortion, the feeling of patriotism is one of connection with the people among whom we live, a merging of our interests with theirs. It becomes destructive only when it takes the form of a narrow pursuit of sectional interests without regard to the interests of others, or hatred of people outside the boundaries we set.

Because of such widespread alienation from the community, many large cities have become nearly ungovernable, political life is ridden with graft, men in positions of power unhesitatingly use governmental agencies to serve their own personal, corporate or political ends, and scandal after scandal rocks the nation. A country or state probably cannot long survive general alienation from the community. Such alienation produces a decline in the quality of both leadership and citizenship at every level. As the Watergate hearings were being held, a recurring question haunted many people: Where has *greatness* gone in our modern world? Where did all these men come from who wanted to use the government of the United States for narrow personal, corporate and political ends?

The outlook is disheartening. To find hope, I have to fall back on what may one day come out of Open Family Living. I know a number of young people, products of the open life-style, in whom I have unbounded confidence. They are intelligent, perceptive, sensitive, creative, sympathetic and thoughtful. They exert little power now and have few possessions. But one day, perhaps, they will have both. Some of them may develop qualities of greatness. For if the purpose of the open family life-style is the fullest development of human potential, the creation of great leaders may be the ultimate test of that style. ►5

ALIENATION FROM THE NATURAL WORLD

"Ecology" is now on everyone's lips although, just a few years ago, the death of an ecologist would scarcely rate a half-inch in the obituary columns. We have been made well aware of how man has recklessly exhausted his soils, cut down his forests, polluted his air, poisoned his rivers, fouled his lakes and seas, wiped out whole species of wildlife, drenched his cultivated lands with pesticides, and upset the balance of nature so that his own survival is now in question. Just how much damage can we do to the life systems on earth and still expect our planet to serve as the homeland of the human race?

This topic seems to carry us far afield from Open Family Living. But there is a close connection. Man's alienation from nature is a part of the same fragmentation of the human personality that gives rise to all the other alienations—the alienation from the emotions, from the body, from people and from the community. If you experience the world of living creatures and plants as something "out there" to be plundered, shot at for your own amusement, wiped out totally if there is money to be made, you are a split human being. One side of yourself—the side that knows itself to be part of the natural world—is suppressed and not permitted to live. That mangrove swamp, for example, full of rare and vanishing forms of wildlife, is where a developer wants to build a tourist hotel. The swamp is part of a shrinking terrestrial heritage of man that has, in one way or another, become the property of its present owner. Can he *feel* this? Regardless of the decision he eventually makes, does the feeling of connection with his natural heritage come through? Or does he dismiss it as of no consequence?

The destruction of our life-supporting systems (air, water and living things) which alienation from the natural world has brought about is now so far advanced that people are tempted to despair of its solution. Perhaps the human species will disappear from the earth. Yet an alarmed citizenry is beginning to respond with political and legal action, some of it effective.

It is but a slight psychological step from the plundering and exploitation of the natural environment to the treatment of human beings as objects for personal aggrandizement, pleasure or convenience. From that position, it is only a slight further step to the loss of capacity to experience one's spouse or one's children as human beings. Subtly, a person who follows this route begins, without realizing it, to confine all people, including himself (or especially himself) in the tight little prison cells of role-conformity. And rigid role-conformity is one of the hallmarks of the closed family living style.

All kinds of fragmentation of the self go together—not that they all manifest themselves to the same degree in an individual person, but they belong together in the total psychological climate that they produce. The breakup of the family is occurring in the same society that is destroying its natural environment—the same society that is suffering from gigantism and runaway crime. The different kinds of alienation are all close relatives—*all are aspects of the split within us.* And until we grasp this fact and begin to allow this brokenness to heal, we will probably not move far towards the enrichment and the freeing of our family life for personal growth. ►6

THE ULTIMATE ALIENATION

To people concerned with spiritual values, the five alienations we have just discussed are incidental to a deeper alienation which some of them might describe as "separation from God." Some would say that this is the only real alienation. We can think of it as a master alienation of which all the others might be considered as outgrowths. It is an alienation from one's own deepest and most profound sense of the meaning of things. With this alienation, man has lost contact with who or what he is.

Man's spiritual search has been a source of strength to him throughout the ages, and although religious beliefs have often separated people from each other, they have also connected people to each other. At its best, the urge that relates man to his God also connects him with himself, with other people, with his community and with the natural world. A spiritually centered community is, or tries to be, a loving and caring community. And so it has proved to be as long as religious feeling was not twisted by closed dogmas, personal ambition, antagonism toward other faiths and the urge to power. I have known former criminals, drug addicts and alcoholics who, in a manner that seemed almost miraculous, have been transformed and illuminated by an infusion of health-giving strength that they could only attribute to the spirit of God coming alive in them.

The belief that there is a power operating at the center of a person's being which can release and transform him, has potent effects for some people, exceeding anything that they feel able to do by themselves. The power may be called "God" or may be given another name. Or it may be looked upon as simply a transformation arising from a new combination of thought and emotion in the person which somehow nudges him off dead center. We have but an inkling of the energies that lie, mostly untapped, in the human being. The power I am talking about operates at a very deep level, and the person experiencing it feels that it is related to the very center of himself, about which the rest of him may begin to revolve. If a person can reach deeply enough into the center of his being to release this energy, he is reconnected and there is little that he cannot accomplish. ►7

At Peace or in Pieces?

The alienated person is fragmented; parts of himself are separated from other parts. It is a kind of paralysis. When someone suffers a stroke his use of a portion of his body or brain is suddenly cut off. He cannot then function as a complete person. Unlike a stroke, the fragmentation that produces alienation comes about gradually and is learned, not imposed by fate. But alienation can in the end, be as crippling as being stricken. Yet it is not, perhaps, as permanent. We can, if we learn how, work individually to overcome fragmentation. Society will not give us much help, for it is as fragmented as we are. But once we learn exactly what has happened to us, we can begin to work on ourselves and resist the divisive pressures that fragmented society brings to bear on us.

To help in this, I have prepared a chart to serve as a guide in self-evaluation. No one is totally alienated, for, if he were, he could not function and would need to be cared for in an institution. But few people are completely whole, either. To be completely whole would mean achieving a state of perfection that most human beings never reach. Not even the Greek gods on Mount Olympus were whole in this sense. The word "whole" comes from the same root as "holy" (Anglo-Saxon "hal," meaning sound, whole, hale). Thus, the word "whole," used as a description of the human condition, implies being like God, the "Holy" Spirit.

Let us not, then, be deceived into thinking ourselves either totally alienated (fragmented) or totally whole. Each of us is somewhere in between. But where are we, in that wide range? It would be helpful to know so that we can pinpoint more clearly the areas where we need to work with ourselves.

Chart II, which follows, shows five continuums, each column

representing one of the alienations I have discussed, and ranging from extremely alienated to whole. You may place yourself high on some of the columns, low on others, or in between. Try scoring yourself.

CHART II How Alienated Are You?

	From the Emotions	From the Body	From People
Ex-tremely alienated	Unaware of emotions. Emotionally dead, or at the mercy of uncontrolled emotions. Or both.	Rejection of the body or total indifference to it. Neglect of its needs. Tendency to self-mutilation.	Treatment of people as objects to be used, exploited, cast aside or ignored. No feeling for people.
Considerably alienated	Sometimes emotionally dead. Or sometimes at the mercy of uncontrolled emotions.	Indifference to the body. Acceptance of injurious habits or addictions; careless about consequences.	Feeling for a few people, but treatment of the rest as objects to be used, exploited, cast aside or ignored.
Some-what alienated	Limited range of emotional awareness. More aware of strong emotions than of gentle ones. Partial control of the passions.	Considerable awareness of bodily needs, but difficulty in overcoming injurious habits.	Appreciation of people who are of your own race or social class, but little feeling or negative feeling for others.
Compar-atively, whole	Broad range of emotional awareness, including many of the gentler feelings. But imperfect control.	Respect for the body. Enjoyment of all its functions. But retention of a few injurious habits (i.e., smoking).	Liking for most people, but some difficulty in feeling close to them or in expressing affection.
Whole	Full awareness of the play of emotions. Strong emotions directed into constructive channels.	Respect for the body. Enjoyment of all its functions. Avoidance of all injurious habits.	Feeling of closeness to and connection with people. Freedom to express love and affection. Respect for persons.

CHART II (continued)

	From the Community	From the Natural World	From Ultimate Values and Meanings
Extremely alienated	No concern for the community or feeling of identification with it. Tendency to plunder or exploit it.	Animals and plants experienced only as objects to be used, exploited or destroyed. No feeling for nature.	No feeling for ultimate values or the meaning of things.
Considerably alienated	Weak feeling of connection with the community, and tendency to ignore its needs.	Some feeling for nature as a hunting ground, but little compassion for animals.	Occasional concern with ultimate values and meanings, but tendency to separate them from ordinary life and work.
Somewhat alienated	Some feeling of identification with one's own people or nation, but general distrust and dislike of "foreigners."	Some feeling for animals and plants if they are one's own (i.e., pets), but little concern for the natural world as a whole.	Acceptance of conventional religious concepts, but loyalty to them not very deep or permanent.
Comparatively, whole	A broad sympathy with many peoples or nations, but some difficulty in accepting differentness.	Love for pets and other attractive animals or plants. Dislike of some. Interest in ecology.	Enough feeling of connection with ultimate values and meanings to have some effect on life and work. But only partial.
Whole	Feeling of identification with mankind; considering the world as a community. Concern for the future of humanity.	Deep feeling of identification with the natural world, of which we all are part. Desire to preserve and treasure it.	Feeling of deep connection with ultimate values and meanings. Entire life is so oriented.

Suggested Interaction Experiences

IE-2. RELEASING YOUR AFFECTIONS (P. 48)

Close your eyes for a few minutes. Try to recall in memory an occasion when you wanted to show affection to a family member but could not, or when you might have shown affection but did not. Relive the experience as it happened.

Now, in imagination, experience the event again as you wish it had been. Let your affection flow freely.

EVALUATION: How do you see yourself expressing affection? Freely, openly, comfortably? Or hesitantly, stiffly, awkwardly? How do you visualize the other person's response to your show of affection: warm and receptive, or surprised and hesitant, or cold and rejecting? Based on this experience, would you judge yourself as tending toward alienation or toward wholeness?

FOLLOW-UP: Could you share your fantasy experience with the family member involved? (A new closeness could result.)

IE-3. EXAMINING YOUR FEELINGS ABOUT YOUR BODY (P. 49)

Stand, nude, before a full-length mirror and scrutinize your body. Imagine that someone else is looking at your body. How would that person feel about it?

In what ways are you pleased with your body and with the care you are giving it? In what ways dissatisfied? Are you uncomfortable with or fearful of any of your body parts or their functions? Do you neglect or have disrespect, dislike or contempt for your body? Do you put anything into your body that might harm it or do anything that might injure it? Or, on the other hand, are you overly concerned with your body and obsessed with questions of health? Do you concentrate on your outside appearance to the neglect of your inner life?

EVALUATION: Are you alienated from your body? Do you want to be? What changes in attitudes would you need to make to reduce your alienation?

IE-4. EXAMINING YOUR FAMILY RELATIONSHIPS (PP. 52–53)

Gather enough teacups to match the number of members of your family. Place the cups on a table (or floor) and identify each: Mother, Father, Bill, Susan, etc. Consider the handle of the teacup to be the person's nose. Now, arrange the cups so that you have a visual display of how members characteristically relate to each other. For example, if Mother and Father usually have a close and warm relationship, you might place their cups "nose to nose." If Mother loves Susan, but Susan usually doesn't listen to Mother, you could place Mother's cup facing Susan but Susan's cup turned partly away from Mother. If the relationship between two family members is distant and detached, you might place their cups far apart facing away from each other.

EVALUATION: When you have arranged the whole family, examine it in terms of who is close and who is distant. What alliances seem to exist? Are any of the members essentially alone and outside of the family circle of closeness? What are our emotional responses to your arrangement? Are you sad or happy about it? Anxious or comfortable?

FOLLOW-UP: After you have examined and evaluated your family relationships as they are *now*, rearrange the cups to eliminate all alienated relationships. Feel the contrasts between the two kinds of family arrangements. Do you believe that such a change could occur? Ask other family members to show how they would arrange the teacups and compare their experiences with yours.

IE-5. BECOMING MORE INVOLVED WITH YOUR NEIGHBORS AND COMMUNITY (P. 55)

Do you ever take the initiative in making the acquaintance of neighbors who are hard to know? When was the last time you attended a public meeting or accepted a job for the sake of your community?

At the next opportunity, initiate a conversation with a hard-to-know neighbor and see if you can find a point of common interest with him in some matter relating to the community. See if he might be interested in a community project such as forming a community association, if none exists.

EVALUATION: How did your approach feel? Was your neighbor friendly or suspicious? Do you feel closer to him now? Are you satisfied with your relationship to neighbors and the community?

FOLLOW-UP: Work gradually from neighborhood concerns to state, national and world concerns. Bring your family into your activities in these areas.

IE-6. BUILDING CONNECTIONS WITH THE NATURAL WORLD (PP. 56–57)

Go to a place, such as the wooded area of a park or a stretch of isolated beach, where the natural environment is undisturbed. Or lie down under a tree. Or, if necessary, contemplate a potted plant. Put your hand on the bark or leaves and feel their texture. Note the movements and changes in the light; inhale the fragrances. If outdoors, observe the animals, birds and insects; listen to their calls. At a beach, listen to the sounds of the water and wind and watch the endless flickering of light on the waves. Relax and let the natural world speak to you.

EVALUATION: Do you feel a connection with the living things around you? What feelings arise in you in this experience?

FOLLOW-UP: Work with others on projects to preserve and protect the natural environment such as cleaning out a pond, removing litter, persuading industry and government to pursue environmental projects, etc.

IE-7. LIFTING YOUR SPIRIT (PP. 57–58)

Have you ever experienced a lifting of your spirit when peace and calm settled upon you and the ordinary day-to-day burdens and conflicts ceased, for a time, to trouble you? Close your eyes. Relax all the muscles of your body. Try to relive in memory that former experience of a lifting of the spirit. It might help to ask yourself: Will all the worries and pressures that are burdening me now make any great difference a year from now? Ten years from now?

Different people find their way toward a lifting of the spirit through different paths. Find *your* path.

THREE

PULLING TOGETHER
THE PARTS
OF THE PERSON _____

Open Family Living calls for families of whole, not fragmented, people. Such people are connected, not alienated.

Connection Is Our Natural Condition

Human beings are designed and built for connection. Alienation fastens upon them like a disease, for it is a learned distortion.

The infant emerges from the mother, still attached to her body by an umbilical cord. The physical cord is cut; but emotional cords come quickly into being, and the baby is soon as completely dependent on them as he was on the umbilical cord while in the womb.

Many years pass before a human being develops the capacity to live to any degree independently of these emotional ties. And does he ever really cast them off? Only partially. He may reduce the intensity of the emotional bond to his parents or to Aunt Molly who brought him up. He may think of them less often, concern himself less with their opinions or their approval. Yet, they are likely to remain forever in the background of his being, influencing him in countless ways of which he may be unaware. No one can ever fully separate himself from this connection, for to do so would mean casting out a functioning part of himself.

It is almost impossible for an infant to be alienated. By the very urgency of his needs he is connected. He has a pipe line into the emotional center of everyone near him, through which feelings flow as unceasingly as the nutritive fluids had formerly moved through the umbilical cord. But alienations felt by his parents or other family members become part of the emotional mix that he absorbs into himself. He senses the fears, the confusions, the inner divisions, the angers, the pressures, the distractions of his parents; but also he feels their love, their wonder, their excitement, their sense of belonging, their peace and their security. He could not describe or articulate any of these feelings, yet they influence him profoundly. His emotional receiving set is wide open. He can withstand the effects of many disturbing emotions as long as there are also gentle, warming, comforting, growth-fostering ones to offset them. But he is very vulnerable. An emotional atmosphere in which the negative (fear producing) emotions outweigh the positive (reassuring) ones can implant in him the seeds of alien-ation. As he grows, his connectedness can become too painful to bear, and in self-defense he may start slowly to close those inner channels through which the feelings naturally flow. The process is a gradual one, rather analagous to that of malnutrition—its effects are not immediately evident, and it can continue gradually through much of childhood and beyond. ►8

You can watch some of the patterns that produce alienation un-folding in any department store or supermarket. An irritable, dis-tracted mother is trying to keep a two-year-old quiet while she shops. He squawks and she shushes him. He reaches out to grasp nearby objects and she slaps his hand. He screams and she threat-ens a spanking. As the scene plays wearily on, the child becomes more and more demanding and increasingly a nuisance while the mother becomes more and more exasperated. Is this the general pattern of the mother-child relationship, we wonder? Or is it a momentary storm to be followed later by an affectionate hug? We hope it is the latter, for if the child gets nothing but irritability and suppression from the mother, the probabilities are that another divided person will have been created in a world too full of them already. The child may become desensitized to feeling, because the feelings he has experienced have been too painful. And he may begin to close off a whole area of his life: that of the emo-tions.

The mother deserves more sympathy than blame for she herself is, no doubt, a product of this same kind of upbringing, consisting much more of put-downs than of build-ups. A person brought up this way tends to think that this is the "right" way to bring up a child, and the mother may have had no other model than her own parents on which to base her style of parenting. But, unknown to her, she has been partially crippled, and she is likewise partially crippling her child. She needs a different model. No matter how tired she is, how frustrated or how irritable, *she does not have to treat her child in this particular way*. The possibility of change exists. There are alternative modes of child care that will foster the growth of the child, not cripple it.

What a Child Has to Have—And May Not Get

A little child has certain clear basic needs for healthy emotional unfolding, denial of which can lead either to a distorted, troubled personality or to death. They are:

Love	Interaction with other human beings
Attention	Stability
Acceptance	Security

These are *needs,* not just nice things to have. Unfortunately, many parents are not emotionally equipped to meet these needs of their children. Middle-class parents often give children, instead, things like clean rooms, pretty clothes, daily baths, comfortable houses, toys, sweets, birthday parties and entertainment to keep them quiet. Children are tough creatures and may survive all this, just as they survive poverty, dirt, cold, war and deprivation. But the needs I listed above are so basic that if not met to some degree, children may not survive, or if they do, may grow up twisted.

Love is the child's emotional food, fully as necessary for the development of his capacity to feel as is physical food for the development of his body. A child may succeed in growing up without much of it, but if he does he is likely to bear scars of the deprivation, possibly for the remainder of his life. Moreover, a baby must not only be loved but must *feel* that he is loved. The *attention* he gets is the way the fact of the love comes across to him. If attention is not freely given when he has needs or wants, he may feel more abandoned than loved.

Acceptance means not only that the parents love their child but that they accept who and what he is. My definition of love would include acceptance; but not everyone, unfortunately, defines love so inclusively. Many parents would claim that they love their children, yet they do not fully accept them. Some parents wish, for example, that their little girl were a boy, or vice versa. If the child has black hair, they wish it were blond. If he is chubby, they wish he were thin. And so on. Yet if you asked these parents if they loved their child, they would say, "Of course!" And, in a sense, they do. But it is not a love that builds a child's belief in himself. A child is sensitive to acceptance, and if his parents wish he were different from what he is, no matter how they may think they hide the fact, he senses it and gets the feeling that he is not an acceptable person. This can be a lonely and crippling feeling.

Interaction with other human beings is the means by which the child is stimulated to grow intellectually and emotionally. Through it he learns about people and develops a sense of his own identity.

Stability and a feeling of *security* are necessary to build a child's faith in life, in people and in himself. He needs to feel that there are things that stay put and people on whom he can depend. He is not yet ready to be plunged into a condition where everything is in flux. Suppose that the people who attend and feed him were to change each week. How could he build enduring emotional ties with them? If he could not build emotional ties, how could he learn to love? If he has started to form an emotional attachment to one individual and that person is replaced by somebody else, what does the shift do to him? He suffers hurt, and if the event happens too often, he may build a wall of protection by turning away from emotional attachment, which he may find too painful to bear because of the subsequent breaking apart of the tie. He may become physically or emotionally ill. He may grow up to be a person who cannot love. He may also lose faith in the dependability of people and thus become alienated.

Considering these emotional needs of the small child and how often parents fail to meet them fully, it is not difficult to understand how alienation arises and why it is so widespread.

How Growth Occurs Within a Person

Now we have a much clearer idea than any previous generation has had of what happens within a growing child, and of how he becomes the adult that ultimately emerges. Knowing this, we can chart the process with some exactness. When we do we discover astonishing things about ourselves.

A baby, as he begins life, is all baby—and we love him as such. But the typical adult view of a baby is patronizing. It overlooks the enormous potential that the baby has in him. Consider: The little wriggling creature comes into the world with no knowledge (unless we adopt the unconventional view that some knowledge is inherited). Yet in three or four years, starting from *no knowledge,* he goes a long way toward mastering the art of language. An amazing accomplishment!

Few people are in a better position to appreciate the magnitude of this feat than are the computer experts who have been working on the problem of getting a computer to translate from one language to another. The computer, of course, does not start from *no* knowledge; the vocabulary and rules of grammar of the two languages are programmed into its memory unit. All it has to do is identify which phrases in one language correspond to a particular statement in the other and print out what it finds. Theoretically the problem is simple, and not long ago it was believed to be only a question of a few years before machines would take over most translation tasks. As the problem is studied in greater depth, this optimism wanes. Present estimates are that it will be many years, if ever, before reliable and satisfactory machine translation becomes a practical possibility.

The cause of the difficulty seems to be that language is an extension of a living organism. It is not a statistical tabulation and does not resemble one. There are expressions in one language that have no exact equivalent in another. There are layers upon layers of meaning and feeling in every language which a computer, with its rigid "yes" or "no" digital structure, simply cannot handle but which a young child grasps intuitively. With the child, language grows out of feeling and experience. But, since a computer has no feelings, it can only make mechanical substitutions of words or phrases which, as translation, can result in ludicrous nonsense or dangerous misunderstanding. A child has no such limitation.

A baby, in fact, has capacities which science is only just beginning to discern. Even before he can utter an intelligible word, the baby is noting and responding to the flow of nonverbal signals that people constantly exchange with each other. When a small child stares at you, you may get the impression that he is looking right through you into your very being; and in a sense he is, for he may be more sensitive to the flow of emotions within you than you are yourself. A child's stare can be disconcerting. We are not accustomed to being appraised with such penetration and acumen.

The magic charm of the newborn baby is that *he is himself*—completely uncontaminated with adult ways, feelings and thoughts. He remains this way for only a very short time, but while he is in this state he captivates us. Then a process begins. He becomes less and less his pure, original self and more and more an *imitation* of us. His imitations, because they are so direct and so discerning, seem to us like caricatures of some of our worst traits. The small child may see his parents struggling against each other, whereupon he may quickly become adept at playing one against the other. ("But, Dad, *Mom* said I could . . .") He can perfect the temper tantrum as a marvelously efficient device for drawing to himself the attention that he craves. If he wants his parents to stay at home when they have planned to go out, he can whip up a fever or produce an attack of asthma. In no time he can throw a houseful of adults into an uproar.

Where does he learn all these tricks? Why, quite simply, the adults around him teach them to him. By failing to give him the kind of attention and care he needs for normal growth, they may leave him no alternative but to draw attention to himself by any means he can devise; and he is bursting with ingenuity.

An infant or very small child has not yet acquired the characteristics of fragmentation or alienation. He is all together—all one. His behavior follows directly from his feelings. If he is angry with you, he hits or yells at you. If he is pleased, he laughs. If he is happy, he dances and sings. If he is frightened, he cries. There is usually little question of how a small child feels. One look at him tells all.

It is otherwise with an older child or grown person. Something has intervened. Some call the intervening process "socialization," but in certain cases it could more appropriately be called "dehumanization." To get along with the people around him, a child is required to modify the behavior called for by his feelings. He may be angry, but hitting will get him into trouble. He may be happy, but showing it too openly may subject him to derision, which is painful. He may be frightened, but if he cries or runs away he may be called a "sissy" or "chicken." He has to set up an internal part of himself that can step between the emotions and the actions about to ensue and say, "Hey there! Watch it!" Life in a family or a society, of course, requires this. People cannot live together successfully if they have not learned to control their behavior.

But clearly, this process of control, if carried too far, leads to suppression of the emotions. Then we produce alienation. Out of it may come the person whose behavior has ceased to match his feelings, as we discussed in the preceding chapter. *Alienation, then, can be seen as a consequence of a necessary process that has gone too far and got out of hand.*

The Persons Within the Person

Sigmund Freud was one of the first to describe what he called "ego states." Actually, anyone who has grown beyond the infant stage tends to act like a different person under different circumstances. Freud found that in each individual he could distinguish three identifiable states which in some ways resemble three distinctive persons wrapped up in a single personality. In other words, a human being may be looked upon as three persons in one.*

This insight has proven extremely valuable both to psychotherapists working with people's emotional problems and to individuals trying to get a better understanding of themselves. The presently popular school of Transactional Analysis† is based on a modified version of Freud's three states, using the simple terms "Parent," "Child" and "Adult."

There are various ways of describing these three "ego states." But, to begin with, I prefer to call them *dimensions* because the

---

* *An Outline of Psychoanalysis,* tr. James Strachey (New York: W. W. Norton & Company, Inc., 1949).

† Eric Berne, *Transactional Analysis in Psychotherapy: A Systematic Individual and Social Psychiatry* (New York: Grove Press, Inc., 1961).

———, *Principles of Group Treatment* (New York: Grove Press, Inc., 1966) pp. 292–319.

Thomas A. Harris, *I'm OK—You're OK: A Practical Guide to Transactional Analysis* (New York: Harper & Row, Publishers, 1967), pp. 1–36.

word "state" implies a static condition, whereas we are referring to a dynamic process unceasingly operating inside a person. Although the three dimensions I will describe have evolved from Freud's concepts, they are not identical with his or with those of Transactional Analysis.

These dimensions describe *us*—they are how all of us operate (although most of the time we are unaware of it). And if we are to understand ourselves, we need to understand these dimensions. They are:

1. **Internalized Others (IO) Dimension:** the part of the self that is directly derived from parents and other important figures in a person's past.
2. **Childlike (C) Dimensions:** the child that still lives in everyone.
3. **Maturing Self (MS) Dimension:** the part of the self that learns to accomplish, adapt, plan, analyze, deal with situations, control excesses, and do all the many things one needs to do to take charge of one's life.

INTERNALIZED OTHERS (IO) DIMENSION

A baby learns about himself and people from his parents and the others around him, and he internalizes what he learns—he builds it in. He develops in himself an internalized parent, or an internalized Aunt Molly, who tells him what he should and should not do, what he may and may not say or think, how he should feel and react in various situations. If not modified by later experiences, these patterns can continue for a lifetime. The most potent of them, for a majority of us, come from our parents, but siblings, other relatives, stepparents, teachers, clergymen, therapists, friends, bosses, peers, and the people we read about or see on TV also can leave powerful impressions. This internalizing process never stops, although its greatest intensity by far is in the early childhood years. From these internalizations, a person acquires many of his rules, values and guidelines for living. Whenever you catch yourself automatically thinking, speaking, feeling or behaving like someone you have known in your past, you may say to yourself, "That person still lives in me; I built him in."

However, what stamps itself upon a child and produces the Internalized Others (IO) Dimension is not so much what the people around him really say or do as *his perceptions* of what they say and do. He may, and often does, interpret his perceptions inaccurately. A parent, for example, is usually many-sided. The side that the child encounters most often may not be the parent's most attractive or mature side—and frequently is not. If the parent's relations with the child are predominantly ones of irritation, frustration, suppression and punishment, that will probably be the side of the parent that is imprinted most deeply in the child's psyche. If it is not offset by a changed picture later, it could be the dominant parent image that the child will carry with him through much of his life. And it may be the irritable, angry side of the parent which the child will take as a model for his own thoughts, feelings and behavior. Then, when the child grows up and marries, he may be an irritable, angry marital partner and, if he has children, an irritable, angry parent.

But suppose, instead, that the parent radiates qualities of kindness, consideration, dependability and helpfulness. In that case, the child builds his perception of those qualities into his Internalized Others Dimension. He then expresses these qualities easily and naturally.

What frequently happens is that the people surrounding a child, whether parents or teachers or both, do plenty of lecturing, criticizing, making moralistic judgments, reprimanding, suppressing and punishing. If that is the way these people come across to the child and that is the kind of image that is formed in him, the child is influenced in the direction of becoming a punishing person, not necessarily (though probably) of others, but almost certainly of himself. He will surely be critical of himself; he will reprimand himself when he is disappointed in what he has done; he will suppress the qualities in himself of which he does not approve; he will consider himself "bad" if he has violated a parent's or teacher's injunction; he will punish his own transgressions by self-denial, by putting himself down or by becoming accident-prone; and he may, in extreme cases, resort to self-mutilation, physical or spiritual. *What he does to himself he is more than likely, eventually, to do to his children, or as an employer to his employees, or as a teacher to his pupils.*

There is a critical, reprimanding, punishing Internalized Others

(IO) Dimension in nearly all of us, for there are few people who have not experienced this aspect of other people's personalities at one time or another. But there is a kind and loving IO image in most of us, too, for with a few exceptions, we have had people around us who loved us. So, as we grew up we experienced *both* moods in those around us and, therefore, both images are built into us.

Our built-in perceptions of the people with whom we grew up can sometimes take over our entire personality without our being aware of it. Our voice then may take on a didactic tone, we deliver a lecture, we view with disapproval, we criticize, we wag our finger, we point with alarm, we opinionate, we quote an old adage that was the favorite of one of our parents or teachers, we utter phrases like "let me tell you" or "may I remind you that . . ." (This is how some of us lose friends.)

Or, in another situation, someone needs help and we fly to the rescue, we give succor, we comfort, we venture a little sound advice, we speak reassuring words, we put our arms around the sufferer's shoulder. We may again be acting the role of a parent or other influential person—this time, a kindly, loving one.

In either situation, we may be functioning in a manner that differs somewhat from the way we ordinarily function when not under stress. The tones of our voice, our mannerisms and our gestures temporarily reveal a quality which, if we were observed closely, would be seen to be not fully our own but borrowed from our past. Those who knew our family well might recognize some of those past people in us. We are reliving some aspects of the lifestyles of those past people.

It is possible to distinguish four aspects of the IO Dimension in most people:

1. *A loving, comforting, protecting aspect* that probably originated when the mother picked up the crying baby, comforted and fed him. This could have been reinforced later as the parents provided a safe, sheltered, loving environment in which to grow up. In adulthood, this aspect of the IO Dimension may show itself in a desire to help the suffering and comfort the sick. Professionally, it can produce the warmhearted nurse, the life-saving doctor, the dedicated social worker or therapist. But, like

all traits, it is susceptible to lopsided development, as may happen in the person whose "heart is bigger than his head" (as, for example, the parent who does so much for his child that the child stays dependent and becomes selfish).

2. *A guiding, helping, teaching aspect* created in a child as his parents, teachers and others provide day-to-day guidance and instruction. In adulthood, this built-in image is expressed outwardly in teaching, training and supervising and may lead to such professions as that of teacher. If not balanced by other sides of the personality, it can also produce the pedant, the dry and uncreative lecturer, the one who "knows all the answers" but whose answers are mostly a rehashing of ideas acquired long ago.

3. *A judgmental, critical aspect* that originated when concerned people tried to correct the child's mistakes, point out errors, guard against foolish actions and the like. We all need this side to recognize where we are at fault and to learn to improve our performance in anything we do. But, with some, the demands of parents, teachers or older siblings have been perfectionistic; nothing the child could do would ever bring full approval. Later in life, this built-in perfectionist image condemns everything the person attempts as "not good enough" and he is unable to bring his creative talents freely to bear.

4. *A controlling aspect,* brought into being by the fact that parents and teachers have to exert control over small children, set boundaries, prevent excesses, stop destructive behavior and the like. The built-in image that results may be a stern authoritarian figure who puts the same kind of curb on the person's activities as his actual parents or teachers did when he was younger. This is desirable and necessary for us all—because the uncontrolled child within us can endanger ourselves and others and disrupt society. But in many cases the control of children by actual parents, grandparents or teachers has been exercised in a punitive manner, containing elements of anger, irritation, exasperation, cruelty, repression and retaliation. These same traits have been absorbed into the child's personality and are used against himself or against others. Out of this background (when it is excessive) come the persons who are obsessed with suppression of dissent, the diehards, the hard liners of any persuasion,

the advocates of war and violence, the punishing moralists, the vengeance seekers, and those unhappy people who are forever punishing themselves.

In a well-integrated person, all four of these aspects of the Internalized Others Dimension operate, but within the bounds set by other parts of the personality. ►9

CHILDLIKE (C) DIMENSION

The Childlike Dimension is the part of us that never grows old and that was immortalized in Sir James Barrie's play *Peter Pan*. It carries many of the qualities that make us most human—our curiosity, our playfulness, our imagination, our fantasies, our creativity, our energy, our affection. But it also has some characteristics that get us into trouble—our impatience, our desire for immediate satisfaction, our demands for attention, our uncontrolled impulses, our avoidance of responsibility, etc. "Childlike" in no way implies "inferior"; that idea is only a cultural prejudice. On the contrary, many of the childlike qualities are indispensable to wholeness. We carry the Childlike (C) Dimension within us throughout life. Therefore, when you catch yourself automatically thinking, feeling or acting as you might have done as a child, you may say to yourself (with no suggestion of self-criticism) "That's my Child in me."

It is not difficult to identify the childlike part of us when it becomes active. It is this side of us that wants its own way, that gets angry when frustrated, that hungers for attention and affection, that is excited by anticipation and surprise, that loves body movement, that is enthusiastic, spontaneous, impulsive and natural. Our intuitive, inventive and creative aspects belong to the C Dimension. This is the part of us that likes to draw, mold clay, paint with colors, build things, make things, seek adventure, go to new places, wear bright clothes, try new experiences, play-act, sing and dance. It is through the C Dimension that we find joy and enthusiasm, and of course, life without this dimension would be barren, dull and unproductive.

But there is another side of the C Dimension that, in some individuals, cowers in fear, wants to please at all costs, is afraid to try anything new, is afraid to be free and to live fully. In some people the Childlike element is evasive, deceptive and dishonest: Their inner Child is a liar. The openness of the unspoiled child has been converted into something else as a consequence of his reactions to the people around him. This is a distorted personality pattern, sometimes called the *reactive child*. Everyone has something of the reactive child in him because none of us grew up in an environment totally free from repression, punishment, anger or neglect. We all bear scars, and there are probably circumstances under which even the most open and honest of us may evade, deceive, cover up and shrink from revealing our true selves.

The reactive element of the C Dimension can come into being as a result of a child's attempts to preserve his self-esteem from attack. Every child does this in some degree, and among his ruses may be "showing off," bullying people weaker than himself, trying to please people to win their approval, hiding his faults, deceiving himself, resorting to bravado, making himself insensitive to pain, and so on. Such defensive operations may be continued long after the need for them has passed and can become fixed patterns extending into adulthood, affecting such aspects of his life as the ways in which he works, plays, deals with people, treats his family and makes love. They can become an embedded part of his lifestyle.

The continuation of defensive patterns such as these after the original need for them has passed interferes with the growth of the adult personality. A man who bolsters his ego by bullying or overriding weaker personalities is actually preventing himself from developing his own inner strength, much in the same way that prolonged use of crutches can limit the growth of leg muscles.

The Childlike (C) Dimension, then, has at least seven significant sides or aspects:

1. *Physical Aspect*—Love of body activity such as running, jumping, tumbling, dancing, swimming.
2. *Playful Aspect*—Love of games, adventure, fun, excitement, thrills.
3. *Creative-imaginative Aspect*—Love of taking things apart and putting them together, building, painting, modelling, playacting, storytelling, fantasizing.
4. *Affectionate Aspect*—Need for giving and receiving affection.

5. *Open Aspect*—Capacity to observe, feel, absorb, explore and learn.

6. *Impulsive-demanding Aspect*—Uncontrolled propensity to demand what he wants when he wants it.

7. *Reactive Aspect*—The "reactive child," as discussed above.

The first five of these are immensely important to a child's future growth; they seem almost to be innate, and collectively they are sometimes called the "natural child." The sixth (impulsive-demanding), of course, requires modification and redirecting to enable the person to function in society. The seventh (reactive) is of a different order, having been produced by the child's reaction to his environment.

Childlike qualities, even the seemingly natural ones, are not always appreciated in the adult world. Parents and teachers, for example, often attempt to root out all childlike qualities and substitute ones that appear more desirable from the adult's viewpoint, such as obedience, self-control, physical passivity, reliability, good work habits, organized activity, responsibility, knowledge and respect for elders. This sometimes amounts to an attempt to suppress the natural qualities of the child. I am not arguing that the qualities preferred by the adult are not valuable—of course they are—but simply that the natural child qualities also need to be recognized as valuable in *their own right*. Two very different and, in some ways, incompatible sets of qualities are *both* necessary to being a whole person and need to be allowed to exist side by side.

The Internalized Others Dimension and the Childlike Dimension in an individual may come into conflict. Your IO image, for example—if you were raised in a closed family life-style—is very likely to emphasize do's and don'ts, should's and shouldn'ts, rights and wrongs, rules, fixed opinions, critical judgments, and very often, disapproval. There is little room in this kind of climate for the inventive, spontaneous, playful, creative, venturesome, exploring proclivities of the natural child. The built-in IO image may try to hold the natural child in check or perhaps suppress the C Dimension entirely. It is hard for the qualities of the natural child to survive long-continued put downs from the actual parents, from Internalized Others, from the educational establishment and from the community. But by suppressing the natural child, we are likely to produce divided, alienated human beings—because the qualities being suppressed are tied in with many of the original potentials with which a human being is born.

Recovery of wholeness in the modern world is to a very considerable extent, the recovery and freeing of the natural child in us all. And we have to begin by accepting, respecting, admiring and working to liberate some of those very aspects of ourselves that we were once taught to suppress. This is the route to producing that openness within ourselves that can ultimately be expressed in open family living. ►10

MATURING SELF (MS) DIMENSION

Along with the Internalized Others Dimension and the Childlike Dimension is an element of the personality that develops as a result of a child's learning to cope with his environment and with his inner life. Coping requires the ability to gather information, size up situations, become aware of feelings (one's own and others'), work constructively with emotions, modify impulses, formulate purposes and goals, appraise possibilities, identify issues, organize data, acquire insights, negotiate differences, select alternatives, make judgments and decisions, and solve problems and plan future actions. These are mature capacities, and I refer to them collectively as the Maturing Self (MS) Dimension of the personality.

The development of these capacities begins in early childhood. Watch a baby solve a problem. His shoe is just out of reach. He stretches one arm toward it but the arm is not long enough. He rolls or hitches himself a little closer. He still can't reach it. He tries the other arm. His fingers touch the shoe and push it farther away. He concentrates, summons up all his resources, wriggles his body, crooks his finger, and finally draws the shoe to him. He knows his foot ought to be inserted into it, and he awkwardly pushes the shoe against his foot. But putting the shoe on the foot is beyond his skill at the moment. It will not remain so for long. He is learning very rapidly, solving one problem after another and, as he does so, increasing his skills. He is laying the groundwork for the establishment of the MS Dimension in which the processing of information and the solving of problems is an important function.

The MS Dimension plays a part in all three basic areas of functioning: thinking, feeling and behaving. It is through this dimension that thought becomes a tool for opening up new possibilities instead of running in old tracks. Thinking thus goes beyond a mere replay of ideas drawn from one's parents or other past person influences. It is through the MS Dimension that greater awareness arises: Sensations and emotions can be sorted out and evaluated. And this is the first step toward control. When the MS Dimension has been only partially developed, emotions can pull the individual every which way. There may be a torrent of sensations and feelings that can neither be understood nor dealt with—a blurred, buzzing confusion. As the Maturing Self develops, the confusion is reduced; inappropriate or destructive emotional drives are identified, examined, redirected, modified, calmed. The individual is less at the mercy of self-defeating, self-destructive urges, and so he is more nearly free to pursue his long-term interests, desires and goals. When annoyed, for example, he can restrain himself from striking out or from sulky withdrawal. He can work with emotions without either repressing them or being overwhelmed by them.

The Maturing Self side of the personality encompasses not only the maturing of thought but the maturing of the emotions and the modification of behavior. We often forget that it is through the intellect that emotions are *felt* because it is in the intellect that conscious awareness exists. Without awareness, an emotion is something that happens *to* a person as if it came from outside. Thus, anger can overtake the unaware individual. In response he may raise a weapon and strike. He doesn't know why. It just "comes over him." The aware person feels anger as it rises, but also feels many other things: respect for himself, respect (or even compassion) for the person who is annoying him, a sense of the meaning of what is going on within and around him, a sense of the proportion of things so that the annoying incident is seen and felt in the context of all the other elements of life. Without this broader awareness, a person might attack someone in fury as a reaction to a small incident, such as an imagined slight, and land himself in jail. Or he might destroy his marriage or family life by some foolish thing done or said on the spur of the moment. The capacity to exert control in the interest of long-term goals is a mark of maturity.

But the effect of the MS Dimension on emotional life goes far beyond the control of destructive urges. As awareness grows, the emotions themselves become less raw and primitive; they are tempered by feelings drawn from a broader range of the psyche. Thus, a person whose principal entertainment is watching football games may find his emotional range gradually broadening; and eventually he may find even greater pleasure in the more varied moods produced by music, literature, dance or drama. Hostile aggressive urges, such as those expressed, for example, by an act of rape, may be softened by the MS Dimension so that the person ultimately becomes capable of tenderness and love. Thus, the MS Dimension is one that not only leads to a clearer perception of reality but opens pathways to new and deeper experience.

The MS Dimension makes it possible to grasp meaning and to envision, formulate and work toward purposes and goals. The child dreams, imagines and experiments, but the Maturing Self gathers these dreams and visions into a meaningful whole, combines them with knowledge, puts purpose into the experiments and finds ways to achieve distant goals. This is not strictly a computerlike operation, for it draws upon and co-ordinates all facets of the person, unifies them, builds them into the whole. The impetus to end fragmentation and become a better integrated person is set in motion by the MS Dimension.

Much of the MS Dimension is a growth, a blossoming and a maturing of qualities that first emerged in the child. Chart III shows how Maturing Self qualities can grow out of the childlike ones. In this chart, each aspect of the Childlike Dimension is paralleled by an aspect of the Maturing Self.

In addition to the aspects covered in Chart III, the Maturing Self Dimension has a quality that does not seem to emerge from any identifiable childlike aspect but rather is a bringing together of the total self. It is the capacity to modify inappropriate or dangerous impulses (such as the impulse to test the top speed of your car), to redirect destructive urges (such as the urge to hit your spouse), and to work toward overcoming the one-sidedness and fragmentation within yourself. ►11

CHART III   How Aspects of the Maturing Self Dimension
   Evolve from the Childlike Dimension

Qualities of the Childlike Dimension	*Qualities of the Maturing Self that Can Evolve from the Childlike Dimension*
1. *Physical Aspect*—Love of body activity, such as running, jumping, tumbling, dancing, swimming.	Concern with the care and optimum development of the body; training in physical skills such as those of dancing or sports.
2. *Playful Aspect*—Love of games, adventure, fun, excitement, thrills.	Development of an enriching and rewarding emotional life; the joy of being with people; the fun of sports; appreciation of art, drama, literature, etc.
3. *Creative-imaginative Aspect*—Love of taking things apart and putting them together, building, painting, modeling, play-acting, storytelling, fantasizing.	Development of original thought, of invention, of new concepts and ideas, of poetry and drama, of the arts and crafts.
4. *Affectionate Aspect*—Need for giving and receiving affection.	Development of mature love, empathy, understanding and compassion.
5. *Open Aspect*—Capacity to observe, feel, absorb, explore, learn and grow emotionally.	Capacity to size up situations, formulate purposes and goals, make plans, gather information, identify issues, organize, analyze, solve problems, make judgments on the basis of facts and feelings.
6. *Reactive Aspect*—Qualities of the "reactive child," produced by his reactions to surrounding people and conditions.	Ability to live and work with other people, to get their co-operation, to avoid unnecessary trouble, to be well-regarded by others, etc.

Bringing Harmony Between the Three Dimensions

For a person to be whole and fully functioning, the three dimensions (Internalized Others, Childlike, and Maturing Self) must be in some degree of balance and harmony. Achieving this balance is one of the functions of the Maturing Self Dimension; yet, without guidelines, the Maturing Self Dimension can make mistakes. Sometimes it allows one part of the personality to overbalance the others, with unfortunate results.

For example, consider what happens if the Childlike Dimension is allowed to dominate. We might have a lopsided condition like this:

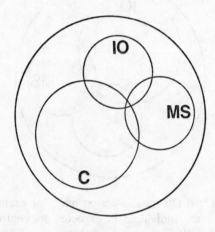

Such a person might do whatever comes into his head at the moment, could not be relied upon by others, would probably not stick to any activity long enough to master it, could become a prisoner of his desires and emotions, might not be able to hold a job, and probably could not achieve anything that required persistent effort and patience. Although much creativity resides in the Childlike Dimension, the production of creative work requires the active co-operation of the Maturing Self Dimension.

Domination by the Childlike Dimension can, under some circumstances, lead to tragedy. Reasoned caution is largely an attribute of the Maturing Self Dimension arising from observation and experience (although the "reactive child" may have learned something of it in an imitative way from other people). The natural child knows little of the kind of caution that is necessary to preserve life in an industrial society. This is why some young people (such as teen-agers whose Maturing Self is not yet completely developed) are insufficiently in control of their impulses when, say, driving a car. They may kill themselves.

Sometimes it is the Internalized Others Dimension that takes over, as illustrated below:

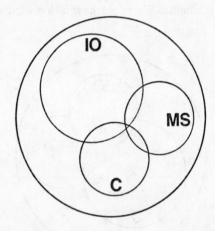

The Internalized Others Dimension may, for example, establish rules to which the individual is expected to conform and may flood him with guilt feelings if he fails to do so. It may even set goals and standards above the person's capacity to meet (at the time) and thus keep him continually feeling incapable, unworthy and miserable. The spontaneity, creativity, originality, playfulness, joy and all the other qualities of the natural child are suppressed.

An example of this might be the perfectionist, mentioned earlier, who devotes his life to trying to do a particular thing in the "right" way according to rules and standards laid down for him by persons from his past. But the perfectionist never satisfies himself, just as, when he was a child, he never satisfied his parents. He has never been freed to evolve his own goals and standards. *He is the captive of a rigid internal system.* An artist caught in this pattern can only produce imitations of other people's works because to ignite the vital spark of original creation, the natural child in him has to be released.

In still other people, the Maturing Self Dimension may take

over in a repressive manner, overwhelming some aspects of the Childlike and Internalized Others Dimensions, as in the following illustration:

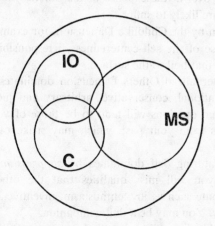

A person too completely dominated by the Maturing Self Dimension may tend to become an observer of life instead of an active participant. Participation requires many of the emotional qualities of the natural child—interest, enthusiasm, eagerness, excitement, desire, drive; also, the energy of the young and the ability to create, to dream and to take risks. With these traits tightly suppressed, life takes on a remote and unreal quality. There are people with brilliant minds who sit on the sidelines, watching, often with amusement, the "antics" and "follies" of the active people around them but who are not moved to do or to risk very much themselves. We see such people occasionally among the overeducated who make a career of attending graduate school, reluctant to take the risks of putting their knowledge to use in the outside world. We see them also among those intellectuals who love to discuss but shrink from coming to conclusions or making decisions.

The way in which these three dimensions relate to each other greatly influences how you, as a person, relate to other human beings. If your inner life possesses a harmoniously balanced relationship between its elements, you will probably have satisfying relationships with people. On the other hand, if any one element tends to take over at the expense of the others, your relationships with people are likely to suffer.

Domination by the Childlike Dimension, for example, can cause upsets because of the self-centeredness, irresponsibility and emotional storms that boil to the surface.

If your Internalized Others Dimension dominates, you may be overly conventional, conservative, arbitrary and judgmental, and your views and opinions will tend to be those of your parents or other persons from your past, which may strike other people as tiresome.

If your Maturing Self dominates by *suppression* of the other dimensions, you will miss qualities that the other dimensions might contribute such as joy, enthusiasm, inventiveness, adventure and creativity. You may be a dull companion.

To bring the dimensions into balance, you need to *recognize* these dimensions in yourself and be aware of when and how they operate. And you need to *accept,* not reject, each of them. These parts of the personality must contribute to and strenghten each other, not be at war with each other. This might be symbolized as follows:

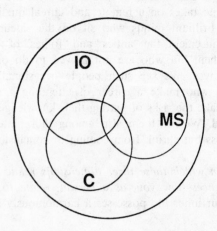

►12

The Head, the Heart and the Limbs

Often in this book I refer to a triad: thoughts, feelings and actions. These are *basic areas of human functioning*. In other words, when something is going on in a human being, it expresses itself in one or more of these three ways—usually (and preferably) in all three.

Symbolically, we can picture the three areas of human functioning in the following way:

FIGURE 2.   Basic Areas of Human Functioning

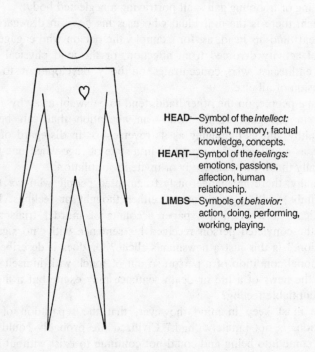

HEAD—Symbol of the *intellect:*
thought, memory, factual
knowledge, concepts.

HEART—Symbol of the *feelings:*
emotions, passions,
affection, human
relationship.

LIMBS—Symbols of *behavior:*
action, doing, performing,
working, playing.

Each of these areas of functioning plays a vital part in every human being; but in unbalanced, fragmented people, as we noted in the case of the dimensions, one of them may tend to be over-developed at the expense of the others. For example, a person may have developed his *head* while neglecting his heart and limbs. He could be highly skillful at solving technical problems (i.e., use his head) yet be unable to get along with his family or co-workers because of clumsiness in dealing with feelings (the heart). When an individual develops such a pattern, his life outside his narrow field of competence tends to become dull and mechanical and he pays the price of emotional starvation and alienation from the people around him.

Or consider the person who pursues an intellectual activity in disregard of the limbs. We see the consequences of this division in the middle-age potbelly, the stooped posture, the flabby arms, the shuffling or hobbling gait—all portraying a neglected body.

Then, there is the individual who uses his *body* in disregard of his heart and his head, as, for example, the person who engages in sexual activity divorced from affection, or the avid physical culture enthusiast who concentrates on body development to the exclusion of all else.

Some people, on the other hand, tend to be swept away by *emotions* in disregard of the head—an alienation that can be as unhealthy and as damaging as its reverse—or in disregard of the body, as may occur, for example, in a state of rage when one may virtually throw away the body or invite its mutilation.

Finally, there are dangerously fragmented people who *act* (use the limbs) with a minimum of either thought or feelings. It is significant how often newspaper accounts of murder trials state that the convicted person received his sentence with "no sign of emotion." Is this just a newsman's cliché? Or does it describe the emotional condition of a person so out of touch with himself that even the news of a life or death sentence may excite but a flicker of identifiable feeling?

We must keep in mind, however, that the separation of the functions is not innately "bad." Civilized life probably could not have come into being and could not continue to exist without it in some form. All accomplishments involving any degree of difficulty require single-minded concentration. Technical work, for example, demands a narrow, intense focus of the mind, shutting out much awareness of either emotions or the body's needs. So do most types of skilled, professional or administrative work. But if the technician who has to exclude emotions from his work situation to get his job done then comes home and excludes emotions from his relationship with his spouse and family, he invites trouble.

Neglect of the head can be equally, or perhaps even more, unhealthy, since a life-style of unrestrained emotionalism is chaotic, and people who release themselves to it can easily become subject to manipulation by the conscious will of others.

Learning to Balance the Different Elements

The inner life, with its Dimensions and its areas of functioning, can be kept in balance only when the person is *aware* of what he is doing at critical moments and why he is doing it. How can you become aware? The problem is essentially one of communication between the elements (the Dimensions) of yourself. The different parts of you have to learn to "talk" and "feel" with each other and negotiate with each other, as we will discuss later.

What either the Childlike or the Internalized Others Dimension tends to do, if you are not vigilantly aware, is to take you over and run your life, just as a recalcitrant child sometimes keeps an adult household in an uproar or a dominating, possessive parent prevents a young person from developing his own potentials. Can you tell whether one element in you is controlling, or whether all the elements are functioning in some degree of harmony? One way to get a handle on this is to watch the outward results of what you say, think, feel and do. Suppose you love your spouse and your children but are constantly running into misunderstandings, angry exchanges and breakdowns in communication. Can you identify which Dimension is controlling you and which is controlling the other family member? Might the problem be rigidity or judgmental pronouncements derived from Internalized Others? Or might it be a demand for instant gratification derived from the Childlike Dimension?

When there is disharmony in marital or family life, the "reactive child" in family members is nearly always involved. Everybody has his own way of defending himself against imagined or actual reprimands, put-downs or rejection by others. Consider the variety and ingenuity of **defense patterns** commonly employed by people—

mostly derived from the way they reacted as children. Here are a few (do they sound familiar?):

> You're a pain in the neck! (Counterattack)
> Oh, dear, I didn't mean it. (Retreat)
> What are you talking about? I never heard of it.
>   (Evasion; covering up)
> It's your (his) fault. (Blame)
> It's entirely my fault. (Self-blame)
> Why should I do it? It's up to him. (Shifting responsibility)
> Nobody can beat me. (Boasting)
> I love your new dress. (Trying to please)
> "Just you wait, Mr. Higgins, just you wait!" (Retaliation)
> Oh, shut up! (Breaking off communication)
> Don't worry, everything will be all right. (Reassurance)
> Oh, that's ridiculous! (Scoffing)

All these, and many more, are ways people defend themselves when they feel attacked. And when any of them becomes an automatic reaction pattern in an adult, it can be a troublemaker. A Maturing Self response to attack is to accept responsibility, to admit fault if the attack is justified, or to respond with something like "I feel attacked—why are you attacking me?" if it is not.

Awareness of the Dimensions operating within you is a vital part of learning who you are. Are you one person or three? Whole or divided? You are clearly a product of your culture and your age (the Internalized Others). But are you *only* this? If you are, how have you been able to deal with change? You are also clearly the child that once was, for the child in you never dies. But are you *only* the child? If you are, does it mean that no psychological growth or inner development has taken place? It is evident that you are much more than any of your Dimensions; you are more than all the Dimensions put together.

Your **feeling of identity** arose from the culture in which you grew up and your interactions with the people around you. What might a person's identity be if he had never interacted with another human being? Imagine a person brought up in a machine age by a machine, totally isolated from other humans. Disregard the fact that a baby would almost surely die under these conditions and assume that this individual somehow survives. What would his mental and emotional state be? He probably would not know that he was a person. Perhaps he would think of himself as another computer. For a person to know who he is, he has to experience himself in relation to other human beings. How those other human beings communicate (or communicated) to him their feelings and conceptions about him is crucial to the development of his identity. A young child, having no independent route to the discovery of who he is, must depend greatly on how his parents and others see him, how they feel about him and experience him, and how they transmit their reactions to him. His mother's frown of disapproval (if he experiences it often) says to him, "You are bad. You are not acceptable. You annoy me." And he, accordingly, says to himself, "I am bad. I am not acceptable. I annoy her." If this is his daily experience and is not offset by other experiences when his mother smiles delightedly at him and lets him know he is loved, he may build his self-concept in terms of "I am no good."

It is impossible to overemphasize what a crippling effect a "no good" self-concept can have on a person. Take Ken, a man of sixty-six who died defeated, heartsick, penniless and alone. His life had completely fallen apart—his money, his health, his job and his family life. To an outsider looking at events, his downfall looked like a blow of some cruel fate. But if you knew how Ken was raised, the sequence of tragic events was not only understandable but almost predictable.

Ken grew up in a family in which the life-style was extremely closed. His mother had rigid ideas about "right" behavior and was consumed by anxiety when her children showed any signs of independence. Her aim was to prevent "wrongdoing" and "wrong thinking." Most parents fail when they try to do this. But she succeeded! Ken was rarely allowed to make any judgments for himself. He grew up convinced that he was incapable of making judgments, and he so structured his life that he rarely had to make any. Thus, he was unfitted for a changing world.

The self-concept, like everything else in the human being, has to be allowed to grow. Otherwise, a person could remain a passive, fearful, insecure child all his life and deny the growing, experimental, daring part of himself. Ken tried to break out of this pattern once. Long ago, when in high school, he became involved in a minor schoolboy escapade—the kind of scrape quickly forgotten in most families. His mother was shocked and let him know how bitterly disappointed she was in him. He resolved never to disappoint her again. And he never did.

The effort to understand who you are, how you got to be you, and what you could become is an appropriate concern of a lifetime. It is often a virtual obsession of the teen-ager who keeps asking himself, "What sort of a person am I? What am I meant to do? What *can* I do?" Much teen-age rebellion is not so much the wish to overthrow parental or other authority as simply an attempt to experience the young person's identity. Even in old age, the question of identity can be of paramount concern. Many people have drawn their sense of identity from their work, and when their work has ended with retirement and their children have grown up, they are again left wondering who they are.

It is a sad mistake for anyone to derive his sense of identity mainly from his work, his class, his position in society or any other situational factor not part of his real self. If I, Tom McGinnis, define *me* as a psychotherapist, what will happen when I retire from clinical practice? Will my identity be wiped out? Or is there a continuing "I" that existed before I became a psychotherapist and will persist after I cease being one? This continuing "I" is a wholeness of which my work is only one aspect, and this wholeness is the "I" which I need to experience if I am not to be at the mercy of external upheavals. Exploration of this "I" means learning not only how I came to be *me* and what I have done with my life, but what I have the potential to do even though I have never done it—what lies untapped in me. And it means approving of what I find. If I hate any part of myself, I will never know my full self, for the same reason that a parent who hates his child never gets to know the child, and the child who hates his parent cannot get to know the parent.

Moving Toward Wholeness and the Open Style

Nearly all of us are fragmented in some way because when we were children we had to defend ourselves against anxiety and all manner of attacks. It is very hard for a child to stay open through all the blows, hurts and disappointments of growing up; he is very vulnerable.

It is possible, however, for a mature adult to open up in a way that he would not have dared to do as a child. He can call on resources that were not available to the child. He can handle the attacks that openness invites and withstand the pain. He need not continue to fall back on the defenses set in motion years before by the reactive child. He does not have to hide, evade, lie, show off, bully, try to please everyone, or desensitize himself to feelings. He can dare to confront, tell the truth, accept responsibility, respect others, do what needs to be done and take the consequences, sharpen his perceptions, let himself feel his emotions. He can continue to grow.

What moving toward wholeness may involve for an individual can be better understood by comparing the fragmented person with the whole person (Chart IV, in this chapter). None of us, obviously, is either totally fragmented or completely whole. We are in between—fragmented in some respects, comparatively whole in others.

The fragmented individual, if he is married and has a family, is likely to be caught in a disturbed and unsatisfying marriage and to have an unhappy family life. The husband and wife cannot communicate effectively with each other or with their children because successful communication requires some degree of wholeness. Everyone in such a family tends to be closed off. The closed family life-style and the directionless style are typical patterns of fragmented people. And the fragmented person, as long as he remains fragmented, is *unable* to develop the open style that might make possible the preservation of family life under modern conditions. To move toward the open style, he is forced to deal first with his own fragmentation.

When he tries to deal with his fragmentation, he may find himself in a kind of no-man's-land. Nobody around him understands what he is trying to do. He is confronted with difficulties thrown in his path by friends, by society (his bosses, co-workers and neighbors, for example), by members of his family, and by parts of himself that do not want to change. If he sets about seeking wholeness, reorienting his life, breaking the rigid patterns that have hemmed him in, thinking anew who he is and where he is going, freeing the parts of himself that have been repressed, learning to become more aware of his feelings and more open in his relationships and communication—he is likely to encounter discouragement and misunderstanding and possibly ridicule and opposition. Family members in closed-style families commonly resist changes in other family members because these disturb existing patterns to which the family has become accustomed. An employee who formerly was a good "organization man" may begin to have problems with his boss and co-workers if he blossoms out too quickly with broadened interests and more open expression of feelings.

On the other hand, the person moving toward wholeness will be freeing himself from much dependence on the approval of others and from the compulsion to be just like everyone else. Liberation was never a simple process for anyone at any time. Yet people can claim freedom for personal growth even in our partly dehumanized world, and it is the initial determination to break the grip of tradition, face up to the Internalized Others and alter long-established habits that is hardest to summon up.

The process requires wisdom. Many individuals who have sought freedom by breaking old chains have only succeeded in forging new ones, sometimes more confining than the old. The resort to drugs can have this effect, freeing one part of a person while enslaving another. Young people who run away from their families to find a "freer" life often find it a disillusioning experience. Escaping from human relationships and obligations by closing yourself off psychologically—that is, by withdrawing into a private world and "doing as you please"—is also costly for it ignores the fact that human relationship is one of the continuing needs of the human being.

Is there such a thing, actually, as freedom?

Yes, I believe there is. Freedom is real, but it is not what most people think it is. It is not the privilege of doing as one pleases. *Freedom is wholeness.* Every form of fragmentation is some form of enslavement. Self-destructive or outwardly destructive behavior —the urge to hurt or injure—is enslaving. Ignorance is enslaving. Rigid, closed opinions are enslaving. Everything that prevents or inhibits the development of one's capacities is a kind of enslavement.

The **whole person** possesses the only kind of freedom that is real: the freedom to grow. His own growth is intimately connected with the growth of those around him. To the extent that he fosters his own growth, he is better enabled to foster the growth of his family members and friends, and vice versa. There is probably no such thing as growing in isolation. But there is such a thing as freeing yourself from the tentacles of others who try to thwart your growth.

A whole person functions fully in every area of human functioning: intellectual, emotional and behavioral. He enjoys the use of his *mind,* looks for challenge, keeps developing and using his mental powers, reaches constantly for new knowledge and deeper understanding, keeps learning more about himself and his world, avoids rigid opinions and prejudices, keeps his mind open and flexible. He also experiences a rich and varied *emotional* life, is aware of his emotions, lets himself feel them, understands and accepts his emotional nature, respects his feelings, enjoys and cultivates them, turns them to creative use, disciplines them when necessary, directs them into constructive channels, uses them as motive power. His *behavior* is a genuine reflection of his thoughts and feelings, takes into account their effect on himself and on other people, is generally constructive and creative.

The whole person has achieved a balance of the three intrapersonal dimensions of his personality—and quite an achievement this is! He avoids the lopsidedness and lack of control that characterize domination by any one dimension.

The whole person is skillful at communicating, both within himself—a process we shall examine more closely in the chapter on communication—and with others. He learns to get his ideas and feelings across to the people around him, and his receiving set is wide open to them. He listens, he feels, he empathizes, he understands. He negotiates with himself and with others. He does not override the feelings of other people; rather, he takes them into account.

The whole person continues to develop his capacities throughout a lifetime. He never sits back and thinks, "I'm big enough. I'll stop growing about here." Yet his urge to develop and grow does not arise from self-disparagement. He accepts himself and fully respects himself. His motivation is simply that growing and developing new skills and talents is a rewarding process in it-

self. He would respect himself much less if he sat back and
watched TV the rest of his life.

The whole person is deeply involved in life, takes responsibilities seriously, is free from ego-centeredness, trusts people
generally, is non-punitive, expresses affection freely, is capable of
love, joy and sorrow, is not afraid to laugh at himself or at fate.

The entire idea of wholeness is neatly summed up in an incident
in the movie version of *Godspell* where a car driver caught in an
incredible traffic jam, surrounded by yelling, cursing drivers, pulls
a recorder out of his pocket and plays on it while waiting for the
tie-up to clear.

I sketch this outline of what it means to be whole, not to make
fragmented people feel inadequate, but to set up a model. We
need a model upon which to shape our emerging and growing
selves. A person evolves toward the model he envisions. Close
your eyes and think what it means to be whole and to live in a
family of whole persons. Live with this model. Think about it often
enough, try to live it, and it can begin to come into being.

Using Chart IV on the next page, check yourself out: how whole
or how fragmented are you? ►**13**

CHART IV   Fragmented vs. Whole Persons and Their Life-styles

Area of Functioning	*Fragmented Person: Closed or Directionless Style*	*Whole (Integrated) Person: Open Style*
1. Feeling of identity	Little understanding of who he is, how he became who he is, or what he may become.	Knows, accepts, and appreciates who he is, how he became who he is, and what he can become.
2. Self-esteem	Low, undermining, self-condemning. Or an inflated, exaggerated opinion of self. Often underlying feelings of inadequacy, failure, or guilt.	High self-esteem and self-acceptance, permitting realistic appraisal of strengths and limitations. Can be himself without cover-up.
3. Self-awareness	Limited awareness of what is going on inside him.	In close touch with his inner thoughts and feelings. Understands and takes responsibility for them.

CHART IV (*continued*)

Area of Functioning	Fragmented Person: Closed or Directionless Style	Whole (Integrated) Person: Open Style
4. Sensitivity	Insensitive to others' needs and feelings. Or too upset to deal with them.	Sensitive, concerned and involved, but able to maintain objectivity.
5. Inner conflicts	Frequent and unresolved; producing anxiety, depression, fear, anger, etc.	Resolved by inner negotiation between conflicting elements.
6. Emotional patterns	Suppressed: emotional deadness, boredom. Or wild, destructive outbursts.	Rich, exciting, lively, rewarding, under control. A source of strength.
7. Thought patterns	Fixed, strongly opinionated, resistant to change. Unreceptive to new ideas.	Open-minded, mentally flexible. Broad interests. Respects differences of view.
8. Behavior patterns	Automatic, routinized, ritualistic, repetitious. Or unpredictable, unbridled and wild.	Aimed at enhancing human relationships and fostering personal growth.
9. Interpersonal relationships	Superficial; oriented around roles, sex, status, jobs, etc. Often contentious, judgmental, exploitive, blaming, punitive, or self-centered, indifferent.	Warm, interested, affectionate, caring. Capable of intimacy, closeness, love.
10. Communication patterns	Poor communicator, insensitive listener. Distorts, misunderstands, and feels misunderstood.	Clear, direct, and skillful communicator. Sensitive listener. Also, helps others to communicate more effectively.
11. Creativity	Largely stifled, or narrowly restricted.	Fostered, developed and applied in many activities.
12. Sexual functioning	Often isolated from love and affection. Compulsive. Often dysfunctional.	Natural, comfortable, enjoyed. Associated with love and affection.
13. Addictions	Tendency to addictive habits (i.e., smoking, drinking, drugs, gambling, etc.)	Free from addictions. Can use certain substances but in moderation.

CHART IV (*continued*)

Area of Functioning	Fragmented Person: Closed or Directionless Style	Whole (Integrated) Person: Open Style
14. Attitudes toward—		
a. The body	Indifferent to and neglectful of the body. Or overly concerned with it.	Body felt as human aspect of the person. Appreciated, cared for, enjoyed.
b. Masculine/ Feminine roles	Rigid, stereotyped, fixed.	Flexible and alterable as circumstances warrant.
c. Freedom	Depends on rules, penalties, structure. Or ignores rules, runs wild.	Welcomes freedom for personal growth. Governs himself.
d. Community	Minimal or exploitive interest. Or tends to extremist positions.	Concerned; feels part of community. Avoids extremist positions.
e. Authority	Blindly obedient, or angrily rebellious. Tends to abuse authority.	Respects legitimate authority, but neither accepts abuse nor abuses others.
f. Newness, change	Fears change, clings to the familiar. Or is unstable.	Welcomes new experiences that enhance personal growth.
g. Personal values	Values externals (i.e., success, status, appearance, etc.) Or makes fetish of rejecting them.	Values most the quality of his relationships with people and the goal of personal growth.

Suggested Interaction Experiences

IE-8. FEELING CONNECTION WITH THE STREAM OF LIFE
(P. 66)

Go alone to a quiet place, relax and close your eyes.

Fantasize the scene of your own conception. Visualize where you are being conceived. Is the process planned or accidental? What is the mood of your parents during this particular time of intercourse? How are they reacting toward each other knowing that they have just started your life?

Then fantasize the conception itself. Visualize the union of the sperm and ovum, the trip through the fallopian tubes, the growth on the uterine wall and the preparation for birth.

Now imagine being born. Visualize the scene of the birth process. Who is present? Is it a difficult delivery? Do you feel the physical separation from your mother with the severing of the placenta? Is the emotional atmosphere filled with a sense of joy, gentleness and warmth? Or is it anxious? Or rejecting? Do you feel vulnerable or secure?

EVALUATION: How did you react to this idea of a guided fantasy trip? Were you able to follow through all three stages of experience? Did you tend to intellectualize the trip or was it filled with exciting moments of feeling? Did this experience give you a stronger sense of connection with yourself and your family?

FOLLOW-UP: If your parents are available (or any other knowledgeable person) ask them to give you some of the actual circumstances of your birth. How do their descriptions compare with your fantasy trip?

IE-9. BECOMING AWARE OF YOUR INTERNALIZED OTHERS DIMENSION (PP. 72–73)

Recall the people you have known who had a strong influence on you and evaluate which of the four aspects of the IO Dimension they principally represent in your life. The following is an example of how you might do this, using pencil and paper:

Aspects of Internalized Others Dimension	Persons that Still Live In You
1. Loving, comforting, protecting aspect	Mother, childhood friend, first steady girl, wife
2. Guiding, helping, teaching aspect	Sister, father, teacher-sixth grade.
3. Judgmental, critical aspect	Brother, clergyman
4. Controlling aspect	High school coach

EVALUATION: Do you feel the influence of these people still? Can you sense how they affect the ways in which you think, feel and act? Which influences would you like to retain and which would you like to get rid of?

FOLLOW-UP: If the person closest to you were to evaluate your influence on him (her), which of the above aspects do you think your name would be identified with? Likewise, share with this person the influence he/she has had on you.

IE-10. Becoming Aware of Your Childlike Dimension
(p. 76)

Close your eyes and imagine you are in your favorite childhood place. Try to recall the feelings you had there as a child. How were you in terms of the seven aspects listed on pages 77–78: physical, playful, creative-imaginative, affectionate, open, impulsive-demanding and reactive? Are all these aspects alive in you still?

EVALUATION: Does this experience help sharpen your appreciation of the Childlike Dimension in you? Which of the seven aspects is most dominant in your personality today? Do you enjoy the child in you? How does it enrich your life? How does it get you into difficulty? Is there any part of your Childlike Dimension that you might wish to expand? Or to reduce?

IE-11. Becoming Aware of Your Maturing Self
Dimension (p. 81)

Refer to the qualities of the Maturing Self that can evolve out of the Childlike Dimension, as summarized in Chart III, page 82. Evaluate which of these qualities you feel to be strong in yourself and which may need further strengthening.

FOLLOW-UP: The next time you encounter a significant problem, try to be more aware of how you use all three dimensions. Pay particular attention to the way your Maturing Adult operates to balance the influence of the other two dimensions.

IE-12. Appraising Your Balance of Interpersonal
Dimensions (pp. 85–86)

Think about how you generally function in day-to-day life. Does any one of the dimensions tend to overbalance the others? Under what circumstances? May one dimension overbalance at certain times and another dimension at other times? Does this overbalancing cause you trouble? Draw circles like those on pages 83–86 to illustrate your usual way of functioning.

FOLLOW-UP: Ask a relative or friend to evaluate your balance of the Dimensions as he sees it. How does his evaluation compare with yours?

IE-13. Appraising the Extent to Which You Are
a Fragmented or Whole Person (pp. 92–93)

Using Chart IV (pp. 96–98), appraise where you are as between fragmented and whole in each area of functioning.

EVALUATION: Do the results suggest that you are basically whole, fragmented or somewhere in between? Do these results generally agree or disagree with the way you see and feel about yourself? Which conditions would you want to change to help you move more in the direction of wholeness?

FOLLOW-UP: Select a family member or friend whom you know well. Using the same procedure, evaluate where he is between fragmentation and wholeness. Would you consider sharing your results with him?

FOUR

WHAT KIND OF MARRIAGE? OPEN OR CLOSED?

Although in this chapter I use the term "marriage," I am really talking about any intimate one-to-one relationship of two people living together and committed to each other, whether of opposite or of the same sex and whether legally married or not.

Of all the marriages or other committed relationships you have known or seen, how many would you select as models for your own? If you have known just one in which the partners were good *for* (as well as *to*) each other, encouraged and supported each other and helped each other to grow as persons, then you have evidence that such a relationship can exist. This is important, for many people do not know this, having never experienced or seen a relationship of this quality.

The route to this growth-enhancing marriage is through the developing "wholeness" of the individual partners.

The Quality of Marriage

It is widely assumed that a marriage that holds together is "successful" ("They stayed together, didn't they?") whereas one that breaks up is a "failure" ("They couldn't make it."). But these attitudes are a remnant of a viewpoint toward marriage that regarded its continuation as a moral imperative and its dissolution a disaster. That view paid little attention to the *quality* of the marital relationship and its effect on the well-being of the partners and the family.

Some more significant questions which might be asked about a marriage, or about any form of human association, are these: *Is it good for both partners? Does it strengthen their relationship?*

Does it nurture their children? Does it benefit society at large? If the answers to these questions are "no," termination of the marriage might be preferable to its continuance. We need ways of evaluating these questions that have more validity than sudden disruptions of a relationship brought about in moments of outrage, discouragement or frustration.

A marriage that is good for everybody concerned could be called an **Open Marriage.** I would describe it as one in which the interaction between the partners *expands* their freedom to be themselves, *enhances* the personal growth of each and *encourages* maximum development of a healthy marital relationship. An example of an open marriage might be one in which one partner, at considerable cost to himself, encourages the other to go back to school, perhaps to develop a latent talent or to prepare for a new career; and the partner so helped later provides a similar opportunity for the first partner. In an open marriage the partners help and encourage each other both in small and big ways.

A marriage that has held together for a long time may not necessarily foster personal growth. Many long-term marriages, in fact, do not. There is a curious popular idealization (by the older folks, not by the young) of the "mature" marriage that has "settled down." Mom and Pop have learned to endure each other all these years and are about to celebrate their twentieth while everybody sips cocktails and jokes, "If you could stand him for twenty years, you deserve a drink!" But this may celebrate not an open marriage in which the art of human relationship has been perfected, but, very often, a closed one where the partners *have locked themselves in and feel unable to escape from each other.*

A **Closed Marriage** is one in which the interaction between the partners *limits* their freedom, *thwarts* their personal growth and *interferes* with the development of a healthy marital relationship. Examples of such closedness are so common that we pay little attention to them although everywhere they stare us in the face. The partners in this kind of marriage follow, in general, a pattern of ignoring each other's wishes, undermining each other's self-esteem, opposing or ridiculing each other's plans and dreams, and interfering with each other's freedom to be himself. For example, one partner in such a marriage may have an undeveloped talent, such as playing the violin, to which the other partner is indifferent or scornful. Or one partner may enjoy friends whom his spouse dislikes and resents. Or one partner's success in some activity may arouse jealousy and hostile reactions in the other.

Closed marriages are not always easily recognized. Some marriages that appear open are, in fact, closed. In these marriages, the partners have adjusted to a condition of limited self-development. They have, in some important respects, given up the struggle to free themselves for growth. As an example, I knew a couple where the husband enjoyed composing music and had considerable talent at this, although his work had nothing to do with music. But during more than forty years of marriage his wife never "let" him work out his compositions on the piano. The noise gave her a headache; she didn't like having him away from her when he was at home; she always had other things for him (or them both) to do, etc. He never felt free to compose music until after her death, by which time he was an old man.

Evaluating the Quality of Your Marriage

It is useful to have a yardstick for appraising the quality of a marriage. Figure 3 and Chart V define eight "marital states" in terms of their quality, ranging from "extremely closed" (least qualitative) to "open" (most qualitative). Nearly all marriages that have been in existence for any appreciable time (say, a year or more) have evolved identifiable and quite consistent patterns of interaction between the partners. I call these consistent patterns "marital states," not because they are static—those high on the scale are, in fact, very dynamic—but because at any particular time they can be identified and described.

On the basis of these patterns, it is possible to judge where any particular marriage fits on the qualitative scale. However, the perception of this "fit" by one partner may differ from the perception of it by the other—a fact that may throw valuable light on the true nature of their relationship.

There is a tendency for the interactive patterns in a marriage to become rigid as time goes on unless some growth is occurring in one or both of the partners. This hardening of the marital arteries may continue until the partners find themselves virtually locked into their patterns. And the rigidification itself tends to move the marriage lower on the qualitative scale because rigidity is a characteristic of the closed style.

FIGURE 3. The Range of Marital States

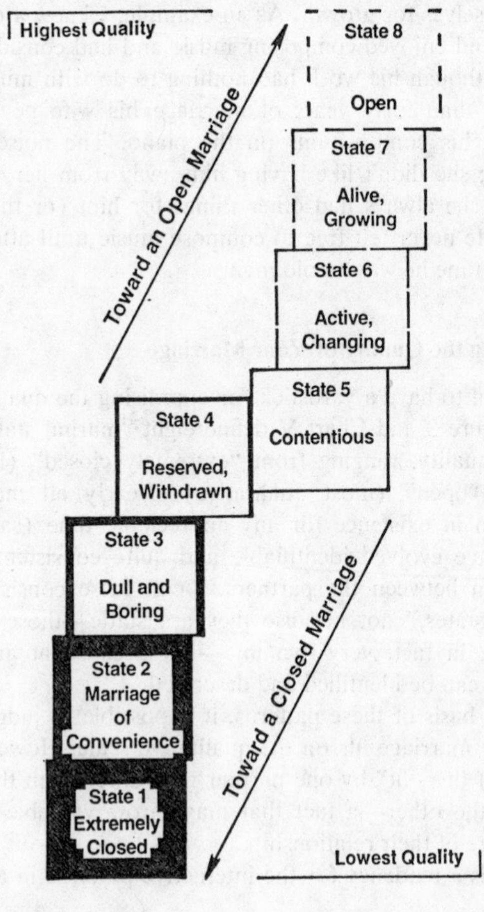

Highest Quality

Toward an Open Marriage

State 8 — Open
State 7 — Alive, Growing
State 6 — Active, Changing
State 5 — Contentious
State 4 — Reserved, Withdrawn
State 3 — Dull and Boring
State 2 — Marriage of Convenience
State 1 — Extremely Closed

Toward a Closed Marriage

Lowest Quality

Figure 3 shows the range of the eight states and the directions in which they often tend to move. Chart V then defines and describes each of these states.

Where does your marriage fit, as you perceive it? How does your partner perceive the marriage? How do your children perceive the marriage? How do these perceptions compare? How clearly have they been communicated between you and your partner and among all family members?

CLOSED OR PARTLY CLOSED MARITAL STATES (NUMBERS 1–4)

State 1, **Extremely Closed,** is at the bottom of the qualitative scale. A majority of closed marriages in real life are probably not quite so dreary as this, though some come close. This is the "dead marriage" that, although it may not necessarily break up, is held together solely by inertia and by the fact that the partners are locked in; they may feel that they have nowhere else to go.

State 2, **Marriage of Convenience,** describes a marriage that, except for its convenience, is nearly as unrewarding as the "extremely closed" marriage. Not all marriages of convenience offer as little as this, but where the relationship between the partners has meaning of its own apart from the convenience element, the marriage would not be classified as a "marriage of convenience" but rather as a marriage fitting higher in the qualitative scale.

State 3, **Dull and Boring,** is common among people in their middle years. It may be an outcome simply of lack of attention to the marriage. Patterns of interaction have hardened to the point that little new or creative is going on between the partners. Yet, unlike the two preceding, it is not totally without a positive emotional component. There are occasional moments when feelings shine through, but these moments leave no lasting impression; the marriage lapses again into dullness.

State 4, **Reserved and Withdrawn,** refers to a common condition where one partner (and sometimes each partner) remains mostly withdrawn, shares little of himself with his spouse, hides his thoughts and feelings, lives by a pattern of formalities and external politeness, and contributes rather little to the emotional side of the marital relationship. Yet caring and feelings are there

CHART V   Marital States Ranging from Extremely Closed to Open

Marital State	Relationship with Partner	How Conflicts Are Worked with
1. **Extremely Closed:** Empty, mechanical. No stimulus to grow. Partners not interested in working on marriage. Condition stagnant. May be referred to as a "dead marriage."	Little display of positive feelings. Frequent criticisms and put-downs. Rarely listen constructively to each other or talk comfortably about anything personal. Sexual relationship very unsatisfactory or absent altogether.	Unhappily. Same old battles over and over. Old gripes dragged up from past. Inability to negotiate. Underlying feelings scarcely identified.
2. **Marriage of Convenience:** Similar to above, except that marriage is convenient because of children, security it provides, or some other reason.	Much the same as above, except that partners manage to work out some practical matters for convenience. Otherwise, either ignore each other or are locked together in mutual bondage.	Same as above, except for compromise agreements on a few practical matters. Underlying feelings occasionally identified but rarely worked with.
3. **Dull, Boring:** Relationship uneventful, unfeeling. Little stimulation of interest or ideas. Occasional spark of life, but this is not sustained.	Often similar to the preceding. But occasionally there is a breakthrough, which suggests possibility of a better relationship. Effects are temporary. Sexual relationship routine.	Often similar to the above, though occasionally a conflict is worked through satisfactorily. Underlying feelings sometimes identified but not taken seriously.
4. **Reserved, Withdrawn:** Superficially polite, distant, cool, rather formal. Feelings are hidden. No real intimacy. Yet some caring underneath.	One or both partners very withdrawn; share little of self or of emotions. Little conversation except on superficial matters. But occasionally some feelings come out. Some basic caring. Sexual relationship is rather passive, not talked about.	Much the same as preceding. Difficulty in getting at the feelings underlying conflicts, but conflicts themselves are occasionally worked through.

CHART V (*continued*)

Marital State	Relationship with Partner	How Conflicts Are Worked with
5. Contentious: Frequent arguments, quarrels, attempts to get the better of one another. Yet also some caring and affection.	Attempts to talk or settle anything usually end up in a fight. But partners don't ignore each other. Sexual relationship often involves aggressive talk and behavior.	Sometimes win, sometimes lose. Same battles fought over and over, followed by peace overtures and "new starts." Underlying feelings seldom worked through.
6. Active, Changing: Changes taking place in partners' attitudes, feelings, values and life-styles. Often tension, but also stimulus to personal growth.	Varied. Roles and expectations changing. Mood sometimes tense and angry, sometimes close and affectionate. Honest feelings fairly openly expressed. Fair communication. Sexual relationship is active, but satisfaction varies.	Varied outcomes, not always happy. Frequent attempts made to deal with underlying feelings. Many conflicts are worked through satisfactorily.
7. Alive, Growing: Moving toward openness. More personal and marital growth than in the above. More trust and stability, clearer goals.	Wider range of emotional responses than in the preceding. More love, affection, joy and closeness in the relationship. More freedom and stability; better communication. Sexual relationship is active and fulfilling.	Usually can negotiate conflicts so that outcome is acceptable to both. Considerable skill in listening, identifying underlying feelings, working through differences.
8. Open: See section in this chapter on "The Open Style." Fosters maximum personal growth of partners and their relationship.	A relationship involving a wide range of human emotions, openly expressed and constructively worked through. Much love, affection, empathy, joy and closeness in relationship. Sexual relationship excellent.	Same as above, but skills are greater, underlying feelings are more clearly identified, and energies released by conflict are more effectively redirected to personal and marital growth.

in some degree, sensed in the background. (Otherwise the marriage would belong in state 1 or 2.)

These are four very unrewarding marital states that, left to themselves, tend to slide downhill. This is indicated by the down-pointed "Toward a Closed Marriage" arrow on Figure 3. Because the "Reserved and Withdrawn" state fails to nourish the emotional life of the couple, it can easily slip down into "Dull and Boring." That state, in turn, can lose the slight emotional content it does possess and slip into the "Marriage of Convenience." And the "Marriage of Convenience," because it does so little to build any sort of satisfying relationship between the partners, can lose even its convenience element and end up "Extremely Closed," where there is little qualitative element left. (A marriage could, of course, break up at any stage along this continuum; or it could hold together indefinitely.)

PARTLY OPEN MARITAL STATES (NUMBERS 5–8)

State 5, **Contentious,** is open, but slightly. The partners fight often and scarcely know why. They experience wide swings from hostility to affection. The fights rarely settle anything for long because the partners lack the insight to identify the deeper emotions underlying their interaction. Nor is their "Maturing Self Dimension" sufficiently developed to work through these emotions in a constructive way. Their fighting is principally a power struggle—an attempt by each to preserve his integrity from attack by the other. The only open element is the fact that the partners do not withdraw as in State 4, but stay right up front with each other where there is a chance of working something out.

State 6, **Active, Changing,** is a marriage in flux. The partners are developing, growing in some degree, trying out new attitudes, feelings, values and life-styles. But they may lack a clear sense of where the marriage is going. One or both partners may decide that the marriage is a hindrance to personal growth and seek to end it. Or they may gain insights as to how the marriage relationship could be made more rewarding, and choose to move in that direction. The "Active, Changing" state is inherently unstable, but it is not, like the first four states, a growth-inhibiting one. It is likely to produce a permanent change of some sort; either a breakup or a much improved relationship.

State 7, **Alive, Growing,** is an active, changing state that has taken on direction and is moving toward openness. The partners are working not only on themselves, but on the quality of their marital relationship. Though there may be much conflict between them at times, they have gained substantial insight into their feelings and into what is going on within and between them. With this knowledge, they can deal not only with the specific matters that precipitate the quarrels (i.e., money, in-laws, sexual difficulties, or whatever), but also with the internal problems (feelings of inadequacy, fear of failure, exaggerated dependency needs, severe compulsions, etc.) that are much less obvious but are vitally important to the relationship. Thus, the outcome of their fights is likely to be more satisfying to both than is true in the preceding states. The Maturing Self Dimension of the partners is strong and growing.

THE OPEN STYLE

State 8, **Open,** is the marital equivalent of the open family life-style which is the main subject matter of this book. It has these characteristics:

1. The partners have a high degree of wholeness as people. Their Dimensions (Internalized Others, Childlike and Maturing Self) are in a healthy working balance; so are their emotional, intellectual and behavioral functions.
2. They are changing and growing, realizing more and more of their individual human potentials.
3. They respect their own and each other's uniqueness; they do not try to remake each other or force one another into prescribed slots. Each gives the other freedom to be himself.
4. They like and love each other (even when they argue) and they like and love themselves.
5. They encourage each other's growth as well as the growth of the marriage.
6. They regard and treat each other with equality.
7. They trust each other and care about each other.

8. They welcome change and are stimulated by new ideas, experiences and feelings. Their relationship is not necessarily peaceful, but it is invigorating.

9. They have enough self-awareness to know (most of the time) what is going on inside themselves and between each other.

10. They are open in the expression of their emotions, wishes, preferences and expectations, so that each generally knows where the other stands.

11. They communicate well at all levels—intellectual, emotional and behavioral (including non-verbal). They listen to each other, give and receive clear and meaningful information and feelings.

12. They are skilled at negotiating differences and working through conflicts.

13. Their marital roles are flexible and negotiable according to the needs of the moment; there are no fixed "man's roles" and "woman's roles." (Internalized Others do not dominate.)

14. They are generally warm, affectionate, loving and appropriately supportive toward each other.

These are the characteristics of a high qualitative level of intimate personal relationship of any two people, whether married or not.

Listed in this way, it might appear that the open style calls for a number of unusual, rather idealistic qualities which few people could be expected to have. Yet there is nothing in this list that is beyond the capabilities of most healthy couples, except that a decision to move in this direction is exceptional, and the couple that makes such a decision becomes, by this very act, an unusual couple.

The qualities in this list combine to make a whole; that is, they all fit together. If you possess one to a significant degree, you probably possess a number of others. Individual wholeness and balance go with personal growth, which in turn goes with respect for each other's individuality and humanity, which inspires trust, which leads to warm human relationship, and so on. *Openness is a total orientation involving the entire personality,* not a boxful of separate, restrictive requirements. If it were the latter, we would be describing not openness but closedness, which is restrictive by definition.

Open people, because they respect individuality, are likely to be strikingly different from each other. They do not demand that all people be alike or fit into precise categories (i.e., good, bad, wise, stupid, etc.). For this very reason, conflicts in an open-style marriage are likely to be less damaging to the relationship than are those in a closed-style marriage. You can probably stand living with someone very different from yourself if each of you gives the other freedom to be himself and does not try forcing the other to meet some kind of "standard" or expectation. If you are neat and he is sloppy, there are certain problems of accommodation; but these can be overcome when the relationship at a *human* level is warm and responsive.

Chart VI, which follows, points up some important contrasts between the closed and open marital styles. You will recognize that many of the differences between the styles are similar to those covered in the charts referring to family and individual life-styles.

Which Way? Up or Down?

A marriage in any of the states, if left to vegetate, will tend to deteriorate. As Alice discovered in the looking-glass world, you sometimes have to run as fast as possible to stay in one place. The difference between the first four states described in Chart V and the last four is that forces come into play in the more open states that, if we allow them to operate and work with them, may increase the degree of openness. Then, instead of sliding downhill, the marital relationship may move up to a higher qualitative level. The force that can bring this about is the discovery by the partners of the rewards and satisfactions of greater openness. Figure 4 illustrates this.

State 5, "Contentious," is precariously balanced; it can go either way—to separation and divorce or to a more open state. State 6, "Active, Changing," also could go either way, but has a better chance of moving upward. State 7, "Alive and Growing," is al-

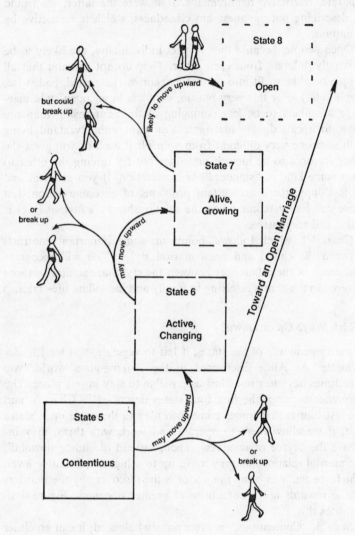

FIGURE 4. The Partly Open and Open
Marital States (Numbers 5-8)

CHART VI   **Marital Life-styles: Closed vs. Open**

Areas of Functioning	Closed Style	Open Style
1. Basic patterns of marital interaction	Rigid patterns centered around roles, duties, rights, oughts and ought-nots, penalties, status, appearances, etc. (i.e., around the *mechanics* of the relationship). Partners may be locked together in a tight twosome, or fighting and undermining each other, or too busy to pay attention to each other.	Flexible patterns fostering personal growth and the *quality* of the marital relationship. They are nurturing and freedom-granting. Partners enjoy and feel close to each other without putting "hooks" on each other.
2. Marital communication patterns	Tend often to be blocked or distorted by withdrawal, overbusyness, indifference, diversions, meaningless chatter, judgmental remarks, argument, blame, suppression, etc. Feelings poorly communicated, rarely listened to.	Open, clear, effective, meaningful. Partners share freely their thoughts, feelings, wishes, dreams, expectations, hopes, victories and disappointments. Listen to each other and check each other out.
3. Marital roles	Roles tend to dominate the relationship as if fulfilling roles were the main purpose of marriage. Rigidity of roles either stifles growth or results in endless friction and dispute.	Roles are subordinate to the human and nurturing goals of the marriage. They are flexible and negotiable to meet preferences, abilities and changing needs and circumstances.
4. Conflicts and decision-making in marriage	Tendency to competitiveness, jealousy, rivalry, blame. Conflicts simmer or flare without resolution. Decisions imposed by one partner, or avoided until forced by a crisis, or reached by unsatisfactory compromise.	Conflicts kept nondestructive by partners' sensitivity and mutual respect. Decisions reached by negotiation, taking needs and feelings of both partners into account.

CHART VI   *(continued)*

Areas of Functioning	*Closed Style*	*Open Style*
5. Expressing affection or love in marriage	Tendency to take partner for granted, not express affection or love (except very infrequently). Love may take distorted forms: be possessive, restrictive of freedom, conditional on behavior, perhaps poisoned by distrust.	Free, unrestrained expression of warmth, affection and love by both partners. Love is accepting and trusting, non-possessive, not restrictive, not conditional on behavior.
6. Sexual functioning in marriage	Routine, sporadic, or no sex at all. Often separated from love and affection. May be dysfunctional (i.e., impotence). Often used coercively (i.e., imposed by one partner as a "right," or withheld by one to force a behavior change).	Natural, spontaneous, mutually enjoyed. Associated with feelings of affection, love, comfort, reassurance, happiness, celebration of an event, etc. Not used coercively.
7. Reaction of partners to outside relationships	Unless shared by both partners, they violate the closed system and pressure is brought to end them.	Freedom to cultivate outside friendships; but care is taken not to hurt a spouse. Partners are responsible, sensitive and trusting.

ready moving toward openness and is very likely to achieve it in some degree. Whether this happens in the context of the particular marriage or requires a change of marital partners depends on many factors, such as whether the partners are growing together or apart, whether they feel they are good for each other, and whether both equally desire to nourish the relationship.

By and large, I believe that as a marriage moves toward openness, the strains that formerly threatened it become much more manageable because they have been brought out into the open where there is a better chance of dealing constructively with them. Therefore, the nearer we come to openness (provided the movement is shared by both partners), the better opportunity the marriage has to become meaningful and secure. ►14

The Traditional-style Complementary Marriage

The marital states we have been looking at do not come into being by accident. For any marriage, the quality is what it is because the partners are the people they are.

Many marriages are actually held together by the complementary one-sidedness of the partners. Thus, an aggressive or strong-minded spouse may be matched with a passive one, an intellectual spouse with a feeling one, an outgoing spouse with an inward-turning one, and so on. Each partner in these marriages is one-sided and therefore, to some extent, fragmented; but the combination of the two may make a rough approximation of wholeness.

Take, for example, the aggressive, decisive, strong-minded spouse matched with a passive, yielding one. Each probably selected the other in part because of this matching of complementary traits. Without quite knowing what was happening, the pair fell into the aggressive-passive pattern from the beginning of their acquaintanceship. The aggressive one feels most comfortable with a passive partner because this gives him scope for playing the aggressive role without disruptive conflict. The passive one depends on the aggressive partner to supply the leadership and initiative he lacks. It is a mutually dependent relationship. Each partner relies in some degree on the imbalance of the other to keep himself in balance. It is as if two one-legged persons were strapped together to make one two-legged person. The pair may not walk well in this way, but somehow they do manage to limp about. So, while this kind of a marriage may not be harmonious or satisfying, it often does function after a fashion; the couple remains together and works out a pattern built on their respective tendencies. If, however, the imbalance of either partner were to cease suddenly, the combined pair might well topple over and the marriage fall apart.

In some ways, the complementarity of opposite types has constituted an element of strength in many marriages we have known in the past. Men and women attract each other by the very reason of *la différence*. Entwined with their sexual polarity is the cultural stereotyping of male and female characteristics and roles. These

stereotypes, taken for granted by the older generations, are beginning to sound absurd today as our culture is moving away from
them. Yet it is important to recognize what these stereotypes represent because they are still deeply embedded in our culture, laws,
life-styles and psyches, and their residual effects will probably be
felt for generations to come.

Traditionally, the man has been expected to be strong, self-
confident, aggressive, masterful, decisive, firm, brave, self-con-
trolled, smart, and not unduly affected by the softer emotions.
Don't laugh. This combination of traits has long been implied in
the word "manly." It has nothing to do with whether men really
are like this. Most are not and probably never were; but the
idealized image persists.

The woman, on the other hand (in this cultural tradition), has
been expected to be sweet, pretty, charming, attractive to men, a
good listener, not conspicuously intelligent, a virgin until marriage,
fairly helpless, dependent on her husband, compliant with his
wishes, fond of children, motherly and free to express such
"female" emotions as fear or affection. If she actually has some of
the qualities generally attributed to the male (such, for example,
as organizing ability or an analytical mind), she has often found
it advisable to conceal the fact.

The two sets of qualities—the man's and the woman's—have,
in the past, tended to complement each other. The man has leaned
on the woman to express his undeveloped "feminine" or tender
side, while the woman has leaned on the man to provide the
"masculine" strength and hard, logical thought she has been told
she needed.

This culturally induced differentiation has made use of mutual
one-sidedness to bring about and secure the marital relationship.
What, then, happens when the partners become less one-sided—
when the man develops more of his so-called "feminine" side and
the woman is no longer so compliant and dependent? Roles un-
dergo a radical change. People no longer fit comfortably into the
old slots. The glue of offsetting differences that once helped to hold
this kind of marriage together begins to lose some of its adhesive
power. Neither spouse leans quite so much on the other for balance. A new balance then has to be found, or even a new kind of
marital relationship, as the basis for the old one gradually passes

away. The changing patterns of society today are thrusting both men and women into a shared need for becoming more whole persons, but, in doing so, the changes have upset many of the old rules and expectations by which people lived.

The paradox we are faced with might be described in this way: the old complementarity that once made marriage both necessary and workable is being undermined by social changes such as the employment of women outside the home, the ability of couples to control family size, the increased education of both men and women, the sexual revolution, the tendency of people's work to pre-empt their time and isolate them from family life, etc. Under the new conditions, one-sidedness or fragmentation, instead of producing a complementary balance that may have contributed to the stability of the marital or family unit, now often has a disruptive effect.

For example, many men, both by tradition and because of business demands, become skilled at impersonal, non-emotional and sometimes manipulative relationships with people. But if a husband uses this same kind of approach with his wife, she is likely to be dissatisfied, hurt and miserable because she wants warmth and affection, she wants to be experienced as a person. So he is expected to be one kind of person at work and another kind at home. At the same time, his wife's feelings of frustration and anger, because she is not getting out of marriage the human interaction on a feeling level that she wants and needs, can lead her to make wounding remarks. When there is no clear and mutually accepted complementarity by which the combined unit of husband and wife can attain some degree of wholeness, the marriage can become as fragmented as the individuals in it. Then the best hope for the survival of the marriage is for *both partners* to become more nearly whole persons.

The complementarity that characterized the traditional closed marriage was never ideal from the standpoint of the mature growth of the individuals in it. The man was generally not encouraged to develop the neglected side of his own nature—the tender emotional side. His "masculinity," his self-control, his tendency to suppress his Childlike Dimension and to be objective and impersonal were admired traits consistent with what society generally expected. And the woman was not often encouraged to develop the intellectual, self-reliant, Maturing Self Dimension of her personality. To do that might have interfered with the compliance and passivity that were supposed to make her a "good wife." *Each partner in the traditional marriage, therefore, tended to keep the other partially undeveloped.*

The Emerging Open Style of Marriage

The dam is breaking now, and one-sided, fragmented people can no longer count on an institutionalized complementarity to get them past the disruptive strains that threaten marriage and the family. The most hopeful course left open to them now, if they wish to stay happily married, is to work toward becoming more whole persons. This involves certain undeniable risks to the marriage. When one partner in a marriage moves toward wholeness while the other does not, there is inevitable strain in the relationship. This happens many times with friendships. We enjoy a close friendship with someone, but one of us slowly grows beyond or away from the other and we drift apart.

Personal growth of one partner, not shared or wanted by the other, can in some circumstances lead straight to divorce. For example, two young college students fell in love and married; and, from the point of view of their families and friends, it looked like an "ideal" match. The young husband had grown up in a textbook example of the traditional closed-style family. His mother had been a meticulous housekeeper and helpmate for her own husband. She agreed with all her husband's many opinions, served him abundant and appetizing meals (which helped enlarge his girth), mended his socks and ironed his shirts. Their son internalized this image of what a husband-wife relationship should be.

The young wife had some of his mother's qualities (which, no doubt, is partly why he chose her). She, too, had been taught by her parents to be a "good" wife and mother, and she (at first) wanted nothing so much as to please her husband, raise children and maintain a nurturing home for them all. But, as the years passed, this aim by itself became progressively unfulfilling. She discovered that her husband expected her to devote herself *totally* to his and the children's wants. Yet he showed little appreciation of her real efforts to do so. He constantly criticized her shortcomings (the judgmental, critical aspect of his Internalized Others). When she eventually accepted a job outside the home he at first welcomed the money she earned; but when she showed signs of expanding her job into a career and began to take courses at a nearby university, he felt increasingly uncomfortable. Soon he became moody, withdrawn and hostile (his "reactive child"). He needed to believe that his position as family head and, especially, as breadwinner was important to the well-being of his wife and children. A dawning realization that this might not be so aroused in him intense anxiety and anger.

The outcome, under the conditions of the closed marital style, was predictable; they divorced. One of the characteristics of the closed style, as we have seen, is rigidity of roles and expectations; there is no room for change. The husband in this case felt betrayed. He had married a person who, he thought, was a certain kind of woman, but she had metamorphized into another kind with whom he could not deal on the old basis.

This raises a question that needs to be faced honestly: Which is more important—to preserve a marriage at all costs or to foster the maximum personal growth of the individuals in it? The young woman we just described made her own decision without qualification; she chose freedom to grow. She feels now as if she has emerged from a prison. Even her former husband has finally become reconciled to the split and has developed a life of his own. But, surprising as it may seem, the children, also, are happier than they were under the conditions of constant parental friction, anxiety and strain.

Are children really benefited when parents whose marriage has deteriorated stay together solely for the children's sake? I very much doubt it. Children have an astonishing capacity to adjust themselves to realities they can *understand,* and an open break between their parents can be such a reality. But children are unequipped to deal with the unarticulated or crudely articulated feelings that rage below the surface in many closed-style marriages like underground coal fires. The children sense the murky atmosphere but may not be able to describe or discuss their feelings about it. Hence, they may fall prey to consuming anxiety. Such anxiety, with its accompanying fears, angers and hostility, which the child cannot fully identify or express, can scar a child's life. A clean open break, in my view, is often preferable.

In marriage, the inner growth and development of one partner demands either an equivalent growth and development of the other or, at the very least, the *acceptance* by the other of the changes taking place in the first partner. Otherwise, there is discord in the marriage. If the spouse of the growing person accepts the change, he himself grows because acceptance demands a certain openness, flexibility, and a kind of wisdom—a willingness to listen, to tolerate the new and to revise expectations. These are all growth attributes. If, instead, the spouse, confronted with a growing partner, remains rigid and holds tightly to old beliefs, attitudes, habits, expectations and role conceptions (the Internalized Others), he places a barrier across the path of his own growth. Thus, the husband I just mentioned missed a chance to share his life with an increasingly interesting, dynamic and attractive woman whom, in actuality, he never got to know. She was becoming a more complete person every day, yet it was this that helped to drive him off.

Despite the strains that inward change can put on a marriage, the long-term hope for strengthening and enriching marriage is the freeing of both individual partners to develop their full potential *as persons*. If anyone is reluctant to move in this direction for fear of hurting his marriage, I can only point out that there is no assurance that the existing closed marriage will hold together any better than a more open one would. Closed-style marriages are increasingly breaking up. *Life does not offer a choice between changing and not changing.* The passage of time, the accumulation of fat, money and experience, the hardening of habits and the fading of youthful bloom all produce changes; and these changes are greatly disturbing to many.

A husband, for example, may have married his bride for her figure and her beauty. How will she keep his interest after she has gained twenty pounds and ten wrinkles? Perhaps she married him because he was the college football hero. What will he be like after fifteen years of sitting behind a desk and drinking beer at lunch?

If neither has found any more durable basis for their relationship than preoccupation with each other's outsides, the prospects for a satisfying marriage are bleak. But if she has discovered qualities in herself that make her more of a person (such as an art or a skill or a capacity to be close to her feelings), and if he has found capacities that challenge and absorb him more than his old exploits as a quarterback and has learned to be a more aware and sensitive person, there is hope for them both. And especially so if each of them observes and welcomes the changes in the other, is interested in what is happening, and empathizes with the needs that give rise to the changes.

To the young, getting older may look like a very unpleasant process, and some young people can scarcely imagine that the life of people "over thirty" could have any spark. A young person's view of the passage of years is expressed in one of the Beatles' songs, asking who needs or feeds a person when he is "sixty-four."

Many of the young have justifiable reasons for their worry about aging. They see around them older people whose lives have gone stale, who have fallen into an unrewarding routine and lost the capacity to respond to the fresh, the new and the challenging. This looks to the young like a slow death. But the fact is that emotional petrifaction has little to do with age. There are very young people whose lives have already congealed and lost the power of growth, and there are very old people still bursting with vitality, interest and excitement. The same is true of marriages. One marriage may reach a dead end in six months, while another may evolve, deepen, develop, become more rewarding and life-enhancing as the years pass. Whether a marriage (or an individual life) stagnates or ripens over a period of time is determined, to a considerable extent, by what happens in the early years, especially the first year. How you live *now* will greatly affect how you will be living twenty and thirty years from now.

The inevitable changes that take place in a marriage as time passes can be taken either as a catastrophe or as an asset. The male-female relationship is bound to alter. In youth it is often sexually driven and may be subject to tremendous swings of mood. A passionate embrace with an outpouring of love can erupt within minutes into a raging quarrel. The passage of time, under favorable circumstances, may bring a tempering and softening of these emotional excesses. Mature people have had the experience and opportunity to learn how to get along together without injuring or destroying each other. To be sure, they may not have used their time and opportunity well; they may have learned little; they may have lost interest in each other or become hostile to each other; they may have ceased to see or experience each other as persons. Yet the fact remains that there *has* been time and opportunity to build an enduring relationship (whether they have taken advantage of it or not); and, to the extent that they have used it to this end, they have moved ahead.

The most satisfying and enduring marriages—those contributing the most to personal fulfillment and community strength—are not usually the ones of the very young. *It takes time for a marriage to develop its full potential,* just as it does for an individual or a business. There is usually a long process of education, adjustment and personal growth, punctuated by innumerable crises. Each major crisis might have ended the marriage there and then had there not been an underlying desire to make the marriage work. But, somehow, the couple learned from each crisis as they surmounted it.

A mature couple has had a chance to discover those values that are most rewarding for *them.* They have had the opportunity (whether they have used it well or not) to find out what kind of a life brings *them* happiness and leaves *them* contented at the end of a day. If they are wise, they have probably made some progress in building their life around those rewarding values and in shaking themselves loose from life-styles derived from their families', their neighbors' or the world's ideas of how people should live (the Internalized Others). They may have grown, for example, beyond the narrow and compulsive pursuit of money, power, prestige or reputation as ends in themselves. They may prefer the freedom that a moderate amount of money can buy to the demands and confinements to which a life totally devoted to money-making would subject them. Or the mature couple may have found that fighting each other about trifles, or resorting to reprisals because of hurt pride, or trying to prove to each other how strong or how smart each of them is (the Childlike Dimension) leads nowhere but to more of the same; and, with their energies no longer poured into these unproductive channels, they may have freed themselves for more creative and enduring relationships.

The Meaning of the Sexual Relationship

It is difficult for young people to believe that the sexual life of a couple "over forty" could still be exciting and rewarding. Even young people married for only a year or two have been heard to complain that their sex life is already getting to be a bore. They can only surmise what it must be like after, say, twenty years of marriage. But couples whose marriages have survived that long have had the opportunity (whether they have profited by it or not) to learn a great deal about sexuality and to experience new levels of sexual awareness and satisfaction. True, many mature couples have not progressed far in that direction, and some have long ceased to have any sex life at all. But when this comes about, my observation has been that the trouble is due, not to their growing older or being married to the same person too long, but rather to their failure to grow in sensitivity, awareness, understanding, empathy and emotional depth. That same failure is one of the causes of many young people's disillusionment about sex. When sex is pursued as an *alienated activity* separated from emotions and from its symbolic and biological roots, it can begin to seem meaningless and even wearisome. But where sex is an aspect of a deepening relationship of two devoted people, it slowly reveals a series of experiential levels, each one deeper and more satisfying than the preceding.

Sexual depths such as these are not revealed quickly even to the most amorous and sensuous couples. The deeper experience may have little to do with sexual techniques as such, although those sometimes help. The transformation occurs primarily in the mental, emotional and spiritual spheres. Few people, even those with extensive sexual experience, are aware of the complexity of the sex act. At its elemental level it is very simple, any dog can do it, and we might argue that it is unnecessary to concern ourselves with all the mental, emotional and physical ramifications. But the fact is that, being the human creatures we are, we *cannot* perform sexual intercourse solely at the elemental animal level. To do so, we would have to strip ourselves of our emotions, thoughts, memories, beliefs, traditions, fantasies, expectations, feelings of identity, moral conceptions and our connections with the past and the future. All these elements, which combine to make us human, enter into the supposedly simple act of sexual intercourse.

The sex experience has enormously powerful psychological consequences, not merely because it is the product of intense physical and emotional reactions, but because it embodies some of the most potent *symbolism* of any experience available to human beings. The symbolism converts sexual intercourse into a ritual with powerful impact in both positive and negative directions.

In its positive aspect, sexual intercourse symbolizes *union*— which places it at the opposite end of the scale from division and alienation. For this reason it has from time immemorial carried a religious significance, symbolizing, for some, the union between man and God or between flesh and spirit. It also symbolizes *creation,* since it is the act that brings new life into the world. It symbolizes and expresses the *love* of two people for each other. It carries associated meanings such as *trust* and *loyalty,* since it is the experience of two individuals being completely open (at least physically) to each other.

The specific physical acts in intercourse are equally loaded with symbolic significance. Kissing suggests *connection and affection;* stroking, *tenderness and love;* hugging, *comfort and closeness;* nakedness, the state of being completely *open and trusting;* petting, the *desire to please;* stimulating the erogenous areas, *aliveness and excitement;* the penetration, a *merging* of two personalities; the orgasm, *peak experience and fulfillment.* These are feelings which the physical actions intrinsically connote, and all are consistent with the blending of two individuals to become, at least temporarily, "one flesh."

Yet, at the same time, in stark contrast to all the above, sexual intercourse can carry powerful negative connotations. For centuries it has been associated with the feeling of *sin;* it is an act that is connected in some minds with the fall of man. In its negative form, it symbolizes *aggression, violence, domination of the weak by the strong,* and even, as Freud showed, *death.* It is no accident that the term "screw" is often employed to mean "victimize." In its negative symbolism, kissing, petting and undressing may represent, not connection, but *conquest;* the hugging, *control;* the nakedness, *opportunity;* the petting, *domination;* the penetration, *invasion.* Each of the physical gestures which, for some, denote love and affection can be twisted to serve a desire for power and domination, an urge to hurt, or a need to prove masculinity or femininity or, simply attractiveness. This may come across to the other person as a fraud, a pretense, a deception, a violation of the personality, a feeling of being used.

These are extraordinary meanings that go deep into human history, society's traditions and man's concept of himself. We cannot, even if we would, ignore them. Nothing could be wider of the mark than to regard sexual intercourse as a "mere" physical act that anyone can do with anyone else at any time. All human experience is against it.

Isolation of sexual intercourse from its emotional and positive symbolic base—such as occurs when the act becomes routine and unrelated to feelings of affection or love—may produce not only a kind of barren dissatisfaction but also can set off disturbances in the personality and in the marriage. If the physical acts of sex do not really express the love that the gestures symbolize, one or both of the partners may feel cheated, disappointed, dissatisfied, hung up, insulted, and there may be a swing to the negative meanings. To numb such feelings, the injured person may suppress all positive emotions and allow intercourse to become merely a physical and mechanical operation which ceases to involve him fully. That is one of the ways in which sexual relations gradually become routine and shallow. But the disaccord between the implied and the actual feelings can damage the integrity of both partners. They may appear to be saying, "I love you," with their bodies while their feelings are saying, "I own you," or "I'm indifferent to you."

A disappearance of the positive feelings symbolized by the sex act is a serious warning signal of a deterioration in the entire relationship between husband and wife. It may be the first clear sign of such a deterioration. It may mean that the human relationship itself is not being nourished, and it demands that attention be paid to it.

The quality of the sexual relationship in marriage, therefore, closely parallels the quality of the intellectual-emotional relationship between the spouses. The same elements that heighten the quality of the one also heighten the quality of the other. In sexual relations it is not enough just to experience genital contact and orgasm. What needs to be experienced is the partner's uniqueness as a person: his humanness, his emotions, his wishes, his fantasies, his humor, his laughter, his tenderness and, of course, his body. But not just a few parts of the partner's body. Experience all of it: the hair, eyelashes, neck, ear lobes, ever-moving hands, breasts, legs, chest, feet. When you learn to experience *all* of the other person, the act of sexual intercourse can take on new richness and coloring.

Chart VII on the following page can be used to appraise where you are in your sexual life and to establish the direction toward which you might need to move in order to bring greater wholeness and satisfaction into both your sexual life and the other phases of your married life. Try out these ideas and share them with your partner.

As an example of how a couple can raise the quality of their sexual satisfaction, I once had as patients a couple in their fifties. Their sexual relationship had become mostly unsatisfying and routine. When they were young they had experienced occasional "red letter" nights when they reached orgasm together. But these times were rare; and, as the years passed, their sexual relationship declined, sometimes vanishing completely for extended periods as the husband became increasingly preoccupied with his work. Yet, once in a while on some special occasion—perhaps two or three times a year—this couple achieved a quality of union that the wife described as "space travel." They could not achieve this at will. It seemed to happen by itself; but over the years they began to discern an identifiable pattern. "Space travel" was achieved after they had either enjoyed doing something together, had shared some achievement or victory or satisfaction, or had quarreled and then resolved the quarrel—a condition leaving them in an exhilarated mood. The key to "space travel," they discovered, was not primarily physical but was, in high degree, a mental and emotional state. When they had achieved a mental and emotional union, the sexual "space trip" followed naturally.

CHART VII   Elements of Satisfaction and Enjoyment in Sexual Intercourse

	Least Satisfying	*Most Satisfying*
1. Quality of relationship	Impersonal or role-centered; treating partner as an object.	Mutually affectionate, loving, caring, sharing, intimate, warm.
2. Motivations for intercourse	Habit, ego satisfaction, jealousy, wish to gain an advantage, need to prove masculinity or femininity, etc. Or just to satisfy partner.	Strong mutual desire growing out of mutual attraction, affection or love.
3. Mental-emotional preparation	Little or none. Partners go directly to genital connection. (In this way, sexual intercourse is alienated from the personalities of both.)	Partners first cultivate closeness by working or playing together, sharing thoughts and feelings, possibly reading aloud, dancing, listening to music, etc. Intercourse follows later as a culmination or celebration of the feelings of union.
4. Physical preparation	Little or none.	Leisurely, sensitive exploration of each other's entire bodies.
5. Atmosphere surrounding intercourse	Ordinary, routine, distracting, insecure, uncomfortable or ugly.	Harmonious, relaxed, secure, unhurried, sensually appealing.
6. Expressions of affection	Aggressive or indifferent hugging and kissing, or no affectionate behavior.	Mutual affection freely expressed, both verbally and non-verbally.
7. Spontaneity	Very little. Intercourse is a mechanical or routine performance.	Spontaneous, joyful, uninhibited.
8. Use of the senses in making love: Touch	Mainly on the genitals. Little sensitive use of hands and fingers.	Touching, stroking, exploring and massaging of each other's entire bodies, enjoying the variety of skin and hair textures and the feel of body movements.

CHART VII (*continued*)

	Least Satisfying	*Most Satisfying*
Sight	Little visual enjoyment; eyes shut or unfocussed; intercourse performed in darkness or in glaring light.	Enjoyment of sight of each other's bodies, skin, color, eyes, facial expressions, movements and gestures.
Sound	Little awareness except of disturbing or threatening external sounds.	Enjoyment of sounds of each other's voices, cries, sighs, breathing, heart beats, body sounds; or of music.
Smell	Little awareness except of repulsive perspiration odors, etc.	Enjoyment of body smells, perfumes, and other odors.
Taste	No enjoyment. Turned off.	Enjoyment of taste in the acts of kissing, licking and sucking.
9. Use of words	Little or no conversation during or after intercourse.	Partners share their enjoyment verbally before, during and after intercourse.
10. Attitudes toward orgasm	Orgasm regarded as the primary object of intercourse.	Orgasm occurs naturally as a part of a complex interaction of the whole man with the whole woman. Orgasm may or may not occur simultaneously.

A number of years passed before this couple was able to achieve frequent "space trips" when they got together sexually. But they did eventually reach that point. Not every couple, perhaps, would require so long a time to do so. The couple in question, when they married, had to overcome the conditioning of very suppressive sexual upbringings. Today's young marrieds would be less likely to have this problem, but they might be handicapped by another problem perhaps more serious. The present young live in an age when sex is widely devalued, cheapened, exploited and separated from love. This older couple did not perform sexual intercourse as a mere physical act isolated from the feelings of affection and love. Thus, the symbolic nature of sexual intercourse as a uniting of two bodies and spirits was not violated.

We hear women speak of "faking" an orgastic response to please a man. The woman we have just described was amazed when she first heard of this. "Faking" would never have crossed her mind. When she had an orgastic response, it was real and her husband knew it. When she did not, he knew that, too. They were able to trust each other and to learn. If a woman fakes an orgasm and succeeds in fooling her husband, he, of course, is prevented from learning how to make the sexual experience more rewarding for his wife.

Nurturing Your Marriage

In view of the fragility of modern marriage and the ominous divorce rate, it is astonishing how little attention most married people give to the building, securing and enrichment of their marriage. A business that received as little intelligent attention as most marriages get would fail in six months. Yet, in a group of young married people who met recently to discuss their problems, not one admitted to putting marriage first in his/her life. When asked what he/she did put first, a number of participants had difficulty in answering. Some put careers first; the rest frankly did not find their jobs that interesting. But their marriages seemed even less interesting.

Yet marriage experienced as a growing, maturing, changing, unfolding relationship between two human beings can, at least potentially, be one of the more exciting activities in human experience and ultimately one of the most rewarding. But a *relationship has to be nourished. It has to be worked at,* just as a career does.

A couple marries. For a little while everything seems idyllic. Then challenges and strains begin to appear. The partners find that their values and their expectations are, in many ways, at odds. He may expect her to cook his dinner and press his pants in the evening, even though she has worked all day at an outside job. She may expect him to declare his love for her several times a day. He may expect her to leave him alone for a half-hour after he gets home in the evening so that he can relax. She may expect him to give a listening ear to her account of the day's crises as soon as he puts his foot in the door. He may expect her to replace the cap on the toothpaste tube after each use. She may expect him to take a shower every evening. There is no end to the number of irritating ways in which conflicting expectations can begin to unravel a marriage in the very first year, as I pointed out in my book, *Your First Year of Marriage.** A couple finds this out quickly, yet, too often does little about it except react in anger, disappointment, withdrawal or retaliation. Small irritations build up into big ones, and eventually the once-loving partners find themselves (figuratively speaking) at each other's throats.

There are at least two reasonable ways to deal with the frustration of disappointed expectations. One is consciously to decide that a thing is not worth getting upset over and then to stop letting it bother you. For example, a husband nagged his wife about her "extravagance" because she did not always get items where they could be bought cheapest. In his view, it was immoral to spend a dollar and a quarter for something that you could get for ninety-nine cents at another store. He found out eventually that saving a few pennies simply was not worth the emotional price of endless arguments, and he gave up this futile struggle.

Another way to deal with disappointed expectations is to communicate them openly to the spouse, listen to the spouse's point of view and try to arrive at an arrangement both can live with. This may require more negotiating skill than many people have. But the development of negotiating skill is one of the requisites of civilized life as well as of Open Family Living, and a couple needs to learn to practice it from the beginning.

How do you negotiate? Do you just argue until you get your way? Some people do, but in actuality, true negotiating ability is one of the higher capacities of the Maturing Self Dimension of a human being. There is no other way for people with differing values and expectations to resolve their differences constructively. The more crowded and diversified the world gets, the more essential it is that people learn the art of negotiation.

To the all-or-nothing temperament, negotiation has the look and feel of weakness. The "strong" person thinks he must over-

---

* Doubleday & Company, Inc., 1967.

come opposition, make no compromises. He has a fear of "losing face." But what he thinks of as strength or firmness is often actually the rigidity, the brittleness, of the closed style. Your spouse's values and expectations are probably as important to him as yours are to you, and you have no inherent right to impose yours on him. **Negotiation** requires open communication; the partners have to listen to each other. It requires respect; neither partner must override the other or allow himself to be overridden. It requires a re-examination of one's own values and expectations and a decision as to which ones are important enough to defend and which can be relinquished in the interest of agreement. And it requires realistic appraisal of what kind of agreement is possible and of what the alternatives to agreement are. If there is no agreement, what will be the result? A dissatisfied spouse? A dissatisfied couple? A period of unhappiness and tension? A wrecked marriage?

On some matters, such as where to go for vacation, the outcome of negotiation may not be critical. You may like the seashore, your spouse might prefer a camping trip. Do you hate camping so much that, if he wants to camp he has to go alone? Or would you accept camping for this summer if he will go to the seashore with you next summer? And how about other members of the family? How do they feel about it?

But on some matters the outcome of negotiations may be crucial to the marriage. An example might be whether one partner should accept a job in a distant city, perhaps requiring the family to move. This could bring to the fore some sticky questions, such as:

Do I want his happiness and success enough to give up my job and friends to follow him to —?

If not, would I demand that he give up his promotion so we could stay here?

Would his willingness to give up his promotion at my request be a test of his love for me?

If he gives up his promotion so we can stay here, what would it do to his future and our relationship?

Clearly, a negotiation that involves questions of this sort calls for a high development of the Maturing Self Dimension, the abil-

ity to judge between conflicting values and appraise both short-
term and long-term consequences.

One enemy of negotiation is the embattled position sometimes
taken by the Internalized Others Dimension. This might lead a
partner to make moral judgments about values that differ from his
own, just as the parsimonious husband felt that his wife's "extravagance" (paying twenty-six cents too much) was "immoral." It
is easy to think that your own values are "good" and "right,"
whereas your spouse's are "inferior" or "wrong"; but a more
effective recipe for disrupting a marriage would be hard to invent. Thus, a disagreement that may be only a reflection of cultural differences, such as, for example, the relative frequency of
baths, can get blown up into a question of who is "better."

A similar problem in many marriages is the habit of indulging
in little digs, pinpricks, critical comments, sarcastic put-downs,
cutting remarks and ridicule. People who do this have generally
been doing it most of their lives and may be unaware of how
damaging to the other person's self-esteem this practice can be.
Many people fall into the habit of using words as weapons. Verbal weapons are two-edged. Qualitative human relationship is
fostered, not by harsh criticism and put-downs, but by encouragement (lift-ups) and the overlooking of shortcomings. Some psychotherapists call these lift-ups "strokes."

On the other hand, a person on the receiving end of the put-
down game does not have to play that game. He can confront the
perpetrator. And the victim can, above all, refuse to incorporate
the put-down into his concept of himself. A put-down may hurt,
but it need not be allowed to undermine. ►15

What About Love?

The clearest sign of alienation in our culture is the lack of love in
marriage.

To be sure, there are still a fair number of ho-hum, workaday
marriages in which the partners have learned to tolerate each
other, be moderately patient with each other, avoid the more
destructive forms of communication such as ridicule or sarcasm,
shun the kinds of fighting that might wound or drive them apart,
listen to each other after a fashion, have sex with varying de-

grees of satisfaction, and engage in common tasks such as rearing children and taking care of a home or a business. But can such a relationship be fairly described as one of *love?* Would the partners themselves so describe it?

Popular wisdom has it that the rosy glow of "love" fades after a few years (or, maybe, months) of married life, after which the question is how to "get along." Not many people expect romantic love to last forever. Yet, there are mature married couples whose love did not wither away but, instead, strengthened and deepened over the years. Is this an oddity, an abnormality, an accident of fate? I do not believe so. I believe that *the capacity for love is inherent in all human beings* and that those in whom it flowers most brightly are the ones who most fully develop the potential for love that they carry within them.

Love has many dimensions. Romantic passion, centered in sexuality, is but one of these. There are also the qualities of caring, interest, concern, devotion, commitment, intimate communication, desire to help one another and to lift one another's spirits, and joy in sharing one another's thoughts and feelings. Love may be said to exist when a person cares enough about another person to want to do something for him, to give him a gift—something to please him or help him or enrich his life—and wants to do it because the doing of it delights them both. If an act is done primarily in exchange for something else ("I'll cook dinner tonight if you'll repair the washing machine") or to buy the other person's regard ("Here are some roses, and let's not talk about our quarrel yesterday") or to exert power over the other person ("I'll go out with you, but you must promise me to stay off the bottle"), there are elements other than love involved, although love may be present, too. These other elements are not necessarily destructive; there is a valid place for *quid-pro-quo* in a relationship, and it is not always injurious to use a gift to purchase something—say, regard. But such gifts should not be confused with the free gifts of love, which, in their pure form, have no strings attached.

The *quality of love* might be measured by five criteria:

1. How strong and how frequent is the impulse to give or to serve?

2. How much does the gift or service demand of the giver? A little or a lot?

3. Does the urge to give proceed from a spontaneous desire to make the other person happy? Or does it proceed mainly from a sense of duty, from a conception of one's role, from a sense of guilt or from some kind of compulsion?

4. Is the gift freely, affectionately and joyfully given, and does it carry no strings?

5. Is the effect of the love on the other person to help him to come alive and bloom?

Any marriage, sooner or later, confronts the partners with tests of their love. One test, for example, is when a spouse becomes ill or disabled. What quality of care does the other give him? Is it given only from a sense of duty ("I've got to serve the bastard meals in bed")? Or because love calls forth even more than duty prescribes ("I'll put roses on the tray")? Another test is when one or both partners gets too busy to pay each other much attention: one is frequently away on business trips, the other is preoccupied with day-to-day problems. In this case, what happens during the short times when the partners are together is crucial.

Love, in the sense of wanting to give freely and spontaneously with no strings attached, seems uncommon in marriage today and, when it does exist, can be very vulnerable. The loving giver who asks nothing for himself tempts the receiver to give nothing. Then giving can become habitually one-sided and potentially destructive. The giver, finding no reciprocation, may begin to resent the imbalance and either tend to withhold his gifts or to make unwelcome demands on the receiver. Then love begins to wither. As is well known, a strong love can turn into an equally strong hate.

When love withers, it is a tragedy—not only because of the hurt that follows but because a great opportunity for achieving new levels of awakening and wholeness has been missed. Love is an essential element of wholeness. It is a peak experience, and retreat from love means a return to alienation—a re-entry into a shuttered, arms-length existence both for the lover and for the loved.

Love is a dynamic process and therefore an unrolling procession of constantly changing states. Because love is a process, the important question at any one time is not so much where the love is but rather where it is going: up or down? Love either grows, expands and strengthens, or it shrinks, weakens and may eventually die. We observe so much of the latter in marriage that the possibility of the former is often overlooked. The fading of the romantic love of honeymoon days is taken to be the fading of all love between the two. Yet this need not be so at all. The growing and maturing love of people who care deeply about each other can be the most rewarding love of all. And this is the love that comes about when the pair reach out toward each other, learn to become more spontaneous and more truly themselves, master the arts of communication and of sharing, and turn each other on—come alive.

A couple cannot produce this love by an act of will. But they can behave in a manner that will foster the growth of whatever love already exists, as one may do with any growing thing.

First, the couple needs to cultivate the love element that was present in the romantic excitement that brought them together in the beginning. There may not have been very much; romantic love is not necessarily love of the enduring kind, and young people are often selfish. But in many cases, some element of real love was present, as was demonstrated by the pleasure each one took in doing things for the other. If the couple can be made aware that this pleasure in doing things for each other is one of the keys to the nurturing of a more mature love, they may take care that it is not allowed to diminish and die. Love is far too valuable to be casually let go, and living without love in marriage is like choosing starvation when there is money in the bank.

Secondly, a couple that aims to be more loving should cultivate the arts of human relationship and communication. The partners need to pay attention to each other, listen to each other, try to be considerate of each other's feelings, respect each other's privacy, look for common interests, and above all, be careful not to allow the giving and serving to be exclusively in one direction. They need to communicate constantly. Over and over, in my work, I hear a person say, "My husband (or wife) does so-and-so which just drives me up the wall!" I ask, "Does he know how you feel about it?" And the answer is, "Well, he *ought* to know by now!" or "It's high time he found out! Can't he *see* that it makes me furious?" This is a very distorted form of communication. It reminds me of a woman in her seventies who said of her husband after his death: "In all the forty-five years of our married life, he never learned that my favorite piece of chicken was the thigh!"

Finally, people who are interested in nourishing an enduring love should try, as best they can, to grow toward being whole persons. They should not neglect their body, mind, feelings or spirit. They cannot only love freely but they can endeavor to be lovable. It is true that loving the unlovable is supposed to be a divine command, and there are some persons who are able to look behind an unlovely exterior to see and appreciate the human being underneath. If we all were perceptive enough to do this, love would blossom more abundantly than it does. But most people cannot do it. Hence, allowing one's self to become unlovable (i.e., selfish, slovenly, dirty, unattractive, unbathed, ill-tempered, ill-mannered, grasping, and the like) is to put a strain on the partner's love which he may be unable to withstand.

Love is undermined when either partner takes the attitude, "I have a *right* to do as I please in my own home." Maybe he does, but what about the rights and feelings of other family members? A person may have a "right" to leave his clothes strewn on the floor, but what about the spouse for whom this practice may be extremely offensive? This is the subject of Neil Simon's amusing play, *The Odd Couple*.

When two people with incompatible life-styles find themselves together, there are five possible choices:

1. Constant struggle, with the issue perpetually unresolved.
2. A compromise satisfactory to neither.
3. One yielding and the other overriding him.
4. Negotiation of a solution reasonably acceptable to both.
5. Splitting up.

Number one means that neither partner will yield any part of his right to do as he pleases. This is incompatible with love, for neither partner wishes to do what would most please the other. Alternative number 2 is often an unhappy outcome because neither partner is satisfied. Alternative number 3 might begin with a loving act of one partner yielding to the other in order to please him. But this works out in the long run only if the yielder is willing to give up his preference, to adapt happily to the preference of the other and to quit worrying about it. Otherwise, the arrangement soon begins to seem unfair, resentments pile up, and the dispute is likely to break out again later in a more destructive form.

The true loving response is not usually a one-sided yielding—it is certainly not martyrdom in any form—but, rather, open communication of each spouse's feelings and preferences to the other, leading to negotiation of a workable solution acceptable to both (choice number 4).

In their book, *The Mirages of Marriage,* William J. Lederer and Dr. Don D. Jackson cut through much mythology about love with the blunt assertion that love is not necessary to a successful marriage. For a marriage to survive without love, however, they assert that certain other elements are necessary, and they list these as tolerance, respect, honesty and the desire to stay together for mutual advantage. To these, I would add ability to communicate adequately and to negotiate differences.

While it is true that a marriage can be held together and can function moderately well in the absence of love (great numbers of marriages, in fact, do), I feel sad that the public is being advised to settle for so low a level of human satisfaction. It means that an element of humanness, a part of an individual's birthright, is being written off. If people are led to believe that enduring love in marriage is a fairy tale or is a mere icing on the marital cake, they will not take the trouble to develop those arts that will nurture it. Thus, they may pass by, unexplored, one of the very great experiences of life.

Love admittedly has its price, and that is why so many people avoid committing themselves to it. Love asks much of a person. It asks, at times, for devoted attention, for warm affection, for intimate sharing of feelings, thoughts, wishes and dreams, for loyal support when the other is troubled or in need, and for offering a listening ear and a sympathetic heart. It asks us to go beyond the *quid-pro-quo* attitude of giving only in return for something. For these reasons, many people who have not experienced mature love or who have been hurt by not having their love reciprocated, think of love as merely a trap set to rob a person of his self-direction. Thinking of it in this way, they naturally seek to avoid involvement.

When two people are open to each other, give their love gifts and services freely with joy, and neither tries to take advantage of the other, a relationship can develop that is unmatched in human experience.

The most implacable enemies of love are indifference, preoccupation with other matters, isolation (alienation), competitiveness between the partners, emotional deadness and lack of healthy communication. How do you feel and behave when you are with your spouse? Are you completely there—mentally, physically and emotionally? Do you listen to what he or she is saying? Do you pay attention? Do you care? Do you look your spouse in the eye? Do you listen to the tones of his voice, inflections, pauses? Are you aware of your spouse's body, gestures, postures, movements, skin texture, color, odor? Do you sense the emotions flowing beneath? Can you accept and respond to those emotions? Does a developing, unfolding human being arouse a sense of wonder in you? If your spouse is confiding something that, to him or her, is meaningful and private, are you aware of the honor and trust that this reveals? Or do you wait out the speech at half attention with one eye on your newspaper?

Love does not and cannot demand all your time and energy. It has no right to do so, and if it did, it would defeat itself. Nor should love annihilate your privacy or your individuality. These belong exclusively to you. But in the loving relationship with your spouse, *while you are with your spouse, even if only a few minutes a day, it asks the best of you.* ▶16

Come the Children

When a couple has children a new set of marital problems arises. Some of the problems are a simple consequence of the fact that the partners' attention is diverted from each other. A new baby usually gets more (and demands more) attention than a spouse.

This can leave a husband or a wife feeling neglected and relegated to second place. The fact that the baby is loved and may be a longed-for addition to the home does not necessarily make up for the shift of focus in the marriage itself. The husband and wife need to be aware of this shift and of its possible consequences and to make a deliberate effort to offset it by showing affection and doing things for each other at every opportunity. On the other hand, the sharing of a child offers them the chance to work together; the husband can learn to care for the baby along with the wife, and this can draw the couple together.

Without question, the coming of children introduces a variety of unexpected complications. Whoever started the rumor that having children helps to cement a marriage? For some, it does. For others, it does not. Yet the creation of a family is a tremendous experience that leaves a person never quite the same as he was before. It connects him with the stream of life. No one who has not gone through this can fully realize what it means. The experience opens up opportunities for new levels of awareness, aliveness, growth and joy. Most parents, I think, looking back on their child-nurturing days, would acknowledge that having children enabled them to become much more human and whole.

The open-style marriage offers a stronger basis for meeting the strains and complications of family life than do the more closed marital states. In the two chapters to follow, some of the major problems and crises of family life are scrutinized and the contribution which the open style can make toward overcoming them is analyzed.

Suggested Interaction Experiences

IE-14. COMPARING YOUR PERCEPTION OF YOUR MARRIAGE WITH OTHER MARRIAGES (PP. 113–16)

Introduce the concept of marital states to someone you know who is married. If you judge it to be appropriate, share with this person (or marital pair) your evaluation (and your partner's evaluation) of your marriage by using Chart V (pp. 108–9) which includes:

a) Marital State

b) Relationship with Partner

c) How Conflicts Are Worked with

If this person is interested in exploring his/her marriage, then give encouragement to go through the same evaluation experience with his/her own marriage.

This kind of constructive sharing can provide you with opportunities to learn more about yourself as a person and as a marital partner. It can also help you more fully appreciate and understand the marital relationships of significant people in your life. Finally, it can enable others to appreciate and understand your marital relationship.

IE-15. DEALING WITH CONFLICTS OF EXPECTATION IN YOUR MARRIAGE (PP. 133–34)

In private, each partner lists those expectations of his marriage which he feels are not being completely fulfilled. Then he lists those expectations about which he feels happy. When this is done, the partners exchange lists. Each reads aloud the lists prepared by the other. Partners should not interrupt the reading or attempt to defend their positions. This is an opportunity for each to learn how the other feels, not to take issue with those feelings.

EVALUATION: Are there any surprises? Any conflicting expectations? Single out the one expectation on each list that has been the most irritating and difficult to manage, and discuss it fully. Listen attentively and meaningfully to your partner and ask him to do the same for you. Likewise, discuss those expectations that have been fulfilled and express appreciation to the partner for his contribution.

FOLLOW-UP: Using the principle of negotiation (p. 133) try to work out the one most irritating expectation so that the outcome leaves both of you reasonably comfortable and satisfied.

IE-16. APPRAISING THE OPENNESS AND CLOSEDNESS OF YOUR MARRIAGE (P. 140)

Using Chart VI (pp. 115–16), appraise your marriage in each of the areas of marital functioning listed. Invite your partner to do the same.

EVALUATION: Where does each of you come out? On balance, where would you place your marriage?

FOLLOW-UP: With your partner, select one area of marital functioning on Chart VI where you both indicated "closed." Communicate about this closed area and decide what might be done to make it more open. Try to work on it.

FIVE

NARROWING THE
GENERATION GAP

In recent decades fragmentation and alienation in families have multiplied like a virus to become a basic social problem all over the world. Millions of estranged youngsters are roaming the streets; millions of embittered, shattered parents are left behind in spiritual poverty and despair.

The poisoning of the rapport between generations is perhaps the most heartbreaking and unnecessary of all the alienations. It robs both generations of the joys and satisfactions they could be finding in each other; it deprives each of the strength and help the other could provide; and it runs counter to the deepest desires of both.

Although alienation between parents and young is becoming so common that it is thought of as almost inevitable, it is actually a highly unnatural, culturally induced phenomenon. There is no place for it in the simpler conditions of nature, as, for example, in the jungle, because Nature's edict is for parents to nurture and care for their children and for children to respond to their parents. Had this not been so, our species could not have survived the harsh conditions of our evolutionary past. Alienation between generations is a social sickness disturbingly suggestive of the disruption of the parent-infant interaction observed among certain animals confined in a zoo. In man, it seems to be a product not only of an artificial environment unsuited to his development, but also of his misdirected thinking and emotional impoverishment which produced that environment in the first place.

In many ways the environment society provides is wretched for children, and more wretched than we realize for the adults those children later become. Too often there is little provision for meeting the six emotional needs of infants discussed earlier: love, attention, acceptance, interaction with other human beings, stability and security. In a society that puts more stress on material than on emotional satisfactions, one or more of these needs may not be met; and when that happens, the seeds of alienation are sown. It is useless to blame parents, or for parents to blame and punish themselves, because many parents themselves were probably denied these needs and are reacting to that deprivation. The deprivation may, in fact, have occurred many generations back, perpetuating itself like a genetic weakness. But there is no evidence to suggest that it is a genetic weakness. It was *learned*. It can be altered, redirected and overcome, and we have to begin to take responsibility for it.

There is probably a connection between the emotional deprivation that has victimized great numbers of people and their inability to feel empathy with the young. Numerous communities provide few if any constructive outlets for youthful energies, vote down proposals for recreational facilities and cut school budgets to the bone.

In our dreams, we envision home and family as a solace for our loneliness, a place of security, love and caring where we can trust those around us and where our needs are fulfilled. This is an almost universal wish fantasy, sometimes most intensely felt by those who have never had such a home.

A teen-age girl who had been abandoned by her mother in her first year of life kept dreaming of a loving mother whom she had never had—a mother always available in time of trouble, always ready to give help and comfort, to dry the little girl's tears and to kiss away her hurts. Perhaps we all have longed for this kind of a parent, and perhaps this girl found more comfort in her fantasy mother than she might have with a real one. For real mothers sometimes get irritated, angry, anxious, preoccupied, careless; they are not always as perceptive or sensitive as they might be; and they often have fears and hang-ups that are upsetting to their children.

Out of the sometimes vast gap between what a family might be and what it is there can arise this pervasive, tragic alienation of the generations.

In many families the generational split is so wide that parents and their teen-age or grown-up children are barely on speaking terms. Or when they speak, they cannot seem to say anything meaningful. Attempted communication repeatedly collapses in quarreling, sarcasm, ridicule, withdrawal, criticism and misunderstanding. Sadly, even after the children have grown up and have had children of their own, there still often remains an estrangement from the grandparents. The old currents of unexpressed and hidden disapproval, doubt, guilt, fear, exasperation and disappointment were never dealt with and the feelings never healed. The overt quarreling may have subsided, but the reactions these generations have to each other are patterned and frozen. Open sharing of feelings, hopes, experiences and thoughts—the real heart of a human relationship—has almost died in such families.

The effect on both generations can be devastating.

Consider, first, the parents. In many cases, they have poured a large share of their physical, emotional and spiritual energies, as well as a substantial financial investment, into the raising of their children. They find themselves rewarded by almost total rejection (as it seems to them) of their teachings, values, hopes and expectations. It is a blow from which many parents never quite recover. Raising children, for some of them, has been the only activity that gave life true meaning. With their children no longer responding or contributing in a satisfying way, it is as if there were no longer a reason to go on living. Some defeated parents take to drink even as their young people take to drugs, and the two generations then seem to strive to outdo each other in self-destructive withdrawal.

But the effect of this kind of alienation on young people can be even more disastrous. The young are in danger of becoming a marooned generation, bereft of constructive models to follow or goals to live by. Their natural idealism, soured by the acid of increasing disaffection, sometimes turns to hate and violence.

What can a youth do when he is estranged from his parents? He emerges from his home into a confusing, frightening, chaotic world. Why, he wonders, can't his parents understand the problems he faces and help him work them through instead of hassling him and restricting him as they do? Because of the near universality of this frustration, young people began after World

War II to draw together to form a culture of their own—a so-called "youth" culture or counterculture. ►17

The Youth Culture

A youth culture had to happen. Its time had come. A society had evolved in which young people no longer worked alongside their elders in common tasks. The work of adults had become so specialized, often so technical and so separated from the home, that many young people knew virtually nothing about their parents' jobs, had never visited the places where they worked, had never heard discussions of the problems encountered on those jobs or learned what kinds of demands the work made on their parents. The young people had come to live in a different and alien world almost unrelated to that of their parents. It was inevitable that the young would find much more in common with their peers than with their parents or with other members of the older generation.

Historically, the emergence of the youth culture occurred only yesterday. Nothing resembling it existed before our time, and it has been difficult, therefore, to put it in any sort of perspective. Youth rebellion is, of course, not new; it has been endemic throughout the ages. Some of our grandparents in the twenties were part of a phenomenon celebrated by Scott Fitzgerald and others, called "flaming youth." But "flaming youth," after introducing some new dance steps, playing lots of jazz, ending corsets and chaperones and removing excess cloth from bathing suits, subsided. The more recent counterculture which came to light in the fifties and sixties struck far deeper. It was concerned more with what life was about and less with fun and frolic. It tied itself to causes such as civil rights, peace, ecology and economic inequities. This recent surge, too, has subsided somewhat; but the effects may be longer lasting than those of earlier youth rebellions. The youth culture has influenced the older cultures in important ways, and we need to look at them.

When the youth culture first began to emerge, it often polarized the generations. The older people of that time either ignored it, reacted angrily to it, or tried uncomfortably to make the best adjustment to it they could. The young people, on the other hand, immersed themselves in it—it was theirs.

Because of the strangeness and disturbing nature of the concepts underlying the youth culture and because of the way most older people had been brought up, a great many parents and teachers were very slow to recognize the exciting potential of the youth culture for opening new paths to self-realization and overcoming of alienation. The older people had not been accustomed to thinking this way. Their first reaction was to try to suppress the youth culture, and thus began the long struggle between the generations on hair styles, beards, clothes and other issues of largely symbolic significance. The parental generation, unable to win this struggle, recalled an old piece of advice: "If you can't beat 'em, join 'em." Many grew longer hair, sideburns and beards themselves, and quite a few of the young people who fought in the hair war have since become parents. (The next youth fashion might be short hair, and I can imagine this being fought by long-haired parents, perhaps just as fiercely and unsuccessfully.)

The youth culture was, and to a considerable extent still is, characterized by informal clothes, rock music, a more open expression of emotions than their parents were used to, much more open attitudes toward sex, an experimental use of drugs for "mind expanding," and an intense questioning of establishment values—many of which aroused hostility from the more conservative older people. The youth culture was (and is) viewed as a threat by leaders in many countries. In France, for example, student riots in 1971 are believed to have nearly brought down the government. In Thailand, later, they actually did. Devotees of the youth culture all over the world (in Soviet Russia, for one example) have been castigated as immoral, undisciplined, unpatriotic, dirty, a threat to socially accepted values, and enemies of law and order. There have been demands in some quarters for putting them down. The shootings at Kent State and Jackson State were logical and probably inevitable consequences of these attitudes of some people.

But suppression, even if total as in the Soviet Union, is usually ineffective in halting a cultural trend. Rather, it tends to stimulate it. The youth culture rolled on like a world-wide tidal wave, growing in complexity, variety, sophistication and emotional scope, and exerting an increasingly powerful pull on the older cultures surrounding it. The more traditional cultures, which had been suffering from a depletion of original creativity and vigor, were enlivened by the enormous vitality that radiated from the productions of the youth culture. Rock music, for example, passed through an impressive evolution from the simple, rather childlike songs of Elvis Presley and the early Beatles to the complex, sophisticated music of the late Beatles and other talented groups that soon arose. Beginning with the Beatles, the top-ranking rock groups often composed their own music and lyrics and made their own musical arrangements, so that the production of the best of rock became a highly complex and creative process using electronic equipment and marketing techniques never before available to musical composers and performers.

Rock carries with it a vibrant, repetitive, pulsing energy, expressive of the energy of youth, which has influenced all the other musical forms of our time. The popular musical show, for example, which had been strong on sentimentality and weak on ideas, was stood on its head a few years ago by the rock musical *Hair*. Later came a new art form: the so-called rock opera beginning with productions such as *Tommy*, which were written largely to be listened to, and evolving into musical pageants such as *Jesus Christ—Superstar* and *Godspell*. The last two, while based formally on the Gospels, brought a new feeling into the New Testament stories, horrifying people accustomed to the solemn, reverent, rather static feeling of the old Passion plays, yet exciting and delighting others. In the two rock operas, Jesus is portrayed as a human being who blends perfectly into the youth culture—a sad and troubled Jesus in *Superstar*, a jubilant, fun-loving, yet serious, one in *Godspell*.

But the feeling and the beat of rock were, at the same time, making their way into highbrow music. Leonard Bernstein's *Mass*, first performed at the opening of the Kennedy Center in Washington, contains a number of rock rhythms with rocklike lyrics. Stephen Schwartz, the (then) twenty-four-year-old song writer who wrote some of the lyrics for *Godspell*, also wrote the lyrics for the rock portions of *Mass*. This is but one example of the way in which the waves originally set in motion by the youth culture have spread outward until they now produce oscillations in the cultural life of nearly all countries.

Intellectually, the youth culture (much like the older culture at which it is aimed) covers the entire gamut from trivialities to serious philosophical reflections and social comment. In its full range, it reflects the variety of the people to whom it appeals: the thoughtful and the foolish, the serious and the frivolous, the egotistical and the social-minded, the lovers and the haters—all are there, all moods are expressed, and the youth culture is varied enough to embrace them all.

The youth culture has centered, to a very large extent, around rock music, which speaks powerfully to the emotional condition of the young. Through this music they discover and find expression for their feelings, their aspirations, their longings, their tenderness, their pain, their search for meaning. It helps fill an immense void that had come into being in a society that puts nearly all its energies into activities related to the production and distribution of goods and services and extremely little into the cultivation of feelings or the nurture of people. I can still see in my mind's eye a boy of seventeen who had just been deprived of his automobile operator's license for two years because of driving while drunk. He loved cars, and the obtaining of this license had meant, to him, the long-awaited achievement of adult status. It was now as if he were pushed back again into childhood. He sat alone in a corner of his home with his guitar, softly singing songs of loneliness and sadness, putting all his feelings into the music which was his refuge.

The inclination toward the use of drugs in the youth culture stems in part from the same need and the same void. Certain drugs loosen the iron grip of the Internalized Others and let feelings and imagery flow more easily. Some young people have found no way to enter the emotional and imaginative realms except by this route, and despite all its dangers and possible "bad trips," they prefer the "stoned" state to the dreariness of the emotional starvation they experience in so-called "reality."

Opening the consciousness to the emotions and images that flow unendingly within every human being can be an immensely worthwhile aim, and if we can teach people to do this by exposing them to an enriched and exciting family life that enhances self-realization, they will have much less need or desire to turn to drugs.

Many of the songs of the youth culture reflect feelings arising from the young people's common experience of not fitting into or being needed by the adult world. The young feel drawn together into a kind of fraternal order or brotherhood of outsiders. Their sense of unity at times is palpable. At the Woodstock music festival a few years ago, observers commented on the vibrating, throbbing presence of a common sharing, not greatly dissimilar to the emotional force that binds people experiencing the sense of salvation in an old-fashioned religious tent revival. At Woodstock the kids shared their food, their bedrolls and their marijuana. A similar feeling pervaded the great non-violent peace demonstrations in the years before these were invaded by extremists seeking to provoke disorder. It also pervaded the civil rights movement at a time when that work was carried on by young whites and blacks working peacefully side by side.

When news of the students killed at Kent State University and Jackson State College reached campuses throughout the country, many students reacted as if members of their own families had been shot. There was anger, there was shock, but probably most of all, there was sorrow.

The song of several years ago by Simon and Garfunkel, called "Bridge Over Troubled Water," now familiar to many parents and teachers, reflects the feelings of sharing and brotherhood that many young people have toward each other.

Empathy, as reflected in such songs as this, is a deeply human quality. It is a process of putting yourself into the skin of another, feeling what he feels and experiencing the world as he experiences it. It is not difficult to practice empathy with respect to people much like yourself, provided the competitive element is removed. Thus, a young person is most likely to respond to "Bridge Over Troubled Water" in terms of his feelings *toward other young people.* For him to feel empathy with, say, his parents and teachers, or with members of the Establishment (if he is anti-Establishment), or for a parent to feel empathy with his rebellious young person, is an achievement of a higher order. Yet, if the "Bridge" is valid for members of a peer brotherhood, it can be valid for everyone.

Through empathy people can really understand and get close to each other. Empathy is the opposite of alienation. Through it we can expand by many fold the range of our emotional experience. All alone, we may be limited to a feeling range, let us say, an inch wide. But if I can get inside the skin of another and feel what he feels, his inch is added to my inch. Yet, somehow, the resulting range is far more than two inches. We both are opened up and our range is expanded.

Empathy often arises spontaneously, even with people who are unlike, if they can free themselves from the competitiveness, power struggles, compulsions and hang-ups that clutter their ordinary lives. When people get together and share feelings on a human level, as they do in certain marathon and encounter groups —and when they get the "crappy" feelings out in the open and discover how absurd and crippling many of them are—then empathy can rise like the sun in the morning. A person will cross the room to touch and comfort another who is going through a hard experience. Reaching out to touch is the physical expression of empathy. It says, "I am here, I care and I can feel with you."

The youth culture is a kind of mirror in which youth sees itself. But it is also a window through which parents and other adults can look into the world of the young. Neglect of this window was a lost opportunity for many of the parents' generation. If you are a parent and you feel separated from the unfamiliar world in which your young person lives, try listening (as I have suggested) to his music. Pay particular attention to the words. If you were to ask your kid directly how he feels about the world, he might not be able to tell you. Feelings are often too confusing and jumbled for clear articulation. But the writers of rock lyrics have, in many cases, found words that express accurately where the young person is. The real music of the young transmits messages that bind the brotherhood of youth together—in some ways against the rest of the world (for that is the way of brotherhoods, especially when they feel conspired against).

If you belong to an older generation, you will find certain of the rock lyrics directed against *you*, *your* values, *your* life-style. It may be hard to take, yet it should come as no surprise because your young people probably have already made it fairly clear that they do not accept your ways of looking at and experiencing life. If you are an overly aggressive person, you may be tempted to counterattack, which will probably lead to a widening of the gap. If you are a withdrawer, you may try to forget or ignore the differences, which can leave the gap as wide as ever. Actually, I know of only one way to reach across the generation gap: listen and try to understand.

Some parents resist the idea that they should listen to and try to understand the young. It is the young, they feel, who should listen to and try to understand *them*. And perhaps the young should. But, unless the parents set an example by being good listeners and understanding people themselves, the young will probably be turned off. ►18

An Adult's Adventure into the World of the Young

A beginning toward reconnecting the generations in a family might be for each generation to take a guided tour, or "trip," into the world of the other. Initially, this action would probably have to be taken by the parents; but once the parents have taken it and responded to it, the young people might later be willing to make a return "trip" from their side. Then the barriers can begin to fall.

Such a trip for each generation could be experienced as an adventure. Each generation's world has contents unfamiliar to the other; each has its own precious objects, values, feelings, laws, rules, ways of thinking. An experience of this sort, if we could detach ourselves sufficiently from our habit of being judgmental, might be as fascinating as the unearthing of a long-buried city such as Knossos or Pompeii. Archaeologists are excited as they uncover all the varied objects that the Roman citizens used two millennia ago or the Aegeans used long before that. It is an absorbing experience to reconstruct what life must have been like in those remote times. So speeded up is change today that the lifestyles of people one generation apart may seem almost as strange in relation to each other as those of the ancients seem to us. Does that fact not offer a stimulating task for the imagination?

Suppose you are a parent concerned about the alienation of the generations and distressed by the breakdown of communication between yourself and your young people. How would you go about re-establishing a connection? You might sit in a chair, close your eyes, and put yourself mentally and emotionally in your young person's place to experience the world as he experiences it. This is difficult because you have your own emotions—worry, frustration, exasperation, suspicion, doubt, fear. How can you cast all these aside? You have potent emotional ties to your young person; you cannot enjoy the objectivity of the archaeologist. Yet if you make a beginning, the process will begin to create its own insights and make further progress easier.

In preparing for the practice of empathy, it helps to enter the world of the young *physically,* to go where young people are, to try to do some of the things they do and to get the feel of their kind of life. You could go to the city park or square, to the coffeehouses, to the movies (listen to the conversation of young people with their dates as they stand in a movie line), to the discothèques, to sports events. Feel the atmosphere, watch the expressions on faces, experience the eagerness and excitement. To whatever extent you feel is appropriate, engage in the kinds of activities which your own young enjoy—swimming, tennis, dancing, cycling, working on a car—or talking ("rapping") until late at night. Or, if you are willing to take the punishment, sit in a school class for a few hours and try to imagine doing this for four or five hours a day every day. Or attend a rock festival if you can stand the crowds and noise.

To prepare further for the adventure of entering the mind and heart of a young person, reflect on the wide differences that exist between (a) the position the young person occupies in today's world, (b) the position you occupy and (c) the position you occupied when you were young. How different these three positions can be is not often taken into account by adults. Have you assumed, for example, that there is a straight road from where the young person now is to where you are, and that all he has to do to arrive at your place in life is to follow it? If so, you may discover that *he* does not see it that way at all. He may not even want to go to where you are. Or do you assume that the problems he now faces are much the same as (or perhaps simpler than) the problems you faced when you were his age? Are you sure? You may find, when you get better acquainted with him, that it is quite otherwise.

How Young People Experience Life

Let us look at some of the ways in which the young experience life, which if you can empathize with them, may throw light on the young people's attitudes toward you, your values, your beliefs and your life-styles.

1. Living on the Economic Periphery

The young tend to live either on the periphery of the economy or at its bottom. Few young people possess any appreciable property or what the adult world considers a "good job with a future." Many do not want such a job and would not take it if it were offered to them. The kind of work and life that the adult has spent a lifetime trying to achieve may look to the young like a bore or a drag; his interests are elsewhere.

The idea of a nine-to-five job in business, industry or government is unappealing to a significant number of young people, not because they hate work (they will work incredible hours on something in which they are really interested) but because, from their point of view, there are better uses of time and energy. Some of those uses (from their viewpoint) may be the cultivation of their own feelings and talents, the making or creating of something their own, the reaching out for new experiences, the discovery of who they are and of who others are, and the building of close relationships. Measured against these goals, the life of a nine-to-five worker who has neglected these human values looks like a starved life.

Older people are apt to make harsh judgments about this attitude when they come up against it; but such judgments have little effect except to close the doors of communication. A more productive approach is to inquire what forces have produced such a widespread rejection of the traditional work ethic. Simplistic answers like "they're all spoiled" get us nowhere.

To begin with, our form of society largely shuts young people out of the prevailing political and economic order. That order has been built primarily by adults for adults. The only jobs available to most teen-agers are the bottom jobs—waitresses, car hops, bellhops, messengers, service station attendants, mechanics' helpers, ushers, and the like. Older people take this condition for granted ("We started at the bottom, didn't we?"), but the young do not. The young people observe that, to reach the better-paying jobs and professions, they must endure long years of schooling during which they either have to struggle without money, living from hand to mouth, or remain for a long time dependent on their parents. They feel like economic parasites. This condition, both emotionally and intellectually, separates the young from the established order. Their response in some cases is to remain perpetually adolescent with a stunted Maturing Self Dimension, and in other cases, it is to reject the social order. Or both.

This is a rather new phenomenon in history, for in the simpler agrarian economy of the past the young were very much wanted and needed. Then they were an economic asset from an early age and became, while still children, a functioning part of the adult world, working alongside their elders and doing work similar to that done by older people. The young could feel accepted by that world; they were part of it. There was little reason then for the young to construct a world of their own which excluded adults and denied many of the adults' values. Today, the adult world virtually compels them to do it and then blames them for it.

The feelings of the young have been quite effectively communicated in recent years in their modes of dress and their hair styles. Nothing could more clearly express the message to the older generation: "We are not with you!" In its more extreme form, the message is: "We have nothing to do with you!" It is as if some of the young deliberately set about to provoke censure in order to bring into the sharpest possible focus the difference between them and the older generation. The feeling that they have no accepted place in a world mostly made by and for adults encourages them to assert their differentness and to play down similarity (except with each other). Their sense of identity is built upon it.

2. *The "Here and Now"*

Another characteristic of the young is their tendency to live in the "here and now." To some extent, this feeling is innate in the mere fact of being young. For many young people, the present seems more real than the past or the future. Doubt about what the future may bring intensifies that feeling. If I do not know whether I will have a future or whether my future will be worth striving for, I am likely to put my attention on what is happening *now;* I will get what I can out of the present and try to forget the future. But that reaction is incompatible with the demands society makes for long years of education and training for a profession or, in fact, for almost any line of work that calls for knowledge or skill. Thus, I am caught in a vicious circle: The more doubts I have about the future, the less interest I may have in long-term preparations for it; and the less I prepare for the future, the more doubts I will have.

In countless families this cycle produces a battle between the parents, caught up in the traditional pattern of working hard to build an established position in the community, and their sons and daughters who may care little about such an "established position." The children probably don't expect to stay in the community—it is not theirs. Their dreams may not envision business success or a comfortable job in the local bank. Some of the more thoughtful young may have as their model a free, uncluttered lifestyle in which comparatively little money, and therefore little work, is needed, clothes are minimal and simple, and they can come and go as the spirit moves them. These ideas blossomed in the "hippie" styles of the sixties.

It is not difficult to see how such attitudes can lead to the actions that worry adults the most: overindulgence in sex and drugs. These are here-and-now experiences. The girl and boy are together now. The pot or LSD are here now, and the future for these young people is distant and easily put out of mind. If there is to be punishment, it may come tomorrow but not tonight.

3. *Frustration*

The young have longings that are difficult, perhaps impossible, to satisfy. So do nearly all of us regardless of age; but older people are more likely to have come to terms with their longings, to have found ways to achieve the achievable (for them) and to have abandoned useless efforts to do the impossible (for them). The young are not (and should not be) ready for this kind of yielding. And the frustrations they feel are of an intensity that may be unfamiliar to many adults—or forgotten by them.

To begin with, the young have been brought up in the TV age in a society that has made a highly developed art out of the creation of wants. TV alone generates an enormous pressure of desires, not merely by its commercials but also because the medium itself wipes out the horizon; it puts the viewer in visual contact with all parts of the earth. TV inevitably will create in almost any young person an urge to travel and to experience. On top of this, the economies of the developed nations are geared to the creation of an ever-rising demand for consumer goods and services, and a formidable array of organized effort is devoted to the stimulation of desire.

But to satisfy the kind of wants that TV and the other media stimulate costs ever-increasing amounts of money. The flow and investment of money is, of course, the ultimate purpose of the whole effort. Demand, therefore, is tied to production and the creation of capital and employment. But young people, as we have noted, are kept largely outside this system or choose to remain outside of it. Many are students, not yet emotionally or educationally prepared for regular, high-paying employment and savings. Many others, particularly some of the more sensitive and perceptive, have turned their backs on the system and feel hostile toward it, as for example, the young man who said to me, "That world out there is just shit!" Even those young people who want to remain in the system find it frustrating to be subjected continually to the stimulation of wants that cannot be satisfied until some distant time, if ever; and some, after years of patient study and preparation, cannot find jobs.

Many older people who have come up the hard way by their own efforts shrug off young people's wants by the comment: "Let them earn it like the rest of us did!" But those adults do not allow for the enormous intensification of deliberately manipulated want-creation since they themselves were young. This might be illustrated by the difference between a pre-World War II Ford and a late-model Lincoln Continental. The present younger generation has been stimulated to want very much more and to want

158 OPEN FAMILY LIVING

it more intensely than any generation before them, yet their capacity to satisfy these wants has not kept pace. Their education is being stretched out farther and farther: junior college, college, graduate school. And much of the burden of this expense is falling on the young themselves. At the same time, tuitions have gone up far faster than incomes. Thus, the satisfaction of material wants is necessarily postponed by many of the young to an indefinite future.

Young people, in many cases, cannot live in the neighborhoods in which their parents live—and a good many would not if they could. Great numbers of the young are compelled by economic pressures not of their making to congregate in poor, run-down sections of cities or to live as groups in communes. That they should begin to question or oppose (or that some should even dream of overthrowing) a social and economic system that operates so greatly to their disadvantage should surprise no one.

The greatest frustrations felt by the young are probably not economic, but rather mental and spiritual. These frustrations are caused in part by the gap between what we claim to be as a society and as people and what we actually are. We claim to be a peace-loving people, yet we were engaged in what appeared, to many youthful eyes at least, to have been an excessively cruel and unjust war in a faraway land—Vietnam. We claim to believe in justice, yet we do not treat rich and poor equally before the law. We claim to have a government of the people by the people and for the people, yet the impression of many young persons is that our government is run by an elite group that, as far as they can see (for many have little faith in their elders), are using it to benefit themselves and their friends. Watergate has hardened that conviction, but the conviction was already there. Our country has an electoral process that was intended to vest political power in representatives of the people, yet the attempts of the young to be heard in one political convention a few years ago were (as great numbers of the young view it) met by suppression and violence. We have an economy that we boast is the best system on earth, but many of the young are disturbed by the fact that its benefits are withheld from sizable elements of the population, resulting in a hazardous and unjustified gap between the poor and the rich.

Many young are far more aware of these discrepancies than their parents were at their age and are often more concerned about them, less willing to accept things as they are, more dedicated to change. A substantial number of young people see the land that they will one day inherit as having been raped and plundered by their forebears with no thought to the well-being of those who will come after; and some are very bitter about it.

Some rock music focuses directly on these failures and injustices. Cat Stevens, for example, wrote a song describing the great advances society has made with its planes and skyscrapers, but ended each verse with the plaintive question, "Where do the children play?"

4. Distrust

This younger generation is not a trusting generation, as many adults are discovering to their distress. The distrust was partly created by a series of betrayals to which most adults have probably given rather little thought. A child feels betrayed if he discovers he has been lied to by someone he trusted; if he has been promised something that was never delivered; if he has been assured of something that turns out to be untrue; if his parents pretend to a love which they do not feel; or if someone on whom he depends abandons him.

Parents are rarely conscious of the extent to which they lie to little children. This is an old practice—our grandparents were expert at it; but many parents do it still. They lie about death ("Grandma has gone away for a while"), birth ("Your mother has gone to the hospital to get a new baby brother"), serious illness ("Dad isn't feeling well today, but he'll be all right soon"), disaster ("Don't worry, everything will be O.K."), and so on. The motive may be to protect the child from shock or hurt, but the effect often is to undermine trust since it becomes obvious eventually that the parent's assurances are not to be believed.

As children grow up, they are exposed to a long succession of lies by authoritative figures coming at them from all directions. The advertising hokum that sells products, the public relations releases of government and other institutions, the lies that leaders of nations unblushingly tell each other and their own peoples, the falsehoods embedded in nationalistic history books, the speeches of political candidates—all these are so studded with half-truths or total falsehoods that no intelligent listener can continue for very long to believe in official statements. Skepticism becomes a way of life—a necessary one if a person is not to be manipulated and have all his choices made for him by others.

The manner in which advertising is alternated with the transmission of legitimate information compounds the distrust. A TV news program in which the newscasters are describing serious or world-shaking events is interrupted every few minutes by toothpaste and deodorant commercials which are an insult to the intelligence and an affront to good taste. The disbelief which one must, in self-defense, attach to the commercials can spill over to the news broadcast. Important events can become trivialized, and in time the viewer may come to scoff at everything, including himself. The distrust is further accentuated by the media's habit of playing up sensational news when more important but less "entertaining" events may be passed over.

Another factor that contributes to distrust is the incessant controversy, much of it self-serving and dishonest, that rages between ideologies, political persuasions, economic theories, religious doctrines, value systems, and academic schools of thought. The young person hears "experts" in almost every field attacking their fellow "experts," each doubting the other's premises and conclusions and questioning the other's judgments. Many of these opinion makers are obviously in the pay of special interests as, for example, the tobacco industry or the drug industry; their viewpoints are bought and are therefore suspect. Other supposed authorities are observed to be in the pay of governmental bodies that have their own policy objectives to pursue—those objectives rarely, if ever, including the seeking of truth for its own sake. Research and communications, as many of the young see them, have both become so contaminated with power struggles and jockeying for position that doubt becomes the only practicable defense.

Many of the young feel betrayed by all this tampering with truth, and an expression of their feeling was given in the "Border Song" of Elton John with the words: "I've been poisoned from my head down to my shoes. Holy Moses, I have been deceived."

5. Rage

The hostility of many young people toward their parents and toward authority in general is often accompanied by suppressed rage. Some of the reasons for this rage have already been explored: the separation of the young from the prevailing system with which many feel little in common; their economic and spiritual frustrations; their feelings of betrayal due to being lied to and manipulated by the many agencies of the established system—these are enough to produce a smoldering rage. But there are other reasons as well.

This is, at times, a terrifying world. Not that the world ever was a calm or secure place. But certainly at no time in the past have so many frightening and seemingly insoluble problems been paraded with full sound and color before our eyes. The present-day young (and some who are now parents) were born in troubled years following a terrible war brought finally to a dreadful conclusion by twin nuclear holocausts. They are the first generation in history to have grown up at a time in which the survival of the entire planet and all its living creatures has come under threat. There have been times, of course, when civilizations were tottering, life was precarious and the future looked bleak. But never before has such a horror as the possible obliteration of all life on earth assaulted the human consciousness. Dragons appear to be closing in on mankind from at least four directions at once: threatened overpopulation of the planet, exhaustion of its food and other resources, ecological disaster from poisons and waste, and the possibility of nuclear annihilation. The young did not create these monsters. The monsters were, in fact, created by a way of life toward which great numbers of us have directed our energies and still do. Therefore, it should not surprise us if some of the blame, unfair though it may seem, is directed by the young squarely at us.

If the world is, in reality, hurtling toward disaster carrying all mankind with it, someone has to pull the emergency brake if any exists. And who is in a position to do this except the responsible members of adult society? It is adults, and only adults, who possess the power to act. But, from the viewpoint of the young, these adults are not acting. They are pursuing "business as usual." The more thoughtful young feel desperately trapped. They have virtually no power of their own except, perhaps, the power to disrupt and make trouble. They possess no board of directors' seats, few executive positions, no chairs in the National Security Council, no chairmanships of legislative committees, and, until recently, not even any voting power in the American political scene. Their voices are not heard. Some become apathetic, some defiant. Some have rioted.

Any society appears much less beneficent from the bottom looking up than from a point between the middle and the top looking down. From near the bottom, where the young, the blacks and other minority groups, the working women and the poor seem to be stranded, the established middle and top layers have the appearance of an entrenched, largely male, white "in group" bent on preserving its privileges and pursuing its own interests. The Establishment can very easily appear to be an enemy to those shut out of it, and a dismaying number of the young see it precisely in that way. The distrust is often mutual because the young, the blacks, the women and the poor are increasingly turning toward the use of organized political and other kinds of power to upset those elements of the *status quo* that work to their disadvantage.

The views of many of the young on war and patriotism are shocking and incomprehensible to many older people. These feelings are a logical outcome of the exclusion of the young from the existing political and social order. The traditional military virtues that envision willingness of the young to serve in defense of their country are eroding, not only in the United States but in a number of other countries as well. Great numbers of the young are openly hostile to the entire military-industrial-governmental system. A considerable number viewed the draft, when it was in effect, as a tyrannical abuse of power by a government which they did not trust. The days of the poor, ignorant greenhorn who simply obeys orders and asks no questions seem to be coming to an end. Today's young people think for themselves, doubt, question, challenge authority, and, if still unconvinced, sometimes disobey and sometimes emigrate.

The older generations are in a weak moral position to lecture the young about obeying the draft laws. Some of us are descended from immigrants who fled Europe to escape conscription. Many of the grandparents of today's youth ignored the prohibition laws in the twenties; and some of their great grandparents participated in the illegal shooting wars between industrialists and strikers in the nineteenth century when labor unions were being built. Educated young people observe cynically that many of the same adults who cry loudest for law and order are the ones who protest busing for desegregation by terrorizing children and destroying buses. Law, apparently, is a good thing when it serves those particular people's interests but can be conveniently ignored when it does not. The Watergate episode and the campaign contribution scandals were examples of this. The young observe, too, that while many of their male members were compelled to serve in the armed forces under conditions of extreme privation and danger, and while good jobs were hard for veterans to find when they returned, many of their elders lived comfortably at home, made good incomes and demanded ever-rising wages and increased privileges. These young people, then, are not much impressed by older folks who berate them for avoiding their military obligations. As many of them see it, the young have been cynically exploited as a group while the older generation has continued to pile up wealth and power for itself. The failure of government to require anything approximating equal sacrifice from all elements of the population in recent years has resulted in a loss of faith in the leadership that may take a long time to heal.

6. *The Sexual Gap*

The young see little connection between what is preached about sex and what is practiced. They read books and watch movies that portray explicitly all kinds of sexual behavior. Yet rarely are they afforded an opportunity to discuss sex sensibly with knowledgeable, unembarrassed adults. Conventional teachings continue to condemn sex outside of marriage as a wrongful act; yet a torrent of written words and visual images in all media present such sex as if it were the biggest thing in life. When the young look at this confusion, they draw conclusions that often conflict with their parents' teachings.

The problem is compounded by the blatant commercial exploitation of sex, not primarily by the young! In earlier times, prostitution was the most familiar route by which money was made out of sex. Today, prostitution is small stuff. The big money is made in advertising and the media; in the production of sex books and films; in the manufacture and sale of drugs, contraceptives and clothes geared to sexual appeal; in abortion services; and in innumerable peripheral industries. Deliberate sexual stimulation has become big business in the same way that the stimulation of other consumer wants is big business. But this is a form of dehumanization because the factors that make sexual activity *human*—the delicate interplay of body, thoughts and emotions—have been crudely amputated, and all that is left in much of the material presented to the public is body reacting to body.

The more perceptive and sensitive young people are in rebellion against dehumanized conceptions of sex. They want human relationships on a human level, and they see sex as a legitimate part of those relationships. Many of them regard the double standard (by which sexual adventures by males are tolerated while those by females are condemned) as indefensible. Increasing numbers of the young (particularly young women) argue that if boys can engage freely in sex without injury to themselves or their reputations, girls should be free to do so as well. In large areas of the young people's world, sexual intercourse by girls no longer carries social stigma.

Unlike the older generations, which engaged in a fair amount of illicit sex in their day but generally admitted that what they did *was* illicit, certain elements of the younger generation are challenging the reasonableness and even the morality of the standards of conduct that forbid sex outside of marriage. This alarms many older people; for, *to break a rule is one thing, but to deny the validity of the rule is another*. The traditional admonitions concerning sexual conduct are deeply embedded in religious, ethical, philosophical and social teachings and are supported by the prevailing political and legal systems. To challenge them involves far more than a little temporary rule breaking to be regretted and patched up later. If such a challenge turned into a general movement, it could mean a revolution in human relationships with unforeseeable consquences.

It is important that adults should understand how this question of sex looks to the young, how confused it appears, how poorly the older generation has prepared the young to deal with it, how dehumanized the sex act has become through its commercial exploitation, and how a number of traditional objections to premarital sex have been weakened by modern contraceptive practices, medical progress and social change. What the young need is sympathetic help, not just rigid rules or strict prohibitions. Proof of this need is the soaring rate of premarital pregnancies (many of them of teen-agers), the torrent of abortions, and the devastating and entirely unnecessary spread of venereal disease. Great numbers of the young are in trouble as a result of evils not of their making, and are getting inadequate help from their elders.

7. *Human Relationships*

A widely prevalent characteristic of young people (and a very hopeful one) is the high value they put on human relationships. The young are drawn to each other, sometimes in opposition to the adult world, but more often simply because they enjoy each other's company. They sprawl on the floor, play guitars, sing, talk far into the night, pass around a "joint," raid the family refrigerator. Their attachment to each other is simple, honest and human. They do not, as so many adults do, base friendships on business associations, social climbing, professional status, money, reputation or politics, where expedience, business advantage and prestige are the objectives rather than mutual enjoyment. To many of the young, the interpersonal relationships of their elders look shallow and superficial.

Many young people enjoy just being together, even if they are not doing anything special. They draw a feeling of identity from each other—something they do not always find in the company of adults. The adult who "takes a trip" into the world of the young may have forgotten what it feels like simply to be yourself in company with another who is being himself—no need to impress, to sell, to persuade or to entertain. The conditions that tend to separate adults—racism, nationalism, politics, religion, ideologies, business competition, money, social status, physical attractiveness, unequal education, etc.—are much less strongly felt in the world of the young than in adult society. For a substantial number of the young, these divisive factors are virtually non-existent. Such matters are looked upon as adult concerns, really, and the young are frequently mystified by the importance adults attach to them.

Because human relationships are so much more important to the young than are institutions and abstractions, an adult who lives in the non-personal world of symbols and mental constructs may have to make a big mental switch when he enters the young people's world. The businessman has to forget, for the time being, his concern with balance sheets, sales and profits. The lawyer or judge has to leave behind his world of interpretations, abstracts, decisions and precedents and pay close attention to a young person whose only contact with the law may have been a nasty bout with an unsympathetic policeman. The governmental official or employee has to move out of his world of policies, power manipulation, records and statistics to converse with a young person who may question some of the basic assumptions under which he carries on his work. It is disconcerting for an older person to discover that his young son or daughter questions the *aims*—the *goals*— of what he does. It is at this point that the relationship between the generations often breaks down and meaningful communication comes to an end.

But if human relationship is important, it must be durable enough to pass this test. The adult may need to listen open-mindedly to ideas radically different from (and sometimes very antagonistic to) his own, and to ask himself these questions: "What is my son's (daughter's) view of the world? How did he/she come to hold these views? Do I respect his/her right to hold these views? Can I help him/her think them through? Can I allow him/her to change my own attitudes or values?"

The adult who believes that his own views are based on a long accumulation of experience and knowledge may be tempted to dismiss the young person's opinions as "shallow" or ignorant and to assume that such immature notions will change "as the kid gets older." This I-know-best attitude infuriates the young person because it seems to say, "You are only a child and your views are of little account."

8. *Life-styles*

A settled, conventionally oriented adult may have some difficulty in understanding the life-style of a modern young person. And, similarly, the young person may have problems in understanding the life-style of his elders. The father, for example, may enjoy living in a house in the suburbs with a large lawn around it. His son may find this choice incredible. "Who wants to live in the suburbs, man? Who needs a lawn to mow?" The son might prefer a "pad" in the big city where he can stow a hi-fi and scatter cushions on the floor. Crossing these life-style gulfs may not be easy.

The mother may enjoy dressing well, keeping an attractive house, being an admired hostess and a sought-after guest, meeting her friends in town for dinner and the theater (if she can afford it), driving a late-model car, and so on. Her daughter may run around in torn dungaree shorts and an old shirt, leave her things strewn all over her room, meet her friends on the street corner near the drug store, and ride a bicycle. Her mother buys her a nice dress and she does not bother to wear it. Can either of these two understand the other?

But suppose the parents examine the assumptions that underlie their children's life-styles. The boy's rejection of the suburban lawn-mowing style might be understandable if the father knew that big houses, fancy furniture and shiny cars add little to the boy's feeling of status among his peers. The shrubbed, manicured lawn that appeals to the suburbanite social set can seem a burdensome nuisance to the young person (who is often saddled with the mowing job). Some young people want to spend as little time as possible in taking care of *things*. Cushions are cheaper and easier to care for than chairs; so who needs chairs?

The girl's rejection of pretty dresses may be understandable if the mother takes into account the changes that have taken place in dating practices. Girls of an earlier era were frequently engaged in manhunting; that was their primary object in life—which is a theme of Tennessee Williams' play, *The Glass Menagerie*. Pretty dresses were, of course, a necessary part of the "bait." This is what the mother probably has in the back of her mind. But the capture of a possible husband has a much lower priority in the minds of many teen-age girls of today. They have less economic need of men; they can get jobs and support themselves. Many would like to get married ultimately, but why should they be in a hurry? They can have fun with boys without being serious about long-term commitments. They don't need to dress up. In any case, they may want to be experienced as persons rather than as sex objects.

As the parents reflect on these differences, they could ask themselves also whether the young person's rejection of their life-styles is a genuine, reasoned choice or a retaliatory, possibly unconscious, reaction to the climate of the home. If, for example, the atmosphere of a beautiful, well-appointed home is cold, impersonal and repressive, the chairs are too antique to be sat on, and the parents are away a great deal, is it surprising that the young person reacts by swinging over to the opposite extreme—perhaps a small, cramped, dingy, messy, but warmly satisfying room on a back alley? Change the climate of the big house to a warm, accepting, joyous one, and the young person's preferences might change.

When adults pay attention to the life-styles of the young, they often find themselves beginning (surreptitiously) to admire certain aspects of those styles. Values such as money, possessions, reputation or prestige, which are so important to many adults, begin to seem less compelling than formerly. They do not compare well with the values sought by the more thoughtful young people: genuineness, openness, honesty, unpretentiousness, sincerity, warmth, acceptance, reaching out. These qualities are prized also in the adult world, yet in the struggle for survival they are frequently lost.

A Youth's Adventure into the World of the Adult

Now, suppose we reverse the "trip" and invite the young to experience the adult world as the adult experiences it. This is a "trip" few young people take for they prefer their own world. Yet, if the young could gain a deeper knowledge of their elders' world, their comprehension of their own world would be enhanced, just as familiarity with a foreign country and its people sharpens one's perceptions and understanding of one's own.

Many of the young show a tendency at times to dismiss their parents' life-styles as dull, stupid, crazy, hopeless, and the like.

And, indeed, sometimes these descriptions hit the mark. But the young have their own hang-ups and limitations; they are rarely as alive or as fully in control of where they are going as they would like to be. Many get trapped in premature, unwise marriages that bind them to years of frustration. Some fall into addictions that closely resemble the addictions experienced by their parents. Alcoholism, for example, is growing at an alarming rate among the young. Great numbers of young people are addicted to excessive cigarette smoking and some, of course, to drug usage. But probably the most common hindrance to personal growth is the slow, imperceptible weaving of the threads of convention and habit which, in the long run, often leave even former firebrands as dull and tame as the older generations they once horrified. The next generation, too often, simply falls in line behind the older one twenty-five years later.

LIVING IN THE ADULT WORLD

One way the young might save themselves from getting caught in this trap would be to expand their knowledge of what it is really like to live in the adult world. If they took a trip into that world, here are some of the things they might find.

1. The "Feel" of Heavy Responsibility

The responsibilities carried by parents are generally of a different order from those to which young unmarried people have been accustomed. The young person may have been raised to take responsibility for his personal life and for the care of himself, his room and his clothes. He may carry out job duties well. But to be responsible for bringing a new life into the world, for the care of a baby, for the raising of a child, for the support of a family, for a family's present and future well-being—that is something of a different order of magnitude. The young person should try to get the "feel" of it.

The limitations this kind of responsibility can place on freedom of action are obvious. A family breadwinner thinks twice before doing things that might cost him his job. If he loses his job, the entire family could suffer deprivation. How much abuse he is willing to take from his superiors and co-workers has to be balanced against his need for the work, his family's needs for his income and the difficulties of finding other work. If the breadwinner loves to fish but has to choose between a fishing trip for himself and buying needed clothes for his children, he may have to give up the trip. Or he may voluntarily forego it because his wife doesn't like fishing and he wants to do something for her. Or he may give it up in order to save money for going back to school to prepare himself for a better job. Or he may be heavily involved in some community service, such as raising funds for the local hospital, and be unwilling to take time off because of this. (Do not be too quick to feel sorry for him; he may be gaining other satisfactions that could mean more to him, ultimately, than fishing.)

There is no doubt that the *habit* of feeling weighed down by responsibilities and anxieties can shut off many of the good things of life. Adults sometimes let this happen without being quite aware of the progressive, loop-by-loop entwinement that is hemming them in. The young, if they are understanding enough, might help their parents to identify this process and to break out of it; for to become unnecessarily burdened by anxiety until all the sunshine goes out of life is to build one's own prison.

But there is another side to responsibility. Carrying heavy responsibilities can be an enlivening experience. It can stimulate growth. Which would you rather be (aside from the difference in earning power): an assembly worker who does only what he is told, or the plant superintendent who is responsible for the operation of an entire plant? The superintendent probably has a thousand problems, headaches and crises to deal with every day. He may develop stomach ulcers. But would he trade his job for the assembly worker's even if the two were paid the same? That depends on how he sees his job. If to him carrying the superintendent's load means learning, growing, meeting challenges, drawing upon more and more of his potential, encountering the new and unexpected—in other words, a real adventure—he might not willingly give it up.

Bringing a family into the world, providing food and shelter for it, nurturing it, helping its members to realize their potential as human beings—that also can evolve into an adventure of a high order. It usually is not experienced as one, but it could be.

2. Defensiveness

Young people sometimes comment derisively on how defensive their parents are—"uptight" is one favorite description. It is not difficult to understand why this is so. The more you have of anything—money, possessions, ideas, opinions, talents, dreams, power—the more disturbed you are likely to be by a threat of their loss.

If you own an expensive hi-fi and a color television set and there have been robberies in your neighborhood, you would probably put a much stronger lock on your door than you would if all you possessed were an old shirt and two pairs of socks. The adult is likely to have possessions—material, intellectual and emotional—which he has spent much of his lifetime accumulating and is not likely to give up without a struggle. Unless you yourself possess something that you cherish, you cannot easily know how he feels. The fact that he cherishes different things from those that are valuable to you should have no bearing on your understanding of his defensiveness.

Opinions may be defended by a closed-style parent even more passionately and strongly than are physical possessions because his investment in them (and therefore the threat posed by an attack) is greater. It may have taken but a few months' savings to buy the TV, but the parent's views about economics, politics and other matters may have been his constant companions for years. They may have been handed down by his own parents (Internalized Others). An attack on his views may trigger a response almost as if he were being held up a gunman and robbed.

Another kind of defensiveness is the clinging to an idea, a feeling or a life-style because it seems "natural" and "right," even though it is difficult to defend with a rational argument. Many adults are very rigid about such matters as how children should behave to their parents ("In my day . . ."), how jobs should be performed ("This is the *right* way"), how late young people should stay out at night, how boys and girls should behave toward each other, and innumerable other topics. The rigidity is due partly to fear of being forced, by argument or other pressures, to retreat from these positions that seem "natural" and "right." Any attempt to change such a person's views may be experienced by him as an attack to be resisted.

Are the young so very different, however? What happens when an older person tries to convince a long-haired kid to have his hair cut? Defensiveness is certainly not a monopoly of any age group. And, by observing how he himself reacts to having his life-style questioned, a young person may gain some sympathetic insight into why adults get uptight.

3. Stodginess

Over and over, the youth sees his parents or his teachers as stodgy or dull. Perhaps they are. There are dulled people everywhere. (I speak of "dulled" rather than "dull" because I am not talking about limited intelligence. People are dulled by a variety of repressive influences that they have not learned to counteract.)

But suppose the parent or teacher does appear dulled. Is he really as deadened as he seems to be? Or is the apparent dullness a consequence of closed communication between him and the young person? It might be that, with someone he can respond to, he lights up. Has either the older person or the youth attempted to make real contact with the other and draw him out?

The stodginess of the older person may not be his real nature but rather his reaction to something either within or outside of himself. It may be a job or boss that he hates, a spouse that he cannot endure, discouragement at the state of the world or at his own lack of progress in it, contempt at his own weaknesses, fear of the future, worry about his income tax—it may be any number of things. Some young people dismiss their elders (including parents) as "hopeless" without making a real attempt to break through the barrier. But a parent might be worth getting to know. To find out *why* he has been dulled and discouraged and to help him emerge from that state could offer a rewarding opportunity for a young person.

4. Becoming a "Stooge of the Establishment"

Young people who are critical of the Establishment for the many reasons summarized earlier may have feelings of disillusionment about their parents' participation in the very things they think wrong. They may be bothered when they see their parents meekly pay income taxes to support a government that they perceive to be corrupt and warlike. They may be disturbed when they see their parents cultivate friends whom they know to be racist; or see them work for a corporation that pollutes the environment or makes materials that maim or kill; or find them compromising with the truth in the promotion of a business venture. Can such a young person take a "trip" into this adult world that looks so corrupt and try to understand it?

Before condemning his parents for a lack of moral perception, the young person might consider the possibility that they are, or have at one time been, as disturbed by some of these moral issues as he is. Many an employee of a corporation or government agency has fought a silent, unhappy inner battle to reconcile his position with the ultimate effects his work may produce. As an example, I think of an employee of a manufacturing company whose son, a conscientious objector, upbraided his father for working for a corporation that supported the war effort in Vietnam. The father, who had doubts of his own about the rightness of that war, had struggled with the same moral question but had come to the conclusion that a compromise was justified. His own work was not directly war-oriented. He therefore did not resign. He had found that *there are few absolutes in life*. He could see no way in a modern industrial state to separate one's self completely from a war effort conducted by that state. He had to satisfy himself with a partial or symbolic separation—an avoidance of too *direct* an involvement.

It is sometimes difficult for the young, who tend to see life in sharp black-and-white contrasts, to appreciate the enormous gray areas in which most adults are forced to operate. For example, to the impassioned young people who opposed the Vietnam war, the conflict appeared an outrage—absolutely evil. Therefore, everyone who had anything to do with it had to be evil, from the President down. An adult who has had to deal with gray areas all his life knows that this is not so. He sees people and issues having both light and dark sides, both good and evil aspects. None is wholly one or the other. And in this generalization, he includes himself. The corporation he works for may have done some things that he knows are wrong; but it has also done some useful, beneficial things. Part of his income taxes go for war, but another part goes for rebuilding the run-down sections of cities. The automobile pollutes the air, but it also carries people to and from work, and so on. The mature adult finds in his world a complex, interrelated system in which everything affects everything else; and you cannot separate certain functioning parts, call them "bad" and treat them as if they worked all by themselves.

Yet, the young person may wonder how the adult has come to live in such a featureless moral landscape; such a web of expediency. The condition probably came about through the cumulative effect of a multitude of little decisions: the decision not to notify the local building inspector of an observed code violation by a neighbor; the decision to install one's own electrical outlet (because one knows how) although, by law, only a licensed electrician is supposed to do it; the decision to exceed a local speed limit on an empty road when no one is around; the decision to use a reasonable but slightly high estimate of business deductions on an income tax return; and so on. Each decision can be defended, each is the kind of decision many people make every day, and yet their sum-total puts a person at the edge of a moral twilight zone. Most day-to-day decisions do not involve a clear-cut, right-or-wrong issue. The young person, if he reviews the day-to-day choices he himself makes, will realize that he, too, makes small compromises. He may discover that absolute truth is what we usually demand of the other fellow but not too often of ourselves. He may then be a little more tolerant of his parent's tendency toward expediency.

As the young person takes his trip into the adult world, he will probably discover another fact: there is no such thing as the Establishment. It is a trick phrase, a stereotype. From outside, the world of those who possess money, power and influence looks monolithic. From inside, it is seen to be a jungle of conflicting ambitions, power plays, opinions, reputations and systems. It rages with competition and struggle; different elements of the Establishment are pitted against each other. So the term Establishment means little more than a particular mode of authority, ownership and control. It is certainly not a fixed group of people, because the people constituting the Establishment are constantly changing.

These, then, are a few of the discoveries that a young person might make in this trip through the adult world. In time, he may make many more which we cannot detail here. As he makes them, his horizons will expand for the adult world is not quite the dreary place the young person may have once thought it. It is exciting and invigorating to confront hard realities that demand all one's strength, knowledge and ingenuity. The hidden motive for the youth's avoiding the adult world may have been fear of inadequacy, fear of failure, fear of being overwhelmed. For, indeed, the adult world can deal mercilessly with those who do not meet its terms.

The Generations Need Each Other

Each generation lives in a world that seems valid for *it*. Neither world embraces more than a tiny proportion of the whole of reality. Each world has gaps, dangers, failures, mistakes, follies; and there is unhappiness and unfulfillment in each. But neither can wholly replace the other. Without the adult world of industry, commerce, government, labor, banking, the professions and the work related to all of these, the world of the young would soon collapse; there would be no cars, boats, skis, houses, hospitals, clothing or food. But without the world of the young with emphasis on personal relationships and fulfillment, the adult world would grow increasingly abstract, dehumanized and violent, as depicted in such horrifying novels as *1984*. Neither generation can live successfully without the other.

Suggested Interaction Experiences

IE-17. EXAMINING THE GAPS BETWEEN GENERATIONS IN YOUR FAMILY (P. 145)

Make an honest appraisal of the gaps between you and each of your parents and (if you are a parent) between you and each of your children. Consider these gaps in terms of attention, acceptance and security. For example, was (or is) your parent too busy to give you adequate *attention?* Did you (or do you) feel *accepted* as a person by your parent or young person? Has constant parental bickering brought about feelings of *insecurity* in your family?

EVALUATION: What effects do current alienations have on you and other family members? Do you feel that you may be contributing, or have contributed, to these alienations? What is the one greatest inter-generational gap in your family now? Do you want to work on it and try to reduce it?

FOLLOW-UP: Discuss your findings with other family members. Encourage them to participate in this experience and compare their ideas and feelings with yours. This can widen everyone's understanding of the gaps.

IE-18. PRACTICING EMPATHY (P. 150)

Close your eyes. Mentally and emotionally, put yourself in the "skin" of another person as you imagine he might think, feel and act in a particular circumstance. This means abandoning your own identity for the moment and adopting the other person's characteristic style of response. Try to mimic, if you can, his body movements, facial expressions, speech patterns, attitudes, values and behavior. You may invent your own experiences using people or familiar characters you know well. Or you may try some of the following suggestions: (1) You are Evel Knieval at the instant he realizes that his rocket is going to fall into Snake River Canyon. (2) You are your mother (as you imagine her in her youth) kissing your father for the first time. (3) You are your father (as a little boy) entering his first day of kindergarten. (4) You are your brother who has just heard that his best friend committed suicide. (5) You are your uncle who has just won the $100,000 lottery.

EVALUATION: Were you really able to shed your identity and feel the way these individuals might have felt? Whose "skin" was easiest/hardest to get into? Which response—thinking, feeling or acting—was the easiest or hardest for you to emulate? What did you learn about your ability to empathize with others? Do you need more practice to increase your capacity for empathizing?

FOLLOW-UP: Although these experiences exemplify outstanding moments in a person's life, we have endless, small moment-to-moment opportunities to empathize with others. Try to apply the concept of empathy on as many occasions as possible.

SIX

FAMILIES IN CRISIS: DOES THE OPEN STYLE WORK?

What tears families apart? Money troubles? Interfering in-laws? Extramarital adventuring? Too much liquor? Rebellious kids? The strains of business life?

On one level, yes. These are disruptive—no doubt about it. On another level, situations of this kind can be seen, not as causes, but as *symptoms* or *effects* of family deterioration. Many families are like tires with their tread worn off; the tire may burst when you hit a pothole, but it had become weakened long before.

Blaming family disharmony on things like lack of money or disagreements about the use of money is really passing the buck. Anyone who saw the movie *Sounder* and thought about its implications should have reason to question this notion. The family in *Sounder* had no money—very little of anything, in fact, except a dog. But they held steady as a family and they stayed loyal to each other (and to the dog).

Practically every crisis in a family, no matter what form it takes, originates with someone's internal problems with himself. This precipitates a crisis of *human relationships*. So consistently is this true that many family counselors have ceased to regard quarrels over finances, mothers-in-law, rebellious kids, or even outside lovers, as basically responsible for family disruption. As a counselor listens to family members unburden themselves, his ears are tuned to what happens as the family members interact:

Do they listen to and hear each other? ("You sound worried!")
Or turn each other off? ("He wouldn't hear me if I exploded a firecracker in his ear!")
Do they communicate their feelings? ("I'm a little uncom-

fortable about this.") Or let the feelings pile up in silence
("Oh, never mind!") until they explode later?

Do they respect each other's differences? ("I know you feel
differently than I do about that.") Or deny each other's right
to be different? ("You have no right to feel that way!")

Do they try to build each other up? ("I'm proud of you—let's
celebrate!") Or tear each other down? ("Your breath smells
like a horse's!")

Are they openly affectionate with each other? ("You're beautiful.") Or indifferent and suspicious? ("What is she after
now?")

Do they grant each other freedom? ("If she wants to go back to
school, I think that's great.") Or are they possessive? ("She's
my wife—keep hands off." "He's *my* husband—stay away.")

Do they forgive each other's (and their own) mistakes? ("Let's
put it back together.") Or try to make each other feel guilty?
("You should be ashamed!")

And so on.

These are the kinds of questions that uncover the roots of
family problems.

Third-person Situations

One of the most devastating of the outer events that shatter family
life is the extramarital affair.

The term **affair** calls to mind a sexual or amorous relationship
with someone other than the spouse. But many family crises are
set off by relationships far short of this. I like to use a more gener-
alized and less "loaded" term, like **third person situation,** which
means any case where a marital partner forms a relationship with
a third person, whether sexual or not, that has potential for
disturbing the spouse. The relationship could be sexual or it could
be primarily intellectual, social or personal such as being
engrossed together in a common interest or hobby. Or the third
person may be a business associate or a co-worker with one of the
partners in some project in which the two are absorbed.

The third person is usually real; but there are cases where a symbol or a fantasy takes the place of a person. In one such case, a woman was very unsure of her husband's love, yet was ashamed to admit this feeling to herself. One evening her husband, playing in an amateur theatrical, took the role of a seventeenth-century gentleman who addressed his opposite with formal, courtly phrases like "my dearly beloved." It suddenly struck the wife that he had never addressed *her* in this fashion, and she suddenly felt lost and betrayed. Here there was no real third person (the actress was not a third person); yet the effect on the wife was the same as if there had been one. Although the immediate effect was great pain and confusion on the wife's part, the long-term result was to strengthen her relationship with her husband. She learned about her own anxiety and fears, found ways to deal with them, communicated these feelings to her husband; and he eventually learned to express his affection to her in a more satisfying way.

This case points up the crucial role that imagination plays in a third-person situation. For what upsets a spouse in many cases is not so much what has *actually* happened as what the spouse imagines and fears might have happened or could happen. ("Why did she get home so late?" "Why does he go on so many business trips?" "What is going on?")

The amount of disturbance produced by a third-person situation has rather little to do with what has specifically occurred. An insecure spouse could be upset by a very slight and innocent happening, as, for example, an admiring look. A more secure spouse might remain undisturbed by a considerable degree of involvement, such as a social or business intimacy over an extended period of time.

Extramarital affairs and other third-person situations are increasing rapidly in the United States as men and women are brought into close association in the work place, in commerce, in schools, in professional associations, in union activities, in volunteer activities, in social life, in neighborhoods and in travel. The extended family, which once sheltered and protected women and gave them emotional support, is vanishing. The double standard, by which men justified their own sexual contacts outside of marriage while denying the same privilege to women, is under heavy challenge. Contraceptives are widely available. Women are demanding equality with men in all areas. And our society is becoming not only more urbanized and suburbanized, but we are turning into a nation of transients; many people rarely live long enough in a single location to put down permanent roots. All these factors are expanding both the opportunity and the emotional pressures (such as loneliness) to engage in affairs.

Available data suggest that more than half of all marriages in the United States have been, or will eventually be, involved in an extramarital affair or some other type of third-person situation. Married women are becoming increasingly active in affairs, a trend with unforeseeable consequences.

A popular idea of "open marriage" is that it invites marital affairs. In fact, quite a few people seem to assume that this is what the term "open marriage" means. But my own observation suggests that the extramarital affair is perhaps more likely to be an accompaniment of closed- and directionless-style marriages than it is of open ones.

A *closed- or directionless-style marriage* sets the stage for an affair by its tendency to fall into dullness and stagnation or into unresolved conflicts. Take, for example, the marriage of Sam and Millie. Once lively, it has become a treadmill. Sam, like many husbands, has forgotten that Millie was once an attractive woman whom he chose to be his wife. She has equally forgotten that she once found him an exciting date. Each takes the other for granted. Neither one thinks when he sees the other, "Why, there is a person I would like to know better." Sam has long ceased to pay the little attentions that he gave Millie in their dating days: the small compliments, the expressions of affection, the good-night kiss. He pays little attention to her at all. He is a TV addict. He spends his weekends watching sports events. She is wrapped up in her activities, also; and, finding him unresponsive to any of her interests, she increasingly goes her own separate way. She cooks the meals and is a mother to the children, and that is about it. Sexual relations between Sam and Millie have become as mechanical and spiritless as everything else they do together.

Sam is not aware or sensitive enough to realize that Millie is ripe for an affair. She is getting almost no emotional nourishment from her husband, no encouragement, no mental stimulation and not even much sex. How long is she going to put up with this? In former days, perhaps for a lifetime. But in present-day society, not for very long. She may eventually find herself a man.

Now, let's suppose she does so. She finds a man whose needs and desires to some extent match her own. As she gets to know him, a change comes over her. She regains a long-lost vitality and interest in life.

Now Sam begins to notice his wife's increased animation and becomes suspicious. He questions her sharply. After repeated denials, she finally admits that she has met someone but insists it is not serious and that "nothing has happened." It is true that, so far, Millie and her friend have not had sexual intercourse. But Sam accuses his wife of lying. She is outraged. He becomes authoritarian and forbids her to see the other man. Thus, the value system of the extreme closed style drives him to precisely the actions most likely to exacerbate the situation.

Ironically, the closed style, which so often sets the stage for an affair, is precisely the style that has the most rigid rules against outside liaisons, especially by the wife. The human reaction of partners in a closed marriage is, in some respects, like that of prisoners in a jail. The prisoner is intent on getting out and will break out if he can. A free person, such as a partner in open-style marriage, would have no urge to break out because he is not imprisoned.

The closed style not only increases the pressures to engage in extramarital affairs, it virtually insures that if an affair occurs, it will damage and quite possibly destroy the marriage. The nature of an extremely closed marriage is such that an outside relationship violates its terms and commitments. An affair, therefore, has to be hidden. The secrecy leads to lying, suspicion and undermining of trust between the partners. And affairs often are very hard to keep secret. Someone sees the couple, someone talks or a change in the partner's behavior is noted by the spouse.

An affair in a closed-style marriage can easily lead to a predicament from which, no matter what he does, the involved partner cannot extricate himself. He can neither confess the truth nor manage successfully to hide it. He shrinks from confession, which could cause unimaginable anguish, upset and anger, and perhaps even lead to violence. But hiding can become more and more difficult as time goes on. The situation may run downhill like a truck with defective brakes.

When an affair in a closed-style marriage breaks into the open, emotional reactions are set off in all family members with which often they cannot deal: shame, outrage, guilt, regret, fear, disgust, disillusionment. Furthermore, a third-person situation is likely to be a closed subject for discussion, especially with the children, not only outside the home but inside as well.

If the affair gets known outside, its undermining effects are often compounded. The family may become the target of righteous indignation of in-laws, unsolicited advice from relatives and neighbors, cold stares in the street (if it is a small town), feelings of being the object of gossip and jokes, and all sorts of other pressures. The partners may find themselves pushed toward the conventional rituals of a wounded marriage: the virtuous display of hurt pride, the rejection of the involved partner by his spouse, the implicit assumption by both partners that the marriage is dead, and self-defeating talk of separation and divorce. A spouse in such a mood may terminate the marriage as retaliation or simply to prove that he is right and the involved partner is wrong.

All this is deeply destructive not only of the marriage and family but of the individuals themselves. When these kinds of reactions occur, there is good reason to believe that the extramarital affair was *not* the cause of the marital breakup but rather a symptom of a disarray already present in the marriage. The forces moving toward breakup had very probably been there all along and had finally found their outward expression in the affair, on the one hand, and the family's reactions to it, on the other. An irate mother who says bitterly to her daughter, "If I were you I'd leave the cheating son-of-a-bitch," probably never wanted the marriage to succeed in the first place. She may be saying, "I told you so!"

But other reactions to the affair also are possible. Returning to Sam and Millie, what are the possible effects of Millie's affair on her marriage?

1. *It could destroy it.* Her husband might throw her out and divorce her—a fairly typical closed-style response.

2. *It could result in tightening her husband's possessive hold on her* (if she allows it). He might, in effect, lock her in, forbid her any freedom, get rid of the third party in one way or another (get him fired from his job, for example), and watch suspiciously his wife's every move. This would be another typical closed-style response. But such a reaction would risk driving the wife into rebellion, possibly precipitating more affairs. On the other hand, if Millie bows to her husband's pressures, the old sterile relationship probably would be resumed with redoubled force and she would be a virtual prisoner (a "dead" marriage).

3. *It could lead to the husband's having affairs, too,* either in retaliation or because he feels freed to do so. If his affairs are retaliatory, the marriage could deteriorate further. But if he feels freed, the couple might arrive at an understanding that neither will interfere with the affairs of the other (the marriage of convenience). The marriage might then survive; but, unless the partners work on the quality of their own relationship, there is little life in it. The marriage would not approach the open style in which marital partners encourage each other to grow as persons.

4. *It could improve the marriage.* If Millie's affair has helped free her for a more genuine emotional response and greater sexual freedom, she might return to her marriage a better marital partner than she was before. She might have learned much about how to communicate with a man on a feeling level. She might, for example, have experienced excitement, anticipation, pleasure, enthusiasm and other emotions that had been missing from her life. She might—perhaps for the first time in years— feel adequate as a woman. If Sam, her husband, can bring himself to accept and enjoy the newly awakened woman his wife has become (and if he is galvanized by the competition from the third person to pay more attention to his wife's needs and desires), the marriage could move upward in the qualitative scale—perhaps up to the middle of the range in Figure 3 (p. 106). But Sam would have to abandon a number of fixed positions of the closed marital life-style, such as the idea that he should punish Millie for her "transgressions," or that he should

avenge a "wrong" by beating up her boy friend. He might even have to recognize that the third person is a human being, too.

This happens to be an illustration involving an affair by the wife. It could just as well have been an affair by the husband; most of the points made would have been essentially the same except that, because of the double standard, wives in the past have been more forgiving of wandering husbands than husbands have been of wandering wives. This inequality is rapidly lessening.

Millie and her boy friend are drawn to each other because both are lonely, unfulfilled people, unhappy in their marriages, unable to reach out to their respective spouses and say, "Honey, I'm lonely. Won't you come to me and comfort me a little?" To do this, they would need to know their own feelings better than they do, and to articulate them clearly, which, in fact, is very difficult for them both.

And for their respective marriages to work successfully, Millie and her boy friend would need spouses who could respond to such an open appeal. When you lay bare your feelings in this way, you are very vulnerable. Millie knows that if she had tried to be open in this manner with Sam, he would have growled, "What the hell's the matter with you? I'm busy, don't bother me."

In the *open style,* the husband would pay heed to the wife's need for affection and her need to be affirmed as a person. ("You feel I've been neglecting you! Let's go out for dinner and talk.")

If Sam and Millie had an open-style marriage, Millie might not have had an affair. Or, if she had one, it would occur for different reasons and produce different effects. Among the reasons for possible affairs in the open style are these:

1. *The open style tends to produce people who are warmer and more outgoing than most.* They are good listeners, good companions, good friends. They are often interested in other people, they like people, they are lively and vital themselves, they are not as inhibited in the use of their bodies as are closed-style individuals. They express affection freely by kissing and embracing. They like to converse, and many of them like to do things that are fun. They form close emotional ties with congenial peo-

ple; and these ties can sometimes lead to third-person situations and possibly even to affairs.

2. *The open style gives freedom to marital partners to develop outside relationships* since it assumes that they are responsible adults. Each partner accepts the obligation not to deliberately hurt or create anxiety in the other. But they also respect each other's privacy: They do not, as in the closed style, demand an exact accounting from each other such as demanding to know, "Where have you been?" They would be more likely to ask, "Have you had a good day?" This freedom and trust, of course, leaves a lot of room for judgment and runs the risk that one of the partners may go beyond the limits that are acceptable to the other. If this happens, the open style encourages on open admission of the fact to the other. Secret carryings-on behind a spouse's back would be incompatible with the open style.

3. *The open style encourages the growth and self-fulfillment of all family members.* The spouse of a political candidate, for example, would encourage him to associate with other people with similar interests. The same would apply to a talent that the spouse may not be equipped to help the other develop. This could possibly lead to an affair. In theory, an open-style spouse who, for some physical reason, cannot satisfy a partner's sexual needs might encourage him to find another person who can. A married woman having such a need is described in D. H. Lawrence's novel, *Lady Chatterly's Lover,* except that the lovers in that case tried to keep their affair a secret. People in the open style acknowledge that it is sometimes beyond the capacity of any one person to meet *all* the physical, sexual, social, emotional and intellectual needs of another.

4. *The open style encourages new experiences, new ways of living,* in contrast to the closed style which resists the new. By always clinging to the old and refusing to change, we block our own personal growth. But this leads to a sticky question: "If seeking newness is a good thing, why not seek fresh sexual partners from time to time?" There are two difficulties with this. The first and most obvious is: What would this do to the marital relationship? And a second, less obvious, question arises: How new would it really be? A series of casual sexual affairs

can become as routine and deadening as any other oft-repeated, uncreative act. Newness, on the other hand, can be found in deepening and enlivening the ongoing sexual relationship with the marital partner.

The open style throws wide many doors of opportunity that marriage in the past has kept carefully shut. But it urges, in return, that people be trustworthy and responsible. If they are encouraged to make new friends, try new experiences, develop new sides of themselves, achieve deeper and more meaningful relationships, they are also expected to take full responsibility for the consequences. If they hurt a spouse, they are obliged to do whatever is needed to help the spouse feel loved and needed and to draw him back into the warmth of the home. There may be room for more than one love in a human life, but there is not room for an unfeeling sloughing off of one intimate relationship to admit another. A spouse in the open style would not say, "I demand that you love no one but me." But the spouse might say, "No matter whom else you love, I want to be loved too."

To expect a spouse who loves his partner deeply not to feel threatened by a developing third person situation may be asking too much of him. If a spouse does not feel threatened, it may mean that he does not care. But if he can bring himself to confront the threat by open communication of his feelings to his partner ("I feel threatened by all those people you are with. Have you forgotten about me?"), the shadows may begin to vanish. Or they may get deeper. Either way, he will know. And it is easier for most of us to deal with what we know (even if it is the worst) than with what we vaguely fear. ►19

Living Together Without Marriage

Living together without marriage has moved out of the urban ghettos (where it was long practiced) into what people a few years ago called the "respectable" segments of society. "Respectable" (now becoming a quaint word) was a cover term for a collection of values considered to be virtues, of which a key element was the virginity of the unmarried girl.

In about two swiftly-moving decades we have leaped into a

social condition in which an unmarried female movie star can live with a boy friend, be photographed with him in the apartment they share together, and be completely unconcerned about any possible negative effect on her reputation.

The idea of mixed dormitories in universities with boys and girls living on the same halls was almost inconceivable two decades ago. This practice has become widespread in a very short span of years. Some observers maintain that it fosters a kind of brother-sister relationship between the sexes that is essentially healthy. This could be; the arrangement is too new to evaluate effectively.

There is no doubt that a great number of unmarried young people in all walks of life are living together openly. Even some churches are being confronted by this change in social practices. Unmarried couples who wish to attend church conferences and religious retreats have, in some cases, asked for the same right to share a bedroom as is granted to married couples. This has posed a dilemma to persons responsible for registration and arrangements. How does it look for a church organization to assign a room to John Baker and Betty Sykes? Or, worse, to John Baker, Betty Sykes, Charles Williams and Marjorie Smith?

Exploration of the effect of this cultural change on family life has barely begun. Many people fear that the whole institution of marriage and the family is being undermined. Will these unmarried couples have children? And, if they do, what will be the effect on the children of such unstable parental arrangements?

"Who's your father?"

"I don't know. I'll ask Mom."

But one very serious consequence of the change in sex customs is a breakdown of trust and acceptance between the older and the younger generations. Families are being split apart by it. Young people in some cases have been virtually driven out of their families or have been ignored (not spoken to) as an expression of their parents' disapproval.

The struggle here, as the parent faces these new conditions, is between closed and open conceptions. In the closed style, the parent is not satisfied with teaching his beliefs about moral conduct to his children. He also insists that the children *must con-*

tinue to live in accordance with them even after they have presumably become old enough to accept responsibility for their own actions. And he uses whatever power he possesses to enforce this. Thus, a parent may cut off educational funds from a college-student daughter found to be living with a boy. And he may forbid her to bring the boy home at holiday time.

In effect, what such a parent is doing is assuming responsibility for the young person's actions *after* that person has grown old enough to take responsibility for himself. Responsibility can only be learned through practice in assuming it. If you keep taking it away whenever the results do not please you, the opportunity for a young person to learn responsibility is repeatedly lost.

In the open style, a parent does the best he can to teach his child what he believes to be true. This might include the idea that a sexual relationship between unmarried persons is wrong, or at least unwise. *The difference between a closed and an open style is not so much in the content of what is taught as in how the teaching is done and how the family reacts to non-compliance with those teachings.* In the closed style, the parent says, in effect, "You must do as I have taught you or I will punish you." In the open style, the parent is saying, "I have taught you what I know. You are old enough now to make your own decisions and take responsibility for them. But I will continue to love you and help you find your place in life whatever your decision is." The father in the open style, then, even if he deplores his daughter's living with a boy, will not cut off her allowance as punishment. And if she wants to bring her boy friend home for a holiday, the family will welcome them both.

But the open style goes further. *It calls for an attempt by the parents to understand, even if they do not approve, their young person's actions.* There are reasons why so many young people today are skeptical about marriage. Many of the marriages they have seen at close range are unappealing: husbands and wives bored with each other, going through the motions of living but feeling no excitement, no joy, no anticipation, no liveliness; or married couples fighting each other, thwarting each other's plans, undermining and hurting each other. The young people are aware that at one time these same people must have thought each other attractive, interesting and desirable. What happened? Unfortunately, many kids focus only on the ugly part of the faded marriages and wonder, "What's the point of marrying?" Yet a boy and girl strongly attracted to each other naturally want to be together. So they live together without marriage.

Young people whose parents have an open-style marriage are in a much better position to evaluate the pros and cons of marriage than are the children of closed-style marriages. The open-style marriage presents them with a model they can understand and appreciate. It may be attractive and joyous enough for them to want to have a marriage like it.

The life of an unmarried couple is far from idyllic. It has an inherent instability and therefore may not satisfy those who want a long-term commitment. It is very easy to walk out of. This is an especially serious problem if the couple has a child. An unmarried mother of a small child may feel extremely insecure. And she has no legal protection. There are numerous problems for an unmarried couple arising from the fact that our systems of laws, Social Security benefits, income tax, social customs, etc. are based on the assumption that a family unit is headed by a married couple, not an unmarried one. The open-style marriage, then, may appear to some young couples as a happy solution that could give them the best of both worlds.

As parents move toward a more open style in their family life, they may realize that the sexual relationships young people are now developing are not necessarily irresponsible, may not injure their future happiness or threaten the stability of their future marriages. Many people of the older generations, particularly women, were married with little or no prior experience in intimate relationships—sexual or otherwise. Dating practices in times past were highly formalized and not designed to help a couple really to know one another. In fact, the old-style dating was a kind of tribal rite intended to satisfy the need of young people to meet but so arranged as to discourage intimacy. This meant that couples often went into marriage on the basis of a very superficial acquaintance.

Having sex together does not necessarily mean intimacy, for sexual partners may know nothing of each other's feelings, values, ideas, hopes, dreams, habits or living styles. Dating couples of former times (more often than they cared to admit) did have some clandestine sexual intercourse. But they rarely had intimacy. **Intimacy** means a real understanding, closeness and sharing between two people. It includes working and playing together, planning together, talking together about all manner of subjects, enjoying things together and, perhaps, sleeping together. Through this process a couple may really get to know each other. This is the opportunity many young people now have for the first time. They do not always take advantage of it. Some young people, especially if brought up in a closed-style family, avoid closeness and pull apart as soon as the relationship looks as if it were getting serious. There are people who greatly fear intimacy. But the person who wants to achieve intimacy and develop a mature love with another human being now has a better chance to do so than any generation has had before. It is possible that marriages contracted after some preliminary living together may be sounder and more enduring than many marriages arising from conventional dating.

Nearly fifty years have passed since Judge Ben Lindsay, drawing on his courtroom experience in divorce cases, wrote a book called *The Companionate Marriage,* advocating that a distinction be made between marriage for companionship and sex and marriage for procreation. He advocated two different kinds of marriage. His book aroused a storm of protest at the time and he was accused of "sanctioning immorality." But much of what the more serious young people are doing today is quite similar (except for the absence of legal and social sanctions) to what Judge Lindsay advocated half a century ago.

On the other hand, some of the young (and older folks, too) are playing what is known as the "singles game," avoiding all commitments and sleeping with whomever they please as long as the emotional involvement is minimal. This is a precarious life, especially for a sensitive person; for his/her emotions are not that easily manipulated and controlled. There are plenty of heartaches in the singles game as old "flames" are supplanted by new ones. While the game may or may not lead to permanent attachments, it can lead to emotional sterility due to the habitual separation of sexual intercourse from emotions. This means that the jaded single person living this life may end up as impoverished emotionally as the partners in a tired marriage, and for the same reasons. He may grow wearied of sex, of people and of life.

The modern situation presents parents with some painful dilemmas. Suppose the parents are tolerant enough to accept the fact that one of their children—a young adult or near-adult—is having sexual relations in a serious "going steady" situation. What should they do about a younger sibling—say, a fourteen-year-old —who wants to imitate his older brother or sister? The age of sexual awakening seems to be creeping steadily downward. The fourteen-year-old says of her eighteen-year-old sister, "My sister is living with her boy friend. Why can't I live with mine?" Yet the parents are very reluctant to permit sexual experimentation by a fourteen-year-old. The young adolescent is unlikely to be mature enough to handle the emotional problems that can arise in such situations. The problem is analogous to that of the teen-age driver. Some teen-agers can be trusted with a car on the road. Others definitely cannot. And there are some for whom unrestricted use of a car is equivalent to a child playing with nitroglycerin.

A similar problem arises with respect to sex education and the providing of contraceptives. Every child today needs to know what sex is about, how the sex organs function and especially how sex is related to the emotional, ethical and other aspects of life. He can learn this either at home, at school, from the media, from his church (if he attends one) or in the street. But the information most kids pick up without systematic instruction is piecemeal, incomplete, often erroneous and much colored by the attitudes of the people who give it to them. Parents have an inescapable responsibility to make available to their children reliable information about sex. But then comes the dilemma: what about the supplying of contraceptives?

Here are David and Debbie, both in their late teens, deeply involved with each other. Their parents don't know for sure, but suspect, that they are having sexual intercourse. One big worry is: What happens if Debbie gets pregnant? Does the young couple know how to avoid it? Would either of them know where to get contraceptives? Yet if the parent gives them this information, he becomes a party to behavior of which he may strongly disapprove.

This is no easy problem to work with regardless of the family life-style. But it is more difficult with the closed style because in that style there is more of a gap between parent and young person; there is less effective communication, less warmth of feeling, less mutual trust. In the open style, the parent can at least communicate his concern.

"I'm worried about you, Debbie."

"Oh, Mother! Why?"

"It's about you and David. What happens if . . . suppose something happens?"

"Oh, come on, Mom! This isn't 1895."

"Do I seem to you like an 1895 Mom?"

"Sometimes."

"We've been pretty straight with each other, haven't we? Can't we continue to be straight?"

"OK, but I think what David and I do is our business."

"Are you interested in why I'm worried? Or do you just want me to go on with no way to resolve my worry?"

"Golly, Mom! You have nothing to worry about. Can't you leave me alone?"

"You want to shut me out?"

"Not really, but I sure resent this prying."

"Wait a minute! I haven't asked a single question that intrudes into your affairs, nor do I intend to. But I ask you to show a little interest in why I'm worried. You haven't even let me tell you."

"Well, tell me."

"Let's stop beating about the bush. Some young people when they go together begin to have sexual intercourse."

(Angrily) "And you think I'm doing it, don't you?"

"I said nothing of the sort. I told you I wouldn't ask prying questions. But let's just suppose that at some very exciting moment you do have intercourse. It's happened to plenty of people. Do you think you could handle it?"

"What do you mean, handle it?"

"The emotions. The emotions can be terrific. Didn't you know that?"

"So you think little Debbie can't handle her emotions?"

"I didn't say that. I asked you if you thought you could."

"Of course I can."

"I'm glad to hear it. But suppose you get pregnant and have a baby. Can you handle that?"

"A baby!"

"You've never thought of that?"

And so on.

By being open, the mother has been able to introduce a very delicate subject with her daughter without turning the girl off. She did it by (1) avoiding a lecture; (2) avoiding prying into the girl's affairs; (3) avoiding judgmental pronouncements; and (4) being honest about her feelings, which were troubling her. With this kind of trusting and open approach many young people can be reached. But it is not easy to do, and to accomplish it successfully the parent needs to be doing much more than trying out a new technique learned in a book. She needs to have worked on herself to become an open, whole person.

A straightforward approach like this is also probably the only way a parent can successfully head off the fourteen-year-old who wants to imitate her older sibling. The success of the effort will depend greatly on how close and trusting the parent-child relationship has been all along. A sudden burst of openness in a family situation that has up to then been closed probably will not work.

What the open family style can do that will help young people the most is to present them, day after day, with an example of a committed, dedicated and loving marital relationship *between their parents.* Young people who have grown up in this kind of environment and seen its rewards are unlikely to be satisfied with anything less for themselves. ▶20

Alcohol, Drugs and Other Addictions

To people who are accustomed to the closed style, the addictions —to alcohol, to drugs or to other harmful agents—seem the most intractable of problems. Some addictions such as those that lead to hard drugs or to alcoholism are, indeed, horrifying and soul destroying. Yet the attempted solutions that arise out of the closed system—tough enforcement, stiff punishment, spying on young people, no-knock forcible entry, cutting off supply, etc.—seem barely to have scratched the surface of the problem and may even have been counterproductive. The only student riot at a well-known university this year was in protest against the university administration for allowing government narcotic agents on the campus. The riot was followed by a "smoke-in," held in front of the administration building, in which some 2,000 students smoked "pot" in defiance of the authorities.

One difficulty with suppressive approaches is that they arise out of the same brand of life-style that often tends to produce addictions in the first place.

The number of possible addictions is unlimited, and if you are going to become addicted to something, you will find a way. Some common addictions are:

Overuse of alcohol
Chain smoking
Other drug abuse
Compulsive overeating
Compulsive gambling
Compulsive sexual behavior
Addiction to passive amusements
Addiction to violence
Compulsive working

An **addiction** might be described as anything a person does repeatedly, automatically and compulsively, and which he continues to do even when it is unfavorably affecting his life. Chain smoking is a typical example. Many heavy smokers are aware that they would be better off if they did not smoke. But they do it anyway.

Some addictions are less easily recognized for what they are: overeating, for example. The overeater may think he merely loves food, but a person free of addictive tendencies can love food without overeating. What motivates a compulsive overeater may have nothing to do with food as such; he may be seeking consolation for something missing from his life—perhaps love, or sense of self-worth, or a goal.

Addiction to *work* is a surprisingly common phenomenon. I am not referring to those fortunate individuals who love their work and are dedicated to it. A person addicted to work may not love the work itself, but he compulsively buries himself in it, perhaps because he does not want to be alone with himself, or because he does not enjoy being with his family, or for other reasons not connected with the work.

The essential characteristic of any addiction is loss of autonomy. The addictive habit takes over and dominates or suppresses other aspects of life. The person is no longer fully free to ask himself what he wants out of life or needs to do to achieve long-term goals. Addiction demands immediate satisfaction of its specific urge regardless of the long-term consequences. The most extreme example is that of the heroin addict who knows (if he dares think about it) that he may end up in jail but goes after his "fix" regardless. He no longer possesses the capacity to make reasoned choices as a free human being.

Loss of autonomy, of course, is one of the characteristics of the closed family life-style. Family members in that style are not encouraged to become self-determining human beings. People who have not developed their capacity for autonomy fall easy victims to addiction.

Our culture accepts addiction almost as a normal pattern of living. A person who doesn't smoke (or smokes only moderately), who doesn't drink (or drinks only moderately), who rarely uses drugs, who doesn't gamble (unless occasionally for small stakes), who is not compulsive about sex, who uses TV only for the particular programs that interest him, and who eats moderately and stays in good health—such a person is often either regarded with incredulity or is an object of amusement. A typical comment is, "What do you do for entertainment—go to church?" We have not yet learned in our society to recognize and appreciate autonomy.

Much of the drive toward addictive habits comes from the Childlike Dimension which demands immediate gratification at the expense of future well-being. Part of the compulsion also comes from the Internalized Others Dimension which has played a part in establishing the major patterns of the person's life. The addict is, in some respects, a person whose Maturing Self Dimension has not developed sufficiently to keep the other two dimensions in balance.

The influence of the Childlike Dimension (immediate gratification) is obvious enough; but the contribution of the Internalized Others Dimension may be less so. Studies of alcoholism and drug addiction among young people have shown quite clearly that drug usage (including that of alcohol) is heaviest among children of parents who habitually use drugs themselves. Thus, parents who drink alcohol to excess may have children who sniff glue, use marijuana or drink alcohol. There also seems to be a connection between parental usage of such drugs as barbiturates (sleeping pills), amphetamines ("pep" pills), pain-killers, tranquilizers, etc., and their children's drug or alcohol use. And this is understandable. The life-styles of both generations have in common a pattern of ingesting chemical substances to produce changes in mood and perceptions.

The message for parents is, "If you want your children to be free from harmful drug habits, the most effective place to start is with your own habits." The children commonly look at the matter very much in this way. Parental advice to avoid dangerous drugs falls on deaf ears if the parent himself is habitually using an addictive substance.

"I hear you've been smoking marijuana. Don't you know that stuff is dangerous?"

"Well, Dad, do you ever read the small print on your cigarette packages?"

The open style approaches addictions in a wholly different way from the closed. Since the goal of the open style is to help family members to grow as persons and to develop their potentials, any addiction that inhibits that growth is incompatible with the open style itself. This does not mean that an addiction could not occur. It could, of course. But the style is oriented away from it instead of toward it. Moreover, the open style aims at wholeness—the development of all sides of the person—rather than one-sided development. The more nearly whole a person is, the less likely he is to be captured by an addiction.

For example, a whole person has too high a regard for his body to injure it by habitual use of a harmful agent or by overeating or violating essential health practices. A whole person respects his emotional life too much to stultify it by becoming a dull work horse, or by falling into excessive passivity (i.e., with too much TV), or by sexual activity divorced from emotions. Also, the open style aims specifically at the development of autonomy. It aims to produce people who not only have high respect and regard for themselves but who know how to handle themselves in an environment of freedom.

But the most powerful force which the open style exerts against addictions is its climate of encouraging the realization of human potential. Anyone who has discovered his own uniqueness, his aliveness, his capacity for love, his creativity, his sensitivity, his awareness and his relatedness, has found keys to growth which make all addictions unnecessary and seem ridiculous. A home in which these human qualities have been called forth is an exciting place to live. There is not the boredom, purposelessness, dependence on others' approval or desire to escape that are so often the motivations for taking up habits that tend to become addictive.

If an addiction were to develop in an open-style family, that family would be much better equipped to deal with it than would one where there is poor communication and lack of trust.

The open approach in dealing with a possible addiction might be something like this:

"Are you expecting to drive home tonight, Jim?"

"Sure, Dad."

"Better stop drinking, then."

"Oh, come on, Dad! I've only had three. I bet everybody else here has had four or five."

"Since when do you let other people's drinking habits determine yours?"

"Don't worry, I'll be able to drive."

"No. Sorry. You can continue to drink or you can drive, but you can't do both."

This dialogue is open because it is honest and direct. No games are being played. There is no sermonizing, no insult, no threats. But the parent is taking control of a situation that is in danger of getting out of hand. And he is encouraging autonomy and responsibility. ("Since when do you let other people's drinking habits determine yours?")

Because the open approach grants autonomy, the parent in that style has to face the possibility that his young person may still choose a course that carries the risk of addiction. In the above example, the parent doesn't say, "Don't drink." But he does say, "Don't drink and drive." The combination is too dangerous—somebody might get killed. Therefore, no option is given here. But the drinking, by itself, may or may not be dangerous. And whether it leads to addiction or not is, to a large extent, up to the drinker. The father is putting that responsibility on his son where it ultimately belongs. ▶21

Rebellious and Runaway Children

Today is the era of the rebellious young—a world-wide phenomenon that makes headlines from places as far apart as Thailand and Greece. No one knows how many runaway and virtually homeless kids are wandering in the streets and highways of the world. The number could well be in the millions.

Running away can be a kid's most eloquent expression of his feelings about his home and his family. How could he say it more clearly—unless by burning the place down? The act of running away is eloquent because it is contrary to the natural inclination of a child or young person. A child normally thinks of his home as the place where he belongs. If he has come to feel that it is a place where he does *not* belong, something in the home's atmosphere or in the interactions taking place there is reversing his natural polarity.

The parent-child interaction that leads to the final act of running away may be one of which the parent is quite unconscious as it slowly builds up in withdrawals, moody silences and half-hidden resentments. Then, suddenly, there occurs a flare-up, and the parent awakens to an almost unbridgeable gap between himself and his children. In near despair, he cries, "Why can't I get close to my child? Why is it that every time I try to reach out to him, he rebuffs me? Good God, I can't even say 'hello' any more without an indifferent or sarcastic response."

Both the closed and the directionless family styles are effective devices for separating people. That is the one thing they do well. The directionless style separates them because there is not enough caring. The family is spiritually fragmented; each member is preoccupied with his own interests and not much concerned about what is happening to the others.

The closed style, while not designed to separate people (though it often does), is rather a system for controlling them. One of its underlying principles has been that of command authority. People accustomed to an authoritarian style have difficulty in conceiving of human relationships based on any other principle. Command authority, of course, calls for obedience. Refusal to obey calls for punishment. The ability to punish requires power of enforcement. The whole system carries an immense weight of tradition and its origin goes back to antiquity. But, although this system is taken for granted by adults in a closed-style household, it may not make sense to teen-agers in the same household. And it may be quite rejected by people in the open style who live by a different set of principles altogether.

Any system of human relationships based on command authority presupposes that the authority is backed up by some degree of recognized enforcement power—moral or physical. Rules and edicts look ridiculous if they are not enforceable. And a power system can never afford to look ridiculous. The closed-style family is in the unhappy plight of trying to live by the vestiges of an authoritarian system in an age when parental and ecclesiastical authority have dwindled to near ineffectuality. The parents in such a family find themselves giving orders that are not obeyed, advice that is not followed, teachings that are not believed; and they threaten punishments they are unable to carry out.

When the closed-style system fails, as is now increasingly happening, what was designed originally as a system for controlling family members evolves into one for alienating and dividing them.

Suppose, instead, that the goal of the parent-child relationship were not control but the creation of an atmosphere of freedom and affection—a human-being garden. Although the ultimate objective of the parent in the open style may not be different from that of a parent in the closed style, the climate is different and the outcome is different.

Let us compare the two styles—closed and open—in the handling of an identical situation. The sixteen-year-old daughter attend an unchaperoned all-night party at a friend's house with a crowd of which the mother disapproves.

CLOSED-STYLE ENCOUNTERS

"Mom, I want to spend the night at Marilyn's." (Not admitting real intention.)

"Have you been invited?"

(Impatiently) "Of course."

(Suspiciously) "Why do you want to spend the night there?"

(Sarcastically) "God, Mom! Do I have to go through an inquisition every time I want to go anywhere?"

"Well, I just want to make sure you'll be all right. Who else will be there?"

(Lying) "Nobody. Just Marilyn and me."

Something in her daughter's tone alerts the mother, who now suspects that the girl is not telling the truth. The conversation deteriorates. The daughter rages at the mother and finally storms out, slamming the door.

Or another version: The daughter is so suppressed that she dares not rage at her mother. She just sits in her room and broods until, acting on impulse, she sneaks out of the house and hitchhikes to a distant city, joining the street crowd.

Or a third possibility: The daughter is an obedient girl not in the habit of defying her mother. She agrees to stay home. But the relationship with her parents slowly deteriorates, and when she reaches maturity she drifts far from the family, adopts a different way of life and rarely communicates with them.

Or a fourth possibility: She accepts the child role (as her mother hopes) and never questions the rightness of her parents' teachings. But, as a result, she does not learn to take full responsibility for her own thoughts and acts. She grows up habitually leaning on others to provide guidance.

AN OPEN-STYLE ENCOUNTER

One way the same situation might be handled in the open style is something like this:

"Mom, I'm invited to a party at Marilyn's tonight. It's an all-night party, so don't expect me home before morning." (No attempt at deception.)

"Cathy, I don't approve of mixed all-night parties." (Clear statement of position.)

"Oh, Mom, it's all right. Don't *worry* about it."

"Whether I worry or not isn't the point. Is it important to you that you go to this party?"

"Mom, my friends are all going."

"I'm not concerned with what your friends choose to do. It's what *you* choose to do that concerns me."

"Mom, you're totally unreasonable. There's nothing wrong with this party."

"OK, I'm unreasonable." (Smiling)

"It's awful having a mid-Victorian mother. I bet not one of my friends has to cope with a mother like you."

"I'm sorry coping is such a problem. Do I frustrate you so very much?"

"Oh, Mom! Sometimes you do and sometimes you don't. I don't know what to do now. Are you forbidding me to go?"

"No, I'm not forbidding you. You're old enough to take responsibility for yourself. But I've told you my feelings."

Two such different ways of handling the same problem are sure to produce very different results. The open-style mother, while making her own position clear, has put the final responsibility on her daughter. Cathy is now thrust into an adult role; she has to decide. The mother's challenge may not necessarily work as she hopes; Cathy may still decide to go to the party. But the mother's feelings are still likely to have an effect and may restrain Cathy from flinging herself into a thoughtless and foolish episode.

It might be objected that in contrasting these two situations I have portrayed two different daughters. Of course I have. A daughter raised in the closed style would be a different person from one raised in the open style. A different interactive process would necessarily have produced a different set of personality traits. Neither of these dialogues stands by itself. Each has within it echoes of hundreds of earlier dialogues between these same persons who have been living with and shaping each other.

These illustrations refer to parent-daughter relationships. But parent-son relationships can be much the same. Who has not seen crowds of boys and girls lounging in parks or on street corners day and night, apparently far out of touch with any sort of parental influence? The parents of many of these young people feel helpless to cope with them and have virtually given up trying.

When things have gone this far, dialogue between the generations may have reached a dead end.

How would an open-style parent handle the problem of a teenage boy about to get out of hand?

"Jim, driving the car on a public street before you get a learner's permit is out."

"Come on, Dad! All I want to do is practice a little."

"It's illegal, Jim. Only a licensed driver or one with a student permit is permitted . . ."

(Explodes) "Goddamit, I know well enough how to drive. Why are you so tight with the car? Dick's father lets him take the wheel sometimes when they go on trips."

"You want me to break the law?"

"Dick's father does."

"Never mind Dick's father. How about me? You want *me* to break the law?"

"If he can do it, why can't you?"

"I prefer not to. But let me make a suggestion. It's on public streets that you have to be licensed by law. On a private driveway or road, it wouldn't be necessary. Why don't we ask Ned Davidson if we could use his private road? I could give you some lessons there and no law would be broken."

"Golly, Dad. Do you think he'd let us?"

"I think he would."

In this dialogue, the parent is firm on law observance, but listens sympathetically to his son and thinks of a way to work the problem out. If there were not such an easy solution, Dad might have to say, "I know how you feel, Jim. You're very impatient to get your hands on the wheel of a car, and I don't blame you. But I'm not willing to break the law or to let you do it. You'll have to wait until you reach the age requirement in this state."

In looking at the examples of these two styles—the open and the closed—some may jump to the conclusion that what mainly distinguishes them is that the closed style prohibits undesired behavior whereas the open style permits it. That would be to miss the point completely. An open-style parent prohibits behavior that endangers a child (such as crossing a superhighway on a tricycle) or that endangers other people or society. But, where a child is capable of taking responsibility for himself, the open-style parent encourages him to take that responsibility and assume its attendant risks, *provided the risks are not too great*. Risk is balanced against the potential for growth. A child who is discouraged from taking any risks whatever ("Never climb trees! You'll fall and break your neck!") is hindered from growing.

The open style, then, uses prohibition where necessary and appropriate, but relaxes it where the challenge of meeting a situation could call forth the child's powers and help him in his development. Also, the open style takes into account the practicability of enforcing a prohibition. It is useless to try to prohibit an eighteen-year-old from drinking, for example, or from taking drugs. You cannot enforce such a prohibition. But you can tell the young person where you, yourself, stand and why you think it is not a good idea to do these things. Thereafter, you have to rely on his respect for you and for himself.

The closed style operates in a rigid framework without balancing risk against growth potential and without much regard to enforceability. When a prohibition is ignored by the young person (as it often is in the closed style), the parent punishes by bitter words, looks of disapproval, withdrawal of privileges, and the like. The generations are driven apart, and eventually the closed-style parent may abandon all attempts to control and may resort to withdrawal and rejection. The battle is lost. ►22

Separation and Divorce

Separation and divorce have moved in about two generations from being a hushed-up event—virtually a disgrace—to a common observed fact. It is no longer limited mostly to young marriages that never got off the ground. A remarkable trend in recent years is the sharp rise in the divorce rate of couples in their middle years. In two decades, the rate at which marriages of more than fifteen years break up has doubled, and the highest divorce rate of the group comes near the twentieth year. Some twelve million Americans now have gone through at least one divorce.

What these divorce rates signify, as I look at it, is the beginning of the death throes of the closed-style marriage. Most of the marriages falling apart in the middle years can be assumed to have been closed style, since the open style is a comparatively new concept that has not been systematically articulated or developed until recently. They are marriages in which the partners have not shared each other's feelings or interests over the years and are no longer happy with each other. The collapsing of these long-term marriages reveals the failure, not of marriage itself, but of *closed-style* marriage. The malaise of this kind of marriage, unless the couple can move toward openness, seems incurable; and increasingly one or both partners in such a marriage reaches a point where the marriage is felt to be dead. About a dozen states have recognized the plight of such people by passing what are known as "no-fault" divorce laws, making it possible to obtain a divorce without proving wrongdoing on the part of either partner.

Separation and divorce are experienced as a catastrophe in many a closed-style family, especially if the family is one of the locked-together type. In such families there are strong feelings of dependency between husband and wife. This dependency is expressed almost in ownership terms; he feels she belongs to him like a possession, and she feels that he belongs to her. Each is intensely jealous of any outsider to whom the other is even superficially attracted. The two go through life with halters around each other's necks, figuratively never letting either one out of the other's sight. This is the closed style in its most extreme manifestation; and, of course, a separation—which means an escape of one partner from control by the other—represents a defeat of the entire system. As the system falls apart it may leave behind feelings of intense anger, outrage, bewilderment, coldness, anxiety and desire to punish. Divorces in closed-style families, therefore, can be exceedingly bitter and hostile—a condition that places a heavy emotional burden on children caught between the battling parents.

The dependency of marital partners can be either economic or psychological or both. As an example of psychological dependency, a husband may expect his wife to take the place of his mother; or a wife may expect her husband to substitute for her father. When people marry before they have fully accomplished their emergence from parental domination, it is natural that they should adopt roles that help them compensate for the fact that they are not yet whole and independent individuals. At first, such substitute-parent roles may be helpful in reducing anxiety and in building a sense of security. But an excessive dependency hampers personal growth. If a woman steps from her parents' home into marriage with a man resembling her father, she may begin to relate to him as she did to her father: She may expect him to support her, protect her, guide her, keep her from mistakes, hold her hand (figuratively) in all situations where danger confronts. And the husband, if he is self-reliant, may fall naturally into this kind of role. (If he is not self-reliant and wants his wife to be his mother, the expectations of both partners may be disappointed and thwarted. Neither, then, can meet the other's need, and they may start fighting in the very first year.)

But, suppose that one partner (either husband or wife) falls unconsciously into the role of a child and the other into a parent's role. The "child" may begin eventually to grow up and start a long-delayed working through of the emergence from the parent that should have been accomplished in late adolescence. Every parent of a teen-ager knows the friction and strain between parent and child that has to be endured during this phase of a teen-ager's development. Now, however, a similar strain may develop between husband and wife. Unless the partner playing the parent role can recognize what is happening and begin to abandon his parental position as the other emerges from the child position, the marriage may be in for rough times.

Here is a husband falling into the father role, "Did you lock the car, dear?" And instead of answering, "Yes," as in the past, she glares at him and says stiffly, "I'm not in the habit of leaving it unlocked!" (Response of the "reactive child.") It may take considerable further emergence before she can smile and say calmly without rancor, "It's O.K." (Response of the Maturing Self.)

Or the wife falls into the mother role, "Be sure and wear your topcoat, dear." And instead of the old, "Yes, dear," he explodes,

"I'll wear what I damn please!" ("Reactive child.") Years may pass before he can smile gently and respond, "I don't need it today." (Maturing Self.)

In the closed marital style, complementary roles such as these may become frozen into a rigid, inflexible system which cannot easily be reshaped—only broken. And when it is broken, the fracture has some of the emotional impact of a split between a parent and a child.

For these and other reasons, separation and divorce in a closed-style marriage can be a shattering experience for both partners. The more tightly the couple is bound into the closed system and its interlocking roles, the more upsetting it can be. The break may not have been foreseen by the partner most habituated to the system and most dependent on it. He may be taken by surprise, since one of the features of the closed style is poor communication, especially of feelings; he may have had no inkling of how his spouse feels. When the prospect of the break dawns on him, he may be overwhelmed with a sense of betrayal and outrage or of sadness and despair. In frustration, he may become vindictive, refuse to co-operate, throw up obstacles to working anything out, draw the children into the fight and try to play them off against his spouse, furiously try to prevent a fair distribution of assets, refuse to discuss problems. His Childlike Dimension may assume full raging control. Underlying his passion is the feeling that he is about to lose a possession that belongs to *him*. When it dawns on him that the loss is really going to occur, he may have a hopeless feeling. His life was built on a system that is now breaking up.

In this atmosphere, which may continue for months or years after the divorce, it is difficult or impossible to work out the best arrangements for all concerned. Everything is a subject of dispute and litigation. Lawyers take over. Children are rarely consulted; their feelings are trampled on. Visitation with the absent parent may become a strain and a trial. There is competition between the ex-partners for the children's affections. The children may take advantage of this to play off one parent against the other. In this situation, the parents and children alike are victims, not so much of the divorce itself as of the breakdown of the *human* relationships involved. If one parent has taken a lover, the children may be piteously torn; the parent wants them to accept the lover while the spouse may expect them to hate the lover.

Separation and divorce in the open-style family, if it occurs, is likely to be less damaging to the partners and to their children. The causes of breakup are different from those in the closed style. An open-style marriage does not bind the partners into a tight system that inhibits their self-development. Hence, dissatisfaction with a restrictive life-style or rigid dependence on roles are unlikely to be among the causes of a split. Nor, probably, would the causes include boredom, irritability, insensitivity, indifference, cruelty, etc. A separation and possible divorce in an open-style marriage could come about because the partners' movement toward self-realization, such as the pursuit of separate careers, might lead them into incompatible life-styles and geographical separation. Or the marriage might end because the partners have outgrown each other, because their goals and needs have changed, because the relationship has ceased to be growth-enhancing or because the old purposes of the marriage are no longer there. But divorce arising from such causes is very different from the brutal slashing of emotional bonds that can occur in a closed marriage. It would be more like the parting of good friends who are about to go off in different directions.

Because partners in an open-style marriage are not locked into a fixed system, they can much more easily seek alternative ways of living. Because they feel less possessive toward one another, each can more easily free the other to go his own way. Because they do love and care about each other, each wants the best for the other; there is less upset at parting, less clinging. Because their communication has been good all along, neither partner is taken by surprise; the decision has been maturely considered and mutually accepted. They can put their heads together to work out the best possible arrangement for each other and for the children so that there is as little hurt as possible. The children's feelings are listened to. The parents continue, after separation and divorce, to share responsibility for the children's care. Differences can be negotiated in a climate of good will. The family is free to act in accordance with what its members feel to be the best interests of all since they are less at the mercy of what other people, such as their parents and in-laws, may think.

Negative emotions do unquestionably occur in open as well as in closed marriages as a breakup approaches, but in the open style negative emotions can be better handled. The partners are better able to ask themselves:

Where are we?
How did this come about?
Can we do anything about it?
Do we need professional help?

In the open style, partners are less likely to panic or to be plunged into despondency. The future, instead of looking black, may be seen as offering a new and exciting challenge. ▶23

Death

Families of closed and open styles are likely to react quite differently to the death of a family member.

In the closed style, even where the marital partners are locked together, there is emotional isolation; for being locked together is not the same as being intimate or close where feelings are shared. When a family member dies, the feeling of separateness or alienation that has existed all along may be suddenly intensified to one of complete, irreparable, hopeless loss. There may be a sense that it is now forever too late, that the relationship can never be retrieved or fulfilled.

These feelings may be further intensified by gnawing regrets and a punishing sense of guilt:

Why didn't we do more together?
Why did I hurt him so much?
Why were we always fighting?
How can I ever make it up to her?
Why was I so selfish?

And there can be additional grief at witnessing the end of what is realized to have been an unfulfilled, half-lived life—the person was cut off before he ever realized his potential as a human being.

He never achieved what he had hoped.

She always wanted to . . . and she never did. (It was my fault.)

Every dream he ever had crumbled to dust.

She went through life without ever knowing who she was.

He only lived for his family (son, daughter) and he was crushed when they . . .

Death that occurs in a climate of guilt feelings, "might-have-beens" and "why-did-it-happen-to-us?" is real tragedy. The feeling of loss is made more unmanageable by the fact that day-to-day living in the closed style provides so few outlets and so little continued nourishment for the emotions. When emotions such as grief, sadness and regret strike with great intensity, the closed-style family is on unfamiliar ground where its habitual reliance on roles and systems no longer suffices. Typically, it tries to systematize and stylize its grief, using the familiar and comfortable symbols of widow's weeds, black arm bands and a "fitting" (often very expensive) funeral.

In the open style, the family members have been emotionally much closer to each other than in the closed. They have shared with each other their hopes and disappointments, their enthusiasms, their insights, their wishes, their dreams and their thoughts. Since the objective of family life has been the self-fulfillment of the family members, there is likely to be less of the feeling of an unlived life that so often haunts people in the closed style. Hence, there may be fewer regrets and less wishing that life could have been different.

The death of a member in the open style is not, then, so often felt as an irreparable loss, nor does it cause feelings of guilt. Death is seen, rather, as a completion of the birth-death cycle to which all created beings are subject. When a human relationship has been rich and rewarding, death does not necessarily terminate it. Everything that made it rich and rewarding lives on in memory, in the works which the deceased left behind, in the things he loved which still survive, and in the impact which his life made on those around him. The survivor may feel the invisible presence of his loved one as he goes about his tasks.

A popular misconception about death of a loved one is that the more deeply you love him, the more desolated you are by his death. But this is not necessarily true. Love is often confused with attachment. It is probably true that the more you are *attached* to a person, the harder it is to be separated from him by death. But attachment and love are not the same. Attachment holds and binds; love gives and frees. If you are tightly attached to someone, you may feel that you cannot live without him. People often call this "love," but actually it is dependency and entwinement.

When, therefore, a bereaved person goes to extremes in "proving" his loyalty and love for the departed—such as by refusing to enjoy life or to live it fully, pledging never to remarry, leaving the deceased's room and effects exactly as they were when he was alive, etc.—it is probably attachment or guilt, not love, that is being demonstrated. In the open-style family, these kinds of excesses, which restrict life instead of enhancing it, are avoided.

Grief, of course, is as real in the open-style family as in the closed and may be felt even more keenly because members of such a family are closer to their feelings. It is experienced as a personal feeling and is less tied to ritual. Funeral arrangements, for example, may be stressed less and would not be designed to impress relatives, friends or the public.

Finally, in the open style the family members have been encouraged to accept their uniqueness and to develop their human potential as individuals. This gives the survivors strength to carry on, which is often lacking in the closed style. They have probably largely outgrown dependency roles. They can take the reins of family life from the hands of the one who passed on and work out their lives. ►24

Human Relationships: Where Family Problems Start

The big question that emerges whenever a family has problems is the one of human relationship: *How do I stand with you, and how do you stand with me?* A family can endure incredible hardships —poverty, illness, accidents, losses, war, imprisonment, separation—as long as its members feel close to one another, care for each other and experience each other as whole human beings. Hardships can, in fact, strengthen a family's solidarity. But when the relationship between family members deteriorates, money, comforts and possessions are of little help.

Curiously enough, such problems as infidelity, drug abuse, exploitive sex, and youth rebellion have rarely been approached as essentially *relationship* problems. Yet, that is what they are. A family member can zero in on any of these problems if he asks himself honest questions about his relationship with his child, his spouse or his parent—such questions as:

What does he mean to me?

What do I seem to mean to him?

How do I feel when he is around? Attracted to him? Interested in him? Proud of him? Glad to be with him? Or repelled, indifferent, disappointed, angry?

How do I think he feels toward me? Affectionate? Interested in me as a person? Happy that he has me for a parent (or a child)? Or annoyed, rebellious, indifferent, frustrated?

Do he and I feel each other's closeness, warmth and love? Do we want to reach out and touch each other, take each other in our arms? Or do we pull away?

Life-enhancing relationships are not achieved without effort. Human relationship is an art, needing to be learned and practiced like any other art. And, of all the arts, this is the one most neglected in the world. It is incredible and tragic that this should be so, for here is perhaps the only art that is universal. Every human being needs to learn the art of relationship with other human beings. There is no way out of this; it is implicit in being human.

Failure in this art is the most dehumanizing of failures. You can fail at painting, at playing the violin, at business, at outguessing the stock market, at making a fortune—yet you are still a person. Your failure, though painful, does not make you less of a human being. But if you fail at human relationships—if you alienate your family, become estranged from your children, let your friendships wither—you have lost something irreplaceable, something essential to the human condition. People, of course, seek substitutes when human relationships fail: pets, TV, books, taverns and bars, superficial human contacts—and it is fortunate that they can. But these are still substitutes, and they do not wipe away fully the sad loneliness that gnaws at the heart.

It is in the home that the practice of the art of human relationship is put to its ultimate test. Strangers and casual acquaintances are relatively easy to get along with. Probably you do not quarrel excessively with most of your co-workers, your subordinates, your bosses or your neighbors. But neither are you very close to them. Most relationships of this nature are highly stylized; we behave in ways that are mutually and silently agreed upon without ever having consciously considered or discussed them. They constitute a code to which we unconsciously subscribe.

We operate according to a code within the family, too, but that code is less evolved, less adapted to the needs of the times than is the one we use in social and economic relationships. Our family code is often derived from a life-style that we inherited from a different age. Most of us have not examined it. Now we must do so. The art of human relationship in a family is a teachable, learnable art, and it is necessary that families everywhere set about learning it. The first essential step is to learn to communicate more effectively.

Suggested Interaction Experiences

IE-19. Understanding a Third-person Situation (pp. 78–79)

Nearly everyone has a friend to whom a third-person situation has occurred and can recall the visible effects it had. Put yourself into the "skin" of your friend who was hurting and imagine how he or she must have felt. Re-enact in your mind a particular scene, such as the family at dinner immediately after discovery, as you imagine it might have happened.

Next, put yourself into the "skin" of your friend's spouse—the one who became involved with the third person. Re-enact the same scene as before, but from that spouse's point of view.

Finally, put yourself in the "skin" of the third party. Re-enact the two scenes as before but from the third party's view.

EVALUATION: Do you think the situation could have been handled more constructively by the three people involved? How do you think you would have handled it if you had been in their place?

IE-20. LEARNING ABOUT YOUNG PEOPLE LIVING TOGETHER WITHOUT MARRIAGE (P. 186)

Obtain the permission of a young person who is living with someone without marriage to talk about his situation.

Inquire how the arrangement came about and why, how conflicts and disappointed expectations are being dealt with, etc. What does the young person consider to be the advantages and disadvantages of this form of relationship? Does he feel it to be an intimate, meaningful experience? Do the couple's parents, other relatives and friends know about the relationship? What would happen if they found out? Do the partners have feelings of guilt? Does the couple expect to marry eventually? (It would be easy to disrupt such a discussion by giving advice or making judgments.)

IE-21. WORKING WITH ADDICTIONS (P. 193)

If a family member is addicted to a habit that could be harmful, imagine yourself attempting to halt or reduce his addiction. In your imagination, try first the closed approach: be critical and intolerant; pile on the blame; accuse him of not wanting to stop the habit; try to make him feel guilty; demand that he obey your rules; and threaten punishment if he doesn't stop. Imagine the responses he might make to this. If you have your own pet addiction, such as smoking too many cigarettes, imagine how you would feel if he used this approach on you.

Next, picture yourself using more open approaches: listening, being non-judgmental, respecting the other person, warning of consequences without being dictatorial, trying genuinely to help the person, admitting the difficulties you are having with your own addictions, etc. Imagine his responses to this approach.

EVALUATION: Can you feel the vast difference between the two approaches? Which is more likely to have positive results?

IE-22. FEELING THE DISTRESS OF REBELLIOUS AND RUNAWAY CHILDREN (P. 198)

While many children fantasize at one time or another how it would be to run away from home, few actually do it. Here is your chance to live (or relive) this kind of experience. Go alone to a quiet place. Mentally and emotionally, place yourself back in a childhood situation in which you felt so lonely or angry or hurt that you wanted to (and perhaps did) run away from home. Imagine where you might have gone (or did go), what you might have done (or did do) while away, and what might have happened (or did happen) when you got back home.

EVALUATION: What was going on in your family during childhood that contributed to your wanting to run away? Were you feeling rejected, unfairly treated, bored? Were you unreasonably jealous, spoiled, provocative? Were your parents neglectful of you, overly punitive, poor listeners? What closed-family characteristics might have contributed to your wanting to run away? Does your present family life contain any such closed characteristics?

IE-23. FEELING THE IMPACT OF SEPARATION AND DIVORCE (PP. 203–5)

Select a divorced couple whom you know quite well. (If your parents have been divorced, you might try this experience with them.) See if the two former partners would talk with you separately. Questions might cover: the causes of their divorce; early separation experiences; reactions of other people (including their children) to the breakup; changes in patterns of living—economic, social, psychological, sexual; feelings (regrets or satisfactions) about having obtained the divorce.

EVALUATION: Why do you think they got a divorce? (Were they too dependent, insensitive, irritable, indifferent, or cruel toward each other? Or did they outgrow each other because their goals and needs changed?) How did each of them manage emotionally during the divorce process? Were the children consulted about the divorce? What is the present relationship between the former partners? Compare their ways of relating to you during the talks.

IE-24. FEELING THE IMPACT OF DEATH (PP. 208–10)

Write the epitaph of a deceased family member or relative. Try to include some references to: the kind of person he was; what he meant to people; the person who probably misses him most; what he achieved and what he regretted not having achieved; which of his personal relationships was most rewarding during his lifetime and which was the most undermining; and finally, how the family members manage without him.

EVALUATION: Was this person closed, directionless or open in his general life-style?

FOLLOW-UP: How would you feel about writing a similar epitaph for yourself?

SEVEN

LEARNING
TO COMMUNICATE

Nearly all troubles that plague family life grow out of or are aggravated by ineffective communication. Quarrels, arguments, misunderstandings, disappointed expectations, dislike, distrust, angry retaliation, sexual problems—a whole gamut of difficulties occur, at least in part, because we have not learned to communicate effectively.

Ordinarily in most families, the family members do not deliberately set about hurting, annoying or frustrating each other. Most hurts, irritations and disappointments come about because somebody did not make something (usually his feelings) clear either to himself or to somebody else. Many people have a great deal of trouble in identifying how they themselves feel; and if they do not clearly perceive their own feelings, they can hardly make their feelings understandable to others. Communication in their families resembles the radio broadcasting of fifty years ago when signals were frequently overwhelmed by static, interference from other stations and fadeouts.

Communication is sometimes defined as the transmission and receiving of signals and messages; and, of course, it is. But it is far more. It is sharing. It is the opening up of one person to another so that each learns who the other is and, in the process, discovers who he himself is. And it is inner clarification; it is an inner opening up so that a person becomes aware of the processes going on within him.

There is nothing uniquely human about signal transmission as such. Fish, insects and computers can send, receive and translate signals. In a simple walk through a wood or meadow, the ear can pick up countless signals from tiny living things; the air vibrates with them. And there are probably countless more outside the range of the human ear. But I am concerned with *human* communication, both inner and outer, verbal and non-verbal.

Communication never stops. It continues as long as the heart beats and the brain functions. It is not something that a person *does* so much as what he *is*. Communication begins at birth with the baby's first cry. A human being cannot *not* communicate. Two persons sitting silently in my waiting room, not looking at or speaking to another, may think they are not communicating. But, in fact, they are. Silent withdrawal is a most eloquent communication. It may be saying, "I prefer the security and comfort of my own thoughts just now to the risk and uncertainty of being confronted with yours." Accompanied by certain facial expressions and body postures, it may say, "I don't like you particularly." With other postures, it may say bluntly, "Keep out." With still others, it may say, "I'm too shy to speak to you, but I'd love it if you spoke to me first."

Communication Within Yourself

Most of us think of communication as an exchange of messages or information between persons. Yet, communication between persons is not the only, or even necessarily the most important, kind of human communication. A more basic kind is that which takes place *inside* a human being before any word or other signal comes through to the outside. This "in-house" communication by which messages are unceasingly flashed from one part of the person to another is the invisible key to all interpersonal communication. Inner and outer communication supplement and reinforce each other. The inner requires the outer; the outer requires the inner. But in our educational methods, it is the inner communication that has been largely ignored.

An example may help make this clear. Here is a husband—call him Dick—who comes home tired and irritable after a rough and somewhat frustrating day's work. He drops into a chair and picks up a newspaper. He wants food, drink and quiet for a while. The last thing he desires at that particular moment is to have to respond to what sounds to him like trivial chatter from his wife.

But Nancy has been cooped up in the house all day with the baby and wants to talk. Her husband only half listens, barely looks at her and continues absently to turn the pages of the newspaper. His seeming indifference annoys her. Her annoyance provokes him. They begin to shout at each other. He finally jumps up in anger and stalks out of the room. What kind of communication has taken place here?

The inner communication in each of these people is faulty, and this guarantees that there will be faulty communication between them. The husband is aware of his own fatigue, frustration and irritability. Those particular messages come through to him clearly, and he passes them on to his wife, but in a distorted form that leaves her feeling angry and rejected. Why are the messages distorted? Because a number of other significant feelings inside the husband do not reach his consciousness and cannot, therefore, be passed on clearly to Nancy. Among these is a longing to be "mothered," to be given a little V.I.P. treatment for a few minutes (he can't get it anywhere else), to be kissed and hugged without much talk, and to have something to eat soon. Another unrecognized feeling in him is resentment because his wife does not give him (and never has given him, he feels) those few simple things he would like. On top of these feelings is a desire arising out of his Childlike Dimension to "show" her, which leads him to insult her by pretending to read while she is talking to him.

In the background of his psyche these feelings are jumbled together to produce a vague sense of dissatisfaction like the distant rumble of highway traffic. Yet he is fond of his wife and family and wishes that his steadfastness were appreciated more. This mixture of feelings is bouncing around in him, affecting his body posture, his responses, the tone of his voice and his facial expression. Yet only a confused background roar is reaching his consciousness. Unable to identify each of these feelings sharply and clearly, he cannot evaluate them; he cannot bring to bear the power of his intellect to decide between feelings that are appropriate to his situation right now and those that are not. His ability to control his actions is limited because his inner communication system is functioning inadequately.

Another difficulty arising from his faulty inner communication is his failure to recognize the onset of a familiar, repeated pattern. The same scenario has been played over and over in his life. He should be thoroughly familiar with it. Why does not a warning light begin flashing in his brain? "Watch out! Here it comes again." Essentially, the problem is that, when inner communication is not effective, warning signals do not always get through to consciousness. Each recurrence of the event seems to strike "out of the blue" as if it had never happened before. Actually, if Dick were to pay attention to his own insides, he has plenty of warning. The setting up of the situation, the way his wife looks and walks as she enters the room, his own feelings as he reacts to her—all these should set bells ringing within him. But they do not. Unconsciously he may even enjoy these set-tos—another unrecognized feeling.

The wife, Nancy, too has faulty internal communication— probably as inadequate as her husband's. She knows he is tired and in no mood for casual conversation; his very bearing conveys this eloquently. But she is not aware that her Childlike Dimension is taking over. This is partly a weakness of her inner communication. Her Maturing Self does not observe soon enough what the child in her is up to. It is as if the child side threw dust in the eyes of the maturing side. The child side wants her husband's full attention right now and all the time, regardless of whether the demand is reasonable and of whether Dick can, in fact, give her his total attention when he is tired after a grueling day's work.

If Nancy's communication system were better tuned, her maturing side would be able to size up the situation with some degree of objectivity and say to the child side, "Hold it, dear! He wants a little quiet for a while. Later, he'll pay attention to us." But her maturing side does not have a clear enough grasp on what is happening to send such a clear message to the child side. Although the situation has repeated itself numberless times in her marriage, Nancy still gets caught in the same pattern. Like her husband, she has an inadequate inner warning system. Her Childlike Dimension comes at her from behind, as it were, and gives her a push at the critical moment.

Neither partner may want this process to continue in this form. It spoils their enjoyment of each other and affects other aspects of their lives. Yet with enough knowledge of themselves and of each other, they could work with it very easily and effectively. The husband could say when his wife enters, "Honey, I'm bushed—and, you know, when I'm very tired like this, I like to be left alone for a bit. Can we wait until dinner time before we talk? I promise to listen then. OK?" She might say, "Of course, sweetheart. I've got some interesting things I can't wait to tell you, but I'll hold off. See you in a little while." And she could kiss him and walk out. But to accomplish this so neatly requires a fairly clear communication of feelings, desires and expectations, both inside each person and between them.

Good inner communication can be taught and learned, just as anything else subject to conscious control can be taught and learned. But the idea of doing this in a systematic way is unfamiliar to most people. Our upbringing and education not only did not train us in inner communication but actually had the opposite effect. Inner communication has been discouraged, and, to a considerable extent, blocked because of the way our schools and our culture have focused on external matters rather than on processes of thought and feeling.

Because of this one-sided approach, communication between people often goes awry, is subject to misunderstanding and confusion, and produces unintended destructive effects. This is one reason why many of us are poor listeners. And it is a major reason why there is a generation gap. The so-called generation gap really has very little to do with age differences. It has, however, a great deal to do with faulty inner communication.

Inner communication operates in very much the same manner as interpersonal communication. We behave often as if there were several separate persons functioning within each of us. It is important that these inner persons (parts of us) be able to communicate with each other. We all talk to ourselves at times, remind ourselves, reprove, criticize, praise and kid ourselves, lie to ourselves and (a few of us) laugh at ourselves. We carry on extended inner conversations with imaginary people. We fantasize. We get angry with ourselves and sometimes punish ourselves. Self-punishment may take actual physical form, as in psychosomatic illness and accident proneness.

When an emotion such as anger or fear takes over and leads to an action we later regret, the cause usually is faulty internal communication. We did not see it coming until—bang! it hit. Yet there were unquestionably many preliminary signals that we might have learned to read. An oncoming storm, seen in time, can be dealt with: an anchor can be dropped, the sails trimmed, the ballast tied, and so forth. But if we do not see or feel a squall approaching until it strikes, we may be unmasted or capsized. This is as true of emotional storms as it is of external physical ones.

There are tested procedures for opening the partly closed channels of internal communication. They are essentially procedures for widening what is already partly open, for if a person's channels were totally closed, or nearly so, he would probably be psychotic. We are talking now about people able to function but not functioning at their full potential.

When communication between two people breaks down, we often observe that one or the other is not listening with full attention. The same is true of internal communication: One side of the self is not paying attention to another side. Most of us have been trained to put conscious attention on matters such as learning subject matter, performing work, making decisions, solving problems and so forth. *We rarely focus conscious attention on our feelings.* We were not taught to do so, and the doing of it seems strange. For many, there is internal resistance to doing so. Yet if we have the capacity to focus attention on a book, we should be equally able to focus on something as close to us as our feelings.

Now is a good time to do it. Stop reading this book and close your eyes. Pause for a moment . . . then, ask yourself, *"What am I feeling now, at this moment?"* Feel this feeling and hold it for ten or fifteen seconds and see if it remains the same or dissolves into a different feeling. Continue this process of catching and holding a feeling for a minute or two.

*   *   *

What were some of your feelings just now? Skepticism at the usefulness of such an exercise? Curiosity at what may come next?

Reluctance to look too closely at your emotions? Eagerness to learn a new technique of the mind? Worry about a current situation? Excitement about being on the verge of a new experience? Or did you yield to the temptation to skip the exercise and go on reading?

Did you recognize any of the above feelings *before* reading the preceding paragraph? Or did you recognize some of them in retrospect after reading it? That in itself may tell you something about the state of your inner communication. ►25

GETTING IN TOUCH WITH YOUR FEELINGS

Here are five steps for getting in touch with your feelings. I have taught these in many college and university classes, in individual, group, marital and family therapy sessions, and in encounter groups. They can be carried out in a very short space of time— just a few minutes, ordinarily. But to be able to use them spontaneously and effectively, they have to be practiced at frequent intervals. Practice them under varied circumstances, such as while watching TV, while going to or from work, while having lunch, after a fight with your boss, after a spat with your spouse, or following some other experience that impresses you. Since the work of getting in touch with your inner life is partly aimed at reversing the habits of a lifetime, do not expect instant expertise. As you apply these steps repeatedly, your skill will grow and the blocked inner channels will gradually clear.

1. *Identify the feeling* you feel at the chosen moment. Do not let yourself off the hook by presuming that you have no particular feeling just then. *Everyone has feelings all the time.* They are numerous and varied, and some may be in conflict with others. At the beginning, unless you are in close touch with the multiple "goings on" inside of you, you will not be able to identify feelings easily. But try to identify at least one.

2. *Hold the feeling* and experience it as fully as you can. Don't let it slip away. Never brush off a feeling as trivial or unworthy or shameful. To paraphrase Gertrude Stein, a feeling is a feeling is a feeling. It has its own right to exist, whether you think it

shameful or not, and brushing it off or denying it is a symptom of that same unclear inner communication that you are trying to clear up. (Remember that you can feel multiple feelings at the same time. Even two opposite feelings, such as love and hate, can be felt simultaneously.)

3. *Report the feeling verbally to yourself.* Give it a name: pleased, annoyed, comfortable, anxious, happy, sad, alive, bored, disturbed, etc. Say to yourself, "I am feeling —."

4. *Explore the feeling.* Now ask yourself some questions about the feeling so that it becomes more than an isolated experience; accept it, respect it and let it take its place as a part of you. There is no such thing as an accidental, isolated or meaningless feeling.

What evoked the feeling? A thought? A remark? A look? An action? A touch? A noise? A sight? An odor? (Note the difference between "evoke" and "cause." Whatever triggered the feeling did *not* cause it, for nobody *makes* an adult feel in a specific way. You think, act, react and feel the way you do at any given moment because of who you are—your attitudes, your values, preferences and expectations, your life-style.)

Have you ever felt this feeling before? If so, how intense was it? Under what circumstances did it occur? How did you manage it? Were other people affected by it?

Is this a feeling that occurs frequently? Does it arise automatically in certain situations?

Does the feeling seem to derive from the past? Can you remember similar feelings being expressed by a parent (or other adult) under similar circumstances?

Does the feeling seem to be more identified with the Childlike part of you? Did you often feel this feeling as a child?

How does it serve you? Feelings, like all behavior, are purposive. They occur in response to inner and outer processes and carry special meanings for the feeler.

5. *Evaluate the feeling.* Does the feeling seem appropriate to the situation now, today? Or is it an inappropriate replay of something from long ago? Do you prefer to hold the feeling intact? Modify it? Or replace it with another more appropriate feeling?

Let us take an example of how these steps can be applied. Here is a couple—call them George and Dorothy—whose marriage seems to be a sequence of angry put-downs by George and hurt withdrawals by Dorothy. The couple fell into this pattern early in their marriage when Dorothy worked in a business office and George was a graduate student. His income was meager and they lived mostly on her salary. George, who had rather low self-esteem, felt diminished by his wife's role in supporting the two of them. He reacted to this feeling of humiliation by dominating his wife. Her passive temperament made this easy; and their life arranged itself into a kind of pecking order where, on the conscious level, it appeared that he pecked and she ducked. At a deeper level, however, she did a good deal of pecking of her own, and it was her pecks that may have caused the deeper wounds.

Their marital pattern did not change appreciably after George graduated and began to earn his share of the family support. His personal life-style seems to be built largely around impatience and anger: he is angry at his parents, his boss, his wife, his children, many of his friends, the world and, above all, himself. He is sometimes even angry with himself for being so angry. After hurting his wife and children by harsh words, he berates himself; but then he turns around and hurts them again. His respect for them and for himself is low.

Dorothy feels she has reached her limit of tolerance. She sits down one day and asks herself what her feelings really are. Some of her feelings—resentment, bewilderment, fear and rage—are very familiar to her. But she is searching for the less identifiable feelings because she is sure that the keys to her predicament lie hidden there. Her self-examination goes something like this:

"What am I feeling beside the fury, resentment and guilt that I always feel when George plunges the dagger into me or takes it out on the kids?"

One feeling comes to mind immediately: disappointment with herself. "I'm such a limp pillow," she says to herself. "I go off and cry when I ought to kick his teeth in. I hate myself for it." This is a familiar feeling, too. She knows it has been around for a long time.

She reflects on her relationship with her husband. "What feelings do I have toward George? Obviously, I hate him when he acts the way he did today. But do I really hate him? If I really hated him, wouldn't I leave him?" She ponders this. "Shall I leave?" And to her astonishment she feels a flood of nos well up in her. The idea of leaving him brings anxiety. Why is that? She is perfectly capable of earning her own livelihood. If she is so unhappy, why doesn't she leave?

"I don't love him," she says to herself, "but I don't want to separate from him, either. Though often I want to hit him, I'm nevertheless drawn to him. What is the feeling I have?"

She cannot identify the feeling at first, but as she reviews in her mind some of their recent conflicts, it comes to her. "I feel like a mother to him. He seems like a bad, angry little boy and I'm a mother whom he can hurt as much as he pleases and I always go back and try to placate him."

Suddenly comes to her mind a picture of George's mother. George hates his mother, yet he cannot break away from her grip. And Dorothy realizes that George's hatred of his mother is being transferred to her. "But I don't want to be his mother," Dorothy tells herself. "Yet I keep acting like one, don't I?"

Dorothy focuses on the motherly feeling and asks herself, "What evokes it? I guess I feel motherly when George does something stupid or clumsy like breaking the handle off the coffeepot. Then he's so like a little boy. He curses and slams the coffeepot down and starts to blame *me*.

"What is going on inside me at the time? Well, I'm trying to show him how to handle delicate things delicately—he's very awkward. It seems like I'm always trying to show him how to do something. And he's very ungrateful.

"Does the feeling derive from past events? Yes, I remember having the same feeling toward my father. He was another one who was always making blundering mistakes and wouldn't take anybody's advice.

"Does the feeling serve me in some way? How could it? Yet if it doesn't, why do I keep on acting this way? Is it because it makes me feel superior? Do I work hard to feel superior because, really, I have such a poor opinion of myself?"

Then she asks a question that leads to a still deeper insight. "Do I invite put-downs because I feel rather worthless and think I deserve to be put down? I seem to have been inviting put-downs all my life—from my father, from my mother, from older brothers and now from George."

She sees now that she needs (1) to build up her own self-esteem, and (2) to help her husband to build his self-esteem. She realizes that by thinking of him as a little boy who needs her help, she has been undermining his respect for himself and for her. These insights do not, by themselves, solve her problem, but they point the direction for her to go.

Of course, insights of this depth do not usually emerge in one bout of self-examination. In real life, a number of such bouts would probably be needed. But this example illustrates how knowledge of your own inner processes can develop out of learning the art of inner communication.

How can Dorothy put these insights to use in her relationship with her husband? If she can keep them clearly enough in mind, she can start treating George as a responsible adult instead of as a child. This may encourage him to treat her also as one and to be a better father. She can help build the self-esteem of them both, cease being so passive, be more up-front with her feelings, communicate her feelings of resentment as they occur instead of letting them pile up, but also communicate her affection for him. If he relapses into his old pattern of put-downs and of not treating her as a person, she can remind him, "Look! I'm a person, see? Have you forgotten that I'm a person?" And she may even be able to do it with a light touch so that he will not feel attacked.

Let's replay the scene now—this time with the husband, George, following the steps of learning inner communication.

George is unhappy with himself. He knows that his recurrent anger is damaging his marriage and his other relationships. But he cannot seem to control it. He is aware that he is often rough on his wife and children, feels guilty about it, but continues to indulge in harsh criticism and cutting remarks.

He tries the procedure for learning inner communication. Asking himself the first question, "What am I feeling now?" he comes up with the answer, "Resentment and bewilderment. I don't understand what's going on with me or with Dorothy."

"What evokes these feelings? Dorothy evokes them with that patient, suffering look she puts on when she thinks I'm in a muddle and need help. I get the feeling she's looking down on me from above, and I can't stand it. I want to pull her down to where I am. I may be a big, blundering fat-ass, but I'm damned if she is any fairy godmother.

"Does the feeling derive from past events? You bet. I've felt this way for a long time. I can remember Dorothy's smug, satisfied look when she brought home a pay check and all I was bringing home was bills. I'd get angry then, and she'd look sadder and sadder with a kind of doglike, appealing look. I wanted to hit her.

"Does the feeling serve me? That's a curious question. How could I benefit by feeling resentful?"

But George realizes that his accumulating anger does serve a purpose for him: It helps offset the feeling of uselessness and worthlessness that otherwise would overwhelm him. "I have to be angry," he says to himself, "or I would go nuts! And bewilderment is useful, too. If I'm bewildered, I don't have to feel so responsible for what I'm doing. I can cut my wife and kids to pieces and say, 'Who, me? I don't even know what it's all about.'

"Am I replaying something from long ago? Yes, no doubt about it. I behaved the same way when I was a kid and mother used to get that same sad, patient look after I had been naughty. I've hated that look ever since.

"Is the feeling appropriate to the present situation? I don't think it is. Something is spoiling our family life, and the way I'm behaving is probably part of it. I'm sure Dorothy doesn't mean to hurt me. I ought to make allowances. And I ought to stop taking it out on her. That's behaving like a kid."

With this self-knowledge, George can begin to control the Childlike Dimension of himself, drawing on the powers of his Maturing Self Dimension. And if Dorothy can summon up her Maturing Self Dimension to prevent her Internalized Others from calling the tune of their relationship, the couple can begin to heal their discordant relationship.

Saying, Feeling and Doing

Communication, both internally and between people, takes place on three levels:

1. *The conceptual-informational level,* in which thoughts, ideas, plans, theories, formulas, beliefs, stories, traditions, procedures and factual information are communicated by means of words, numbers, codes, symbols, diagrams, pictures or direct sense impressions. All such data can be translated into what, in computer terminology, are called "bits" of information. Such information can be stored, processed, analyzed, reproduced and evaluated.

2. *The emotional level*—the transmission of feelings. Feelings are communicated (or sometimes masked) in an incredible variety of ways: by vocal inflection, eye contact (or averted eyes), facial expression, tilt of the head, body posture, gait, hand grip (in a handshake), hand wringing, foot tapping, nodding, eyebrow raising, smiling or frowning, giggling, laughing, turning toward or away from the other person, gesturing, hugging, kissing and many other physical signals, many of them unconscious. Also by physical reactions which may be uncontrollable, such as trembling, teeth chattering, blushing, turning pale, stiffening, becoming frigid or impotent, developing headaches, breaking out in rashes or stomach ulcers. Further, by shouting, screaming, crying, whispering, singing, whistling, belching, sounding a "Bronx cheer" and so on. And finally, by the person's manners, such as his way of speaking and choosing words, of greeting or responding to another, of eating, sitting, entertaining, etc.

Each of these actions and signals can have a variety of meanings. Thus, a laugh—depending on its tone and context—can signify enjoyment, appreciation, good humor, excitement, embarrassment, triumph, contempt, a threat or an insult. Crying may mean despair, grief, joy or excitement. Every signal, therefore, needs to be interpreted, not only by the receiver but often also by the sender who may not always be certain of the meaning of his own signals or necessarily be aware of these signals at all. Moreover, the same signals that communicate emotion can be used equally well to hide it. Thus, a smile can hide a broken heart; polite gestures can hide a desire to attack.

In addition to all these personal ways of expressing and communicating feeling, there are the more complex and sophisticated creative processes that express emotions in art forms. Picasso's "Guernica" is an example of an intense emotion (hatred of war) incorporated into an art work. Such creative works may include poetry, stories, music, dance, drama, painting, sculpture, and, in fact, any creative work which expresses and communicates feeling.

3. *The behavioral level*—communication through behavior—generally reflects and helps to express the other two levels (as a hug and a kiss express affection). But behavioral communication may also be distinct from the direct communication of thought and emotion. For example, telling someone you love him communicates on the conceptual-informational and emotional levels; it expresses a feeling and conceptualizes that feeling in words. Hugging, cuddling, fondling, kissing the person, smiling into the person's eyes and so on, communicates on the emotional and behavioral levels but not on the conceptual-informational one. Cooking dinner for the loved one, taking him or her to the theater, giving up a fishing trip to be with the person, and a multitude of other acts may communicate more specifically on the behavioral level (what a person *does*) while not necessarily expressing thoughts or feelings directly.

When communication functions on all three of these levels, and the same message comes across on all three, there is rarely any problem of being understood. Love expressed in words, tenderness *and* unselfish actions does not leave gnawing doubts in the loved one's mind that he is loved. Doubt arises principally when one of these elements is missing or is discordant with the others. A man who kisses and has sexual intercourse with his wife but never tells her he loves her may leave her in doubt; the kissing may be only a gesture and intercourse may be only for his own enjoyment. A man who speaks words of love but shows no tenderness or consideration is soon not believed. Communication that leaves out any one of the levels or operates with the signals at different levels in conflict with each other is a distorted communication. It does not produce understanding; rather confusion, estrangement and doubt.

WHAT YOU SAY

Words are the common vehicle for conceptual-informational communication and for much communication of emotions as well. Yet, communication by words has been so stressed in our culture that many people are conditioned to respond to words and to little else. On the other hand, in many families the most significant communication is not through words but through behavior and non-verbal signals.

This is a curious anomaly since our educational system is largely based on communication by words, and the world of productive work, except at its least skilled levels, requires this kind of communication at every stage. Yet in many closed-style and directionless-style families, it is communication by words that seems to have dwindled most. The members have little to say to each other. Some feelings are communicated non-verbally; but, without words to accompany the non-verbal signals, the communication can get distorted and misunderstood.

We need words. Words fix themselves in our memory. They can bring comfort when we are distraught. Prisoners have been buoyed in spirit by the recollection of words spoken in love, or by a perception which some poet expressed in words, or by the lyrics of some song. People contemplating suicide have been brought back by remembering words that they had read or heard. The beautiful words of the Psalms or the Gospels or other inspired writings have nourished the minds and spirits of multitudes through the ages.

But words also have power to damage or destroy. Hitler used words to arouse an urge to kill. Family members carelessly use words that injure and wound. A middle-aged man still remembers with pain when his older brother called him "stupid." Hurtful words can hang in memory for a lifetime, injuring self-esteem and clouding joy.

Communication through words, then, is a powerful force, either to lift or to tear down. Words can be either chains or wings.

In Open Family Living, the goal is to use words as wings. Family members willingly share and discuss thoughts, problems, plans, insights, wishes, dreams, fears and frustrations. Young and old alike bounce ideas off each other. Their minds are stimulated. Their flights are free.

The common failure of word communication in closed-style families is emotionally caused. Family members gradually cease to share their thoughts for fear of criticism, ridicule or blame, or they meet with indifference and inattention. If you don't listen to me, why should I talk? ►26

HOW YOU FEEL (AND HOW YOU COMMUNICATE IT)

People communicate emotions in an endless variety of ways, and, in the case of the stronger, harsher emotions, they may do it freely but often very crudely. Most of us are much less skillful in communicating the gentler emotions; yet it is the gentler emotions that are in greatest need of expression in family life.

The problem most people struggle with is how to get the rougher emotions under control so that the gentler feelings have a chance to be heard. Suppressing the strong emotions or trying to cover them up usually works poorly. Like fire in a basement, such emotions are likely to burn through the walls and burst out. Giving them free rein works badly, too. We are apt to "dump" them on someone and produce resentment, outrage, hurt feelings, withdrawal, strained silence, useless argument, disrupted relationships and other untoward effects. What can a person do? He *has* the emotions. He must accept the fact that he has them. It is often not possible to hide them.

Let us begin with the *acceptance*. If I am angry, that is how I feel. It only fuzzes up my awareness to be caught in a web of feeling guilty about feeling angry, or feeling upset about feeling guilty about feeling angry. These chains have no end, and their result is a confusion of feelings like a bubbling pot of witches' brew. If I feel guilty about feeling angry, I need to remind myself that anger is a legitimate feeling and I need not feel guilty about it. But the guilt also is a legitimate feeling, and if I feel guilty about feeling angry, I must acknowledge that, too.

Once I am sure of how I feel, I must *articulate* it, at least to myself. This articulation must reflect my feeling, but stop there. I must not use the feeling as a charge of dynamite to blow up somebody else. If I say, "You bastard!" when I am angry at you, I am doing much more than articulating my anger. I am hurling an accusation at you, which is different thing. Articulating only the anger means saying, as much to myself as to you, "I am angry." I must be careful about saying who or what I am angry at. Anger is so often projected upon innocent or partly innocent people or upon circumstances or events having nothing really to do with it that the expression of anger must be kept separate from blame or insults. It is sufficient to say, "I am angry," or "I feel myself getting angry." This articulation in itself helps to keep the anger from flying loose senselessly and destructively.

For example, a father had been repeatedly annoyed by his son's demands for use of the family car at inconvenient moments, and the father's response had been to explode in irritation and refuse use of the car altogether. The boy felt unfairly treated and was overheard to call his father a "grouchy old fool." The father, fortunately, awoke to the fact that he had been handling the matter poorly. One evening, after the father had gone to bed, the boy woke him at midnight and demanded the keys to the car. Instead of reacting in outrage as he had done in similar situations in the past, the father said, "Are you trying to make me angry?" The boy, in surprise, said no. "I'm beginning to feel angry," said the father, "and, if I get angry enough, I might forbid you the use of the car for several days. Do you want to push me to that point?" The boy again said no. "Then consider the position you put me in," continued the father. "By your demand, you are putting me in a spot where the only way I can keep my self-respect is to say 'no.' If I were to say 'yes' while under all this pressure you are putting on me, I wouldn't feel much like a father. If you want to negotiate with someone, don't begin by backing him into a corner. Do you understand what I am saying?" The son did understand, stopped pressuring his father, and the two of them were able to work out an arrangement acceptable to both. This single event helped to restore meaningful communication between father and son.

There is another useful approach in the handling of insurgent emotions. That is to *look for the opposite or complementary emotion*. It must be there—it nearly always is. The angry or hating person also can feel forgiveness and love. These feelings may be deeply buried, but they probably exist. We are complex, many-sided creatures, and our emotions are rarely pure; they sometimes contain their opposites. Return to George and Dorothy. George expresses anger and resentment with great force, but scarcely ever tenderness or sympathy. Yet George does have tenderness and sympathy. Dorothy has affection, which she does not often show. The couple's failure to reach down to those depths where these gentler emotions reside does heavy damage to their relationship. But if they are ever to learn to communicate effectively, the communication must be comprehensive, not lopsided. The tenderness, sympathy and affection, as well as the irritation, must be communicated. Failure to communicate both ends of the emotional spectrum is responsible for the failure of many marriages and other human relationships.

WHAT YOU DO

Behavior is perhaps the most revealing of all the forms of communication. Words can lie, distort, twist, deceive, hide. Emotional communication can mislead because the more violent emotions may outshout the gentler ones. *Behavior, in the long run, rings truest*. Short-run behavior, of course, can be as suspect as anything else; it may be aiming strictly at seduction or deception, as also may words and emotional communication. But in the end, a person's behavior day in and day out is a true statement of who he is. If I love you, I will do things to make you happy—little things and big things. I will kiss you when we meet or part; I will bring little gifts to please you; I will work for you, plan dates with you, go out with you. As long as I continue to act in this way, you can have reasonable assurance that I love you. When I cease doing these things you may have reason to wonder. You then ought to check me out. I may be simply absorbed in my own problems or work; but my failure to *behave* as a lover ought to ring a warning bell for us both. The reason for the change in behavior may be something unrelated to the quality of my love. But whatever it is, it ought to be explored, brought into the open, not left to fester.

In many marriages, the partners' performance of loving acts for each other diminishes gradually until the couple becomes stranded in a loveless routine. The partners may work, as before, to keep the family in steaks and clothes and to keep the household going. But doing things for each other has lost its former spontaneous quality. Duties have taken the place of love gifts. But duties are not adequate replacements. Without voluntary and spontaneous expressions of love through behavior, people may well begin to feel that they are no longer loved. And perhaps they are not. But, again, their love may simply have been sidetracked by other pressures. The problem may be one of communication. It is important to find out.

Parents who interpret "discipline" as making strict demands on their children but who never think of making spontaneous "gifts of love" to them are sometimes appalled when they discover that their children do not believe their parents love them. What has been missing are the behavioral signals of love. Giving children a comfortable home, good food, adequate clothing, spending money and "education" falls more in the class of fulfilling duties than of spontaneous giving. Such acts are not sufficient to carry the message of love. Doing things *with* children, taking them on excursions, listening to them, giving freely of the parent's time, and expressing affection openly, count for far more.

Communication on the behavioral level is a major force in the creation of life-styles. It accounts also for many other phenomena in modern life: the spread of fashions, fads, behavioral "epidemics" (such as the campus riots of the 1960s and the prison riots of more recent years), smoking, drinking, drug taking and the like. The influence of parental drug and alcohol habits on the use of drugs and alcohol by kids is a striking example of behavioral communication.

WHAT YOUR BODY DOES

In all communication, the body participates because it has an eloquent language of its own. Body signals are, to a considerable degree, unconscious. The transmitter of body signals is often not quite aware of the signals he is giving off, and the receiver also may not be conscious of his reactions to them. When, for example, a man remarks that a certain girl is "sexy," he has probably been responding to some very subtle body signals from her and she may have been responding to equally subtle ones from him. Maybe they both can identify them. Maybe they cannot.

Body signals can, however, be misread. They are strongly influenced by a particular culture and by changing fashions. The way an English boy and girl signal each other may be quite different from the way an Italian boy and girl do it. An Arab or Chinese boy and girl would probably do it differently still. When cultures are mixed, as in many metropolitan regions of the world, unconscious interpretation of body language, which is likely to be based on experience in one's own culture only, can lead to trouble. And changing fashions can produce misinterpretations. The extreme mini-dress styles of recent years, for example, exposed an amount of female thigh which only a generation ago would have signaled a "come-on" by a prostitute, and in some parts of the world still would.

When you have a general feeling about someone, such as that he is trustworthy or untrustworthy, strong or weak, a good sexual partner or an unwilling one, or any evaluation not based on direct knowledge, it is wise to check the impressions received non-verbally against other information. Can you identify the body signals on which the impression is based? Can you be sure they mean what you think they do?

Body signals, like words, can cover up feelings and signify the opposite of what they appear to mean. A man trying to seduce a woman may engage in elaborate gestures of love when his real purpose is merely to spend a night with her. Body signals that seem to portray dislike or indifference may only be reflecting fatigue. Or signals that seem to convey bravery may actually arise from fear. To base impressions of other people on non-verbal signals *alone* is risky. They need to be compared with other data.

But body signals can be of help to an individual in recognizing *his own feelings*. Often, a person's only clue to a deeply repressed emotion is the reaction of his body. When you suspect the existence of an emotion that lies below the threshold of consciousness, turn your attention to your body. Is it tense anywhere? If so, where? Do you have clenched fists, for example? Do you have psychosomatic symptoms which might appear in the form of sweaty palms, a headache, a tightness in the chest, a trembling, a skin rash or breathing difficulties? Any of these can signify an unrecognized emotion. Have someone give you a massage and note the sore or tense spots that are revealed. By closely watching the reactions of the body, much can be discovered about the emotional state. The body may not immediately tell you *what* the hidden emotion is, but it reveals its presence and in time you may observe a correlation between certain emotional conditions and certain body states. For example, when I get a headache I suspect that I have not dealt satisfactorily with a situation of conflict. The headache often means that I suppressed some of my anger. A headache might not necessarily mean this to someone else, but I have found from experience that this is what *my* headache often means. So then I know better what to do. I retrace the events of the day, identify (if I can) the situation in which the anger arose, acknowledge its existence, allow myself to feel it, ask myself if it is appropriate, and try to work more constructively with my anger. And lo! The headache often vanishes. ►27

WHEN SAYING, FEELING AND DOING ARE AT ODDS

Because we have been taught to hide and falsify many of our feelings we commonly use words not to express our real feelings but to cover them up. At the same time, our supposedly hidden feelings are revealing themselves indirectly in ways ranging from a harsh tone of voice to an impatient foot tapping—a fact of which we may be quite unconscious. In this conflict of signals, conventional etiquette adds to the confusion. In social situations, it is considered bad manners to articulate too honestly an emotional state (such as saying, "I'm annoyed with you"), whereas the nonverbal indications of the same feeling (such as a frown or impatient gesture) are ignored. The whole thing becomes a game. And similar games are sometimes carried on in the home. Thus, we have the man who says "sweetheart" to his wife while sarcastically upbraiding her for overdrawing their checking account, or the mother who says "dear" to her teen-age son while making disparaging remarks about his choice of friends.

Conflicting signals from the different levels are a familiar cause of family troubles. A wife says to her husband as they are about to go out, "How do I look?" He says, "You look fine." The words convey approval. But as he says them, he gives her only the most cursory glance, and his manner seems to say, "I don't much care how you look." The feeling she gets from him, however, is, "I don't care about *you*." She suspects that he is about to play an old game. Sure enough, later in the evening when they are at a party, he looks at her critically and observes that her lipstick is crooked, or he finds something else wrong and refers to it publicly. She is furious. This is an example of marital game playing, and one of its characteristics is that some of the things that are said are not really meant, and some of the things that are meant are not said.

It is essential in family life to bring all three levels of communication into agreement. This is partly a matter of simple honesty. In social situations where certain well-acknowledged social games are played, this may not be so important. But in the family it is. Game playing in the family is destructive. Family members are entitled at all times to know where they stand with each other. Children and young people, especially, need to know how they stand with their parents, and the parents need to know how they stand with their children.

A person who puts out different signals from different functional levels does so because he is not all of one piece. The marital game player, for example, who embarrasses his wife at a party, is probably not being intentionally mean. He may not be conscious of the satisfaction he gets out of embarrassing her and how this "builds" his own ego. He may not be aware, either, that this pattern is repeated over and over. She might help him become aware of it by insisting that he inspect her carefully before they start out and warn him, "If there is anything that doesn't please you, *tell me now and don't embarrass me later.*"

Artificiality and closed-off communication develop when a person tries to cover up how he really feels. This fools no one in a family situation, for family members know each other's patterns too well. What happens is that they may get an impression of insincerity or even of dishonesty. It is a common belief that honesty refers to how one deals with other people. That is only partly true. Its real roots are in *how a person deals with himself*—in whether he acknowledges his own faults, limitations, self-centeredness, inadmissible impulses and "shameful" feelings—in whether he can say, "I have problems with myself." If he habitually covers up and hides from himself what he regards as "bad" or weak, he is not trusting himself. He then tries to hide that part of himself from others, puts on a "front," and thus undermines other people's trust in him.

Often what underlies this inner dishonesty is fear. Many people do not dare risk letting their family and friends see them as they really are. They dread being laughed at or not being loved or respected; and so they hide behind a mask. This can become an embedded life-style, and such a person may reach a point where he can scarcely even imagine coming out from behind the mask and letting himself be open and exposed. He would feel naked. Yet the work that has been done in group therapy, sensitivity training groups and encounter groups has shown repeatedly that it is the *mask* that elicits distrust from others and quenches their feelings of affection and love. A mask does not successfully conceal for long what a person truly is. On the contrary, its mere presence reveals that the individual does not like or trust himself. In these group experiences, the mask gradually drops off and the person eventually reveals what he has been trying to hide. And, lo!—instead of turning against him and taking advantage of his exposed position (which he has feared all his life), the group discovers that he is a human being very much like themselves. Those "weaknesses," those feelings or qualities he was so ashamed of and didn't want others to see, are perceived as part of his humanness; and perhaps for the first time, people are able to get close enough to him to feel warm toward him.

The same transformation and opening up that occurs in the group experience can occur in a family. The process may, however, be more difficult and take longer because many families have developed fixed patterns in which the masks have an important role to play. If the father has habitually covered up his feelings, everybody in his family is accustomed to it and expects it. For him suddenly to become an open person might produce a crisis in family relationships. No one would know how to deal with it. Some family members might become uncomfortable, and pressures would very likely be exerted to push him back into his former style. Family members and friends might even insist that something is "the matter" with him, for, curiously enough, signs of increased psychological health in an individual are often mistaken by people close to him for signs of disturbance. ▶28

Full Communication

Full communication brings it all together: the mind is working, the emotions are felt, the body participates. Full communication is exciting. Instead of the feeling, "He doesn't know what I'm getting at," there is a warm response, "He understands!"

There is an impulse to hug a person who "understands." For something of you has entered into him and vice versa, and there is a desire to complete the connection. Full communication is an intellectual and emotional interpenetration and, in some degree, a physical one, too. I am talking now, not about sex, but about connection. About the child who runs up to you and throws his arms around you. About the friend who puts his arm across your shoulders as he listens to a private confession. About the married person who hugs his spouse when they have worked through a difficult situation together. About the soldier who holds a wounded buddy in his arms.

We always know when the communication has been complete. It *feels* complete. It is satisfying. The responses are right. We know, too, when it has failed. The responses are indifferent or hostile or inappropriate, and we have a sense of defeat ("I can't get through to him").

Full communication, for most of us, is a rare event. But we can learn to make it a more frequent event. We begin with self-training in inner communication (the Dorothy and George technique) to become aware of the flow of our feelings. We try to become aware of the three Dimensions in ourselves—the Internalized Others, the Childlike and the Maturing Adult—and we practice identifying which of these is having the most influence on what we are saying and doing at a particular time. We watch out for evidences of our own alienations and work on overcoming them.

Finally, we learn to listen to the other person, to catch the feeling that lies behind what he is saying (which means listening to emotions as well as to words). We respond to his emotion. ("You feel strongly about that don't you?" "You're disappointed, aren't you?" "I see you feel very good about it.") This leads to a totally different conversation than does argument or taking issue, and a much more rewarding one, because argument or disagreement frequently results in breaking off real communication. This is not saying we should not disagree, but simply that the emotion behind what has been said needs to be heard first.

For example, suppose a pre-teen-age girl in your family makes an outrageously untrue statement like, "*all* boys are brats." If you say, "No, they're not," you get the answer, "Yes, they are." A silly argument can go on and on, solving nothing. But suppose, instead, you respond to the feeling: "Boys annoy you, don't they?" Then you get, "Yes, they sure do. Why, yesterday . . ." And you may eventually learn why boys annoy her.

Arguments with adults are not really that much different. Your spouse says, "You *never* give me any help around the house." You are indignant because you washed the dishes yesterday (maybe for the first time in a month) and therefore she is being unfair when she says "never." But when you point this out, she is annoyed because you picked on her words while missing the feeling behind them. Responding to the feeling would be more like: "You feel the load is too heavy?" Then you might get the answer, "I'm tired out and you are just sitting there watching that damn 'boob tube.'"

Full communication has six characteristics:

1. *It is open.* Small children often communicate beautifully. When your baby reaches for something and says, "I want that," you haven't the slightest doubt of what he wants. His voice, gestures, body movements all say the same thing. Adults, who are less open, communicate less well. Communication is inadequate when there are forbidden, closed-off areas (such as the discussion of sex or politics); when there is any hiding or pretending

or distrust; or when there are attempts to control, to manipulate or to "win" an argument.

2. *It is a process of the whole person* involving all three functional levels: intellect, emotions and behavior. The signals on the several functional levels supplement but do not contradict each other.

3. *It is a process of people who are in touch with themselves.* It arises out of effective internal communication. The signals are clear and true, not distorted.

4. *It is two-way.* A monologue cannot be effective communication because the speaker is not in touch with his listener's state of mind and feelings; he is not getting feedback (we will discuss this shortly). Good communication requires the ability to interpret incoming signals, both verbal and non-verbal (listening, observing, being touched, etc.) as well as to signal outwardly.

5. *It is a process that, to some extent, integrates the Internalized Others Dimension and the Childlike Dimension with the Maturing Self Dimension.* An outgoing message that comes solely out of either the Internalized Others Dimension or the Childlike Dimension without being modified by the Maturing Self Dimension is likely to be an incomplete message—too one-sided, too distorted. It may bore, annoy or mislead.

6. *It is a human process between unique human beings* who respect each other and reach out toward each other. We too often break off communication or withdraw from it when the process gets uncomfortable, long before a true connection is made, before issues are resolved, before emotional conflicts are dealt with. To achieve effective communication, many old habits (such as that of withdrawal) may have to be abandoned and new approaches practiced and learned. But without effective communication, Open Family Living is impossible.

KEY METHODS IN COMMUNICATION BETWEEN PEOPLE

Communication in only one direction with no signals coming back is like the verse:

> I shot an arrow into the air.
> It came to earth I know not where.

Random arrows can hurt. And communication without a signal coming back to check it by is blind. A writer, for example, is seriously handicapped. The only final check on whether he is getting through to his readers (except for the few who read his manuscript) is the verdict of the critics and whether the book sells. This may come too late to help him much. This is the chief reason for my request on the inside cover that you, the reader, write to me about your experiences in applying the system of open family living.

When I speak of **feedback** in communication, I mean a response to a message that indicates whether the message was received and how it was interpreted. We often put out special messages to draw feedback, and I call this process **checking out.** We need to do this to be sure that our message is coming through clearly and without distortion. We do it by asking and answering questions about our communication.

Suppose, for example, you suggest to your wife, "Let's just the two of us go off tomorrow and have a holiday." You think you are proposing something very nice. But she hesitates. You ask, "What's the matter, dear?" This is checking out. "Well, I wish you had let me know earlier. I have no clothes ready," she might say. This is a first feedback. Now you know that your spontaneous suggestion was not as welcome as you expected. You had intended to communicate a delightful, spur-of-the-moment idea. But you had forgotten that she is not so fond of surprises. She likes to plan.

Now you try again: "What I had in mind wouldn't require dressing up." "Oh dear," she says, "but I *love* dressing up. You only have to give me time to get ready." With this feedback, you discover that a holiday without dressing up would not be a holiday for her. So you ask, "How much time would you like?" "Two or three days," she answers. "Three days would throw me into next week," you point out, "and I can't make it next week. I have a whole pile of appointments. Could you perhaps make it day after tomorrow?" "O.K.," she says, "day after tomorrow it will be." And she is happy.

This is an example, not only of checking out and feedback, but also of negotiation. **Negotiation** occurs when two (or more) people work together to develop some kind of outcome that is reasonably satisfying to both. They do this by sharing their ideas and feelings; by determining available alternatives; by deciding together what action to take; and by agreeing how the decision will be carried out.

In the above situation, your checking out ("What's the matter?") brought feedback that told you your original plan was not quite satisfactory to your wife. Her request for three days is not satisfactory to you. The two of you seek a solution that is acceptable to both.

This might not have worked out so well had either of you reacted differently. You might have become angry at your wife for not appreciating your surprise proposal. She might have been angry at you for springing a surprise without giving her time to prepare for it. You and she might have quarreled and the plan might have been abandoned. You might have permanently dropped the whole idea of impromptu holidays ("I'll never offer anything like that again!")

Failure to check out, listen to feedback and negotiate is at the root of an enormous amount of family friction and unhappiness. Just as communication proceeds on three levels—the conceptual, the emotional and the behavioral—so also does feedback. Let's return to Dorothy who is upset by George's continual put-downs, and George, who is angry at his wife's superior attitude toward him and feels he is not treated as a person. This couple is at loggerheads, not only because their inner communication has been faulty, but also because they do not know how to check out, they do not hear the feedback that comes through, and hence they cannot negotiate. They only fight.

Without feedback, people make incorrect assumptions about each other. One rule for meaningful communication is: *Don't assume. Check out.* George, in the preceding example, assumes that his wife is deliberately trying to undermine him by tearing down his self-respect. He assumes this, but he has never checked it out. If he did so, he would find that this is not true. She is reacting to his reactions to her reactions to his reactions, and so on; and, up to the time she begins to work on inner communication, she is not clearly aware of how she undermines him. His pattern is to react angrily to the undermining, but never to say to her, "You are undermining me." So she has been left without a clear picture of how she affects him.

Dorothy assumes that George is angry because he is a guy who never grew up, but she has not checked this out either. If she did, she would find that he has understandable reasons to be angry with her.

Unchecked assumptions about other people's feelings are hazardous and very often wrong. No matter how well we think we know our spouses and our children, we step into quicksand when we make assumptions about how they feel. *Always check out, get feedback and pay careful attention to the feedback signals.*

Most of us, if we are accustomed to the use of feedback at all, think of it as *intellectual feedback.* Suppose I state an opinion. You respond to my statement. Your response shows me that you did not quite understand what I wanted to convey. This leads me to reformulate the statement. Again you respond. I gather that you came closer this time to understanding my meaning, but I see also that my statement was not quite accurate. I have to change it a bit and expand on it. The interchange has pinpointed errors in my thinking. I reformulate it still again, and again you respond. With each interchange we theoretically come closer to understanding each other, and we also may change each other's thinking. You may point out faults in my logic or gaps in my knowledge. True communication with clear and honest feedback can be an exciting learning process.

But it may not actually work out this way because along with the intellectual feedback goes *emotional feedback.* Your criticism of my statement disturbs me. I bristle slightly. You note the bristling and hold back on your next criticism. You don't come through quite honestly because you are afraid I might take offense. I hear the hesitation in your voice and the "ah's" and "ums." I see your eyes shift away from mine. Now I am getting emotional feedback that is beginning to interfere with the intellectual learning process, and I need to work with myself to overcome my feeling of a wounded ego. If I do not do this, your intellectual feedback fades out and I can learn little more from it.

There can be *feedback on the behavioral level* also. George verbally attacks his wife in one of his angry outbursts, and she withdraws, crying. If he then goes off by himself, there is no opportunity for feedback. It is an interrupted communication. But suppose, instead, he goes to his wife's room, stands behind her as she sobs, and puts his hands quietly on her shoulders. If she pushes his hands roughly away, that is one kind of feedback. If she leans her head back against him, that is another. George, like many people in our culture, has a pattern of withdrawal after he has expressed his own feelings, and so this kind of feedback is not usually allowed to take place. But if he can break the withdrawal pattern, the behavioral feedback of his wife might tell him much about their relationship.

There are a number of ways in which instead of facilitating feedback people cut it off, thus aborting their communication. One is by "laying down the law." Who is going to respond to a pronouncement that says, "This is it—there's nothing more to be said"? Often, nothing more *is* said. Another way of stopping feedback is by judgmental criticism: "That's wrong and I won't hear of it!" True, you don't hear of it; but you aren't getting feedback, either. Still another way is to give unasked-for help ("Oh, let me do that for you") or unsolicited advice ("If I were you, I would . . ."). You take over then, and you may be uncertain later whether your help or advice was wanted or not.

The drawing of feedback is facilitated by interspersing one's conversation with *checking out* phrases such as: "Do you follow?" "Do you see what I mean?" "Do you hear what I am saying?" "Do you get my feeling?" "Am I coming across?"

The listener, too, can draw feedback from the speaker by such phrases as, "How's that again?" "I'm unclear about . . ." "Would you repeat . . . ?" "I understand." "I assume you mean . . ." "I hear you saying . . ."

Feedback on emotional and behavioral levels is facilitated by eye contact. If, when talking with you, I do not look at you, I may miss many of your signals.

Communication skills, like those of any art, require thought and practice and cannot be learned overnight. But every failure can be turned to good account and used as an opportunity for pin-pointing faults. ("How could I do better next time?")

An instrument of potential value in this is the tape recorder. The recorder may not always be handy when a situation blows up, but if it is possible (perhaps through the co-operation of another family member) to record a family discussion of an important issue on tape, the replaying of it later can be a revelation. "Did I sound like that?" you may say. "Did I really say that? It's unbelievable." But it happened; the record is on the tape. When you hear it, you learn your own personal and family lessons from it.

We proceed now from this discussion of communication itself to an examination of how it can be used (particularly inner com-munication) in developing some of the qualities of humanness that lie at the core of open family living, and in preparing the ground for a greater realization of our human potential. ►29

Suggested Interaction Experiences

IE-25. FEELING YOUR FEELINGS (PP. 221–22)

Ask a family member or friend if he would participate with you in an experience designed to help people get in better touch with them-selves. If he agrees, then sit facing each other. Reach across and take his hands in yours. Now, close your eyes till the end of the experience and ask him to do likewise.

Give your partner the instruction to "feel the feeling you feel at the moment you feel it and describe it in one word." Promise him you will do the same. Take turns in sharing a moment of feeling. Continue the experience for several minutes, at least, long enough to give each of you a chance to identify and share several different feelings.

EVALUATION: Did you think you were really in touch with your "in-sides"? Was your partner? Did you observe a feeling sequence, such as: from silly to self-conscious, to annoyed, to anxious, to uncom-fortable, to a little intrigued, to silly again, to interested, to warm, to excited, to fun, etc. Were you able to listen to each other with full at-tention? Did your partner's sharing of his feelings influence what you felt and how you shared? Did you influence him? What did you learn about yourself and your partner as communicators?

IE-26. COMMUNICATION THROUGH WORDS (PP. 230–31)

Pick a partner and sit facing each other. Talk to each other in the manner suggested below. Observe how you feel as you do so. Also, be aware of how your partner is giving and receiving these messages.

(1) Talk two or three minutes to each other using only statements that begin with the word "you." (Examples: "You seem tense." "You look very attractive.") Ask no questions during this interchange. Then discuss the experience with your partner.

(2) Now talk to each other using only statements that begin with "I." (Examples: "I am nervous." "I am wondering what you're thinking.") Again, ask no questions during the interchange. Discuss and compare it with your previous experience with "you."

(3) Now talk to each other using only statements that begin with "we." (Examples: "We need more recreation." "We are getting tired.") Again, no questions during interchange. Discuss and compare it with your previous experiences with "you" and "I."

(4) Now make any statements you wish, as long as the word "but" is included in each sentence. (Example: "I'm enjoying this, but I'm also bothered.") Discuss what effect the "buts" have on the statements.

(5) Now make any statements you wish, using the word "and" in each sentence. (Try repeating some of the sentences you made with "but," substituting "and" for "but" and notice the effect on the message. Example: "I'm enjoying this and I'm also bothered.") Discuss and compare what "but" and "and" do to statements.

IE-27. COMMUNICATING WITH YOUR BODY (PP. 233–35)

Pick a person (family member or friend) toward whom you have, or would like to have, a closer relationship. Stand and face each other. Ask him to stay perfectly still with arms at his side and say nothing until the experience is completed.

Look intensively into each other's eyes, without blinking if possible, for at least a minute. Use your eyes and facial expressions to communicate, "I like you and want to feel close to you."

Next, take some physical position toward your partner that again communicates without words, "I like you and want to feel close to you." (This may be shown by a hand on his shoulder, an arm around his waist or a hug.) Hold this position for a minute or so.

EVALUATION: Which approach impressed each of you most? How

were your responses similar or different? Was there any masking of feeling? Identify any body signals which gave clues to how each of you were feeling.

IE-28. ACKNOWLEDGING YOUR WEAKNESSES AND STRENGTHS (P. 237)

To acknowledge our own faults, limitations, self-centeredness and shameful feelings is very difficult for most of us. Challenge yourself to consider these areas and write down what you believe to be your three most glaring personal weaknesses. Next, write down your three most important personal strengths.

EVALUATION: How do you feel about these six personal characteristics? Were they difficult to acknowledge? Are you more in touch with your strengths than with your weaknesses, or vice versa? What are your thoughts on how these particular weaknesses and strengths came into existence?

FOLLOW-UP: The next time you are with someone, try to "feel" one of your "weaknesses" in operation. Stop at that instant and verbalize what you are feeling. This kind of acknowledgment, instead of hiding, will provide you an opportunity to work more constructively with your weaknesses.

IE-29. A COMMUNICATION EXPERIENCE WITH YOUR FAMILY (PP. 240–46)

Round up as many family members as you can and, with their permission, tape record a discussion of a current family issue such as, where to go on vacation, who should do what around the house, how should money be spent, what guidelines can be set for dating practices, who should get the car and when, etc. (If family members are not available, you may wish to discuss a current concern with one or more friends.) Start recording as you begin to talk about what particular issue might be discussed.

EVALUATION: Ask everyone to listen to the replay of the recording with the purposes of learning not only about how they communicate individually but, also, how the family (or group of friends) interacts as a unit. Consider the following questions:

1. Was information clearly communicated?
2. Were feelings openly and clearly expressed?
3. Did people listen carefully?
4. Were assumptions being made? Did they seem valid?

5. Did you observe deliberate attempts to get feedback?

6. Did you hear "checking out" phrases being used?

7. Were power struggles, compromises or negotiations evident?

8. What comparisons do you make between the group's determination of the issue to be discussed and their actual discussion of that issue?

9. Was there a clear outcome to the discussion? Any problems solved? Any strict rules laid down? Any guidelines established?

10. Would you say your group demonstrated some of the characteristics of full communication described on pages 238–40?

EIGHT

BECOMING MORE HUMAN AND ALIVE

You and I are human and alive. But are we human enough and alive enough? Do we make excuses for feeling half-alive?

How often does our humanness emerge in ways like these?

A husband looks at his wife in wonderment as if seeing her for the first time, and a feeling comes over him that she is unique, precious and attractive.

A wife hears emotions in her husband's voice that she had never heard before and suddenly realizes that he cares about her.

A teen-ager observes tears welling up in his parent's eyes at the sight of something beautiful that the teen-ager has made and exclaims in amazement, "Why you're crying!"

The "everydayness" of a person's life is unexpectedly and abruptly transformed into a succession of miracles, and what had previously merited scarcely a glance becomes an occasion for astonishment and awe.

What reason could anyone ever have for feeling apathetic? Can the mere fact of being alive and able to function arouse in us the emotions of excitement, appreciation, hope and joy?

Here is a woman. She is not glamorous, her hair is sometimes in disarray, her clothes never came from Dior, she is obviously no movie star. Does anybody love her? Yes, most everybody who knows her loves her because she is a nurturing person and she vibrates with life.

Here is a man. He is no athletic marvel, he would take no prizes in a strength contest, he has never made a million dollars, he never got through college, he has no inclination to be a romantic hero. Does anybody love him? Yes, most everybody who knows him loves him because he is kind, understanding and alive.

Here is a child. His clothes get dirty, his table manners need attention, he is sometimes rude to his parents, and his school report card is marked "Not working up to full ability." Does anybody love him? Yes, most everybody who knows him loves him because he is very much himself.

Knowing the whole human being means looking beyond the rather superficial criteria by which people are commonly judged. A person who is becoming more whole (as we have defined wholeness) is making growing room within himself for special qualities of humanness; and as they come into bloom, he will be much less dependent on the kinds of assets that the world most admires. He may possess some of the worldly assets—he does not scorn them—but the regard in which he holds himself (and others hold him) does not rest significantly on them.

The Humanness and Aliveness of a Child

We love a child because his eye is bright, his laugh is infectious, his enthusiasm knows no bounds. We love the breadth of his curiosity, the charming spontaneity of his reactions, the energy of his passions. To look at a free, unspoiled child is to get a fleeting glimpse of what a human being really can be.

But, all too frequently, in the growing up process, something happens to the child. He loses this verve, this excitement about life. His energies, which were aimed in a life-enhancing direction, are slowly diverted into anti-human paths. Capacities that emerge with such promise and hope begin to languish. His eye loses some of its brightness and sometimes takes on a vacant look. His enthusiasm, instead of intensifying, wanes. His curiosity, instead of expanding as his knowledge increases, becomes narrower, and to things outside that reduced range, he gradually becomes indifferent or contemptuous. His senses, instead of growing keener with use, become dulled. His strong emotions, instead of functioning as the dynamo of his personality, go underground and begin to turn against himself and others.

Why does this happen? What reason is there for it? Many people assume that such deadening of the life processes is a natural consequence of moving into adulthood, growing up, learning to work, assuming responsibilities, "meeting life," acquiring knowledge and experience, outgrowing the child's propensity to play. In this way they convince themselves that a loss is actually a gain, that retrogression is "progress," that down is up. People accept this belief because to admit that they have lost a part of their humanness in the growing-up process might be unbearable; they might go into mourning for that element of themselves that has vanished, assuming it to be dead.

But this loss of childhood's flame is neither inevitable nor irretrievable. It is not part of the nature of human beings that the process of growing older and entering adulthood should dampen enthusiasm, narrow the range of interests, deaden the senses, anaesthetize the emotions, kill delight, fog up awareness, result in feelings of emptiness or apathy. Growth can produce exactly the opposite effects. A person who is emotionally mature is able to experience (that is, consciously "feel") nearly every emotion of which a human being is capable. *All* emotions are a valid part of life. The mature person's interests and enthusiasms broaden with the expansion of his knowledge. His perceptions become keener, not duller, his awareness more intense. This is what "growing up" in its true sense means. The powers that first emerged in rudimentary form in the small child can unfold, blossom and bear fruit as the Maturing Self Dimenson grows. The fact that so often they do not do so but remain stunted and unfulfilled is one of the tragedies of our world.

What so often aborts this process of growth? One reason for it is that a child is very vulnerable, easily hurt, often forced to close himself in to protect himself. The little child learns early that his eagerness, his enthusiasm, his wholehearted approach to life, his curiosity, his experimentation, his openness, his spontaneity, and the honesty of his emotional expression make him highly susceptible to getting hurt.

"See flower, Mummie."

"You idiot! You pulled it up by the roots. Keep away from my flower pots!"

She might have said, "Darling, when you pull a flower up like
that it will die. You must leave it in its little home where it can
live."

Or: "Look, Mummie—pretty, pretty."

"For God's sake, give me that! That's my antique peachblow
vase."

She might have said, "Yes, darling, it's beautiful, but it breaks,
oh so easily. Be very, very careful. Put it back now."

The child who is reprimanded for doing what any child would
naturally do soon learns to cover up, to lie, to pretend, to take advantage of people, to manipulate and punish (including punishing
himself), to imitate instead of being himself, to try to please those
having power over him, and so on. In short, he becomes corrupted. Next time he goes to the flower pots, he will look around
to make sure his mother doesn't see him. When he wants to feel
the satiny surface of the peachblow, he does it when Mother is
otherwise occupied. And he so fearful that he drops it! Crash!
"You naughty, *naughty* child! That vase is worth two hundred
dollars!" ("But what," the child might have reason to wonder, "am
I worth?")

Many parents and others, without quite knowing what they are
doing, conspire in the child's corruption; and, to the extent that
the child is corrupted, he is launched upon a process of slow
dehumanization. Feelings are dangerous. Curiosity is dangerous.
Showing things to Mother is dangerous. Don't touch! Don't investigate! Don't learn! Hide! Lie!

Yet, those life-enhancing qualities that are being choked and
distorted are never quite killed in most of us. Our psyche is tough
and resilient. It bounces like a rubber tire on a bumpy road.
Unlike the tire, it develops ways of protecting itself. Moreover,
some of the suppressed and smothered portions are trying to
emerge and function again. If an adult sets about recovering the
human qualities he has partly lost, he will be working with powerful forces within himself that eventually can become his ally. He
can also be working toward the rehabilitation not only of his personal life, but of his family life and, more broadly, the life of the
human race.

What Makes Us Really Human?

Here are eight qualities of the human being that, if nourished, could transform personal life, life in the family and life in the world.

1. *Individual Uniqueness*

There is only one person in the world that is *you*. Only one that is *I*. Each of us is unique. But it is not enough to be unique. Each of us also needs to *feel* that it is good to be unique and to be accepted as "special" by others. But, alas, the feeling of uniqueness is not always a comfortable feeling. Many people let themselves be ashamed of their "different" or "odd" qualities, feel embarrassed by them; and so they try to be as much as possible like everyone else. If you can feel your own unique value as a person, the pressures to conform can cease to have power over you.

2. *Aliveness*

To be alive is to be awake, to respond, to vibrate, to feel, to think, to be "turned on," to be exhilarated at times, to experience a full range of human emotions, to work enthusiastically, to laugh, to play, to fulfill your potential. This is the birthright of the human child. But what do we do with it as we grow up?

3. *Capacity for Love*

This is the capacity both to love and to be loved, to give of yourself to a person, a work or a cause, to be fully present to another, to be involved, to be devoted, to seek closeness, to experience the full richness of a human relationship. Without it, life lacks meaning.

4. *Creativity*

Not the monopoly of a gifted few, but the broad human capacity to put the elements of your life together in such a way as to produce something of value: a home, a garden, a dinner, a song, a knitted sweater, a picture. Or a thought, an idea, a dream, a story, a solution to a problem, an answer to a dilemma.

5. *Sensitivity*

Sharpened sense impressions and the capacity to experience your own feelings (emotions) and the feelings of others, without which people can circle endlessly around each other without really seeing, hearing, touching or caring about one another.

6. *Awareness*

Sensitivity combined with understanding, so that the meaning of what you see, hear, sense and feel comes through into consciousness. Without awareness, people are automatons.

7. *Relatedness* (*opposite of alienation*)

A feeling of being connected to the stream of life, of being a part of nature rather than outside of it and pitted against it, of sharing the greater life of mankind, of having a relationship to the people around you. Without this quality, people may annihilate the natural world and each other.

8. *Capacity for Personal Growth*

Willingness to accept change, to be open to new insights and new experience, to let go of unprofitable ways of thinking, feeling and acting. Without this, people cling to static, outmoded forms and ultimately fall victims to forces they cannot manage.

These are qualities that appear to emerge spontaneously in unspoiled children and also arise naturally in adults who are free to be themselves. They come out strongly in the releasing and liberating environment of group therapy, of sensitivity-training sessions, of marathon groups, and of similar experiences of group dynamics. This suggests, to some of us who work in this field, that such qualities are a part of the basic human heritage and that, barring disease or the distortions of a repressive upbringing or a suppressive society, they might be expected to unfold in many human beings, just as apple blossoms do on healthy apple trees. Their rareness in the world suggests a pervasive social sickness comparable to the failure of a vast fruit orchard to produce any fruit worth eating. But man, unlike the fruit, can act upon himself and seek a path of healing.

BEING A UNIQUE PERSON

Society and its institutions are often not friendly to unique persons. People tend to be suspicious of the unusual or the different. To stand out too much—to be too dissimilar from the crowd—is to invite trouble. The crowd equates the different with the inferior. To dress unfashionably is to be criticized, laughed at. To think unusual thoughts is to arouse antagonism. To feel differently from most is to be looked at askance.

The family, where of all places uniqueness ought to be respected and cherished, is often as suppressive and unfeeling in its efforts to force conformity as is the crowd outside. A child who enjoys intellectual pursuits but not sports may be made to feel inferior by his father as well as by his schoolmates because he does poorly on the playing field. Or a child who loves to work with tools but does not respond to books may be referred to scornfully by his parents and teachers as a slow learner. Or an introverted child may be hurt by people who do not understand why he is not more outgoing. Or an outgoing, affectionate child may feel rebuffed because a person to whom he expresses affection (maybe a parent) does not respond in kind. Or a child may possess an unusual gift (say poetry or music) that is unappreciated by those around him who do not share that gift.

Whenever we reject, belittle or ridicule the uniqueness of another person, we lose sight of the similarities he shares in common with us. In our minds, we dehumanize him, we throw him into a mental waste basket. To think of him as an "oddball" is effectively to dismiss him. This is the attitude that people living in the vicinity of schools or colleges sometimes take toward students whom they neither know nor understand. Annoyed by the hair styles, beards and sloppy appearance of the students, people forget that these students are their neighbors' sons and daughters and the friends of their own children. Preoccupation with dissimilarities can obscure likenesses and even tend to make people totally blind to them.

Very often the denial of individuality in families is an unintended consequence of something else, such as economy. In some families, the younger children get hand-me-down clothes—a useful saving for the parents because children frequently outgrow clothes before they are worn out. But, to the child who is made to wear these cast-off clothes, the practice can feel like an indignity, a denial of his individuality. Sometimes twins are dressed alike because it is "cute"; but how do the twins feel about it? Are they ever asked? Does the practice undercut their individuality?

The children may have no clear feelings about this, but it is possible that they may resent it later.

Beside being unique, each person is also similar to other people, sharing with them a common heritage: all are human. There is probably no emotional state you have experienced which I have not experienced also, and vice versa. Our bodies and their organs have been constructed very much alike. Why should we not know similar feelings? Who could honestly state that he has never in his life experienced the extremes of joy and misery or the infinite gradations in between? Or love and hate? Or adequacy and inadequacy? Or freedom and constraint? Or calm and excitement? Or closeness and separateness? Or innocence and guilt? Or strength and weakness? Or attraction and repulsion? What human being has not felt all of these and more, as well as the intermediate conditions, in endless combinations?

Because we are, at the same time, unique yet similar to others, our feelings about uniqueness are confused and ambivalent. This is because likeness and unlikeness are merely different ways of looking at the same thing. Humpty Dumpty in Lewis Carroll's *Through the Looking Glass* complained because Alice looked to him exactly like everybody else.

" 'I shouldn't know you again if we *did* meet,' Humpty Dumpty replied in a discontented tone, giving her one of his fingers to shake; 'you're so exactly like other people.'

" 'The face is what one goes by, generally,' Alice remarked in a thoughtful tone.

" 'That's just what I complain of,' said Humpty Dumpty. 'Your face is the same as everybody has—the two eyes, so—' (marking their places in the air with his thumb), 'nose in the middle, mouth under. It's always the same. Now if you had the two eyes on the same side of the nose, for instance—or the mouth at the top—that would be *some* help.' "

The distinction between likeness and unlikeness rests in the observer's frame of mind. To one person, a beard is a mark of distinction and each bearded individual looks different, whereas clean-shaven people look very much alike. To another person, bearded men are members of a category (the bearded ones) and look alike; clean-shaven ones have individuality. ("If he'd only shave that beard off, I'd be able to recognize him.") A person loses capacity to appreciate uniqueness when he lumps people in any category—bearded or shaven, white or black, old or young, rich or poor, Republican or Democratic—and ceases to see them as individuals.

Every person has his own unique pattern of reacting to his life situation. He is unique in how he thinks and lives, how he feels in the morning and at night, how he eats, talks, works, has fun, handles crises, relates to the opposite sex. He is unique in how he relates to nature, acts with kids, spends money, protects himself, fights, laughs and cries. He is unique in how he handles his age and sex roles—how he feels about being a man or a woman. If he were not unique in such ways as these, you could scarcely think of him as a person.

We come, then, to a paradox. Uniqueness is universal. *Everybody is unique.* There is no "typical man" or "common man" or "ordinary man" or "middle-class man" or any other kind of mass man. The human race is a collection of individuals or, as some people might put it, a "bunch of freaks." If we were free enough, we could be proud of this. Who wants to be one of a million robots, all alike? Yet, we are all caught in the same bind: We want to be individuals and yet to be accepted by the group. Many people cannot face this. They disguise their differences or oddness, try to look, act, think and feel like the people around them, and so gradually become reflections of them. The Internalized Others Dimension in them grows huge; the "natural child" is suppressed. Gradually people like these cease to be persons in their own right —they become just a mishmash of others' values, thoughts and behavior patterns.

Anyone who senses that he may have moved in this direction needs deliberately to seek out what is unique in him, cultivate it, express it and let it grow. You can learn to appreciate your differences and oddities. They are *you.* If you have stubby fingers, you need not hide them and hope nobody notices them; there is no rule that says everybody's fingers have to be long and slim. Suppose you have a receding chin. What of it? Another person may have a trigger temper. Is he any better? If you are ashamed of a differentness or even a deformity, it is probably because someone teased and ridiculed you about it long ago, and you gave that person power over you. Take that power back. ►30

COMING ALIVE

Great numbers of people, for a variety of reasons, are locked up, closed in, functioning at only a fraction of their full capabilities. They need to emerge and learn to live fully. And this they can teach themselves to do.

What is it **to be fully alive?** It is to be awake, aware, responsive, vigorous, capable of enthusiasm and excitement, able to throw yourself fully into an experience or activity, able to draw on all your potentialities of thought, feeling and action. The fully alive person is capable of a mental state that can best be described as "exhilarating." Picture a condition in which the senses are sharpened, emotions are more intense than ordinarily, the mind is released to move in new directions and the body feels free. In this state, the sound of music or of falling water or of the chattering of birds can bring an inrush of joy. So can the sight of a wildflower or a leaping squirrel or a work of art. So can the smell of pine smoke or leather or bread baking. So can the taste of vintage wine or a crisp salad. So can the feel of wind or rain on the body or the touch of a caressing hand. It is difficult to be in such a state continuously, and you might not want to be—you might need alternating periods of inward and outward turning; but the condition to which I refer allows the alive state to come into being spontaneously with increasing frequency and intensity, generally without need for the use of drugs or other artificial aids. It is similar, in some respects, to the state which the drug user calls "turned on."

Under what conditions may you experience coming fully alive? Here are some:

When you interact with other people in ways that involve, simultaneously, your mind, your emotions and your physical body, such as in a passionate "affair" or an exciting "happening."

When you are moved by a powerful and absorbing love, such as love of a person, of nature, of music, of art, of a cause or a dream ("I have a dream . . ."), of your country, of your

work, or of anything in which you experience not only contemplation but involvement.

When you are engaged in an exciting and all-absorbing endeavor involving thought, feeling and physical action, such as
participation in a sporting event, a fight, a political campaign,
or the creation of some work of craft or art.

When a long-continued endeavor, such as scientific research (or
writing a book), finally results in discovery or completion ("I
have it at last").

When you become stimulated or deeply moved by a performance, whether a rock concert, a musical recital, a drama, or
something else that reaches you and stirs your imagination.

When the excitement of a religious revival or service in which
there is a strong emotional element "gets to you."

When you are under the influence of certain hallucinogenic drugs
("stoned").

These various ways of "coming alive" vary in quality and per-
manence. A drug-induced high, for example, may be intense for a
limited time but it wears off. On the other hand, something like a
deep love of nature (such as that which motivated John Muir) or
the dedication of an artist to his art can be lifelong.

The "stoned" state is included in this list for a reason. It differs
from the others in the fact that it is not a natural response but is
artificially heightened by a chemical agent. The reason for including it in spite of its special nature is that these various ways of
"getting high," including the drug route, are somewhat interchangeable. The drug user, having become acquainted with the
"turned on" state, is often unwilling to give up his drugs for an ordinary everyday state. However, he might be willing to trade the
"stoned" state for one of the other "alive" states. Thus, some religious movements of the young such as the "Jesus Freaks," which
send their members into ecstasy, have successfully attracted some
of the "street people" away from their drugs. The religious route
to becoming "turned on" is cheaper than the chemical route, does
not injure the body and is less likely to rob life of other values.
Another promising means of attracting drug users from their habit
is the use of fantasizing, stimulated by such means as music, dance,

dramatics or other avenues of imagination. Experiments in consciousness raising through music are being made with addicts in a few hospitals.

A true "coming alive" experience involves the whole person. Excitement of the mind primarily, as in the discovery of a solution to an "impossible" mathematical problem or a brilliant chess move, may be very rewarding, but if it stops with the intellect, there is no coming alive. Often, however, mental excitement brings emotional excitement with it, and the body responds spontaneously. The person might jump from his chair and dance around the room, or go out for a fast walk or a game of tennis.

Excitement of the emotions only, not involving the intellect—such as winning the jackpot when operating a "one-arm bandit"—is momentarily fun, but this is not coming fully alive. Nor is excitement of the body only, as in sexual intercourse divorced from affection. For a person to come fully alive, all three areas of functioning (mind, emotions and body) must be involved, all of them tuned to a high pitch.

This condition of heightened aliveness is not to be confused with euphoria—a deceptive feeling of well-being brought about in some people by drugs or alcohol, or sometimes occurring in certain pathological states. Euphoria, in contrast to the fully alive state, distorts reality so that the sensation of well-being displaces most other feelings and short-circuits the warning system that protects a healthy person from danger. Driving a car while in a state of euphoria, for example, could result in a fatal accident because the person might drive as if there were no other cars on the road. A mountain climber in a euphoric state might step off a cliff into space because he feels "at one with the universe" and thinks nothing can hurt him.

The feeling of coming alive does not suppress the grim and dangerous aspects of reality, but it charges all aspects, both pleasant and unpleasant, with excitement and meaning. An automobile racing driver, for example, while competing, feels intensely alive. His brain, sense organs, muscles and emotions are tuned to a fantastic pitch. His eyes are alert for slight irregularities in the road ahead for which he must compensate. His ears hear every change in the sounds given forth by his engine, his transmission and his tires.

His hands, wrists, arms and legs feel the road and the motion of the car on it. Many messages are pouring into his brain at every moment, and his brain works at incredible speed to sort out and evaluate them. The tiniest mistake in handling the car or an error of a fraction of a second in timing can bring disaster. The faultless co-ordination of so many nerves, organs, and muscles directed to the one goal of winning is truly a miracle. Obviously, a racing driver cannot afford euphoria. Failure to recognize and react to danger signals would almost certainly cost him his life.

The "turned on" state seems to be connected both with meaning and with fantasy. The research scientist who makes a new discovery is enormously excited by it and fantasizes about it. Meaning has been added to his life. Anything that is deeply meaningful to a person tends to "turn him on." Conversely, when we are turned on (as by a hallucinogenic drug), the intensified experience itself seems to have meaning—sometimes one that cannot be translated into words and may not long survive in memory or be usable afterwards, but is felt to be very real at the time.

Many people in our culture, especially among the young, have used various drugs to turn themselves on. It is an alluring path because it is undemanding at first and, for some, it can bring a powerful "alive" feeling. For others, it can unleash a state of terror—a "bad trip." What often is overlooked is that a chemical does not put anything into the mind that was not already there. The chemical seems in some way to neutralize certain inhibiting processes in the brain so that visions, perceptions and feelings ordinarily repressed are allowed into consciousness. This is not necessarily bad—many people are far too repressed—but it can be dangerous. Drugs are commonly taken without control either of the potency or the dosage, and this can be rather like opening a locked door with a dynamite cartridge. Smashing one's way into the unconscious has its disadvantages; and one of them is the question of whether we can control what emerges. Other methods of coming alive can be just as effective as drugs in the long run, but are much better controlled, more long-lasting and much safer. They could be likened to using a key to open the door rather than an explosive.

A natural capacity for intensified experience, whether positive or negative, seems to be latent within every human being. Drawing forth such intensified experience is one of the objects of sensitivity training, encounter groups and marathon groups. After a group sensitivity-training session involving some joyous, freeing experiences in relating to others, a college student told me that when she emerged from the building where the exercises had been held and walked across the campus, "I wanted to hug everybody in sight. But I couldn't, you know," she added, "because they hadn't had the experience."

If we can be "turned on" this easily by a simple, directed group experience, surely a family can learn to "turn on" through the interaction of its members without need for drugs. Each family can find its own approach to coming alive—can choose some activity which all family members enjoy and which can involve them fully. This works best if the activity draws upon all three areas of human functioning (head, heart and limbs) and stimulates the imagination. For one family, it might be a gala party where the entire family gets together with a ceremony and the playing of games. For another, it might be a work spree where family members all work together sprucing up the house and yard, planting flowers or creating something in the workshop. For another, it might be singing or dancing together or writing poetry together, etc. Coming alive is much more a product of doing than of watching and hearing, although there are exceptional performances by gifted artists that can bring an audience alive.

You cannot know for sure what *new* experience may bring you alive. You may, like many of us, tend to avoid new experiences; yet you cannot be sure that one of them might not unexpectedly enrich your life. For example, you might love the taste of sweet-and-sour pork in a Chinese restaurant, but you will never know this unless you try it. You might discover that skiing turns you on more than your bowling and poker ever did, but you will never find out unless you put on skis and get out into the snow. You may think that music and ballet have nothing for you, but how do you know you are not cutting off the possibility of enormous pleasure? Your dislike of people who dress oddly (as you view it) may be limiting your acquaintances to people sharing your own prejudices, yet others may be interesting, too. The limitations you habitually set on modes of travel and the kind of hotels you choose may be keeping you enclosed in a very restricted area of experience.

Your fixed adherence to conventional behavior may be placing you at the mercy of your neighbors' opinions. Actually, you might tremendously enjoy something they would think foolish or useless, but you would never know for sure.

The "turned on" feeling is not a condition that you need to struggle for or develop through intense effort. On the contrary, self-conscious effort often tends to kill it. Coming into this state is somewhat like spontaneous combustion: the event takes place at unexpected times and places when mind, body and emotions are open and receptive and the inner Child enjoys a bout of freedom. Then the problem is to stay open and receptive because almost everything in the life most of us live tends to close us up again, and we find ourselves creeping back into our shells like frightened turtles. ►31

LOVING

Love is the path through which many people experience coming alive. To fall in love—with a person, an acitvity, an art, a vision or a thing—is always to come alive, possibly for the first time since early childhood when each new experience of an unfolding world was wonderful. Love is a discovery of wonders. Watch the man in love with a woman, how he is delighted and thrilled by every expression and movement of his loved one, carried away by the sound of her voice, enthralled by her scent, moved to ecstasy by the soft feel of her skin. Everything within him responds. He wonders if he had ever lived before. Everything that happened before he met the loved one seems like life in a dark tunnel. Only now has he burst into the sunlight.

But the sunlight is where he belongs, not the tunnel. Yet he will crawl back into the tunnel unless he learns a different style of life. To stay in the sunlight for long requires staying open and receptive so that the discovery of wonders can continue; for if the man can remain sufficiently open, discovery can continue for a lifetime. But staying open is no easy matter. Habit reasserts itself. The pressures of daily life—the bills to be paid, the leaky faucet to be repaired, the laundry to be gathered, the boss to be satisfied, the baby's mess to be cleaned up—tend to push him into a desperate kind of trudging with his head down and his eyes half shut. Like a dray horse, he becomes hitched to a load—mostly of his own making—which he is obliged to pull, and he forgets the open fields in which he once frolicked in joy and freedom. Slowly, this dreary trudging smothers love and quenches aliveness.

But, in fact, a person does not have to respond to life's load, no matter how heavy, in this unimaginative manner. Although loads are unavoidable, your way of handling them is very much within your control. Some people run away from their loads—husbands flee from their wives, parents from their children, young people from their homes. Great numbers of people of all ages try to seek refuge in drink or drugs, usually not very successfully. The more satisfying solution lies in the opposite direction: getting as much involved in life as possible, sharpening your perceptions, increasing your awareness, becoming more receptive, more open, more interested and active. If a load has to be carried, you can learn to carry it without getting a bent back. And if there is someone to love, you can give your heart to that person.

Love is avoided by people who have had bad experiences with possessive attachment, which is a destructive distortion of love. They may think of "love" in terms of the jealous husband who will not let his wife out of his sight or the overanxious mother who will scarcely let her children breathe without her help. Real love, of course, not only grants freedom but grows out of freedom. Without inner release and openness, love is a crippled, wingless bird.
►32

CREATING

Almost every person has the desire and capacity to put something together that did not exist before. It may be a thought, a feeling, an activity, a plan, a game, a song, a dance, a life-style. Or it may be something constructed or formed, with or without tools: a garden, a window box, a dress, a boat, a work of art. Homes in past eras seem to have been more creative, at least in certain respects, than most are today. The work that people did in their homes had creative aspects. They often used artistry and ingenuity in the decoration of their homes and barns, producing such results as the charming Pennsylvania "Dutch" hex signs. The Shakers made beautiful, highly prized furniture. Mountain people and the plainsmen of the West produced folk music. Almost every people has produced some kind of folk art.

Observe a child who is given modeling clay, or crayons and paper, or a water-color set. His productions may lack sophistication and skill, but the urge to create, to make something, wells up in nearly every child and is a part of the Childlike Dimension of most adults. It is a natural urge, one so close to beng universal that when it is seriously absent we suspect mental illness. The natural creativity and imaginativeness of the human mind is evidenced by the incredible richness of dreams during sleep. If you think you have a dull, unimaginative mind, try an experiment: keep a notebook and pencil by your bed and write down your night-time dreams. You will find that you are extraordinarily imaginative and creative, for those dreams all came out of *you*— who else?

Creativity is so deeply embedded in the human being that it expresses itself even in the face of fierce suppression, as is observed in countries having totalitarian governments. Yet modern life is often more damaging to human creativity than are suppressive environments because it entices people to spin away their lives in passive entertainment and other non-creative channels. The machine has eliminated much of the creativity that once characterized such skilled crafts as those of pottery, printing and cabinetmaking. Industries have gone to mass production, denying workers an opportunity to contribute their unique and individual touch. Work has largely ceased to be a personal expression of the worker's pride in his skill. So we get building foundations that crack, pipes and roofs that leak, furniture that falls apart, clothes that separate at the seams, appliances that do not work, and so on. Since creativity has departed from work to such a large degree, the home is now the one place where there is the greatest possibility of keeping it alive. Since the home is where creativity originally centered, the process has come, in a sense, full circle.

But far too few homes are creative today. Some are little more than places to sleep, procreate and, occasionally, eat. Husband

and wife, in many instances, both work outside. Meal preparation, which in earlier times was a highly creative task, has been reduced largely to opening cans and frozen-food packages. People increasingly go out for meals, watch TV, live in small apartments or trailer homes where there is little space to pursue interesting self-directed tasks. Their creative urges are allowed to atrophy until, except for a vague sense of emptiness and uneasiness, there may be scarcely any external sign that the urges ever existed. But there is a penalty to be paid: Life begins to seem increasingly meaningless. A wide generation gap can develop between parents who have smothered their creative urges and young people who still possess those urges but are not equipped, skilled or given the means to find satisfying outlets. This deprivation alone could account for much of the unrest and rebellion among the young.

One of the most urgent tasks that parents can undertake is to bring creativity back into the home, not only for their children's sake but for their own. To do so will require alterations in the lifestyles of many families. Parents need to band together to stop letting commercial interests decide what kind of toys children should have. Mechanical toys which imitate trains, tractors, airplanes, guns, etc., and break in a day or two give little impetus to a child's creativity. What a child of either sex needs is toys that stimulate his imagination and allow him to make, to build, to construct, to rearrange, etc., such as blocks, boxes, construction toys, paper, crayons, paints and the like. (Not books to be "colored in," by the way; let the kids draw their own pictures.) Much time spent in passive TV watching could be reclaimed for creative pursuits. Household drudgery jobs could be rotated so that no one family member, such as the wife or daughter, gets stuck with all the dreary work like cleaning the oven or washing the bathroom floor. Cooking can be made creative again, and all family members can learn to enjoy concocting new dishes.

The number and variety of possible creative pursuits for adults as well as young people is endless: dressmaking, woodworking, decorating, making pottery, growing plants, learning a musical instrument, painting—the list could go on for pages. Information and training courses on such activities are widely available. People are increasingly seeking these outlets. A family in which parents, children and teen-agers are all busy doing something they love is a family that already has erected a bulwark against the disruptive and dehumanizing forces from outside. ▶33

BEING SENSITIVE AND AWARE

Being sensitive to what is going on within and around you is a step to being aware. **Full awareness** is reached when a person is functioning harmoniously on all three levels: emotional, behavioral and intellectual.

For example, suppose a person who has been accustomed to traveling a certain route by car walks it instead. He sees things he never noticed before: a gnarled tree in a back yard with a child's swing hanging from it, a window box full of geraniums on a rundown house, a peace symbol scrawled on a concrete sidewalk, a horrifying glimpse of poverty through the uncurtained window of a building. He catches odors that he misses when he travels by car: the fragrance of a dooryard flower garden, a whiff of frying bacon from a house, the perfume of a woman who has just passed by, the less pleasant scent of garbage awaiting collection. He hears sounds ordinarily unnoticed: someone trying to play a flute, the chirping of birds, the barking of a dog, the noise of hammering in a building, a mother calling her child. He experiences a greater variety of touch sensations than he usually does in the car: the different feel of concrete under his feet as compared with asphalt, the texture of a picket fence which he touches as he passes, the coolness of the wind on his face and the warmth of the sun on his head.

If, when he walks, he is withdrawn into a world of his own thoughts, he might be oblivious to all these sense impressions. We could then say he is insensitive at that particular time because these sights, sounds, smells and sensations, although picked up by his sense organs, are not getting through to his consciousness. He is shutting them out to concentrate on something else. Insensitivity carries with it unawareness: He is not paying attention to what is going on around him and makes little response to it. Nothing much is happening inside of him as a result of these impressions reaching his sense organs. Perhaps he is concentrating on a business problem. His Maturing Self is temporarily overpowering his Childlike Dimension, not allowing the latter to function.

Let us suppose, now, that instead of remaining untouched by these sense impressions, he responds to them. He enjoys these sights, feelings, sounds and smells that he usually misses. He has emotions of pleasure, surprise, shock, distaste, wonder, hunger, curiosity. If he stopped to ask himself, "What am I feeling now?" he might be able to identify some of these feelings. But he does not ask. At the end of the walk he has the general impression that it was a different experience than the one to which he was accustomed and that it was moderately enjoyable. He has some sensitivity, but still very little awareness.

Let us now imagine that this man is quite aware, not only of the sights, sounds, smells and touch sensations as they occur, but also of his own reactions to them. He consciously feels his pleasure in the flowers and birds, his enjoyment of the perfume, his repugnance at the squalor and the garbage, his sensations of well-being in the exercise of the walking, and so on. The feelings set off trains of thought and memory as he walks. He wonders what kind of woman was wearing that perfume and who in that neighborhood might have chalked a peace symbol on the sidewalk. He now has a considerable degree of both sensitivity and awareness. He has a feeling for what is happening around him as he walks, he senses the throbbing of life everywhere and he responds to it. He is aware of these responses, and they have meaning for him. His Maturing Self and his Childlike Dimension are both functioning.

Awareness, however, can go deeper. It can involve participation. Suppose the walker sees a small boy swinging from the gnarled tree and stops to chat with him. Suppose he sees the owner of the dooryard garden and asks her what some of the flowers are. Suppose he notices that garbage is not being regularly collected in that neighborhood and raises questions about it at City Hall. Suppose the poverty he sees stirs him to volunteer his services to a social agency or an educational or religious organization. Awareness without involvement does not reach full depth although it is incomparably superior to unawareness. Awareness plus involvement lead to meaning: the walk, instead of being merely a series of random experiences, begins to relate to the life

of his town. It may have started out as random, but, if he participates, it will end up with a purpose.

There are, then, several kinds of awareness:

1. The awareness of sensations. ("This is what I see, hear,
touch, taste and smell.")
2. The awareness of emotions. ("These are the feelings I
have.")
3. The awareness of behavior, including body postures and
habits. ("There I go again! I do it every time.")
4. Conceptualization of the meaning of the experience. ("I feel
this way or do this because . . .")

Awareness, when it has expanded to include all four of these
aspects, is a royal road to freedom, though a rough one because
through it we are brought face-to-face with our patterned rigidities
("I did it again"), our prejudices ("I can't *stand* people who do
thus-and-so"), our obsessions ("I'm a nut about this or that")
and our compulsions and addictions ("I've got to . . ."). The
fully aware person sees these forces working in himself—many of
them a product of his Internalized Others Dimension—and can
appraise them. To reach this point is a step toward becoming
liberated from subjection to them and therefore freed to claim
one's full humanness.

Consider another example. Suppose you are suddenly very annoyed at your child because of a casual remark he made. You
know you are annoyed, but you recognize that your feeling is
more intense than is justified by a child's remark. This is a partial
awareness. Realizing that your annoyance is unreasonable, you
guess that there must be a hidden cause of which you are not quite
conscious. Even if you never identify the true cause, this partial
awareness is useful and may head you off from some unwise reply
or action. But you continue to think about it and try to replay the
action in your mind, and suddenly it comes to you what upset you.
It was the ridiculing, contemptuous tone of voice that your child
used toward you—not the words he said. This inflection carried
you back to a time in your childhood when you were ridiculed and
made to feel foolish and rejected. When you understand this, your
self-awareness has deepened. Now you are much better able to

deal with your annoyance. You know it is absurd to refight the
battles of your childhood with your own child. You are even able
to laugh at yourself. You no longer feel impelled to say something
nasty to him. Awareness has not entirely calmed your feeling, but
it has helped to defuse it, to diminish any power it contained. You
can tell your child frankly how he affected you. That is communication. He, too, may then become more aware himself and
learn to avoid offending by ridicule and contempt. ►34

FEELING RELATED

Although connectedness is the natural condition of man, our need
for connectedness is at war with an environment that is constantly
trying to disconnect us. The condition is most evident in the
congested cities, but is spreading rapidly into suburban areas as
apartments and condominiums replace open spaces. The city or
suburban dweller lives largely insulated from the earth, from
climatic extremes, from growing things, from hard physical effort,
from incentive to exercise his body, from many kinds of discomfort
and pain, and from other people. He may go through a lifetime
rarely experiencing his uniqueness, his aliveness, his creativity, his
capacity for love, his sensitivity, his awareness or his relatedness to
the life around him.

Part of the problem is the fact that our work often isolates us
from the realities of human interaction. Much of what we do is
impersonal, oriented to institutional requirements. When we deal
with people in our work, we often do it in terms of their roles and
may not think of them as individual, unique persons. Managers
think of employees as "labor," workers think of managers as
"bosses," business men think of other business men as "customers" or "competitors," politicians think of constituents as "voters,"
and so on. Human relationships in society have turned into a vast
web of role interconnections in which the purely human element is
pushed far into the background. You are caught up in this; you
cannot help it. But you can, if you choose, develop an ability to
see through any given role to the human being behind it. A simple
way to begin is with the waiter or waitress in a restaurant. Do you
look the waiter in the eye? Would you recognize him if you saw
him again, say, in the supermarket? Does he look *you* in the eye—

does he recognize you as a person? Or are you, to him, merely "table No. 5"?

The same thing applies in a family. Do the members see and experience each other as persons? Or merely as husband, wife, father, mother, kids? The tendency not to experience individuality (uniqueness) is increased by our incessant busyness and chronic fatigue. To become whole persons, we need spaces between our activities—time to find ourselves. What chance does the overburdened mother have who is on the go from early morning until late night carrying a full-time job outside the home, doing much of the family shopping and housework (as many do), preparing the meals and taking care of the children? Or what chance does the hard-working husband have who combines a daytime job with moonlighting to earn extra cash, squeezes in night-school courses, helps where he can with the housework and children, and spends most of his weekends performing these various tasks? People like these certainly have a most difficult problem. They are victims of social and economic pressures that take little account of real human needs. A certain amount of free time, time for recreation, time simply to feel and think are essential to human beings. Children need this, too. Overbusy people have to sacrifice something, carve out some stretches of time, even if it amounts to only one or two hours a week, and endeavor during those precious hours to raise the qualitative level of their inner and outer life.

Isolation is largely self-imposed. But urban life increases the tendency to self-impose it. Millions of city people do not know their next-door neighbors. People become closed in upon themselves. And this closed-in state shuts out not only neighbors and strangers, it also shuts out, in many cases, members of their own families. Closed-in people wear an invisible sign that says KEEP OUT.

While great numbers of people in our society fear being close to others, they are, at the same time, terribly lonely. They long for, as well as dread, closeness to another human being. The longing and loneliness arise from their suppressed humanness; for it is human to want to reach out to another and to have the other person respond. Human beings are not built psychologically to live in isolation. When they do so, it is because of fear—a dread of being entrapped, possessed, smothered, overcome, broken into, deflected from the course they have set for themselves. Like any other fear, this fear feeds upon itself. The more one yields to it, the more paralyzing it gets. It is necessary for your emotional health to break out of isolation: to call on your neighbors, invite them to tea, talk with strangers in the supermarket or laundromat, telephone your friends, write notes, give people flowers from your garden—whatever will draw you closer to others. It is ultimately through human relationships that life is felt to have meaning.

To feel **relatedness** is to feel a connection with other people and with the whole world; to care about what happens to people and to the world. It arises from an inner relatedness, the feeling of being all one. If you are at one within yourself (i.e., whole), you are not afraid that your emotions might betray or run away with you or that your thoughts will misdirect you or that you might act foolishly with your body. You can feel, most of the time, at one with your family, your community, your nation and mankind as a whole. Beyond this, you can feel yourself a part of the natural world. You will not want to shoot song birds or students, tear down trees, dump poisons into the rivers or litter the landscape. You will understand that you yourself are part of the world around you and that when you damage nature you damage yourself.

This kind of feeling can arise spontaneously in a person who lives close to nature, as the American Indians did, not to exploit it but to dwell in it and with it. The artificiality of so much of our life tends to smother this feeling. Yet the feeling is still there because it is part of our basic humanness. Only our upbringing and the kind of life we lead sets one part of us against another. As we rethink our values and simplify our life we can move toward this feeling of relatedness; and as we do our family life becomes enriched. ►35

GROWING

If our family life is to be a kind of garden in which human beings grow, we must have a fertilizer to nourish their growth. That fertilizer is a combination of all the qualities of humanness that we have discussed. Growing and maturing are natural processes. We do not have to pump air into a baby to make his body grow. All we do is feed him, love him, talk to him and meet his needs. Many children in the Western world, except in poverty areas, get enough physical nourishment, but not many get enough emotional and spiritual nourishment. They do not get enough freely given love, enough feeling of being wanted, enough security and sense of self-worth to be able to let go of the defenses with which they try to protect themselves. Cooped up behind those defensive barricades, they are hampered from growing emotionally and, therefore, from fully living. A person's capacity to love, to give, to help another, to lift someone out of his despair, to be a friend, to be a good parent or a good son or daughter—all these capacities are crippled if the person has to keep defending and bolstering a weak ego that never quite found itself.

To grow is to be willing to consider new ideas, to develop new skills, to accept new feelings, to try new experiences, to experiment with new life-styles that contribute to the full development of one's capacities and talents.

Intellectually, we cannot travel through the twentieth century exclusively on nineteenth-century ideas. The tighter the grip outgrown ideas have on us, the less room we give ourselves to think and innovate. This does not at all mean that the old ideas are wrong and should be abandoned. Many are valid and constructive. Some are products of great minds of the past and we would ignore them at our peril. But we must be free to re-examine and reinterpret all thoughts, to test whether they apply under the new conditions. We cannot afford to accept any belief just because "this is what Mother and Dad taught me," or, "this is a teaching to which I have always clung." It may be comforting to feel that there are principles or truths on which one can eternally depend without question or reflection, but to take this position without constant re-examination is to crawl into an intellectual shell in which we have a false and deceptive sense of safety. Even the crab, who lives in a shell, has to make himself a new and larger one from time to time. How else could he grow to full size? Our present age is not a safe haven for people who insist on hanging onto ideas developed under other cultures and conditions, and this kind of fixation is especially risky for parents whose children are exposed to a be-

wildering confusion of conflicting ideas beating upon them from
every quarter. The old, protected, homogeneous community of
commonly accepted ideas is vanishing, and our best defense (and
offense) in the times that lie ahead is to keep as open as possible
to new knowledge and insights.

Emotionally, too, we need to open ourselves if we are to grow.
The motto on our desk pad should be: *"Feelings are human;
never be ashamed of them."* If I feel sad because of the death of a
dear relative and I want to cry, let me cry my heart out, even if I
am a man and even though I was taught that it is unmanly to cry.
If I do not cry on the outside, my distress on the inside can make
me sick and weak. If I am angry, let me admit it. There is nothing
shameful about feeling angry. But let me learn to work with my
anger so that I do not foolishly destroy a person or a friendship. I
can handle my anger much more effectively if I am conscious of it
as it mounts, than I can if I suppress it until it bursts forth uncon-
trollably like dynamite touched off with a cap. Let me learn to feel
and express affection by all the little words and touches that outwardly convey that feeling.

Finally, there is the need to try new experiences and to break
through some of the rigidities in our life-styles. When we feel stale
and static it is time to do something different, make a change in
our routine, go somewhere else, meet somebody new, try a new
job, learn a new skill, read a new book, go to a museum or play or
a circus, take a bicycle trip, do something we never did before—
not as an escape but to nudge ourselves out of our tight little bas-
tions.

Parents who refuse to open themselves to growth are heading
for trouble with their young. To stay with the young today
requires an agile parent, free to acquaint himself with new aspects
of life, not one who is rigidly bound by ideas and life-styles that
he cannot or will not change. ►36

Enlivening Family Life

Becoming more human and alive is not only a matter of individual
growth. It is a family concern as well. A family made up of lively
individuals might not necessarily be a lively family. For the family

to be lively, the family members need to turn *each other* on. Sometimes one member of a family "comes alive" while other members do not. This may produce tensions that close off communication instead of opening it. The passion and enthusiasm of the more alive member may be experienced by the others as a threat or reproach. They may be jealous of his openness and freedom and try to pull him down.

The ability to come alive in a pursuit or career is clearly not the same as the ability to turn on *with people*. A person may possess the first ability in high degree and be seriously lacking in the second. Yet, *the family that does not know how to come alive in the relationships of its members is heading for trouble.*

Let us take a look at a couple that fell passionately in love ten years ago, married and now have two children. At the beginning they were entranced by each other. Now their view of each other is less rose-colored. The lady's figure is not as slender and graceful as it once was; she is anything but beautiful in the morning; her clothes are sometimes poorly chosen and unbecoming; her teeth are irregular (which used to fascinate her husband but does not now); her voice is occasionally shrill (which he had not noticed before); she parks the car with the keys in it no matter how often he remonstrates. But her husband's disillusionment with her is fully equalled by her disillusionment with him. She hates the way he sleeps in his underwear, strews his clothes on the bathroom floor, drops cigarette butts in the sink, buries himself in the newspaper at night, refuses to help with the housework, pays little attention to the children, and rarely takes her anywhere. Each thinks, "What came over me to marry that slob?"

Now, what has happened here? Some would say that the couple has recovered from the romantic illusions of their honeymoon days and that they now see each other as they really are. This view assumes that the disagreeable features these people now see in each other are a truer picture than the rose-colored image they had at the beginning. But is this correct? Have the partners now discovered the "real" person each married, whereas before they only saw a creature of their dreams? That is very doubtful. Actually, neither knows the other at all well. The qualities in each that annoy the other are superficial and have almost nothing to do with either's identity as a person. The husband's qualities add up to a certain insensitivity and inconsiderateness, but if he can be made aware of this without feeling attacked, he probably will change. What the couple lacks is the ability to look behind the outer covering to see the real individual underneath—to share each other's interests, loves, passions, expectations, hopes, dreams and ideas about life. Even after ten years of marriage, this husband and wife remain almost strangers to each other and to their children. Like the steak lover who has never tried a Chinese dinner, how can either of them know whether he can love the other if he does not experience the other?

Blemishes and minor flaws become less annoying when people get through to each other as persons. If the husband discovers his wife's delightful sense of humor, or her courage when threatened on a dark street at night, or her skill at refinishing furniture, or her ability to speak French, then perhaps he can forgive her carelessness with the car keys. If she discovers her husband's surprising ability to manage people or to repair a broken washing machine, or learns of his dream of some day owning his own print shop, she may not be so bothered by his habit of leaving his clothes in a mess. Real annoyances, such as the car keys or the strewn cigarette butts, can be handled by negotiation. He might try to remember to put his cigarette butts in the ash tray and she might be more careful in parking the car. The transformation this could bring in their marriage could brighten their children's lives as well.

The facets of a human personality are endless and ever-changing. No person needs to appear dull or uninteresting to another. The dullness is not usually in the person observed but in the limited interests, attention and perceptions of the observer. The person who gives an impression of dullness is incompletely seen and only partly experienced. He may well be a person who has not mastered the art of inner and outer communication. He may not be fully in touch with his own emotional life and therefore may not make it easily available to others. It may therefore require some effort to get to know him. You may not think this worth the bother, but if he happens to be your husband, son or father, or if she happens to be your wife, daughter or mother, taking the trouble to break through could be worth everything it costs.

What does it mean "to treat people as persons?" There are, in general, two ways to treat people: (1) as persons; (2) as objects. Being treated as a person, even within one's family, is exceptional in our society; we long remember and appreciate it when it happens. Much of the time (perhaps most of the time) many of us are treated as objects. Great numbers of children are treated as objects from morning to night. I have referred earlier to the tired, irritable mother with a small child in a supermarket. She jerks her child's hand away from a pile of fruit. He screams and she slaps him. He complains and she growls curt commands: "Stop that!" "Get away from there!" "Shut your mouth!" and so on. Observe the husband (perhaps a similar child grown up) who ungraciously doles out petty change to his wife, forcing her to beg for anything she wishes to purchase. There is the married person who treats his spouse as property, as, for example, the old-fashioned husband who demands his marital "rights" whether the wife is in a mood for it or not. Or the in-laws who demand to know why a couple haven't any children yet. And so on.

All these people are treating the human beings closest to them, not as persons, but as objects to control, manipulate, push around, shout at, smack, cuff or punish. Whenever the treatment of a person—whether child or adult—ignores his feelings, thoughts, dreams, hopes, aspirations or wishes, it is treatment as an object.

How could the irritable mother in the supermarket have treated her child as a person? She could have recognized that being in a supermarket is a marvelous learning experience for a little child. From the child's point of view, all his food comes from there. He is enthralled. She cannot let him explore as freely as he would like, so she firmly guides him while she explains the different kinds of foods he is seeing. She prevents him from upsetting a precariously balanced pile of cans, explaining, "It would be fun to see all those go rolling down the aisle, wouldn't it? (Laughs) But you'd better not. The man over there would be very cross. And I would be, too." The child is far too interested to cry or make a scene. His mother is treating him as a person.

It is not hard to "turn on" with other family members. The basis of emotional connection is already there. You could begin the process at the family dinner table. What do you customarily do with your eyes while you are eating? Many people look at their food, their plates, their glasses to make sure they are clean, the tablecloth to see if there are spots on it, the view out the window if there is anything to see there; but they are not in the habit of looking closely at the other people sitting at the table.

Pick one family member and look at him as if you were seeing him for the first time. Observe the flow of expressions on his face and note his body movements and gestures. Is he tense or relaxed? Happy or sad? Excited or bored? How aware is he of you? Does he notice that you are looking at him with unusual interest? How does he respond? Is he annoyed or suspicious? ("What are you staring at me for?") Is he sheepish? ("I feel as if you were appraising me.") Does he look back at you with interest? ("Gee, you look nice tonight, Mary.") Is he curious? ("What do you have up your sleeve?") Or does he merely stare at you and shrug?

Unless yours is an open-style family accustomed to its members looking at each other as if they saw each other, a look of this kind is likely to strike a new note. It could open the way for communication, "What's on your mind, Donald? I saw you looking at me." Or it could close off communication: "For God's sake, stop staring at me like that." But the latter response might cause you to ask yourself, "What was I really feeling? Was I feeling resentful or hostile, and did I transmit that feeling by my look?"

Another approach could be to do with the ears what I have just described doing with the eyes. Choose a family member and listen closely as he speaks, hearing not only the words but the subtle inflections, pauses, hesitations, rhythms, voice tones and variations of emphasis that communicate as much as the spoken words. Words listened to in this way take on meanings largely missed when one only half-listens. Behind the words (which may be quite commonplace) there might be feelings that are exciting to sense, to watch, to hear.

When you listen in this way, the responses you make will be more to the point and perhaps closer to the other person's feelings than they might otherwise have been. He might notice this. "Gee, you're sharp tonight."

As you develop these skills of looking and listening and, of course, combining them so that you are doing both at the same time, something will happen to the relationships in the family. Some family members might not like the attention you are giving them; they are not used to it, and it may even seem to them like a kind of prying, a disturbance of their privacy. They may erect barriers. You have to be sure that your motive is not a prying motive. But people need also to share their feelings with others, to be listened to, to have a response from the others—from you. A teen-ager complained, "I wish my mother, just for once, would look at me as if she *saw* me."

If the response of other family members to your sharpened attention is negative, then it may be necessary to back off for a time and return to the practice later, perhaps less obtrusively. But don't give up. The attempts to make human contact are valuable and necessary and, in the long run, are likely to bring positive results. When the family member is drawn closer to you by your showing interest in him, the foundations for turning on are being laid.

If yours is one of those families where no one touches anyone else, try putting your hand on a family member's shoulder, give him a hug or a kiss when you greet him or part from him, and watch the result. If this has not been a previous practice, it will surprise him and he may draw back or stiffen up. But you are out to break down the rigidity and stiffness that has been keeping family members apart. If your approach is genuine and you are not just playing games, the stiffness will begin to melt. People do not really want to be separated; they want to be together. Your spouse may have been conditioned to think that if you hug or kiss him, this is a signal that you want sexual intercourse. Disabuse him of this idea. Tell him you are just being affectionate.

The next step is to share. How broad is your range of interests? How willing are you to try out someone else's interest? Suppose a person in your family is excited by, let's say, playing the guitar. You never held a guitar in your hand before. This family member —perhaps your daughter—would love to share with you the excitement of learning to play the guitar. You might say, "Oh, don't bother me. I have no use for the guitar," which would probably dampen your relationship with her. Or you might say, "I've never tried it. Show me how." It might be that, after a few tries, you decide that playing the guitar is not for you. But it also might happen that, after you learn a little bit about it, the activity turns out to be delightful. Then you have discovered not only a new way to turn on, but also a person with whom you can do it. It goes without saying, however, that no one in a family should try to force or impose his interests on someone else.

Can people turn each other on by quarreling? Under some circumstances, they can. A rousing fight can be a turning-on experience for some people; perhaps leading to increased closeness afterwards. But a healthy fight requires—

(1) That feelings are honestly and fairly expressed, yet are not used as weapons against each other. ("I am angry," but not "You louse!")

(2) That each respects the other as a person.

(3) That neither is trying to destroy the self-respect of the other or injure the other.

(4) That the fight is between equals, is not waged to establish supremacy, and is not the kind of fight one person "wins" and the other "loses."

(5) That the quarrel is not left hanging, unresolved, but is followed through, maintaining adequate communication, until some resolution of the dispute is reached either by mutual understanding, negotiation, compromise, or, if necessary, by good-natured acceptance of disagreement.

Here, as in all other aspects of human relationships, a certain openness and willingness to listen is crucial. How is it possible either to love or to fight someone if you never listen to him or he to you? His feelings may seem unjustified or distorted, you may think his arguments absurd, but if you ignore those feelings and do not listen carefully to those arguments, how can you take issue with either one? Even a fight (provided it is not a mere power struggle) requires some openness. Consider where the completely closed person is in a verbal argument. You cannot reason with him because he does not hear or pay attention to your reasons. He ignores, denies or overrides them. You cannot reach his feelings because, except for anger, his feelings are bottled up! You cannot negotiate for a resolution or compromise because he will not yield any points. Actually, he does not fight at all. He issues pronouncements and directives. He reiterates fixed opinions. All you can do with him is defy him, ignore him or yield to him.

I have rarely seen a successful family life in which the members never quarrel at all. If they never quarrel, the reason almost certainly is suppression of feelings. *Successful families are generally ones where the members know how to quarrel constructively.* If I am annoyed by something you do or say but I never tell you so, you will soon sense my annoyance in my bearing, facial expressions, tones of voice and actions (or by the way I break dishes or slam doors), but you may have no clear idea of what caused the annoyance. We will soon both be indulging in petty bickering and feeling resentful. Yet both of us will probably have only a vague idea of what is going on within and between us. We are like blackboards that are never erased. The new material is written over the old, and presently neither of us can read anything written there. A constructive fight that leads to a resolution is a cleansing process like the erasing of the blackboard. Whatever is at issue can be spotlighted, pinpointed and dealt with. Then it is far less likely to distort future communications. Both parties know where they stand with each other. Dr. George R. Bach and Peter Wyden have written a useful book called *The Intimate Enemy,* that gives helpful guidelines on how to fight in ways that strengthen instead of undermine a marital or family relationship.

Parents need to learn to fight constructively with their kids. The closed parent cannot do this. He is frozen into immobility by certain of the traditional ideas of parenthood, such as these two clinkers:

1. The parent is always right (hence, the child is always wrong). Period!
2. The parent's word is final and the child must never argue (i.e., fighting is strictly prohibited). Period.

What can a child do with this except ignore his parent, defy him if he dares, or pretend to yield but defy him behind his back? Any system better calculated to produce dishonesty would be hard to imagine.

Fighting within a family can be constructive only when it operates within the five conditions mentioned above. Otherwise, relationships quickly deteriorate. Any fight, for example that aims at undermining or destroying your opponent or at injuring his self-esteem is out of bounds in a family. Family feuds can turn into ruinous, bitter quarrels, in which communication is manipulated and distorted until no one knows where he stands. Words and actions do not jibe. There is no willingness to listen to both sides. Feuds are generally a product of conflict in a closed or partially closed family life-style. In an open life-style, a feud is almost impossible because the avenues for constructive settlement of disputes are kept open. ►37

Meditation

Being whole means having the capacity to come alive, but it does not mean being in an excited state continuously. We need also to turn inward at times to "get ourselves together." There is a way of doing this even when pressures are intense and conditions are hectic.

A research technician, for example, had a narrow escape from stomach ulcers because the pressure of his job tightened him up. Realizing that he could not afford to let the job "get" him, he worked out a successful response to deadline pressures. One morning the head of the firm telephoned him and requested some information that would ordinarily take about a week to assemble, but asked for the results in *three hours!* The man's stomach contracted, he felt an upsurge of resentment at the unreasonable demand, and he came close to panic. Then he leaned back in his chair, put his feet on the desk, took several deep breaths and fixed his eyes on the distant view of hills beyond the city. For five minutes he relaxed his body completely and let his mind go blank. Then he returned to the problem at hand. His brain worked smoothly and at high speed. He planned a procedure that would bring the results needed, and in two hours and a half he had the data requested.

A certain long-distance runner uses his running time for meditation. A certain housewife takes a five-mile bicycle ride before breakfast and uses this time for meditation. A commuter meditates when going to and from work. Many people meditate while listening to recorded music.

In meditation, the mind does not wrestle with immediate practical problems. The technician who put his feet on the desk and had a five-minute meditation was not thinking about how to perform his assignment. That would have tightened him up. Instead, he let his mind become completely relaxed, as one lets a muscle go limp. Had he not done so, his thought processes would probably have gone round in ever-narrowing circles with the pressure and confusion steadily rising. After this short relaxation, he was able to pull the elements of the problem together, rethink his position, ask questions that might otherwise have been overlooked. In some kinds of meditation one relaxes and quiets the mind by focussing on a neutral object, word or sound. In others, one deals with basic issues like: Who am I? How do I feel? Why am I doing what I am doing? Is it right to do this? Should I be doing something different? Does my life make sense? Meditation of this kind deals more with *why* questions than with *how* questions. And, finally, there is religious meditation in which the focus is on God.

Meditation is slowly being rediscovered in our time by both young and old. We have hitherto been a society almost exclusively of doers. Now perhaps we will swing back toward a more healthy balance between doing, thinking and feeling. ►38

Suggested Interaction Experiences

IE-30. DISCOVERING THE UNIQUENESS OF MEMBERS OF YOUR FAMILY (PP. 255–57)

This, preferably, is an experience for the entire family. Ask each family member to write down what he feels to be the three most significant personality characteristics of each other family member: i.e., how that person comes across to him as a person. Examples might be: passive or aggressive, outgoing or withdrawn, noisy or quiet, critical or tolerant, flexible or rigid, etc. Then compare your appraisals.

EVALUATION: Which family members seem to be alike? Which seem to be different? Is there a member who appears to resemble none of the others? Do you tend to reject, belittle or ridicule the differences you see in other members? Which members are you more comfortable with—those different or those similar to you?

IE-31. COMING ALIVE IN YOUR FAMILY (P. 262)

There have probably been times when you felt dull and apathetic and other times when you felt very alive. Try to remember an occasion when you felt the former and one when you felt the latter. Can you identify the circumstances or conditions that led to each of these contrasting states? Where and when do you feel them most often? Who is involved with you? What influence does your family have on these circumstances?

FOLLOW-UP: Discuss with family members possible new ways for coming more fully alive through family interaction. Try to cover all three areas of human functioning—intellectual, emotional and behavioral.

IE-32. FEELINGS OF LOVE AND RESENTMENT TOWARD ANOTHER FAMILY MEMBER (P. 264)

Select a family member and sit facing him. Ask him to remain silent while you look directly at him and tell him some of the moments when you *feel love* for him. Use brief sentences that begin with "I" such as: "I feel love for you when you share your hurts," or "I feel love for you when you are showing warmth and tenderness." Then let your partner reply similarly with some of the moments he feels love for you while you remain silent.

Next, use the "I" sentences to express those moments when you *feel resentment* toward the other, and vice versa. For example, you may say, "I resent you when you criticize me in public." Or your partner may say, "I resent you when you make lame excuses not to be with me."

EVALUATIONS: Compare the two sequences of "I feel love" and "I feel resentment." Which group of feelings was harder to express? Do either of you ever take love for granted? Are feelings of resentment kept hidden? Can you have negative feelings toward a person and still love him at the same time? What is the outcome of this experience? Do you feel closer to him or more distant?

FOLLOW-UP: Try this experience with another family member.

IE-33. FOSTERING CREATIVITY IN YOUR FAMILY (P. 266)

See if any family members are attracted by the idea of creating something—an original construction, an activity, an art work, a game, etc. Discuss with them what tools, materials, equipment, space, instruction, etc. they would need to get started. Work out with them a specific plan, arrange for any lessons or other help needed, and assist in getting tools and materials, if possible.

EVALUATION: Did the idea take fire or fizzle out? Was something actually created? Did the members involved enjoy it?

IE-34. DEVELOPING AWARENESS OF YOUR FAMILY'S PATTERNS (P. 269)

In the context of this book, a "pattern" is a thought, feeling or action that occurs automatically and repetitiously with little conscious awareness.

Write on three separate sheets of paper a patterned way of family living in each of the following areas:

(1) *Thinking,* such as: "My family thinks that getting an education is the most important goal in life." (2) *Feeling* such as: "My family feels discouraged at the state of the world." (3) *Behaving,* such as: "My family reacts very angrily toward any outsider who criticizes one of its members." Pass each of these sheets to as many family members as care to participate and have them add one pattern to each of the lists.

When the lists are completed, read and discuss them with the family so that all can become more aware of how the family functions in terms of thinking, feeling and acting. Consider how these patterns might have developed. Are individual family members still influenced by these patterns? If so, in what ways is the influence constructive? What ways undermining or limiting?

FOLLOW-UP: Consider what changes might be made in patterns of family functioning to enable your family to be more open.

IE-35. INCREASING THE FEELING OF CONNECTION WITH ANOTHER FAMILY MEMBER (P. 271)

Set aside at least half an hour to be alone with a family member. Pretend you are strangers who are going to interview one another. Decide who will be the first interviewer.

The interviewer asks the interviewee questions about: his present life-style; early childhood and family relationships; current feelings about himself, marriage and his family; satisfactions and dissatisfactions; a critical health problem; greatest secret; most intimate experience; a period of loneliness; a time of joy.

Interview as if you know nothing about each other. Make no assumptions and give no opinions or evaluations. Inform the interviewee that, as in any good interview, he doesn't have to answer a particular question.

When you have finished, reverse roles and let the interviewee become the interviewer.

EVALUATION: Discuss this experience together. Do you feel you know more about each other? Was the experience exciting or boring? Did you experience each other as real persons? Did it result in any special feeling of connection or greater involvement with each other?

FOLLOW-UP: Try this with other family members.

IE-36. STIMULATING PERSONAL GROWTH OF MEMBERS OF YOUR FAMILY (P. 274)

"How is our family involved in the personal growth of its members?"

Raise this issue with at least one other family member and, with his agreement, explore the following questions:

(1) Are the children urged to grow for themselves or just for the sake of the parents' convenience or reputation? (2) Are parents as well as children, encouraged to experiment with new life-styles? Or do the children press their parents to maintain the typical stereotypes of "Mom in the home" and "Dad at the office?" (3) Is the whole family "anti-change"? Or "change no matter what the risks"? Or neither? (4) Is there more concern about saving the family from embarrassment in a situation than about how to help a member achieve greater personal growth?

EVALUATION: Do you feel good about your family's involvement in the growth of its members? Or dissatisfied? How do your impressions compare with those of other family members?

FOLLOW-UP: Have a general family discussion of how the family might encourage, to a greater extent, the personal growth of its members.

IE-37. LEARNING TO FIGHT CONSTRUCTIVELY (P. 281)

Recall a marital or family quarrel that took place in the recent past. Evaluate it in terms of the rules for fair fighting listed in this chapter. Did it end with bottled-up rage or resentment? Or did it clear the air? Did it involve denigration of either participant? Or did the participants respect each other throughout? Did it end with either participant over-riding the feelings and wishes of the other ("win" vs. "lose")? Or were feelings and wishes respected on both sides? Did communication break down? Or was it openly maintained throughout?

Review the quarrel in retrospect and see if it could have been handled more constructively so that it ended with an improved relationship instead of a bruised one. Discuss the question with the other family members. Ask for their ideas as to how family quarrels might be more constructively handled and get their reactions to the rules of fair fighting here presented. Would they be willing to try to follow them in the future?

FOLLOW-UP: The next time a quarrel erupts, remind yourself and the others of the rules agreed upon and try to stick to them.

IE-38. MEDITATING ON YOUR BASIC FAMILY SYSTEM (PP. 282–83)

Go alone to a quiet place. Close your eyes and relax mentally and physically. Meditate on these basic family issues:

(1) What is my family's basic system? (Refer to Chart I, pp. 21–23.)
(2) How do I feel about this system? Does it make sense? Do I want it to continue as it is?
(3) What part do I play in my family's system?
(4) How might the family react to a change in its basic system?

FOLLOW-UP: Check out how other family members feel about these questions.

NINE

REALIZING OUR
HUMAN POTENTIAL

Where Has Joy Gone?

We live in an age when (until recently) everything seemed possible. Everything, that is, except achieving the full status of human beings. Our astronauts have gone to the moon. Space vehicles have reached some of the planets. Technologically, there seems to be little that the mind of man cannot ultimately master.

But ourselves? Here we are far less sure. While scientists and engineers pursue the conquest of the material universe, great numbers of us are feeling small, helpless and hemmed in.

Take simple joy. Is each one of us not entitled to joy? Is it not a human heritage? With all the mechanical appurtenances and aids to living—the equivalent of a dozen electrical servants in an average middle-class home—why should a simple feeling like joy seem out of reach? Why do so many people feel driven, lonely, insecure, fear-ridden, self-absorbed, empty? Our ancestors' ghosts, if they happen to be hovering around peeking at us, must be astonished and concerned. "With all *that,* they are still unhappy," they might exclaim in wonder. The ghost of the pioneer woman who had to get up at five A.M. to build a wood fire in her stove and who spent a large part of her life washing, ironing, cleaning, cooking, canning, clothes making, helping her husband on the farm and taking care of babies, could scarcely be expected to understand why her modern emancipated descendant is unhappy. Nor could a man of a century ago readily comprehend the frustration of the modern male who, to an observer, appears to possess more freedom than his ancestors, who worked eighty hours a week, ever dreamed of. In a sense, he does. But, in another sense, he does not.

An unnecessarily heavy price is being paid for the privileges of modern life. Children pay the price first. Everybody pays it later. Who needs children in the world of work—which, in the eyes of many adults, is the central activity of life? Who can use what the child has most: curiosity, spontaneity, imagination, keen sense perceptions, strong and varied emotions, infectious joy? Since these qualities do not particularly help the child to find his place in the adult world, the child's curiosity gradually declines, the spontaneity is repressed, the imagination and sense perceptions are dulled, and the emotional flow is submerged. Joy fades out.

So accustomed are many of us to a joyless flatness in our lives that we do not often question whether this flatness is necessary or makes any sense. We accept it mechanically, take it for granted. And this is our undoing. Someone ought to stick a pin in us, step on our toes, twist our arm, make us aware of our own joylessness and force us to ask, "Do I have to be like this?" There is only one answer, "Of course I do not! I have carelessly let myself drift into it."

Within all people is a gnawing desire, a barely recognized craving, for the element of joy that they so largely miss; and it is a *good* craving. Human beings have the potential for joy. But they are too easily satisfied with less. They give up too soon. They fall back on half-satisfying palliatives to which they quickly become addicted; overuse of alcohol, tobacco, drugs, gambling, exploitive sex, TV watching (as a substitute for living), accumulation of superfluous possessions, compulsive work (or loafing), and many other activities or inactivities that afford a temporary relief but must be continually and ever more frequently repeated to keep life endurable.

How did this loss of natural joy ever come about? People did not always depend on artificial aids for their well-being. As children, they certainly did not. If you were fortunate enough to be loved and to have had security in your childhood, joy came to you naturally along with a lot of other feelings. You had no need to search for it.

When you were a small child, you delighted in your body, in

your sensations of touch and movement, in the flow of your feelings, in your triumphs and accomplishments, in the attentions of the people around you, and in the trees, the sky, the wind and the rain. When happy, you skipped, shouted and sang (or weren't you allowed to?). When miserable, you cried. The adult delights in the child's delight, but he also has a condescending attitude toward it. He knows it will not last. He knows the child will outgrow it, and of course, the child soon does. Parents are proud that their child is "growing up." But should they be? Should they not, rather, mourn because the child is losing his birthright and may never know such untrammeled joy again?

Yet this does not need to happen in the way it does. Some walling in of the child's perceptions, some dulling of his emotional awareness, is bound to occur because parents are imperfect, because an indifferent society makes demands and has built an environment not well adapted to a child's needs, and because the child does not have the personal resources to deal with the unfavorable conditions he finds around him. Everyone, therefore, receives some wounds and scars in the growing-up process. But as a person matures and gains in self-awareness, he can take steps to heal the old wounds and he can avoid imposing *unnecessary* obstacles to the growing and maturing processes of his own children.

What Has Happened to the Sense Perceptions?

How about **touching?** That is where a baby begins. Studies have shown that a baby *must* be touched, picked up, cuddled and hugged if he is to survive and grow. Deprived of such physical contact, no matter how well-fed and otherwise well-cared-for he is, it appears that he will languish and, in a few weeks or months, may die. The implications of this discovery are far-reaching and barely beginning to be understood.

Every mother knows how a baby seeks to feel and touch the objects and people around him and his own body. In this manner he acquaints himself with his surroundings and with himself. Touching is fully as important to him as seeing, hearing and tasting—perhaps more so, because a baby who is blind or deaf may survive and develop (with the help of others), as Helen Keller did, but a baby deprived of touch evidently cannot.

Fortunately, for the human race, people enjoy cuddling babies, and the babies revel in the joy of it as long as they are not frightened by the emotions and tensions they absorb from those holding them. But the period of time for this is brief. When babies begin to run about, adults in our culture cuddle them less and, instead, begin to punish them for touching. Forgetting that touching is one of the child's major gateways to the outside world, the parent sets up a series of prohibitions. Some, like forbidding the touching of stoves or matches, are necessary for the protection of the child, but others, such as keeping fingers off furniture and drapes, merely serve the convenience of adults. The child wants to experience the delightful feel of fur or velvet, the hard coolness of crystal, the warmth of human or animal skin, the fluttering of a bird's wings, the pleasant sensations of his own body. He gets a series of no's from the people around him: "Keep your grubby little hands off my things," "Don't muss my hair," "Leave that alone, you'll break it." Parents are fussy about finger marks on the white paint. Store owners glare at the child for handling the merchandise. Teacher reprimands him for touching the girl in the seat ahead. He learns to feel uncomfortable or even guilty about almost any kind of touching.

As he reaches adolescence, the child runs into a series of social taboos about touching. If he feels like throwing his arms around a friend of his own sex, he gets a raised eyebrow or a frown. If he feels like doing the same thing with some of the opposite sex, he risks having the action misinterpreted—what is meant as a gesture of friendship might be taken to be a sexual overture. Some adults shrink back or push away if touched by their child or any other person. The effects of this conditioning are noticeable in the way people sit in public gatherings or in public vehicles—often as far apart as possible. A kind of mistrust operates here, even among people who know each other well. Each one shrinks from touching the other, afraid of the possible reactions, afraid of being misunderstood or rejected. Thus, each intensifies the feelings of alienation already strong in himself and prevalent in the world.

So deep-seated in our society are suspicions aroused by touching that a certain teacher who loved children and sometimes hugged or patted them affectionately was hauled into court on a charge of "child molestation." Although promptly acquitted for lack of evidence, this teacher found himself the object of bitter antagonism and suspicion on the part of the community. He was fired and his career as a teacher was ruined. Touching (especially by males) as an expression of affection is often confused in the public mind with sexual "molestation." And this is understandable; it would be easy to confuse them. Yet touching as a warm, non-sexual gesture could be a teacher's way of saying to the student, "I like you and it is a pleasure to teach you." The student's response could be an increase in his motivation to learn and in his capacity to respond to people.

There are five acknowledged senses—sight, hearing, touch, taste and smell—all of which make vital contributions to a child's learning experience, and all of which, in different ways, he is discouraged from using. Consider **taste.** The baby tries to put everything into his mouth, and the people who care for him have to cure him of this habit to protect him. Many things, of course, are dangerous if put in the mouth; some are filthy. But people go much further than keeping out dangerous and dirty things. They violate a child's sense of taste by urging him to eat foods he does not like, insisting that "they are good—yum, yum!" (They are not —to him.) Worse, adults exploit his taste organs by offering him sweet-tasting non-foods, such as candy or soft drinks, as bribes or tranquilizers. The child runs into trouble if he uses his tongue to find out what people taste like. A dog does this naturally—licking is one of his ways of getting acquainted with a new individual and expressing his fondness. But for a human being such an act is considered disgusting. By the time the child has grown up, his sense of taste often has been reduced to near-uselessness as a means of receiving communication from the outside world and has become unreliable even for the appraisal of food because of distortion by chemical flavorings and overconsumption of sugar.

Smell is another discouraged sense. Smelling too often is regarded as an animal trait. And truly, for many animals, smell appears to be the most important of all the senses; the primary means by which they can identify the creatures near them. The fact that our own eyesight gives us enough information to render the sense of smell less necessary for us than for them is no reason to neglect it as we do. By letting the sense of smell fall so largely into disuse, we close off one of the paths of communication from the outside world. Most of us, for example do not know what *people* smell like; we are rarely permitted to find out. We have been taught to think that the odor of people is bad and offensive. We do everything possible to mask and hide it. Yet how ironical that is. The same person who covers up his body odor with a deodorant may be smoking a cigar that smells worse than a bus terminal, or he may pitch an alcoholic breath like the exhaust from a chemical plant.

Of the five senses, then, three are so severely restricted and distorted in use that they cease to be of much value in the expanding of awareness. The child must rely mostly on his **eyes** and **ears.** But here, too, stifling restrictions are imposed. To learn what a person looks like, you need to scrutinize him at some length; a mere glance is insufficient. But scrutinizing is called "staring" and leads to unpleasantness. People prefer to be casually glanced at, not closely scrutinized. The sensitive child soon learns this and, if he is a people-pleaser, he eventually scarcely looks at anyone. We have a whole society of individuals who, for a variety of reasons, rarely actually look at each other. This is one of the reasons why witnesses of a crime are often so unreliable in the identification of suspects. Only very observant people, such as artists or certain policemen trained in the use of their eyes, have developed the habit of looking at people closely. What most of us see is a blurry mental image that in many cases is quite different from the individual standing in front of us. If you doubt this, try the following experiment: When with a friend, close your eyes and try to form in your mind the image of your friend's face. Fix this image in your mind, then open your eyes and look at the actual person. How clear and accurate was your image? You may be shocked at its inaccuracy and fuzziness.

Children learn early that it is best not to see or hear certain things. Some activities that go on in the household are not acknowledged or talked about. Certain body functions, certain orifices of the body, are among the unspeakables; you pretend they do not exist. Bathroom doors in most households are closed, and the child is not supposed to hover outside with his eye to the keyhole or his ear to the door. Certain facial expressions, in a closed family life-style, are best not observed or commented on: mother's suppressed rage, for example, or father's boredom. When a parent gets drunk or abusive, the child is better off not to notice. When parents are quarreling or are hostile to the rest of the family, too much seeing and hearing is painful. The child learns to close off whole areas of his perception.

As the child grows up, his senses may be used less and less as means of becoming aware of the real world outside and more and more as preselected signals relating to an extremely limited range of phenomena in which he is particularly interested. His attention becomes like a very narrow searchlight or radar beam. Whatever the beam (his attention) lights up, he sees. Everything else is in darkness, and although objects pass across his field of vision and his eyes record them, his consciousness does not register. I know a lonely woman who checks every car that passes her house and notes it occupants. This is because (1) she fears strangers, and (2) she keeps looking for a visit from her grown daughter who has come to see her only twice in ten years. She does not notice the peeling paint and loosening plaster in her home. Another woman on the same street does not observe cars, but she notes every bird that flits across her field of vision.

Hearing is subject to the same kind of selectivity. We learn to shut out what we do not wish to see or hear. Selectivity is, of course, necessary to avoid endless confusion and distraction. Only by the process of concentration and mental elimination of distracting elements can we pursue an orderly course in what we want to do. But, necessary as our narrow selectivity of perception is, there is a price to be paid for it. If we carry it too far, we become perilously imperceptive to matters that happen to be outside our restricted range of interests at that particular time. While looking for the first robin of spring, the bird watcher may miss the desperately troubled look on her daughter's face.

What Do We Do with Our Emotions?

Emotions occupy a very peculiar place in our culture. People find them inconvenient, interfering with personal objectives, upsetting peace of mind, leading to regrettable actions, seemingly incompatible with logic or reason. People's emotions at times resemble powerful engines with no one at the controls, driving them to do things they did not at all want to do, such as striking a child. There is good reason to fear and mistrust uncontrolled emotions, for they introduce an irrational element with which the intellect may not know how to deal.

The old solution, popular in the Victorian era (from which we are gradually emerging), was to suppress all emotions as much as possible, and this especially applied to men. The masculine ideal, epitomized by the captains of industry and finance, was the "iron will." A mature individual was expected to control his emotions, and the degree of his maturity was measured by how well he kept them under control. This was not an altogether successful lifestyle. Suppressed emotions have a way of sneaking in by the back door and wreaking vengeance in hidden, often unrecognized and sometimes devastating ways. This has been exhaustively dealt with in treatises on psychoanalysis and other forms of psychotherapy, and we need not go into it extensively here.

Because of their fear of emotions and of the disconcerting if not disastrous effects that powerful emotions can have on their lives, great numbers of people in our culture have turned away from the life of the emotions and refuse to give feelings their legitimate place. These people have forgotten the sources from which folklore, legends, poetry, literature, drama, music, art, religious devotion, ceremonies of all kinds, and their own night-time dreams have arisen: the incredible richness of the inner emotional life of the human being. It is the emotions that put all the color into life, that give it all its drive and, in the end, its meaning.

Imagine a robot, all computer brain and no emotions. He would be a tool for others to use, but he could have no wishes of his own, for these arise out of emotions. He would have no will or intent, except as programmed, for emotions give the will its force.

He would have no interest in anything for interest comes from feeling. He would have no concern about anything, for without emotions, everything, from the trivial to the serious, is on a dead level. He would have no sense of humor and no comprehension of play; for laughter and play bubble up out of feelings. He would have no sense of the right or the beautiful, which are grounded in feeling. He would have no conception of meaning, for without emotions nothing matters.

An emotionless robot might seem, at first, to be the perfect servant: He would do exactly what you tell him, would never intrude, complain, rebel, get tired, loaf on the job, talk back, strike for higher wages, have aching feet, let his attention wander, mix with the wrong crowd or become addicted to drugs. But his obedience to your instructions would be literal and totally unimaginative. If you made the slightest error, used a wrong word or symbol, or an incorrect number, or put your instruction in the wrong place, he would do something absurd or go haywire. As a companion, he would be far less interesting than a housefly because unless you gave him a job to do, he would do nothing— forever.

We human beings ought to be proud of our emotions. They set us apart from the computer. In conjunction with our brains, our emotions enable us to do all the things that the robot cannot do and that most animals cannot do: appreciate, understand, select values, become excited and interested, be compassionate, love, dream, enjoy, conceive of a better world, develop moral principles, arrive at insights, see meanings, experience awareness. But emotions also may drive a person to destruction, crime and every kind of folly. Emotions separated from the brain, running wild by themselves, can be disastrous. So can brains separated from emotions. Either extreme produces a one-sidedness capable of tearing an individual, a family or a society apart. Clearly, the brain and the emotions were designed by nature to work together. Yet much of your life energy may be devoted to trying, mostly unsuccessfully, to keep them apart.

Despite the great advance during the past seventy years in our knowledge of the vital part which emotions play in all human activities, our culture still downgrades emotions, relegates them to the cellar of human affairs, pays little heed to people's feelings in general, and, worst of all, ignores the emotional needs of children. A child's feelings are rarely taken seriously. His toy is broken, and the parent laughs, or ignores the child's distress, or reproves the child for breaking it. Few parents would say, "You feel bad about that, don't you?" What does a parent do with a raging two-year-old? The parent may be amused—for an angry toddler can, indeed, be funny to watch. He may distract the child with a lollipop or play "peek-a-boo" until the child laughs. Or the parent may get angry and punish the child. *But how often does a parent pay his child the respect of taking his anger seriously?* How often would a parent say, "You're angry, aren't you?" Among the unarticulated presumptions of our culture is the belief that the feelings of little children (or of big children, for that matter) do not warrant being taken seriously—that, whatever the emotion may be, it will shortly vanish and be replaced by another, that the little person will "get over it," that he will "grow up," and so on. The climate of our culture is one of disrespect for feelings, and this disrespect pervades our entire society. *We do not even respect our own feelings,* which is a natural consequence of the way our personal feelings were treated in childhood. And the individual who does not respect his own feelings impoverishes his life and the lives of others.

Racism offers one of the most glaring contemporary examples of pervasive disrespect of feelings. Racists are often quite unaware of their own attitudes. They hurt without intending to, and they are hurt in turn by their own insensitivity and unawareness. A woman in my community who had devoted a long life to various philanthropic endeavors suggested that her organization could raise money by putting on a "blackface minstrel show"—her idea of delightful comedy. That those Amos-and-Andy stereotypes which so amused white audiences of a former generation might hit a modern black audience like a hurled insult never entered this lady's head; and even when the probable consequence was pointed out to her, she insisted that it was all harmless and "in good fun." The argument that people's feelings of self-respect might be hurt brought the answer, "Don't be absurd! Nobody was ever hurt by a minstrel show." This lady was not only a perpetrator but also a victim of a disrespect for feelings which was so much a part of her upbringing and life-style that she could not see it for what it was.

The ultimate result of disrespect for feelings is that a person becomes detached from his own emotions. The thinking function operates in one isolated compartment, the emotions in another, and because the thinking function dominates consciousness, the emotions do their work to a large extent on the periphery of or outside the conscious area. This removes the emotions from the moderating influence of the intellect working through the Maturing Self Dimension. Thus, the person who has lost touch with his emotions finds himself being propelled from behind, as it were, toward goals not a part of the Maturing Self's plan. People who believe themselves to be wholly rational are blind to their own capacity for irrationality—a dangerous state of mind. If the civilized world is destroyed by a nuclear holocaust, the people who will push the buttons will act from the most "logical" and (from their viewpoint) "rational" of reasons to perform the ultimately irrational and fatal act.

One of the most fascinating aspects of the Watergate episode in Washington was the evidence that a large number of highly trained minds were operating with very little knowledge of the emotional forces underlying their own actions. They evidently did not know why they were doing what they did. When asked why, the answers of some were variations of "I was ordered to do so" and "I was trying to serve my President [or my party, or my country, etc.]." These, of course, are like the reply of a child reprimanded by teacher for punching a classmate: "Well, *he* started it." Others appeared to be motivated by the feeling that life is a war you either win or lose—a thoroughly irrational conception wrapped in the language of rationality. It is irrational because it rules out some reasonable options, such as an attempt to negotiate with opponents. Working with the "enemy" is felt by "bitter enders" to be weakness; you must, instead, grope for his throat while he gropes for yours. This kind of person may destroy his own family life just to prove he is "right."

Minimal awareness of the emotions affects people in various ways. One type of person may lead a life of dull routine or trivial fussiness into which emotions rarely enter except when the routine is broken. Another type of person, in which the thinking function is highly developed, may immerse himself in a cerebral activity, such as engineering, accounting, or the physical sciences, in which he can function efficiently with a minimal need (he thinks) for cultivating his emotional life. A third type, geared more to outward activity than to thought, may become a doer of deeds that have a peculiarly amoral quality; such people make possible such events as the My Lai and Bangladesh massacres, the Nazi concentration camps, Stalin's purges—all kinds of mindless violence. In the family, this may take the form of child abuse. Still another type of person out of touch with his feelings (and also with his intellect) is the bigot—the confirmed racist, the persecutor of anyone who is different, the hater of Jews or Catholics or Protestants or Communists, the individual who naturally gravitates to an extreme position—the political right or left—but cannot abide the middle.

All these people, of whichever type, live a life of emotional impoverishment. Their consciousness is detached from the incredible richness that flows beneath; it floats, as it were, in space. People of this sort often have little awareness of the gentle, life-enhancing emotions that are expressed in poetry, art, music, literature and drama. Only the roughest, crudest, most violent emotions get through into their consciousness. Yet these same people, at a deeper level, may be crying out to recover their humanness.

The Dulling of Our Perceptions of People

Any fragmentation of the human personality, such as the dimming of the sense perceptions or the blocking out of the emotions, diminishes both our perception of ourselves and our perception of other people. The two go together.

Let us return to the baby: A baby learns about objects by being allowed to touch, handle, lift, push, pull, throw, scrutinize, explore with his fingers, listen to, look at, smell and taste them. With people, he is not allowed to make many of these investigations—at least, not for long. One possible consequence is that people may seem less real to him than inanimate objects. He has had a chance to become thoroughly acquainted with a variety of *things,* but not with a variety of people. Sight and sound alone seem to be insufficient to transmit the sense of full reality. Thus, a parent who rarely touches his child and is rarely touched by him may not seem real to the child; he may remain a kind of apparition, a remote god, powerful but not felt as human.

Such a child may grow into an adult whose car seems more real to him than his teen-age son or daughter. He can touch the car, feel the smoothness of its finish, the coolness of the metal, the toughness of the tires, the softness of the upholstery. The roar of its engine excites him. Its sleek lines please him. The new-car smell delights him. Can this person's teen-age son or daughter delight him as much? Yes, the teen-ager could delight him far more if the parent had learned, long ago, to acquaint himself with people. But people, including his own teen-ager, do not seem fully real to him.

If people are less real to you than theoretical concepts and inanimate objects, you tend to substitute for your perceptions of people mental images that often are very poor approximations of the real person. You may no longer see, hear, touch, smell or taste the actual person. If the person you are looking at (perhaps a child) is troubled, you may easily miss noticing it, unless he does something unusual, forcing it on your attention. Then you may be embarrassed and try to make a distraction. If he is quieter than usual, you may be unaware and merely fill the gap with your own talk. Without seeing him clearly or touching him, you cannot know how tense he is, how tightly his muscles are contracted, how his emotions are boiling up and his thoughts are racing.

Human beings do not seem to have the capacity some animals are believed to have to smell another's fear. We shut ourselves off. There, in front of you, may sit a troubled child or spouse or friend; yet all you may observe is the mental image of that person which you formed at some previous time. From his point of view, you are half asleep. To get your attention, he has to shock you: grow long hair or a beard, dress in a manner of which you disapprove, join a demonstration or get bashed by a policeman. And even after all of this, you still may not see *him*. You may avoid looking and seeing by applying a label to him ("dropout," "pacifist," or whatever), so his efforts to make *you* look at *him* as a unique human being fail.

One of the consequences of fogged perceptions and blocked-off emotions is that we see people, not as individuals but as members of categories according to the roles they play or the groups they belong to: parents ("squares"), teen-agers ("brats"), workers ("hard hats"), policemen ("pigs"), strike-breakers ("scabs"), black people ("niggers"), white people ("honkies"), people in responsible positions ("the Establishment"), and so on. Each group is labeled with an epithet which is applied to *all* the persons in the group, blocking out their individuality. And these epithets are nearly always derogatory or carry a derogatory feeling. Students or children are seen as "spoiled," business men or workers as "greedy," parents as "Victorian," politicians as "crooked," blacks as "impudent" or "lazy," whites as "oppressors," and so on endlessly. The perceptions of a person who sees things in this manner are no longer focused on reality. He is living in a simplified mental construct which he assumes to be the "world" but which actually is moving farther and farther from the world of objective fact. He has cut off communication with the real world which contains unique, individual people.

The tendency to see only groups and not individuals is a profoundly dehumanizing process. This is why the labels applied to groups tend to be derogatory. The process has dehumanized the name-caller himself by limiting his perceptions, and it dehumanizes the individuals in the group by wiping out (in his eyes) their individuality.

The end result of the dehumanizing process is to confuse a person's perception of himself. Just as he sees others in terms of generalities and derogatory group judgments, so, likewise, he sees himself. He sees, not the unique person he really is, but a caricature of that person. He appraises himself in terms of the roles he plays, the groups he belongs to, the color of his skin, his social status, the work he does, the church he attends, what the neighbors think of him, and so on. These are external reflections of his identity and bear a certain relation to who he is, but they do not define or describe it. He is really someone in his own right, not encompassed at all by this kind of description. A story that points up the distinction between who a person appears to be and who he is, is the novel, *Mr. Sermon,* by R. F. Delderfield. The novel tells of a school teacher whose life has become cut-and-dried and thoroughly unsatisfying. Suddenly he quits his job and takes off on foot with a pack on his back to find out what life really can offer (which is equivalent to finding out who he is). What he discovers, to his own amazement, is that he is far more of a person than he had thought he was; he discovers in himself unsuspected depths, feelings and talents.

Few of us can read such a story without a tinge of envy—a wish that we too, could snap the invisible chains that keep us in lock-step like so many prisoners in a road gang. This is not as easily done in real life as it was for Mr. Sermon; yet the achievement is possible, though in a different way.

It is not so much people's external roles and responsibilities that keep them prisoners. It is the internal ones: long-settled habits (the same old thing); embedded prejudices ("I don't want those people for neighbors"); inertia ("why bother?"); excuses ("I don't have time"); addictions ("I need a drink"); unwillingness to change or to try the new ("I've gone to the same place every summer for thirty years"), and so on. The psychological equivalent of leaving home with a pack on your back is to cast off all these self-forged mental, emotional and behavioral chains.

Experiencing Newness

Modern life, despite the boring nature of much work, offers unprecedented scope for enrichment and personal growth. *But we have to be open to it;* we have to learn to look at everything afresh, as a child does. Change itself cannot be avoided; and in some ways we seek it—we change jobs and residences, move to new towns, travel to far places, perhaps try different sexual part-ners. Yet, even as we do this, *we avoid experiencing the newness of the change.* Too often we remain securely locked into an old system that prevents either the physical or the imagined change from producing a permanent imprint. We ourselves end up es-sentially unchanged. This is our closedness.

We poke fun at the tourist who hops from country to country (*If It's Tuesday, It Must Be Belgium*) and never experiences the individuality of the country he visits. He stays in hotels that are as identical as possible with those he has known, meets mostly other tourists from his own country and his own social stratum, eats the foods he is familiar with, plays bridge or rummy every evening, and reads newspapers from his own city. For a lot less money, he could stay at home. The opportunity for new experiences surrounds him like a cloud, yet he clings to the familiar. Real newness may frighten him. He enjoys being somewhere in its vicinity, and he likes to watch it on TV from the safe vantage point of his living-room sofa or read about it in *National Geographic*. But that is as close as many people care to get.

It is not close enough. The tourist who makes his travels really worth the money they cost is the one who meets and talks with the people of the countries he visits, sees them in their homes and at their work, eats their food, travels among them in the same manner they do, absorbs the atmosphere of the region, finds out how the people think and feel. This is *experiencing* a country, not merely passing through it. The same principle applies to a lot of matters besides travel. It applies to nearly all of life, and in particular, it applies to the relationship between individuals in a family. It is not enough to have individuals share a dwelling and eat at the same table. They have to learn to *experience* each other.

The move to a new community—increasingly common in this age of mobility—and the new friends one finds there offer unprecedented opportunities for the experiencing of newness. But we can kill off these opportunities by choosing localities and homes as nearly as possible like those we have had in the past (only slightly more expensive). And, for friends, we pick people very much like ourselves—approximately the same economic level, compatible opinions, similar beliefs, interests, prejudices, ways of dressing and wearing their hair, the same manner of talking and entertaining, the same ideas about doing business and about recreation, similar value systems. People radically different in any of these respects make us uncomfortable and we avoid them. By selecting our homes and our friends in accordance with fixed patterns, many of us minimize the effects of change. Standardized homes and friends, like machine parts, are interchangeable. After a while, we may not distinctly remember one from another. ("Remember Betty? Or was it Edith? No, I'm thinking of . . .")

Even in that most physically intimate of experiences, sexual intercourse, a succession of new partners may not involve any real experiencing of these people as unique human beings. An individual who is constantly seeking new sexual partners is often one who has difficulty in sustaining for long a relationship of depth or in experiencing the whole of another person. He shuts off much of the experience of newness by limiting his attention to genital action, with which he is already quite familiar. The more subtle differences of personality, ways of responding and thinking and feeling, and even of body structure and skin texture, may escape his notice.

Newness is experienced by opening all the senses—seeing, hearing, smelling, tasting and touching—and letting the sensations pour in, free from rigid selection. It is experienced by sharpening the awareness of emotions as they are felt, not hiding or repressing them or pretending you do not feel them.

You may begin by performing some act to which you are entirely unaccustomed. How do you usually move about? For most of us, it is by car. Suppose, then, you walk or ride a bicycle or a motorcycle. Any of these means of travel is a totally different experience—not necessarily better, but different. The sights, sounds, smells, touch sensations and emotional responses are all different. Try, for example, a bicycle trip or a pack-hike as part of a vacation. You may have the experience of being caught out in the open in a heavy rain or thunderstorm. Instead of the usual panicky sprint for shelter, try relaxing and enjoying the coolness of the rain on your body (if the weather is warm), the pelting of the shower on your head, the look of the lowering clouds overhead, the excitement of the lightning and thunder. Take off your shoes and feel the soft mud and wet grass under your feet.

If you are a restless person who feels a compulsion to go out every evening, try staying at home for a change and really experience the event. Look at the familiar objects you have always taken for granted and let them speak to you. Stay away from the TV—that is experience filtered through a tube, and what you need is experience firsthand. Listen to the sounds audible in your home. Lie on the floor and put your ear to the floor boards, or put your ear against a wall. Sounds are thereby magnified. There will be strange creaks, snapping sounds, sounds like the patter of tiny feet, the "clink" of a dripping faucet. A mouse may be loose in the house. There may be muffled voices, traffic sounds from outside, dogs barking, car doors slamming, car engines starting up, children shouting in the distance, music. Let the imagination play on these sounds. Things are happening all around you. Immerse yourself in them. Do you feel part of them in any way? After all, these are sounds of events taking place in your home or very near it. Do you feel connected? Do you feel any fear? Excitement? Curiosity?

If a member of your family or a friend is with you, look at that person as if you had never seen him before. (Perhaps you never have.) See how many things about him you can observe that you had not previously noticed. See if you can communicate with him without being defensive. See if you can experience his personality as a whole instead of reacting to some single part of it that may have formerly irritated you, such as his habit of picking at his nose. See if you can enlarge your view of him.

If your usual recreation is watching TV at home, try something new. Not that TV in itself is bad. TV can enlarge our lives by bringing into our home views and sounds of experiences we have never had and perhaps could never have. But it also can become an escape, a substitute for living. Used in that way, it constricts life instead of expanding it. You may not be aware of how your creative energies, your imagination, your capacity for first-hand experience, can slowly atrophy under the hypnotic spell cast by the flickering tube. You have to break this spell, like the fairy-tale prince waking the enchanted princess. So turn off the tube for a while and turn to other forms of recreation.

The variety of possibilities is endless. There is conversation—it seems to be going out of style, but it has its points. There are books—an incredible variety for every interest. There is music, either in the home or in the concert hall; and you can either listen to it on the hi-fi or learn to play an instrument yourself. There is the theater with its live drama, musical shows, opera and ballet. There are games—an enormous variety, from chess to parchesi, from poker to monopoly. There are sports (to participate in or to watch) from skiing to bowling, from football to tennis, from sailing to motorcycle racing. There are hobbies of every color and shape from stamp collecting to gardening or the study and purchase of antiques. There is the pleasure of growing things in pots or gardens. Best of all, there is a vast array of choices along creative lines: wood-working, pottery, painting, sculpture, jewelry making, knitting, crocheting, dressmaking—the list has no end.

There is one fact to consider, however: doing something requires effort. A weary person who has poured out effort all day is tempted to spend his evenings passively enjoying someone else's effort. But passive entertainment is insufficient exercise for the inner self, and if you rely on it too exclusively, your mind and emotional responses will become deadened. On the other hand, absorption in an interesting creative effort is an *energy producer*. One can begin tired and end up brimming with energy.

Our whole gamut of fixed opinions, habits, preferences, tastes and life-styles need to be examined from time to time to determine how they may be limiting us. A meat-and-potatoes man, for example, limits himself in the choice of foods. Because he was brought up on meat and potatoes and liked his mom's cooking, he may turn his back on lobster, crab imperial, caesar salad, French, Italian, Scandinavian, Chinese and Japanese dishes, etc.—a whole universe of delectables that he will not even try. Likes and dislikes, unless tested by actual trials over a period of time, may be little more than excuses for refusal to experience newness. There are music lovers, for example, who will not listen to anything except Baroque or classical music; some others are interested only in rock or jazz. Many of these narrow tastes betray rigidity or snobbery or sometimes a simple lack of desire to try anything new. The fewer things you enjoy, the more restricted your life is and the more it tends to close in on you.

Small children are sometimes (not always) more open than are adults to the inflow of impressions from the outer word. Watch a little child explore an area he has not seen before—a park, for instance. He kicks the gravel on the walkway, throws stones and hears them "plop" into the water, feels the rough bark of a tree, looks underneath a rock to find ants or a turtle, tries to catch a butterfly, sits in the middle of a mud puddle, feels the wind on his neck and the sun on his back, rolls down an embankment.

He has not yet learned to close himself in, though his parents quickly begin that process so that he will stay clean and avoid messing up his clothes. That marvelous openness and curiosity that makes life appear to him a constantly unfolding series of wonders can be yours too. An adult can learn to be open. The openness he may achieve can actually be more rewarding than the child's, because what is a buzzing confusion to a little child can be built into a meaningful structure by an adult who, with the aid of his Maturing Self, is able to integrate the new impressions with what he has learned in the past.

Being Aware of Feelings

Because we have had little education in recognizing, cultivating and handling our emotions, most of us stumble through life trying to hold emotions in check, on the one side, and being victimized by them, on the other. People easily experience the intense emotions—anger, irritation, excitement, sexual attraction, fear and, sometimes, love—which break through in spite of all the bulwarks erected against them. But the lives of many are, nevertheless, emotionally impoverished because they generally have little conscious awareness of the subtler, gentler feelings that flow at a deeper level like underground springs. If we could reach these with awareness, our entire life could be illuminated with new color. We could be revitalized. To reach them, we need to cultivate two areas of activity that our culture has neglected: (1) some form of the arts or skilled crafts in which the body, the mind and the emotions can function together, and (2) human relationships on the feeling level.

I have referred to the dehumanization of work and the separation of the person from his craft. People must have work they can put themselves into. Since most work in the commercial, industrial and institutional world makes little provision for this, an individual needs to find a craft or art to which he can devote spare time and involve himself. If it is an art, it need not be "longhair" art, and it must in no case be art for snobbery's sake or to impress someone. It can be simple, such as the design and knitting of an afghan or the turning of a simple pot. It must be something you do because you love to do it and because the feelings it arouses in you are nourishing and life-enhancing. Learning to play a musical instrument can be such an experience if it is taken as fun, not as an ordeal. Singing and dancing are such experiences. The human being, if he is to realize his full potential, must be released to create something.

All of us create while asleep, or while nearly asleep, in our dreams. The function of dreams is still a matter of dispute, but there can be little doubt, from a variety of experimental evidence, that dreaming is essential to the maintenance of psychological balance. When dreaming is prevented by outside intervention (based on eye movements which signal the beginning of dreaming), a pressure seems to build up which, if long continued, begins to take on some of the characteristics of psychosis. I do not wish to go into details here, but some dream research seems to indicate that dreaming acts as a kind of safety valve of the psyche, allowing expression of parts of the psyche that are given no outlet in ordinary daily life.

Suppose, then, that this is true. Are dreams enough? What kind of a life is it that would dehumanize us while we are awake and allow us to recover our humanness only while asleep? To be sure, we are part of a society that has little use for those dreamlike, symbolic, emotion-laden fantasies that inhabit the deeper levels of our mind. It is difficult to integrate them into much of our daytime existence. But, it is possible to give them conscious expression through the arts and crafts and through meditation. You can play or listen to music that transmits these fantasies and feelings. You can experience them through contemplation. You can feel them in art works by others. And you can give expression to them in creations of your own. You can paint these fantasies and symbols on paper or canvas, mold them in clay, carve them in wood, weave them into tapestries. We need to do these kinds of things.

Then there is human relationship. Work in the arts and crafts tends to be solitary; you work alone. But it is not enough to work alone. You also have to experience people on the level of their feelings. What is new and different about this is not the expression of the strong passions: anger or sexual passion, for example. These are communicated, though crudely, even in a superficial human relationship. What characterizes a human relationship on the feeling level is the open interchange of the gentler emotions: appreciation, concern, comfort, affection, wistfulness, happiness, sadness and the like, such as in this interchange between a parent and a child:

"That's beautiful, Jimmie [referring to his guitar playing], but it makes me sad."

"Why sad, Mom?"

"I'm not quite sure. I think it reminds me of something that happened a long time ago before you were born."

"Must have been awfully sad for you to remember it so many years."

"It was. But a lot of good things have happened since."

"Was I part of the good things?"

"You certainly were."

Effects on the Family

What does all this have to do with collapsing family life, the generation gap and the drug threat? Everything. Family life suffers when the people who comprise it are not realizing their potential as human beings. The generation gap becomes unbridgeable when closed-in parents whose sense perceptions are partly anesthetized and whose emotional life is impoverished lose the capacity to feel, understand and empathize with their young people. The threats of drugs, crime, corruption, poverty and human deterioration grow steadily more unmanageable when family life lacks the qualities that foster the growth of humanness in its members. To reverse the process of dehumanization may be the only chance the world has now, the only "solution" that exists. For police power, harsh parental authority and hard-line policies have certainly made little enough impact on the problem. But the nurture of the neglected qualities of sense perception, awareness and emotional enrichment in family life could lift us above these disturbances.

TEN

EMERGING INTO
OPEN FAMILY LIVING _____

Moving from the closed style toward a more open one is like emerging from a prison. You may not have been fully conscious of the prisonlike qualities of the closed style. You had been accustomed to living in it, had probably always lived in it and had never known a different style. But many younger people today experience the closed style as a kind of incarceration. And somewhat similar feelings arise in older people who have in some degree freed themselves from the restrictions and rigidities of that style. The farther you move away from the closed style, the more prisonlike it looks in retrospect; and the idea of returning to it after a successful venture into a more open way of living is quite inconceivable.

There can be no dodging the fact, however, that trying to transform a basic life-style challenges everything in you. It brings into question your former ways of thinking and reacting, it disturbs previously fixed emotional patterns, it alters the things you have been accustomed to doing moment by moment and day by day. Nobody makes these kinds of changes easily. So take a deep breath. You are about to plunge into what can be the most difficult, yet rewarding, experience of your life.

Changing Your Personal Life-style

THOSE TIGHT, TIGHT PATTERNS

Unless you are a very unusual person, your patterns of thought, feelings and behavior are so fixed that someone watching you might almost feel he could predict how you would react to a particular situation.

Are you, perhaps, a worrier? The chronic worrier is habitually uptight, afraid something may go wrong (and it often does). He fusses over details, he wonders if others are doing their part properly ("Has the ground crew remembered to put fuel in this airplane?"), he panics for fear he has overlooked something, and so on. This is a pattern that yields him very little in long-term satisfaction; he does not do his work better because of it, but rather, he pours so much energy into unproductive fretting that his creativity, vision and relationships are impaired.

Over there is a person who is relaxed and confident, trusts others to do their part, takes reasonable precautions against things going wrong but does not dissipate his energies by useless fussing. He has a wide range of interests, he likes people and enjoys life.

The worrier and the relaxed person could conceivably be working side by side in the same organization. But one functions with far less wear and tear on himself and on the people around him than does the other.

The first is an example of a closed-style and the second of an open-style *emotional pattern*. A movement from the closed to the open style would involve a change of patterns equivalent to the change from the first to the second. If you are the worrier, this is your challenge. Impossible? No. Changes of this magnitude have been made by people who, when they fully understood that the more closed style was an obstacle in their path, were willing to work over a period of time for their own release from its limitations and rigidities.

If you are to change an emotional pattern, you first must recognize the pattern for what it is. This is by no means easy. A pattern can seem so natural that you may never have considered other possible ways of responding to a situation. You may even think that the way you habitually respond is the only possible way to respond. But it is not.

Remember George and Dorothy? George had a pattern of anger that was disrupting his marriage and all his relationships. He was using anger rather self-indulgently as a substitute for facing himself. I illustrated how he could learn to get in touch with himself through the practice of inner communication. He might then begin to guide his emotional responses into more constructive patterns.

Here is something that looks like a contradiction. Emotions, of course, are the way you feel, and everyone has a right to his feelings. Nobody can properly ask you to feel differently than you do. Or can they? Suppose the *pattern* of your emotions—the habit of feeling in a certain way—is inappropriate, limiting and restrictive, as was the case with George. Should you try to change it? If so, how is this compatible with accepting your emotions as legitimate?

The individual emotions that make up an emotional pattern need to be recognized, accepted and respected, and this is necessary before you can even make a beginning at changing the pattern. Part of the trouble with the closed style is that the emotional patterns are often not recognized as such. The person who constantly worries about things going wrong and fusses over details may not be aware of the fear, anxiety and distrust that pervade his life. He needs to become aware of these very real feelings that lie behind his fussing. He needs to know, too, that emotions in themselves are neither good nor bad. They just *are*.

But once you recognize your pattern of feelings, you do not have to accept it as a permanent part of *you* if it is hindering you from being the kind of person you want to be. You need to learn where it came from, how it arose, how it manifests itself in your life now, and what it is doing to and for you. And then you can draw upon the powers of your Maturing Self to bring about gradual alterations in your life-style and the emotional patterns that are part of it.

Suppose you are repeatedly upset because, day after day, a member of your household leaves soiled underwear on the bathroom floor. You remonstrate about it, you get into a rage, you tell the person he is being inconsiderate, and it continues to happen. Knowing that you are upset is not enough. You need to know where your anger and related feelings came from and why other responses do not occur to you. Is being upset the only possible response? Does it accomplish anything for you? A different response might be to laugh. Underwear on the floor makes a droll sight. If you add another soiled garment, it will be droller still.

Moving from the closed style to the open one means, in general, substituting a more relaxed emotional pattern for a tight, tense one; an enriched emotional life for an impoverished one; an attitude of celebrating life for one of hemming life in.

Thought patterns can be just as tight as emotional ones. Moving into the open style involves an alteration much more basic than throwing away old ideas. It involves a change in attitude toward *all ideas,* new and old. It may not necessarily mean throwing away any ideas at all. The open style means freedom to draw upon and examine all ideas, to evaluate them and reintegrate them into your life.

If you are open, you do not repudiate your past, for that is a form of alienation. You maintain connection with your roots. You treasure the richness of accumulated wisdom, insight, experience and inspiration from the past. But you also respect the new knowledge, the new thoughts and relationships that are being developed to deal with new situations. You try to integrate the old with the new. You are careful, however, not to be carried away by the latest "ism" because most "isms" are closed systems.

How about *behavioral patterns?* Suppose a family member brings home the family car with an empty gas tank and the next person who uses it runs out of gas. How does the family react to this? A common closed-style response is to attack the careless one with a tongue lashing: "Don't you know any better?" "When will you learn?" "How many times have we told you?" In the more extremely closed-style families, the pattern of response to a faulty action goes something like this:

Admit you did wrong!
Expect to be punished!
Take the punishment you deserve!
Say you are sorry for what you did!
Promise never to do it again!
Now, feel ashamed and bad about yourself! (If you feel badly enough, we'll forgive you.)

The careless one feels badly, all right. But he also may feel resentful, pushed down and unloved. He may sense that the attack on him was to satisfy an emotional urge of the attacker, not to help him be a more careful person. The attacker may have been playing a closed-style game that Eric Berne* called "Now I've got you, you son of a bitch" (NIGYSOB).

This is the closed style in one of its darker manifestations. In the open style, the person who had to walk ten blocks with a container of gas lets the careless one know he is angry but does not "dump" on him. Forgiveness is quick. The person at fault is not made to feel bad about himself.

FEELING BETTER TOWARD YOURSELF

The open style fosters good feelings toward yourself. This contrasts with the closed and directionless styles in which people, especially children, frequently suffer put-downs from parents, relatives, teachers and peers, such as:

> You aren't very important.
> You're just a kid (or: You're only a girl).
> You don't know much.
> You're a joke.
> You'll never amount to much.
> People haven't time for you. They're busy, you mustn't bother them.
> Haven't you any sense?
> Where are your brains?
> Stop that senseless chatter!

Many of us who have had to suffer from such put-downs know quite well that they had nothing to do with valid appraisals of us as human beings. Nevertheless, the scars may still hurt. Some part of us may even now believe these old messages and may be holding us back from what we might otherwise achieve.

If you suffer from low self-esteen (or from its converse, inflated esteem that has no connection with your real abilities), the first step is to identify, if you can, the crippling messages that were implanted in you as a child. This does not necessarily mean that you need to remember the occasions when the messages were delivered or even who delivered them. You may be able to recognize the kinds of messages that put those scars on you by your emo-

---

* *Games People Play* (New York: Grove Press, 1964).

tional reactions to situations today. For example, if you always find yourself apologizing and putting yourself in subservient roles, you can be sure that somebody once impressed on you that you were not very important. If you find yourself always asking other people's advice about matters where it would be more appropriate to rely on yourself, you know that somebody once convinced you that your own judgment was not to be trusted. If you frequently suffer from feelings of guilt, you know that you were called "naughty" by someone long ago and were made to feel ashamed. If you keep reprimanding yourself for being "stupid," this is evidence that someone once called you "stupid" and you believed it.

When you identify the messages, watch your reactions when the emotions carried in these messages are activated in you. Then give yourself realistic counter messages:

I *am* important—to me, to my family and to my friends.

Everyone was a child once and was probably laughed at by somebody, just as I was.

I have many assets now.

I am worth knowing and worth loving, and there are people who love me and respect me.

I can have happiness and claim the good things in life.

No one has or ever had the power or the right to put a limit on what I might someday accomplish; nor have I the right to put such a limit on myself.

The counter messages have to be truthful; it does no good to claim assets you do not have. It helps to work with someone who believes in you and can affirm positive views of you with conviction.

As you grow in self-esteem and become more aware, you begin to realize the extent to which you yourself are responsible for your reactions to events. You stop using expressions like:

He drives me up the wall.

She makes me furious.

He brings out the worst in me.

My parents bug me.

She has me in the hollow of her hand.

She arouses me sexually.
My boss upsets me.
Dogs scare me.

All these expressions imply that you have no autonomy. You are thinking of yourself as a puppet: pull one cord and you get angry; pull another cord and you are happy. An open person moves beyond this. Not that he is independent of the need for human interaction. He wants love, affection, approval; he needs them, of course, as all human beings need them. But he is not at the mercy of people or of forces outside himself. He can intervene when he feels manipulated. He can say to himself:

I don't have to climb a wall.
I don't have to be furious.
I don't have to let anyone bring out the worst in me.
I don't have to be bugged by my parents.
I don't have to be in the hollow of anyone's hand.
I don't have to get sexually aroused. (The question is: Do I
    want to be?)
I don't have to let my boss upset me.
I don't have to be frightened by dogs.
What the open person claims and makes his own is autonomy.

GROWING AND BECOMING MORE CREATIVE

As you move toward the open style, you become more creative and help those around you to become so. You foster creativity in your children by the choice of toys, by limiting TV watching, by bringing art, music and literature into the home, by supplying materials for creative pursuits, by encouraging (but not forcing) children to learn musical instruments, by engaging in family projects of a creative nature, etc.

When you encourage creativity and imagination you nurture personal growth. A person grows naturally when he is able to draw upon his powers and is given the tools and encouragement do it in his own way. The open style gives a young person freedom to find his own growth pattern. Thus, in the open style, the son of a contractor is free to try to become an artist or musician if he chooses; whereas, in the closed style, the father might try to maneuver his son into the contracting business, or might want to "upgrade" him to lawyer or doctor. Strong pressure would probably be brought against any contrary ideas the son has.

A girl in the open style would not be pushed into marriage if her choice were not to marry. The old parental question, "Isn't it time you found a nice boy, got married and settled down?" would not be heard in the open style. Nor would a parent inquire of a married daughter, "When are you going to have a baby?" The daughter would be expected to make these decisions for herself.

If you are open, you do not resist change provided the change is necessary or desirable. Nor do you fight change that is clearly inevitable and cannot be held back; there are better uses for your energies. You learn to see change as an opportunity and a challenge. But not only do you face up to external change—you *seek* changes within yourself. You do not say, "I am thus-and-so and I always have been." You say, "I am thus-and-so right now, but I was different last year, and next year I may be different still." Also, you may say, "Thus-and-so does not describe the *whole* of me. It is only one side of me. I have other, different sides as well." And you say, "There are sides of me that I want to develop further. I have not finished growing yet. I hope I will continue to grow to my dying day. There are new things to experience, new feelings to cultivate, new ideas to explore, new people to know."

CHANGING YOUR ATTITUDES AND VALUES

The open style accepts the body with fewer hang-ups and less self-consciousness than does the closed. You accept body contact naturally and do not necessarily associate it with genital sex. A husband and wife in the open style may frequently do pleasant physical things such as hugging, holding hands, massaging each other, washing each other's feet or hair, and the like. These may presage sexual relations or be enjoyed simply for themselves.

You learn to care for your body in the open style, to respect and love it as an expression of who you are. You do not let your body deteriorate from carelessness or abuse, grow flabby from lack of exercise or from overeating or drinking. You pay attention to nutrition; you select foods carefully and prepare them properly, and you avoid "convenience" foods that have had most of their nutritive content removed.

If you are closed, though you may not be aware of it, you probably tend to think of people in much the same way you think of objects: as either useful or in the way, valuable or worthless, beautiful or ugly, well-made or poorly made, high-powered or low-powered, and so on. You could just as well be describing a washing machine or automobile. The contemporary habit of describing a girl by her dimensions is a case in point. Many colloquial descriptions of people are names of animals or things or are unflattering descriptions: "Broad," "doll," "chick," "hen," "bitch," "clod," "jock," "egghead," "schmuck." These are disparaging terms, and their common use says something about our ways of perceiving and experiencing people.

As you move toward a more open style, you begin to experience people less as objects and more as human beings—generally interesting, attractive, unique and worth knowing. This evolves out of learning to accept and feel warm toward yourself. It is natural, then, for you to feel warm toward others.

In the open style, people enjoy each other simply because they like each other, both in the family and outside. They are not trying to use each other, force each other into roles, make deals (in personal relationships) or perform any other sort of manipulation.

As you become a more open person, your values change. In the closed style, you were probably accustomed to putting the highest value on jobs, success, material possessions, appearances, status, reputation and, often, money. We nearly all do. As you move toward openness, these values begin to seem less important. You may still enjoy these outer trappings; and of course, your job—your work—is likely to continue to occupy a major place in your life. Yet your highest values become increasingly *qualitative* ones: your relationships with people, the development of your human capacities, your family life, your ability to help others to grow and to flower. You are also likely to become involved to some extent in public work to give expression to your feeling of connectedness to the community, to society and to nature.

Changing Your Marital Style

As you become more open as a person, your marriage will change
—inevitably. It will either become a more open marriage or a
more strained one, depending on how open your spouse is willing
to become.

One problem that comes up very quickly is that of roles. It is
around the question of roles and partners' expectations of each
other's roles that many marital disputes revolve. This has become
an increasingly acute problem with the shifting position of women
in our society. A man can no longer blithely assume that when he
marries his wife will necessarily do all the housework, laundry and
baby care. She may expect him to share this work, especially if she
has a job outside the home, and all these matters may need to be
negotiated. Nor can the woman necessarily assume that the man
will support her all her life—something that once was taken for
granted. That, too, may have to be negotiated. Some men feel that
breadwinning ought to be shared by both partners, and some
women desire this, too.

Roles are among the key areas in which the closed marital style
is breaking down and in danger of collapsing into the directionless. The closed style, with its tight, unbending attitudes that
draw rigid distinctions between "man's work" and "woman's
work," is ill-adapted to dealing with this kind of problem.

In the open style, there is just "work," and it is divided between
the partners as seems appropriate. They have to negotiate the
question of what work they want done and who is to do it and
when—and especially they have to negotiate the sharing of work
that neither likes (like cleaning the toilet bowl). They negotiate
from positions of equality, and if they are sufficiently sensitive to
each other's feelings and needs, they can arrive at solutions satisfactory to both.

Conflicts, of course, are inevitable in any arrangement where
two people with independent minds and wills live together. There
is no such thing as both always agreeing on everything unless one
is passive and continually yields to the other—a closed-style practice. The question, then, is not whether there will be conflict, but

rather *how* the conflicts will be handled. To move toward openness in your marital relationship will require developing listening skills, communication skills, negotiating skills and, most of all, a willingness to consider your spouse's point of view.

Affection has to be freely given in marriage. Its life-enhancing effect is lost if it is made conditional on acceptable behavior. One problem of the closed style is that people often withhold affection or love as a means of controlling behavior, not only of a child but of a spouse. One partner may do this by withholding sex, another by withholding warmth or love.

I think of Bill, a high-school science teacher, who had a highly developed capacity for negative criticism. For a long time he used it to devastate his students, his children and his wife. One of his troubles was that he loved (as well as lived) "by the rule." He followed three assumptions that made sense to him:

1. Overt affection is a woman's trait. ("I am a man, and men don't show affection outwardly.")
2. Affection must be earned by good behavior. ("I will be affectionate toward my wife and children when their behavior meets my standards of approval.")
3. When a man's wife or children behave in a way of which he disapproves, he ought to punish them. ("Not only do they not deserve my affection, but witholding affection is a gentleman's way to make them toe the mark—i.e., better than knocking their blocks off.")

Bill set up rules in accordance with these assumptions despite the fact that, as he could easily see for himself, they did not work. Withholding affection did not produce anything like the behavior he wanted. Instead, his wife became increasingly exasperated and his children sneaked around behind his back, ignored his directions and, when caught in misdeeds, lied expertly. It is characteristic of the internal rules by which many people operate that the rules themselves are rarely examined, the assumptions underlying them are scarcely ever questioned, and the rules continue to be followed even when their use may threaten marital and family disruption. Eventually, Bill's wife threatened to leave him. He had already lost all control over his children. To preserve his marriage and family, Bill had to toss out his "rules" and learn to express his love freely and unqualifiedly.

In the open style, you do not love conditionally or possessively, and you do not constrict the other person's freedom. You openly and freely express love by such means as affectionate words, touching, stroking, hugging, kissing and doing things for the other. Your sex life is truly part of your love life, not separated from it.

An outstanding difference between the closed and open marital styles is that open style places no barriers in the way of either partner developing outside relationships or friendships that can contribute to the fullness of the person's life. Such friendships come about naturally in consequence of participatory activities such as rehearsing and performing plays, singing in a choir, developing a hobby, working with others in a cause, etc. They are a result of a marital style that fosters self-realization of the partners.

In the closed style, such outside relationships could put a severe strain on the marriage. In the open style, they would be less likely to do so because the partners have individually developed enough wholeness as people not to need to use each other as ego-bolsterers, as targets for each other's aggressions, or as partners in any psychological game playing. They have a relaxed and straightforward relationship with each other, they do not make a practice of wounding each other, they trust each other and each wants the best for the other.

Changing Your Family Style

TRANSFORMING THE EMOTIONAL ATMOSPHERE

The emotions in both family styles—open and closed—are the ones with which we are all familiar, but they do not arise in the same proportions and they are not handled in the same way. The emotional climate in the two styles is so contrasting that people entering homes having the different styles often can notice the difference quickly.

In the closed style, the atmosphere tends to be tense, repressive, distrustful, freedom denying, possessive, guarded, and often dull and boring. This climate may be manifested either in an authoritarian tightly controlled setting, or in an irresponsible, uncontrolled and possibly violent setting.

Feelings in the closed style tend to be disregarded and downgraded. Life is full of "shoulds," "shouldn'ts," "musts" and "mustn'ts," and how anyone feels is likely to be considered irrelevant. If it is your duty to be cheerful, you are cheerful, by God, and you are expected to smile. Little in the emotional patterns of this kind of a system is straightforward or honest. Unwritten family rules specify how you *should* feel about everything: loving toward your mother and your rich aunt; respectful of your father, your teachers and the judge downtown; happy about the career your family has chosen for you; interested in your school work; and so on. One consequence of this discounting of genuine feelings is that family members begin to lose touch with their own feelings. They may have difficulty in identifying what their true feelings are ("Let's see, how do I feel about that? Am I happy or unhappy about it?"). They confuse the feeling they have been taught they should have with the one they really have.

Other consequences often are a deadening of feelings generally and perhaps a pile-up of resentments. Closed-style people, whether they show it or not, tend often to be angry people.

The open style, on the contrary, when at its best is characterized by more of such feelings as trust, caring, acceptance, reassurance, affection, love, warmth, interest, eagerness, excitement, joy or sadness and understanding. It is a much more relaxed style. But this does not mean that negative feelings are absent. Open-style families have them, too. When negative feelings boil up, however, a family in the open style deals with them differently than one in the closed style. The feelings are more likely to be acknowledged and accepted. They are less likely to pile up and overheat, as do the more suppressed or disarrayed emotions of the closed style. Members of an open-style family are not afraid that if they express themselves honestly, they might risk losing the love and respect of the other family members. Feelings are acknowledged to be O.K., and it is permissible to get them out where they can be talked about.

"I'm furious."
"I can see you are." (Recognizing the feeling.)
"I hate Dad."
"You really do, don't you?" (Again recognizing the feeling.)

"Why didn't he . . . ?"

"Why don't you ask *him* instead of me."

"I will, by God!"

Then:

"Dad, I'm very angry at you." (Open statement.)

"I can feel it." (Acknowledgement.)

"Why did you . . . ?"

"I'll explain it if you'll cool down."

"You could have . . ."

"You're really hot under the collar, aren't you?"

"I'm angry as hell!"

"What do you want me to do now?"

"I don't know, but I want you to know how I feel."

"I understand how you feel."

Anger can dissipate when it is recognized and acknowledged and nobody is saying things like, "Now, now, there's no reason to be angry," or, "Come now, you can't talk like that to your father," or, "Control yourself, son," or, "What on earth are you so angry about?" When the anger is acknowledged as a feeling to which a person (even a child) has a right, its destructive power declines, understanding can be reached and the anger may soon be forgotten like yesterday's dream.

The relaxed atmosphere of the open style allows the free play of many of the softer, pleasanter, more life-enhancing emotions that tend to be submerged by the tensions and angers of the closed style. Life takes on new coloring; there is a new music in it.

OPENING UP MINDS IN THE FAMILY

The freer emotional patterns of the open style are accompanied by freer intellectual patterns. These freer patterns do not mean flabbiness of conviction or, necessarily, the rejection of what most other people believe. You may have strong convictions of your own, which may or may not be in harmony with conventional ideas. What distinguishes the open from the closed style is in *how* you react to views contrary to your own. If you are closed, you have great difficulty in tolerating uncongenial views of any sort, you do not allow them breathing room, you shut them out of your hearing, you may attack or ridicule them before you understand them, and if they are forced too strongly upon your attention, you may react with indignation, outrage or scorn. In addition, the closed person often tends to be suspicious of people who harbor views or feelings contrary to his own or who behave in ways he does not understand. He questions their motivation. A person in the turbulent mode of the closed style may see such people as evil—as enemies to be outwitted, struck down, removed, perhaps even imprisoned or killed.

If you are open, on the other hand, you experience an opponent as a human being and respect him while differing from him. In an open-style family, a dialogue might go something like this:

"Dad, I'm thinking of going away to live in a commune."

"You astonish me!" (Expressing own feeling.)

"Are you against it?"

"Hold everything! You haven't told me what it's all about yet."

"I met a guy who lives in one. He says it's the only life."

"He does?" (Echoing.)

"Yeah. What he told me sounded fascinating."

"What did he tell you?"

"Oh, a lot of things."

"They really turned you on, eh?" (Acknowledging other's feelings.)

"Wow!"

"Tell me more about it." (Opening door to further communication.)

Or in a devoutly religious family, a child may drop a bombshell like this:

"Mom, I don't believe in God."

"You don't?" (Acknowledging child's statement.)

"No. He's just like Santa Claus—a fairy tale for children."

"Does it make you feel better not to believe in God?"

"I don't know what you mean."

"You used to believe in Him. Now you say you don't. Do you

feel better not believing in Him?" (Helping child to identify feeling.)

"No, not better. But I just can't believe any more."

"Does it make you feel more grown up not to believe?" (Continuing to help child to identify feeling.)

"Yes, that's it."

"So the people who believe in God aren't quite grown up? This puzzles me because I'm grown up and I believe in God." (Pointing out own position.)

These are examples of effective communication. In the first conversation, the parent is open to receiving information, and in the second, each person has clearly stated his position without rupturing the communication. It is easy to imagine what would have happened in either case if the parent had snapped, "What nonsense! You don't know what you're talking about."

As you become more open, you find yourself genuinely interested in the question of *why* another believes as he does. You have curiosity about it. You find it fascinating, this human propensity of two people to look at the same set of facts and arrive at opposite conclusions. How does such a thing come about? You could learn to enjoy the exploration of differences as one of the more exciting aspects of a human relationship.

Many closed-style persons tend to fall into one of two categories: the anti-intellectual and the intellectually arrogant. These are generally thought to be opposites, but they both share the same essential ingredient: rejection of opposing views. In politics this attitude is typical of the extremist of either right or left, the totalitarian, the "hard liner" of any persuasion. In religion, it describes the person for whom one doctrine, and only one, can possibly be correct. In family life it characterizes the person who would rather have his relationships with other family members permanently disrupted than accept the existence of opinions strongly differing from his.

In the open style, you regard the relationship between family members and the acknowledgment and acceptance of feelings as far more important than any ideological or philosophical differences. For example, Elaine believes in the doctrine of the redemption of mankind's sins through Jesus Christ. Husband, Joel, does not. They are deadlocked on this point. In the closed style, Elaine would get thoroughly upset by Joel's arguments and suffer from anxiety and suppressed anger, or Joel would become exasperated and tell her, "For Heaven's sake, lay off!" Or, by mutual agreement, they might keep off the subject and never discuss it (closed area).

If the relationship is open, Elaine can have her belief and Joel his, and each can be respectful of the other. Neither would try to force his position on the other. Yet they can talk about their differences openly. It is not a closed area. Such a discussion might go like this:

"That was a great sermon this morning, Joel."

"It really sent you, didn't it?" (Acknowledging feeling.)

"Did it! I wanted to kiss the preacher."

"Wouldn't he have been surprised!"

"Honestly, now, can you really say that the sermon didn't move you?"

"I didn't say that. But you understand that my reactions are rather different from yours."

"I know. Sometimes I can't help wishing that we both believed the same. But you have to be you, and I have to be me."

"Yes, and I appreciate your saying that. Is it so terrible that we have different viewpoints?"

"Not really. It's just that I get lonely sometimes, being the only believer in this family."

"You're not the only believer, Elaine! I have my beliefs, too, except that they're different."

"Of course! I wish I hadn't said that."

The conversation does not get into the points of religious doctrine. On that level these two continue to be far apart; they have been over that ground many times and each knows what the other thinks. They have learned to let doctrinal differences go and deal strictly with feelings. On a feeling level they can give each other encouragement and support; and that, as they both view it, takes care of their relationship in a positive way.

ALTERING FAMILY PATTERNS OF BEHAVIOR

Closed-style patterns are automatic and repetitious, and because of this, they undermine the autonomy of family members. Instead of being free, unique individuals, all are geared into the family system. This subjection to the system can take either of two forms or a combination of both: It can lock the family members inextricably together so that no one can function as a person in his own right, or it can drive them apart so that they are deeply alienated from each other.

The locking of family members together amounts to a kind of imprisonment, no less so because it is self-imposed or imposed by the rules under which the family operates. Nobody is quite free to have his own friends, interests, hobbies, sports, or to enjoy doing the things he loves most. If the father likes to play golf while the mother prefers playing bridge, either he has to give up the golf or she the bridge so they can do whatever they do together. They assume that the family has to march in lockstep. This is what Eliza's father dreads in the scene in *My Fair Lady* when he enjoys his last all-night fling and sings "Get Me to the Church on Time."

What is wrong here is not that the family does things together—it can be very satisfying to do things together—but that they subscribe to an arrangement that denies the freedom of each to be an individual. One consequence of the arrangement is that family members who go their own independent way are made to feel guilty. Association of either spouse with someone of the opposite sex presents a particular problem because this violates the family code, and so, in order to avoid trouble, it has to be kept hidden. Few conditions are more destructive of family life than secret areas that no one dares bring to light.

The lockstep leads logically and inevitably to separateness and alienation. Entanglement and alienation are among those conditions of the closed life that appear to be opposites but actually are not. People in lockstep may be virtual strangers to one another. The lockstep refers to external activities, not to emotional sharing.

"I had a queer dream last night."
"Come on, we'll be late."

"I don't feel so good."

"Are you coming or aren't you?"

"Do we *have* to go to this damn party?"

"Of course we do. They're expecting us."

"I don't feel like it."

"Are you letting me down again?"

"What do you mean—again! I've gone to these things with you
until they give me a headache."

"You've got to go, and that's all there is to it."

This is the closed lockstep, and neither person has the remotest
idea of what the other really thinks or how he feels.

Try this dialogue in the open style:

"I had a queer dream last night."

"What was it?"

(Tells dream.)

"Do you really feel as pushed as the dream sounds?"

"Well, maybe I do. I'm not keen on going out tonight."

"I'll miss you. But I promised Helen I'd be there."

"You go ahead. Would you feel bad if I didn't go?"

"As I said, I'll miss you. But I don't want you to go if you don't
feel like it."

"I really don't."

"O.K. See you later." (Kisses him and goes.)

A family system that compels a person to do something he does
not feel comfortable about doing—except for those things that are
necessary for survival of the family or the individuals in it—is
closed. Take music lessons, for example. The closed style goes like
this:

"It's time for your music practice."

"Aw, Mom, I want to play baseball."

"You know it is practice time."

"But why does it have to be *now?*" (Whining.)

"Stop arguing. Get at it."

"I hate music lessons."

"Do you hear me?"

The open style:

"I notice you haven't been practicing your flute lately."

"Well—you know—I've been awfully busy."

"Do you want to learn the flute?"

"Um—I guess so. When I get time, I'll do some practicing."

"Do you think occasional practice is enough?"

"Sure."

"You are kidding yourself, and you know it."

"Well, there are so many other things, Mom."

"How about sorting them out and deciding on how to use your time?"

The outcome may or may not be flute practice, but the young person is being helped to make a responsible judgment about it. In the open style, you would consider it more important that a child learn to make responsible judgments than that he learn to play the flute. The objective here is not to produce a concert flutist but to encourage the development of autonomy. The open family style envisages a self-actualizing human being. And the only way a person learns to be self-actualizing is by practicing it (and sometimes failing.)

IMPROVING COMMUNICATION AND DECISION MAKING

Communication in the closed family style tends to be distorted and incomplete. There are likely to be areas in which independent thinking or non-conforming emotions are taboo; hence communication in those areas is shut off. These closed areas often include morals, sexual behavior, feelings, roles, religious beliefs, politics, women's rights, money, manners, ways of working and various others. Probably no family is closed in all these areas at once, but many are closed in one or more of them.

A closed area—one in which open discussion is avoided—is the result of fear, distrust and other disturbing feelings with which the family cannot deal. The difficulty is emotional, not intellectual. The communication of emotions in a closed family is tightly inhibited. No one is sure how any of the others feel. No one is even sure of how he himself feels. Family members are continually making guesses or assumptions about each other, and their guesses, since they are rarely checked out, are often wrong. As a result, communication in the closed areas where there is intense negative emotional reaction tends to fall to pieces. There is avoidance of feedback because feedback may involve questioning, doubts, opposing opinions, disbelief, etc., and the closed person cannot handle the emotions these arouse.

During World War II a gentle, peaceable man who was deeply concerned about political matters and was (or thought himself) open and reasonable found himself in an argument with a friend who began to defend certain of Hitler's policies. The supposedly reasonable man began ranting incoherently, pacing the floor and belligerently shaking his fist at his friend. They had stumbled into a closed area.

Members of a closed family tend not to listen to each other, whether they are involved with a closed topic or not. Listening is not their style. Or, if they do listen, they do it poorly. Partly, this habit is a result of a lack of respect for each other's humanness and uniqueness; it is a consequence of the closed-style tendency to experience people (including themselves) largely in terms of roles. Some closed families and individuals avoid listening by talking incessantly. Others do it by not paying attention, by being preoccupied, or even by being willfully deaf. Failure to listen is often felt by the speaker as rejection. Since many people in the closed style tend to do this, family members often feel rejected and not much cared about. Yet, at the same time, members of closed families can be very much entangled with each other, unable to escape each other—which, actually, is one of the elements underlying the avoidance of listening.

In the open style, on the other hand, effective two-way communication is a basic part of the life-style. Without it, the style could not be said to be open. Members of a family with the open style are accustomed to listening to and being available to each other. They listen not only to ideas, but to feelings. They check out constantly:

"Gosh, I'm tired tonight!"
"Do you mean you'd like to be left alone?"
"For a little while, yes. Let me relax a bit and I'll tell you about it later. Did you have a good day?"

"No, it was a lousy day."

"I thought you looked upset when I came in." (Gives spouse a hug.)

"I'm very upset. I see you are, too. Let's get dinner on. We can talk about it then."

The style in this same family before they learned to listen was more like this:

"Gosh, I'm tired!"

"Me, too. Everything went wrong today."

"I lost that order I had worked so hard for."

"Mary broke our best dish—the one your mother gave us for our wedding."

"Do you realize what it means to me to lose that order?"

"Aren't you going to punish Mary?"

"You aren't listening!"

"You don't even care!" (Stalks out and slams the door.)

In the open style, people keep in touch, yet do not intrude. There is a fine line between intimacy and entanglement, and people in the open style stay on the intimacy and involvement side while avoiding the entanglement and intrusion side. They may feel very close to each other, but they do not let themselves become locked together.

The open style is not necessarily an easy one to make work. Children who are allowed to express their wishes and feelings openly can, at times, become difficult. They may push their parents to the point of exasperation. It would be a mistake to imagine that the open style insures smooth, harmonious, quiet and unruffled living like the calm of a library. The open style is a workable way of making family life an exciting, rewarding, stimulating growth experience, not a recipe for tranquility.

But, because the open style lifts from children the frustrations of being suppressed and treated as less than persons, it can produce children of great charm, originality and appeal—children who are interesting to know, stimulating to have around, and exciting to watch as they discover their unfolding powers.

The open-style approach to decision making is to discuss the issue with the whole family, listen to the preferences expressed by each member, consider all the pros and cons, and try to find a solution that will be acceptable to all. This requires effective communicating and negotiating skills. It requires, too, that all members be honest about their preferences. If somebody is reluctant to say what he would like, the negotiation may proceed in disregard to his preference because nobody knows what it is.

In the open style, you learn to express your preferences freely because: (1) you are not afraid to and are not hung up on the notion that it is impolite; (2) the family style encourages you to do it; and (3) the other family members do it, so why not you? On the other hand, the open style does not encourage anyone to override another's preferences. Family members are accustomed to taking each other's feelings into account. Hence, they work at the question until all are reasonably satisfied.

Suppose the father wants an outboard motor, the mother wants a new dress, the daughter wants singing lessons and the son wants a bicycle. All agree that there is not enough money in the bank for more than one of these at a time. Should one person get what he wants and the other three wait? If so, which one? Or should the family go into debt sufficiently to satisfy two members? Or three? Or all four? Somebody, if care is not taken, could easily feel unfairly treated.

The father argues that with all the overtime he has been working recently, he has earned the right to a little relaxation, and the outboard motor would make it possible for him to get to a good fishing area. The mother has been conscious of being less well-dressed than her friends and would appreciate one really lovely dress. The daughter is thinking of making a career out of singing and feels that she is entitled to help from the family in getting her career started. The son wants a ten-speed bicycle to accompany his friends on cross-country bike tours. Each position has a strong emotional component.

One possible outcome is for the most persistent and aggressive pleader (often a child) to get what he wants and the others to give in. But in the open style the less aggressive but perhaps more mature members are given a hearing, too.

What can the family agree on? They agree that it would be unwise to go too deeply into debt. The father points out what the interest payments would have to be and how debt repayments would tend to constrict family life later. Now, the advantages and disadvantages for the family of each alternative are explored. Obviously, the family would benefit from a more relaxed father, a more self-assured mother, a daughter happily preparing for a career and a son able to enjoy healthy outdoor sport. So all four wants are, in one way or another, in the interest of the family. The family comes to the conclusion that all four wants are reasonable and that all should be satisfied if possible, but not all at one time. They calculate that in about eight months they can accomplish all four without running into unmanageable debt, so the only question is: in what order?

The seasons help settle it for this family. It will be three months before fishing season starts, so the father can postpone getting the outboard. Same with the son's bicycle. The mother could use the new dress right away, so she is urged to go ahead and get it. The daughter's singing lessons would start in the following fall, so the payment for these can wait, but she should sign up for them now. The decisions are satisfactory for all concerned and the family stays solvent.

Such a fortuitous outcome is not always possible. Differences may arise that are not susceptible to neat solutions. In the open family, all interested parties are at least listened to, although decisions may have to go against some of them. In that case, the ones who lost the current decision may be given a preferred hearing next time around. The focus is not on winning or on losing but on what is appropriate and best for all.

One of the problems may be that certain family members are more generous and unselfish than others and thus repeatedly come out with the smaller share of the good things. If the family is wise, it will watch out for this; for this can be a hidden threat. If one member makes a habit of yielding, apparently because of unselfishness, the real cause might be low self-esteem ("My wishes don't count," or, "I don't count.") In that case, hurt feelings and resentments can pile up undetected and unacknowledged until they begin to reveal themselves in little digs, put-downs, and self-pitying remarks. These over the long term can be much more damaging to family life than the original self-denials were helpful.

LOOSENING UP ROLES IN THE FAMILY

In the closed family style, roles are rigidly prescribed. They are likely to be stereotyped, based on the traditions and values of the subculture in which the parents were raised. In nearly all older cultures, the roles of men and women are sharply differentiated. There were good reasons for this in times past when men performed much of the work that was exchangeable for money while women bore children, prepared meals and took care of the home. Despite the fact that the old conditions have, to a large extent, passed away and great numbers of women are working outside the home, the role expectations in many families still adhere to those old patterns. Men in such families continue in many cases to dump all the child care, housecleaning, food preparing and dishwashing tasks on their wives, even when the women have been working outside the home all day. The men do this without giving much thought to its unfairness because those tasks have long been regarded as "woman's work." And many women have accepted the burden because they, too, were brought up to think of the homemaking jobs as "woman's work." At the same time, women in business and the professions are rarely paid salaries equal to those of men and are even more rarely awarded promotions to high administrative levels. Hence, women are faced with discrimination both at home and at work, against which they are only now beginning to fight.

But the sexually apportioned roles go deeper than this. Some of these roles derive from a very early period in human history when the male was primarily a hunter and fighter, and one of his main functions was to protect and defend his village and his family. This put a premium on fighting qualities in the man: physical strength and agility, aggressiveness, competitiveness, courage, ability to remain calm in the midst of an uproar (Kipling expressed this in the ultimate statement of the British version of the masculine stereotype, "If you can keep your head when all around you are losing theirs . . ."), and of course, mental acumen so as not to be outwitted. The woman, on the other hand, was expected to be relatively submissive, helpful to the man, obedient to him, fertile, nurturing and life-enhancing.

Although the conditions that originally produced this sexual dichotomy have passed away in much of our society, the role expectations based on them stubbornly survive. Physical prowess has declined in social importance, but the imperturbable, unflappable man, who, when pressed, takes a long draw on his pipe while thinking out his position—this man is still very much with us. So is the excitable, animated woman who can afford to be scatter-brained because no one expects her to think in a systematic way.

There is nothing wrong with people like these—I am not attacking them. I am simply pointing out that one of the characteristics of the closed family style is that the man (if it happens to be the tradition of his people) is *expected* to be this way whether it is his natural inclination or not. The wife is *expected* to be emotional, excitable and non-analytical whether it is her nature or not. These stereotypes are passed down from parents to children. A very bright girl, then, may be warned by her mother, "Don't be too clever. It will scare the boys away." And the eager, excitable boy may be told by his father (in actions if not in words): "Cool it! A man keeps in control of himself in all situations."

This model of the closed style (which might be called the "Anglo-Saxon model") is far from the only kind there is. A strongly contrasting one that I sometimes think of as the "Mediterranean model" features an excitable, emotionally expressive man and a rather submissive, self-abnegating woman. Some of these characteristics were shown in the movie, *The Godfather*—an illustration of an extremely closed family style which, nevertheless, was different in many respects from the Kiplingesque closed style.

What makes a style closed is the *inflexibility* of the style and the force, moral or otherwise, exerted to compel family members to conform to it. In *The Godfather*, the force was physical as well as emotional: Conform or find yourself at the bottom of a river. In less violent styles it is mostly moral and judgmental: Conform or be criticized and, if you persist, excluded from the family circle.

In all closed styles, the role of children is to do what they are told, be respectful of their elders, never question their parents' judgments, never argue or talk back, and never do anything to embarrass or bring criticism on the parents.

In the open family style, roles are less important and can be negotiated. There must, of course, be roles. People need to know what their functions are. But the roles can be flexible. They can be adapted to the needs of the moment. If the wife is working, the husband can do some of the housework so that burdens are more equally shared. There is no such thing in the open style as "woman's work" (except childbearing). And even childbearing is not forced upon the woman against her will; there are a number of ways for a couple to avoid unplanned pregnancy. There is no exclusively "man's work," either, except work that may exceed a particular woman's physical capabilities. What comprises the husband's and wife's roles may change from time to time, depending on the physical or emotional condition of each. If the woman is sick or pregnant, the man cares for her as needed and takes over any tasks that she might find difficult. If the man is sick, the wife cares for him. This kind of adjustment is made in many closed families also, but sometimes reluctantly and with grumbling and friction.

The principal role of both men and women in the open style is to encourage, support and nurture the family members. The home is experienced as a "human being garden." The objective, as Virginia Satir* puts it, is "peoplemaking." (Factories make *things;* homes make *people.*) The role of children in the open style, therefore, is not necessarily to please the parents or feed the parents' egos, but to develop their own capacities, learn to think and feel for themselves, expand, grow and flower.

NURTURING CHILDREN

The aim of child training in the closed style is to produce a child who will conform to the parents' (or the family's) ideas of what to

* *Peoplemaking* (Palo Alto, California, Science and Behavior Books, 1972).

think or believe, how to feel, and how, where, when and with whom to act. A closed-style parent, for example, is likely to regard obedience, good manners, courtesy and neat appearance as among the more important qualities to develop in a child. The child in such a family is not expected to have independent ideas of his own; or, if he does, he may find it advisable to keep them to himself.

In the open style, on the other hand, you encourage a child to wonder, question, speak his thoughts, express his feelings, broaden his interests. You help him to work through and redirect emotions that might be a problem to him and others. You provide a nourishing environment for him to unfold and to discover his own powers. This does not mean that good manners and appearance are ignored; for these are important qualities that make it tolerable to live in society. But you put the development of the child's potential first. You encourage your child to be genuine; to be honest about his feelings. You help him to know and experience himself and to develop the qualities and talents with which he is endowed (intellectual, mechanical, artistic or whatever).

In the open style, even the smallest child is regarded as a *person* and is treated as such. What he says is listened to, his wishes are considered, his feelings are respected. This does *not* mean that the child always gets his own way. Far from it. If your child wants to do something you don't want him to do (such as taking apart your brand new record player) you can respect his wish to have the fun of dismantling something while still dissuading him from doing it in that particular way. ("Let me give you something else to take apart, but that record player is a no-no.") Children learn quickly this way. But if you say, "Godammit, keep your dirty hands off my record player!" the child may conclude: (1) that you don't like him, (2) that he is a naughty boy, and (3) that you love the record player more than you love him. He might be tempted to take out his resentment on the record player.

The sad thing for a child in a closed family style is that his parents do not see or experience him as fully human. They see him as an object of attention, concern, worry, responsibility, etc.—as a

kind of unruly pet, like a shaggy dog, that has to be continually
trained, shaped, warned, reprimanded.

"Careful, dear."
"You'll get your hands dirty, dear."
"Don't do that, dear."
"Watch out, dear."
"Don't make a noise, dear."

Some of this, of course, is necessary in bringing up any child,
but the closed-style parent carries it to the point of being counterproductive. It becomes almost the only form of relationship between parent and child. The idea of simply enjoying companionship with the child does not occur to most closed people, for that
is an open approach. In the open style, admonitions become
much less frequent and less necessary:

Instead of, "Careful, dear," you might say, "Oops!" followed by
   a laugh.
Instead of, "You'll get your hands dirty, dear," you could say,
   "Let's wash 'em up, shall we?"
Instead of, "Don't do that, dear," you could say, "How about
   doing this instead?"
Instead of, "Watch out, dear," there might be, "We do this."
Instead of, "Don't make a noise, dear," you could say, "Now
   let's be very quiet."

The attitude in the open style is that a child is a unique individual for whom the parents have been given the privilege and responsibility of caring. They do not own him. Even when tiny, he is
a person in his own right. In the closed style, on the other hand,
there is usually a feeling, often unconscious, of ownership. A
parent speaks of "my child" as he would of "my house" or "my
spring coat." Perhaps this feeling of the child being a possession
explains, in part, why so many closed-style parents disregard
children's feelings. I have earlier referred to the way in which
some parents yank little children this way and that, slap them
when they protest, insult them in the presence of other people,
and so on. Much of what goes under the name of "discipline" is

simply the overriding of a child's feelings by a physically and mentally more powerful adult:

"Hurry up, what's the matter with you?"
"Shush! Keep quiet!"
"Get out of my way!"
"Don't touch that!"
"If you do that again I'll . . ."

All this belongs to the closed style.

The corresponding communications in the open style might be:

"Please move faster, Jane. Mother is in a hurry." (A request and an explanation, not an order.)
"Let's be quiet, Jane." (Finger on lips and a smile.)
"Just move to one side, won't you, so I can pass?"
"We don't touch things in stores, Jane. They don't belong to us."
"I am annoyed when you do that. I don't want you to do it."

A common response of the closed style to unapproved behavior is to withhold love. It is an unjust as well as a cruel weapon, analagous to the withholding of food or water, because a small child must have love to grow. The parent may be deliberately taking advantage of this fact, knowing it is a weapon that the child cannot resist. If love is withheld, a child seeks the next best substitute: attention in whatever form he can get it, including the inviting of physical punishment. He may be "naughty" hoping to be punished, just to force a parent to pay attention. ("If you won't love me, I'll make you at least look at me.")

In the open style, you do not withhold love. Your relationship to your child is not, "Do as I say, or else . . ." It is "Let's work together on this." Suppose your child has gone on a rampage and carelessly broken your record player. If you are open, you might handle it like this:

"Oh dear, the record player is broken." (Avoiding an accusation.)
"Yeah. It doesn't work any more."
"That makes me sad. I brought it home for the family to enjoy."

"Oh well, we can get another record player."

"What shall we do with this one?"

"We can fix it."

"Let's try."

The parent and child work together for a time trying to repair the record player. It still won't work.

"I guess we'll have to have the repairman fix it."

"Will it cost much?"

"Quite a lot, I'm afraid."

"I could help pay for it by doing things for Mom."

"That's a good idea. I'll take you up on that."

They reach an understanding. The family agrees to a schedule of work by which the child can "earn" the cost of repairing the record player. The child learns responsibility. Next time he may be more careful about taking things apart. He feels closer to the family now. The work he has agreed to do is not considered "punishment." It is merely an arrangement by which he can feel that he is making good. There is no need for him to feel guilty or "bad."

In working with teen-agers, parents have to accept the fact that they cannot hope to exert authoritarian control over children of that age. Open-style parents know that they must either build a bridge of love, trust and respect between themselves and their children or they will lose much of their constructive influence with them. It helps for parents to recognize that their own life-styles have made, and are still making, an indelible imprint on the way their young people view life. They now have to trust the result. If the parents are people whose word can be trusted, their children are likely to be, also. If the parents are kind, considerate and understanding, the children are likely to develop similar qualities. If the parents are broad in mental outlook, the children are likely to be broad. No one can say that these influences are total, for every child is exposed to other influences as well. But parental influences are still powerful.

Knowing this, if you are an open-style parent, you can look at your children's behavior with some perspective. Sometimes even very good children get into trouble of some sort: they may drive too fast, smoke "pot," do things that you would prefer they didn't do. You may have to hang on to the faith that your children are basically sound. They probably are. And if you believe in them, it is much easier for them to live up to your expectations. A young man so treated once said gratefully to his parents, "Thank you for believing in me."

Broadening the Family's Interests and Goals

A family interested in a variety of things has much to offer its members, provided the interests do not draw the members away from interrelationship with each other. If family life is exciting and there are feelings to share, new things to do and places to go, or if the family becomes absorbed in some deeply engrossing activity in which all its members can participate (such as making music together), there is less likelihood of a serious gap between the generations.

One impetus to a broadening of family interests is the educated woman. Since fewer women today are content to limit their activities to scrubbing floors and washing dishes, our floors and glassware may not be as clean as our grandmothers kept them. On the other hand, many women are reading more, taking more courses, doing more volunteer work, embarking on careers of their own, doing a variety of things that are interesting and stimulating. When they return to their families from all these activities, they are often brighter, more engaging people than their grandmothers were.

Men, too, find that a life devoted exclusively to wage-earning or the details of business, relieved only by the Saturday football games and Sunday's trip to the shore, is unsatisfying; and they also are seeking a broadening of interests. If the woman moves in this direction, the man has to do it too, or he may get left intellectually and emotionally behind; and vice versa. These trends, in themselves, may have little directly to do with the open family style, but they merge with the movement toward greater openness. The broader your interests, the easier it is for you to move into the open style. And, conversely, the more open you become, the broader your interests are likely to get.

The broadening of interests leads to a greater involvement in the outside world—the world of people and events. The world, in the open-style family, seems much less "outside" than it does in the closed. The open-style family regards itself as part of the community, part of mankind, part of the cosmos.

This feeling of belonging goes beyond ethnic or religious boundaries. There is a problem here; for people need close relationships with others, and it is natural that these "others" would tend to be people much like themselves with whom they feel most comfortable. Yet the "in-group" is almost always exclusive; it is inherently closed. The open-style family, then, needs to strive to expand its "in-group" relationships to embrace individuals of all races, nationalities and ethnic groups.

This sense of being part of a greater humanity has its effect on the open-style family's attitude toward individual people other than family members. There is less of the arms-length attitude or the habitual suspicion that often accompanies interpersonal relationships in the closed style. The open-style individual trusts most people. But he also may be more perceptive than most because of his development of sensitivity to feelings and non-verbal signals. Hence, he is not easily taken in by swindlers or demagogues.

The open-style family, knowing that the fate of the world is also its own fate, is concerned about world problems and participates in whatever ways it can in seeking means of ameliorating them. Such a family thinks in broader terms than merely serving its own immediate interests. Thus, if there is widespread unemployment, its members do not grumble at the taxes they have to pay to keep the unemployed from starving. They know that a civilized society has to find means of solving the problem of people's livelihoods.

LOOKING TOWARD CHANGE

Perhaps the sharpest difference between members of open- and closed-style families is their attitude toward growth and change. The closed person clings to and defends his mental-emotional condition, whatever it may be. He may hate it, it may make him miserable, it may threaten other aspects of his life, but still he defends it. "I am thus-and-so," he declares, "and always have been. I'm the kind of person . . . [fill this in] and always was like that. I like . . . and always did. I hate . . . and always did. I believe . . . and always did." He extends the same attitude toward his family. "In my family we . . ." or, "My family has never had a . . . [scandal, arrest, non-believer, etc.]"

To have a firm conviction of who you are and to be proud of what your family stands for can characterize the open as well as the closed style since this is not the element of the pattern just described that makes it closed. What makes it closed is the door it shuts and bars against change. The closed individual is not only strong in his convictions but determined never to allow any change. This tends to be his attitude toward most things.

In an open-style family, on the other hand, you accept the inevitability of change and look upon it as an opportunity for fostering personal growth. You may learn even to turn a disaster to good account. Loss of your job might galvanize you to seek more rewarding work which is better suited to your needs. Loss of money or of a home might stimulate you to re-evaluate your life-style, to think through what is really important to you, to discover new values, to make fundamental changes that perhaps you would not have made without the stimulus of a disaster. Your openness may enable you to look for ways of overcoming the immediate problem and making plans to avoid similar catastrophes in the future. If you were flooded out because your home was on low ground, you may consider moving to higher ground. The closed person, on the other hand, tries to restore his life as nearly as possible to what it was before. He might rebuild on the same spot and thereby expose himself to being flooded out again.

The open style encourages experimentation with new ways of living and doing things provided such approaches offer reasonable promise of enriching family life and fostering personal growth. It would promote activities that call for mental application and manual skills, such as the arts and crafts, because these develop the capacities and talents of family members. It would not encourage experimenting with drugs or with new kinds of passive indulgence or amusement because these do not result in the increase of human capacities. In the open style, you place a high value on stimulating and training your mind, sharpening your perceptions, getting in touch with your feelings, and maintaining the vigor of your body. Any practices that might confuse your mind, dull your perceptions, undermine your feelings or weaken your body, or that might become addictive and difficult to control, you would avoid. This guideline prevents the true open style from becoming a hodgepodge of freakish, disorderly, directionless living. (It is a collapsing closed style that is more likely to head in that direction.)

In moving toward openness, people can, as individuals, become more relaxed, more truly themselves, more free to find their own paths to growth, better able to encourage and unfetter others to find theirs. Discovering this road increasingly becomes the central purpose of their lives. Many young people today are farther along this road than their parents were, and their children may be farther along still. The move away from closed patterns is worldwide and inevitable. Some may not find this road for a long time, but they will keep stumbling until they do because the closed and directionless styles are becoming unworkable in a changing world. The prisons of the mind are crumbling everywhere. Do not let their place be taken by a jumble of debris but plant a "human being garden" in which people can flower and produce their endless variety of fruits. ►39

Suggested Interaction Experience

IE-39. TAKING STEPS TOWARD MORE OPEN FAMILY LIVING (PP. 342–43)

Gather together all available family members for a major family discussion. (Use as your frame of reference Chart I, Family Living Styles: Closed versus Open, pp. 21–23.) Here are some possible questions you may wish to consider as a family group. Select one to implement with the hope of fostering family growth.

1. What changes are needed in our *basic family* system?
2. How can we make the *emotional atmosphere of the family* more open?
3. How can we develop freer *family intellectual patterns?*
4. What changes can be made in *family behavioral patterns* to increase the autonomy of family members?

5. How can *family communication patterns* become more effective?

6. How can *family decision-making patterns* be based more on open negotiation?

7. What *family roles* could be more flexible?

8. How can *parent-child relationships* become kinder, more considerate and understanding?

9. How can the *range of interests of family members* be extended to offer more variety, excitement and family growth?

10. Can the *attitude of the family toward other people and the outside world* develop a stronger sense of belonging to the community?

11. How can the *attitude of the family toward change and growth* be expanded to foster personal growth and enrich family life?

EVALUATION: Did your family identify many family style areas where change is indicated? Was it difficult to select only one for implementation? How can you work to contribute to your family's growth?

FOLLOW-UP: After some time elapses, reassemble the family and evaluate your success in making the changes and fostering family growth. See if the family wants to select additional family style areas for implementation.

EPILOGUE

What the Family Can Mean in the Future

At midnight on December 31, 1999, bells will ring as we never heard them before; for Western peoples will be celebrating the beginning of a new millennium. Mankind has had a seemingly endless struggle against limitations imposed by his environment, his ignorance and his greed. Is it possible that the third millennium, A.D., will bring man's realization of his humanity?

Something very new and very big may be about to happen. Never before at any time in history has there existed a society in which great numbers of people have had an opportunity to develop all sides of themselves and become whole, unique individuals. The "civilized" norm has always been to try to force people into slots prepared for them by others and, especially, by their station in life. Their roles, their occupations, their styles of living have nearly always been predetermined, and in many cases have been in conflict with the individual's real nature. The people who were able to overcome these limitations, even partially, were a very privileged few. But, if Open Family Living takes hold and becomes the norm, such a privilege will be extended to far greater numbers. What will society be like when gentle and sensitive men are not pressured to engage in war; when aggressive, self-reliant people are not wounded in spirit by job obsolescence and unemployment; when children with original minds are not shoehorned into conventional molds of thought; and when women are not pushed into the roles hitherto considered as exclusively feminine?

It boggles the imagination to consider what could happen in the new millennium if the principles of Open Family Living have by then become widely understood and practiced. What would people and society be like?

I see *people* who would stand straighter, walk with more grace and assurance, feel more at home with themselves than do most people of today. I see them as friendlier, less stand-offish, communicating more easily with those they meet, having less hesitation in opening conversations with strangers, being generally more interesting and attractive. I see them having more spontaneity, being much more relaxed, enjoying life more, being less "touchy" and defensive. I see them showing greater individuality in their speech and manners, dressing with more variety, exhibiting more personal flair and style.

The young, in my vision of the future, have more of a feeling of being part of the world around them. They have been brought, to a large extent, into the decision-making processes in their families and schools; they have less of the sense of being unwelcome intruders in a world designed to benefit adults. They show more self-respect in their bearing and their personal appearance.

There is less feeling among all age groups of being helpless pawns in a game played by others. Many have the attitude that their lives matter, that what they think and do has an effect on society. They are interested in what is going on around them, feel closer to nature than did their forebears, and are concerned with the preservation of a liveable world.

Marriage has changed. It has grown in status and honor. The marital condition had been held in declining esteem during its closed and directionless phases, and many people had fled from it. It is now recognized as a step toward a high-quality, enduring human relationship for which there is widespread longing; yet it is also acknowledged that this is not usually achieved without training and practice. People who have not yet developed skills in human interaction are not encouraged to embark on long-term marriages. There are, for them, shorter, limited-term relationships to help prepare them to affirm the deeper commitment required for a truly successful marriage.

The task of bearing, nurturing and educating children is looked at in an entirely different way than it had been in the closed-style era. In the older style, the emphasis was on the right of the *parents* to raise children as they saw fit. But in the open style, the right of the *child* to be loved, accepted for what he is, given a stable and secure environment, recognized as a unique person, and encouraged to develop his human potential is as fully acknowledged and protected as is the right of the parents to help shape his future. Parents have now come to realize that it is not enough simply to "want" a child, to "look forward to having an heir." Bringing children into the world is serious business, and those couples that are not yet prepared to develop a high quality, long-term relationship do not, in most cases, have children. Consequently, the proportion of children raised in an unfavorable family environment is greatly reduced.

The attitude of many married people toward their relationship and their interaction in the marriage is that of an artist toward his art. Good relationship, like good art, needs training, dedication and practice. The romantic illusion that "love is all" and that lovers can find lifelong happiness in a "vine-covered cottage" simply because they are lovers has been quietly buried. Couples look forward to a rewarding, fulfilling life together, but they do not expect that it will come about automatically without thought, planning or effort.

Many of the old role expectations around which so much marital conflict once revolved have passed away with the change in the times. If the husband supports his wife and she stays home to raise a family, it is because *both* prefer it this way at this particular time, not because either of them, or social custom, has imposed these roles. In a different family the roles might be reversed. Or both partners might choose to work. Or they might carry on a family business together. Or at one point in the marriage, such as when they have small children, the husband might work, whereas at some other time the wife might work. Or the husband might prefer caring for and nurturing the small children at home, changing the baby's diapers and preparing the "formula," while the wife works. Or he might like this plan for a while, and she might want to take over later. Or neither might like it, and they will hire someone to do it. Or they might live in a commune and share the child-care with other members. Or the couple might have other adults living with them in their home who would help out. All these, and others, will be recognized, socially acceptable arrangements; and the marriage of the future will allow a couple to negotiate the arrangement most suitable to its own needs.

Marriage has ceased to be a battleground of the war of the sexes. On the contrary, it allows the contrasting natures of men and women full scope of expression. Men and women need each other for wholeness. The confrontation of their differences helps each to know who he is. The partners sometimes fight in the sense that each may feel a need to protect his own individuality, autonomy and integrity from invasion by the other, and such fighting may even be angry and intense for a short time. But it is the fight of lovers, and when it is over the combatants feel closer than before.

The day-to-day marital state is generally relaxed, companionable, affectionate and often joyous. People no longer say, as they did in the closed and directionless era, "Who would want to get married? I've never seen a happy marriage yet." Young people of the new millennium do see happy marriages, and they desire the same for themselves.

When trouble develops in the marriage, the couple of the future promptly tries to deal with it according to the guidelines of the open style; and if the partners cannot do this successfully, they seek help. There are a number of helps available: marriage clinics, sex clinics, marital enrichment seminars, training courses in Open Family Living, weekend marathons for couples or individuals, encounter groups, consciousness-raising groups, group therapy, and a variety of forms of individual, marital and family therapy. (These all exist at present, but in the future will be more widely available and better known.) And the partners do not necessarily wait until they are in trouble to draw upon these resources. Many couples use counseling or group assistance as regularly as they visit their doctor or dentist. An annual marriage and family checkup is considered an important part of an ongoing family mental health program.

If all help fails and the husband and wife find themselves growing apart and increasingly unable to make their relationship meaningful and rewarding, they may decide on separation or divorce. Legal divorce has, in this future time, ceased to be an adversary proceeding unless contested by one of the partners. As marriage was undertaken voluntarily, it can be ended voluntarily.

I visualize *family life* in the new millennium as (at its best) evolving into something very different from the crumbling, disordered, confused family life of our present era. The directionless phase has been largely worked through for many couples. Home has once again become "home" in the meaning that the term conveyed in poetry and song: an oasis of love, warmth and solace—the place where a human being belongs. Expressions that have come down from the past—"homelike," "no place like home," "home, sweet home," and "want to go home"—reflect the wistful loneliness, the longing of the wanderer far from home for what he has left behind.

But "home" may come to mean even more than it did in the sentimental memories of mankind's past. It may come to be a place, for many families, where people enlarge and enhance each other and help each other find fulfillment. I see it as the ongoing emotional center of many people's lives—the environment in which they can find the most rewarding and stimulating human relationships. Home is where people can grow.

Architects and home-furnishings designers have finally come to the family's aid and designed dwellings and furnishings that help to reduce the natural conflict between a child's way of life and an adult's. The newer houses and apartments are so arranged that adults and children can find mutual privacy when they need it, yet not be isolated from each other. Furnishings are such that small children cannot easily damage them; and all delicate objects, such as fragile glassware, are placed out of little children's reach.

The "generation gap" has largely vanished in open-style families. This does not mean that there is no friction or argument or that young people do not have private lives from which their parents are, to some degree, excluded. Such separations are a part of the healthy growing-up process in which a young person is freeing himself from being tied to his parents. But the old "generation gap" in the sense of a nearly total breakdown in communication, a wall of resentment and judgmental disapproval, is gone. The family, whatever strains may temporarily develop between parents and young people, is still a family, and the basic ties of loyalty, respect and affection survive. The generations continue to communicate.

The family has found ways of integrating the breadwinners' work outside the home with the family life inside it; and far-sighted employers are co-operating in this process. Instead of a total separation of work from the home, as had prevailed since most money-earning work was removed from the home, there is now a planned interaction between the two. Care is taken to see that the children know what kind of work their parents do, have visited the plant or the office, have met the parents' bosses and co-workers, have heard their parents discuss their work problems, happenings, disappointments and plans, and have shared in the parent's emotional reactions to their work. The children, too, are included in any consideration of proposals such as a job change or transfer which may directly affect the children's lives.

As the products of the open-style family have moved more and more into the fields of education, industry, trade, politics and the arts, the climate of all these activities is changed.

When I look, for example, at *education* as I see it evolving in the future, here is what I see:

Schools have ceased to be mass-production organizations, like big factories, with overworked teachers struggling to handle classes far too big for personal attention to individual pupils. Taxpayers have at last acknowledged the need for higher-quality education and have become willing to support a much lower pupil-teacher ratio than now prevails. They have been convinced of this necessity by the frightful toll of crime, illiteracy and unemployability allowed to come into existence by widespread past failures of family life and education.

The repressive, regimented atmosphere of the mass-production school has vanished. Teachers and pupils have an affectionate, informal and trusting relationship. Teachers are given freedom to shape the education process to a particular child's need. The children's feelings are respected; they are not ordered about arbitrarily to suit the convenience of teachers and administrators.

Discipline is handled, wherever possible, by trying to establish communication with the child, to find out what is on his mind and how he feels. If this is not successful, recalcitrant students may sometimes be transferred to special classes in which they can get even more intensive individual attention or, if necessary, individual tutoring or counseling. Discipline has been separated from punishment.

There is better balance between the intellectual and emotional elements in the educational process. Students may get specific training in handling their emotions through methods derived from experience with encounter groups, marathons and other processes of group dynamics. Because of better emotional balance, intellectual learning proceeds much faster, and the time lost to subject matter teaching as a result of these innovations is more than made up.

The schools and the family are more closely connected than in our time, with adult family members continuing their educations throughout their lives. There is, in particular, a great expansion in education of the elderly to help give their lives meaning after retirement from active work and from child raising. School buildings and other facilities, too, are made available for community recreational and cultural purposes when not in use for their primary educational function.

In this future time, human values have come to be more fully recognized in the *industrial-commercial world*, partly as a consequence of the movement into these fields of persons nurtured in the open family style, but also because of increasingly clear evidence of damage to the entire social fabric when family life collapses. Deterioration in the cities and suburbs alike, the enormous costs of crime, corruption and environmental damage, the growing hordes of unemployables, and the costs of excessive absenteeism, poor workmanship and low morale, have convinced even the most profit-minded that corporate business must do more to make qualitative family life possible.

Stockholders are taking a broader view of a corporation's function, realizing that the quality of family life, not only of empoyees but also of customers and of the general public, has effects throughout the community that directly affect profits. Business managers are somewhat less subject to pressures for quick profits at the expense of long-term stability. They can take more realistic account of the threats of resource exhaustion, ecology damage and pollution. Managers, too, are willing to take the time to visit with family members of employees in pursuit of the family-work integration process that has come to be generally accepted.

As I look into the future, I see the importance of family life recognized, world-wide, at the highest *levels of government*. I see a Secretary of the Family, with cabinet rank, co-ordinating those governmental functions at state and federal levels which have a bearing on family life, such as housing, child care, nutrition, social welfare, birth control, marriage and divorce laws, consumer affairs, the conditions of migrant workers, and many other areas having to do with the family. It has finally been recognized that the quality of family life determines the quality of every other human activity and that providing legal, administrative and financial help toward the improvement of family life is as important a governmental function as is, say, defense.

Parallel with the concern for family life at the highest levels of government is a growth of private, *non-government organizations* supporting family life. Families have organized themselves into family unions, analogous to labor unions, to provide a center for information, research and other assistance and to win for themselves a greater voice in government policy. (Note: Such unions already exist in a number of European countries, and these have now been brought together, in association with governmental and other non-governmental bodies concerned with the family, into an international organization: the International Union of Family Organizations.)

I see in the future a "World Family Organization," perhaps functioning as an agency of the United Nations, providing the interchange of information, research and resources relating to the family. I see this organization becoming necessary because the need for revitalization of family life is felt in all countries.

As people from open-style families rise to *high posts in government* in many countries, the climate of governing and lawmaking processes begins to change. These leaders are better able to work with people very different from themselves than were their predecessors. Their listening and communicative abilities are more highly developed. They can, for example, listen to a wide range of views, including those of partisan opponents, and yet respect those opponents and have no desire to destroy them as human beings. By considering a broad spectrum of opinions, they are less likely to make serious miscalculations or errors. They can be close to people, avoid the mistake of secreting themselves behind closed doors, judge the people's moods and needs more accurately. They are less partisan, less rigid in their opinions, better balanced in their approach to issues.

The open-style leader has another great advantage over the closed-style one: He can often work constructively with people with whom he is politically at odds. He can, for example, find the right spot for an able opponent where the person's abilities can be used constructively. He can do this because he can respect an individual without agreeing with him.

The leader who comes from the open-style family is likely to lead rather than maneuver, to look into the future instead of being at the mercy of short-term considerations, to consider the larger good rather than the good of a few. When asked to favor a special interest, he inquires, "How does this square with the aim of building a better country and a better world?"

The open-style family is, in my view, the best long-term hope for world peace. The world today hangs on the brink of nuclear war, given temporary respite by a balance of terror. Who thinks the world can, for all time to come, remain precariously balanced in this way? And who now thinks that civilization could survive a nuclear war between superpowers?

From families, somewhere, must come the future leaders who can soften the rivalries, extend a hand to former enemies, base policies on realistic appraisals of possibilities instead of on unrealistic, jingoist dreams, and build a basis for international co-operation and trust. The closed family styles tend to perpetuate old hostilities, heat up ancient hatreds, condemn as "traitorous" all attempts to understand or to appreciate the enemy's position. War is the most likely outcome of such attitudes.

The leader who rises above these limitations comes to realize that no single nation or party can claim total right on its side; and he seeks to find what appropriate arrangements are possible so that the former enemies can live side by side and contribute to each other's well-being instead of tearing each other apart. He keeps his eye, too, on larger considerations such as the effect of his policies on peoples in other parts of the world, on the world's resources, on the ecology of the oceans, rivers, and marshes, and similar matters. He learns to be, to a considerable extent, planet-minded.

At the family level itself, there is a great increase in personal associations between individual *families in different countries*. Families throughout the world exchange family members so that many people can get the experience of living in different cultures. Through these and other means, people of varying races and nationalities come to understand each other better, appreciate each other's problems and become emotionally involved with each other.

Religious leaders, too, are more humble, less doctrinaire, less insistent that only their conception of theology is the true one, more willing to allow a variety of views, more willing to listen to other interpretations.

When the open style has taken hold, I see an explosion in all the *arts*. I see, too, a shift in the climate of artistic and literary expression.

Literature and the other arts today give the impression of being the products of frustrated people who take a dim view of man and all his works. Many of these expressions portray human beings as weak, indulgent, self-destructive, corrupt, lustful and decadent. Writers and other artists in both communist and capitalist societies have often tended to express anti-Establishment attitudes because of their antipathy to the dehumanizing forces in modern life.

But I visualize that as the open family style humanizes child care and produces people whose emotional needs are better fulfilled, the artists and writers nurtured by these families will have a greater affection for man and for the society he has built. Their works, then, instead of reflecting disgust and despair, will begin to express a conception of the human being as capable of growing and assuming responsibility for his own destiny. In place of contempt will come faith. The artist and writer then may help mankind to discover his humanness.

Literature and the arts may once again portray heroism, but from their work will emerge a different kind of hero. The ancient hero was a great warrior—Siegfried, King Arthur, Theseus. But the new one may be a gentler hero (or heroine), a wiser, more tender, more compassionate one who embodies what humanity means and what mankind may ultimately achieve.

The world is obviously a very long way from the dream I have described, and it is, in some respects, moving away from it, not toward it. We live in a confused era—a time of uncertain values, collapsing hopes and threatened disaster. Yet in all this turmoil I believe that fruitful seeds are being planted.

A vision cannot become a reality all by itself; it is manifested through people's efforts. Yet without the vision, people's efforts may be futile.

Working out the vision is your job and mine. In this book I have tried to set forth the guidelines as I see them. I now pass the baton to you. Your personal growth and development constitute the first heat of the race. From this grows the quality of your human relationships in marriage and outside. Finally comes the quality of your family life.

Put all this together, and the outlines of the vision begin to emerge like a panoramic scene coming into clear view beneath a rising fog. Won't you join in this adventure toward openness?

RECOMMENDED READINGS

Chapter 1

Bernard, Jessie. *The Future of Marriage*. Cleveland, Ohio: World Publishers, 1972.

Cooper, David. *The Death of the Family*. New York: Pantheon Books, 1970.

Cottrell, Fred. *Technology, Man and Progress*. New York: Charles E. Merrill, 1972.

Cox, Frank. *American Marriage: A Changing Scene?* Dubuque, Iowa: William C. Brown, 1971.

Cudlipp, Edythe. *Understanding Women's Liberation*. Chicago: Paperback Library Division of Coronet Communications, 1971.

DeMott, Benjamin. *Surviving the 70's*. Baltimore, Md.: Penguin Books, 1972.

Dentler, Robert A. *Major Social Problems*, 2nd Ed. Chicago: Rand McNally, 1972.

Etzioni, Amitai. *Social Profile: U.S.A. Today*. New York: Van Nostrand-Reinhold, 1972.

Farrell, Warren. *The Liberated Man*. New York: Random House, 1975.

Feldman, Saul D., and Thielbar, Gerald W. *Life Styles: Diversity in American Society*. Boston: Little, Brown & Co., 1972.

Gabor, Dennis. *The Mature Society*. New York: Praeger Publishers, 1972.

Goode, William J. (ed.). *The Contemporary American Family*. Chicago: Quadrangle Books, 1971.

————*World Revolution and Family Patterns*. Riverside, N.J.: Free Press, 1963.

Gordon, Michael (ed.). *The Nuclear Family in Crisis: The Search for an Alternative*. New York: Harper & Row, 1972.

Hunt, Morton. "Is Marriage in Trouble?" *Family Circle*, January 1971.

Kahn, Herman, and Bruce-Briggs, B. *Things to Come: Thinking About the 70's and 80's*. New York: Macmillan, 1972.

Kanter, Rosabeth Moss. "Communes," *Psychology Today*. July 1970.

Levey, John, and Munroe, Ruth. *The Happy Family*. New York: Alfred A. Knopf, 1962.

McGinnis, Thomas C., and Finnegan, Dana G. *Open Family and Marriage: A Guide to Personal Growth*. St. Louis: C. V. Mosby Co., 1976.

Mead, Margaret. "The Future of the Family." *Barnard Alumnae Magazine*, Winter 1971.

Otto, Herbert A. (ed.). *The Family in Search of a Future*. New York: Appleton-Century-Crofts, 1970.

Queen, Stuart A., Habenstein, Robert W., and Adams, John B. *The Family in Various Cultures*. Philadelphia: J. B. Lippincott, 1961.

Reiss, Ira. L. (ed.). *Readings on the Family System*. New York: Holt, Rinehart & Winston, 1972.

Rimmer, Robert H. *Proposition 31*. New York: New American Library, 1968.

———(ed.). *You and I Searching for Tomorrow*. New York: New American Library, 1971.

Sussman, Marvin B. (ed.). "Variant Marriage Styles and Family Forms," *Family Coordinator*, Vol. 21:4, October, 1972.

Toffler, Alvin. *Future Shock*. New York: Bantam Books, 1970.

Wortis, Helen, and Rabinowitz, Clara (eds.). *The Women's Movement*. New York: John Wiley & Sons, 1972.

Chapter 2

Belgum, David. *Alone, Alone, All Alone*. St. Louis, Mo.: Conordia Publishing House, 1972.

Di Salvo, Charles, with Cox, Claire. *Faces People Wear: Today's Identity Crisis and How to Cope With It*. New York: Hawthorne Books, 1968.

Fuller, R. Buckminster. *Utopia or Oblivion: The Prospects for Humanity*. New York: Bantam Books, 1969.

Hoopes, Ned E. (ed.). *Who Am I? Essays on the Alienated*. New York: Dell Publishing, 1969.

Laing, R. D. *The Divided Self*. Baltimore, Md.: Penguin Books, 1965.

McGinnis, Thomas C. "Sensitivity Training in a Partly Dehumanized Environment," *Marriage Guidance*. London, England: December 1970.

Pearce, Jane, and Newton, Saul. *The Conditions of Human Growth*. New York: Citadel Press, 1969.

Chapter 3

Berne, Eric. *Games People Play: The Psychology of Human Relationships*. New York: Grove Press, 1964.

——— *Transactional Analysis in Psychotherapy*. New York: Grove Press, 1964.

——— *What Do You Say After You Say Hello? The Psychology of Human Destiny*. New York: Grove Press, 1972.

Erickson, Erik H. *Childhood and Society*, 2nd Ed. New York: W. W. Norton, 1963.

Fane, Arthur, and Fane, Xenia. *Behind Every Face: A Family*. Waltham, Massachusetts: Ginn and Company, 1970.

Freud, Sigmund. *An Outline of Psychoanalysis*, tr. James Strachey. New York: W. W. Norton, 1949.

Harris, Thomas A. *I'm OK—You're OK: A Practical Guide to Transactional Analysis*. New York: Harper & Row, 1967.

James, Muriel, and Jongeward, Dorothy. *Born to Win: Transactional Analysis with Gestalt Experiments*. Reading, Mass.: Addison-Wesley, 1971.

Jersild, Arthur T. *In Search of Self*. New York: Teachers College, Columbia University, 1952.

Jourard, Sidney M. *Disclosing Man to Himself*. New York: Van Nostrand, 1968.

———— *The Transparent Self*. New York: Van Nostrand, 1964.

Malamud, Daniel I., and Machover, Solomon. *Toward Self-Understanding: Group Techniques in Self-Confrontation*. Springfield, Ill.: Charles C. Thomas, 1965.

Missildine, W. Hugh. *Your Inner Child of the Past*. New York: Simon and Schuster, 1963.

Montague, Ashley. *The Humanization of Man*. New York: Grove Press, 1962.

Mullahy, Patrick. *Psychoanalysis and Interpersonal Psychiatry: The Contributions of Harry Stack Sullivan*. New York: Science House, 1970.

Newman, Bernard Berkowitz, and Owen, Jean. *How to Be Your Own Best Friend*. New York: Lark Publications, 1971.

Perry, Helen Swick, and Garvel, Mary Ladd (eds.). *The Collected Works of Harry Stack Sullivan, M.D.*, New York: W. W. Norton, 1953, (2 Vols.).

Powell, John. *Why Am I Afraid to Tell You Who I Am?* Chicago: Argus Communications, 1969.

Rogers, Carl R. *On Becoming a Person*. Boston: Houghton-Mifflin, 1963.

Wees, W. B. *Nobody Can Teach Anybody Anything*. Garden City, N.Y.: Doubleday, 1971.

Chapter 4

Allen, Gina, and Martin, Clement G. *Intimacy: Sensitivity, Sex, and the Art of Love*. New York: Pocket Books, 1972.

Buscaglia, Leo. *Love*. Thorofare, N.J.: Charles B. Slack, 1972.

Casler, Lawrence *Is Marriage Necessary?* New York: Behavioral Publications, 1974.

Chartham, R. *The Sensuous Couple*. New York: Ballantine, 1971.

Clinebell, Howard J., and Clinebell, Charlotte H. *The Intimate Marriage*. New York: Harper & Row, 1970.

Constantine, Larry L., and Constantine, Joan M. *Group Marriage*. New York: Macmillan, 1973.

Davids, Leo. "North American Marriage: 1990." *The Futurist,* (Vol. 5), October 1971.

DeLora, JoAnn S., and DeLora, Jack R. (eds.). *Intimate Life Styles: Marriage and Its Alternatives*. Pacific Palisades, Cal.: Goodyear Publishing, 1972.

Drakeford, John W. *Games Husbands and Wives Play*. Nashville, Tenn.: Broadman Press, 1970.

Duberman, Lucile. *Marriage and Its Alternatives*. New York: Praeger Publishers, 1974.

Ellis, Albert, and Harper, Robert A. *Creative Marriage*. New York: Lyle Stuart, 1961.

Fisher, Esther O. *Help for Today's Troubled Marriages*. New York: Hawthorne Books, 1968.

Fromm, Alan. *The Ability to Love*. New York: Ferrar, Strauss and Giroux, 1963.

Fromm, Erich. *The Art of Loving*. Chicago: Harper & Row, 1956.

Garrity, Joan Terry (Under the pseudonym of "J"). *The Sensuous Woman*. New York: Lyle Stuart, 1969.

Garrity, John, and Garrity, Joan Terry (Under the pseudonym of "M"). *The Sensuous Man*. Lyle Stuart, 1971.

Hamilton, Eleanor. *Partners in Love*. New York: A. S. Barnes, 1968.

Hart, Harold (ed.). *Marriage: For and Against*. New York: Hart Publishing, 1972.

Hunt, Morton. *Sexual Behavior in the 1970s*. Chicago: Playboy Press, 1974.

Kaplan, Helen Singer. *The New Sex Therapy: Active Treatment of Sexual Dysfunctions*. New York: Brunner/Mazel, 1974.

Katchadourian, Herant A., and Lunde, Donald L. *Fundamentals of Human Sexuality*. New York: Holt, Rinehart & Winston, 1972.

Lederer, William, and Jackson, Don D. *The Mirages of Marriage*. New York: W. W. Norton, 1968.

Lee, Robert, and Casebier, Marjorie. *The Spouse Gap*. Nashville, Tenn.: Abingdon Press, 1971.

Masters, William H., and Johnson, Virginia E. *The Human Sexual Response*. Boston: Little, Brown, 1966.

May, Rollo. *Love and Will*. New York: W. W. Norton & Co., 1969.

Mazur, Ronald. *The New Intimacy: Open-ended Marriage and Alternate Lifestyles*. Boston: Beacon Press, 1973.

McGinnis, Thomas C. *Your First Year of Marriage*. Garden City, N.Y.: Doubleday, 1967.

Montague, Ashley. *Touching: The Human Significance of the Skin*. Irvington, N.Y.: Columbia University Press, 1971.

Moustakas, Clark E. *Loneliness and Love*. Englewood Cliffs, N.J.: Prentice-Hall, 1972.

O'Neill, Nena, and O'Neill, George. *Open Marriage: A New Life Style for Couples*. New York: M. Evans and Company, 1972.

Perutz, Katrin. *Marriage Is Hell*. New York: William Morrow, 1972.

Peterson, James A. *Married Love in the Middle Years*. New York: Association Press, 1968.

Reuben, David. *Everything You Always Wanted to Know About Sex** But Were Afraid to Ask*. New York: David McKay, 1969.

Rogers, Carl. *Becoming Partners: Marriage and Its Alternatives*. New York: Delacorte, 1972.

Rosner, Stanley, and Hobe, Laura. *The Marriage Gap*. New York: David McKay, 1974.

Roszak, Theodore, and Roszak, Betty (eds.). *Masculine/Feminine*. New York: Harper & Row, 1969.

Shedd, Charlie W. *Letters to Karen: On Keeping Love in Marriage*. Nashville, Tenn.: Abingdon Press, 1965.

—— *Letters to Phillip: On How to Treat a Woman*. Garden City, N.Y.: Doubleday, 1968.

Snow, John H. *On Pilgrimage: Marriage in the 70's*. New York: Seabury Press, 1971.

St. André, Lucien. *The American Matriarchy: A Study of Married Life in 1997 A.D.* Madison, N.J.: Florham Park Press, 1970.

Chapter 5

Ackerman, Nathan W. *The Psychodynamics of Family Life*. New York: Basic Books, 1958.

Andrews, Matthew. *The Parents Guide to Drugs*. Garden City, N.Y.: Doubleday, 1972.

Bricklin, Barry, and Bricklin, Patricia M. *Strong Family, Strong Child*. New York: Delacorte Press, 1970.

Briggs, Dorothy Corkille. *Your Child's Self-Esteem*. Garden City, N.Y.: Doubleday, 1970.

Earisman, Del. *How Now Is the Now Generation*. Philadelphia: Fortress Press, 1971.

Fletcher, Grace Nies. *What's Right With Us Parents?* New York: William Morrow, 1972.

Gelinas, Robert, and Gelinas, Paul. *The Teenager in a Troubled World*. New York: Richard Rosen Press, 1973.

Ginott, Haim G. *Between Parent and Teenager*. New York: Macmillan, 1969.

Kirkendall, Lester A., and Whitehurst, Robert N. (eds.). *The New Sexual Revolution*. New York: Donald W. Brown, Inc., 1971.

Laing, R. D. *The Politics of the Family*. New York: Pantheon Books, 1971.

Le Shan, Eda J. *How to Survive Parenthood*. New York: Random House, 1965.

McGinnis, Thomas C. *A Girl's Guide to Dating and Going Steady*. Garden City, N. Y.: Doubleday, 1968.

Niemi, Richard G. *How Family Members Perceive Each Other*. New Haven, Conn.: Yale University Press, 1973.

Office of Child Development. *Teenagers Discuss the "Generation Gap."* U. S. Government Printing Office, 1970.

Rimmer, Robert H. *The Harrod Experiment*. New York: Bantam Books, 1966.

Roszak, Theodore. *The Making of a Counter Culture*. Garden City, N.Y.: Doubleday, 1968.

Salk, Lee. *What Every Child Would Like His Parents to Know (To Help Him With the Emotional Problems of His Everyday Life)*. New York: David McKay, 1972.

Stevens, Anita, and Freeman, Lucy. *I Hate My Parents*. New York: Tower Publications, 1970.

Woodward, Kenneth L. "The Parent Gap," *Psychology Today*. September 22, 1975.

Chapter 6

Becker, Russell J. *When Marriage Ends.* Philadelphia: Fortress Press, 1971.

Bird, Lois. *How to Be a Happily Married Mistress.* Garden City, N.Y.: Doubleday, 1971.

Bohannan, Paul (ed.). *Divorce and After.* Garden City, N.Y.: Doubleday, 1971.

Bredmeier, Harry C., and Jackson, Toby. *Social Problems in America.* New York: Wiley, 1972.

Donelson, Kenneth, and Donelson, Irene. *Married Today, Single Tomorrow: Marriage Break-up and the Law.* Garden City, N.Y.: Doubleday, 1969.

Engleson, Jim, and Engleson, Janet. *Parents Without Partners.* New York: E. P. Dutton, 1961.

Fisher, Esther. *Divorce—The New Freedom.* New York: Harper & Row, 1974.

Fletcher, Joseph. *Situation Ethics, the New Morality.* Philadelphia: Westminster Press, 1966.

——— *Moral Responsibility: Situation Ethics at Work.* Philadelphia: Westminster Press, 1967.

Glasser, Paul H., and Glasser Lois N. (eds.). *Families in Crisis.* New York: Harper & Row, 1970.

Grollman, Earl A. (ed.). *Concerning Death: A Practical Guide for the Living.* Boston: Beacon Press, 1974.

Hamilton, Eleanor. *Sex Before Marriage.* New York: Bantam Books, 1970.

Hill, Ruben, and Hansen, Donald A. "Families in Disaster," in Christensen, Harold (ed.). *Handbook of Marriage and the Family.* Chicago: Rand McNally, 1964.

Hunt, Morton. *The Affair: A Portrait of Extramarital Love in Contemporary America.* Cleveland, Ohio: World Publishing 1970.

——— *World of the Formerly Married.* New York: McGraw-Hill, 1966.

Jackson, Edgar N. *When Someone Dies.* Philadelphia: Fortress Press, 1971.

Krantzler, Mel. *Creative Divorce: A New Opportunity for Person Growth.* New York: M. Evans and Co., 1973.

Langsley, Donald G., Kaplan, David M., et. al. *The Treatment of Families in Crises.* New York: Grune and Stratton, 1968.

Le Shan, Eda J. *Mates and Roommates: New Styles in Young Marriages.* Public Affairs Pamphlet No. 468, 1971.

——— *Sex and Your Teenager: A Guide for Parents.* New York: David McKay, 1969.

Lindsey, Judge Ben B., and Wainwright, Evans. *The Companionate Marriage.* Garden City, New York: Garden City Publishing Co., 1929.

Macklin, Eleanor D. "Going Very Steady," *Psychology Today.* November 1974.

Maddox, George L. *The Domesticated Drug: Drinking Among Collegians.* New Haven, Conn.: College and University Press, 1970.

McGinnis, Thomas C. "Sex Education and the Battleground of Controversy," in Silverman, Hirsch L. (ed.). *Marital Therapy.* Springfield, Ill.: Charles C. Thomas, 1972.

————, and Roesch, Roberta. "Marital Chaos in the Middle Years," *Weight Watchers Magazine,* to be published.

Mead, Margaret. "Marriage in Two Steps," *Redbook Magazine.* McCall Corporation, July 1966.

Morris, Sarah. *Grief and How to Live With It.* New York: Grosset & Dunlap, 1972.

Nelson, Jack L. *Teenagers and Sex.* Englewood Cliffs, N.J.: Prentice-Hall, 1970.

Neubeck, Gerhard (ed.). *Extramarital Relations.* Englewood Cliffs, N.J.: Prentice-Hall, 1969.

Neuhaus, Robert, and Neuhaus, Ruby. *Family Crises.* Columbus, Ohio: Charles E. Merrill, 1974.

Ogg, Elizabeth. *When a Family Faces Stress.* Public Affairs Pamphlet No. 341, 1963.

Pavenstedt, Eleanor, and Bernard, Viola W. (ed.). *Crises of Family Disorganization.* New York: Behavioral Publications, 1971.

Ray, Oakley S. *Drugs, Society, and Human Behavior.* St. Louis, Mo.: C. V. Mosby, 1972.

Scott, E. M. *Struggles in an Alcoholic Family.* New York: Charles C. Thomas, 1970.

Spotnitz, Hyman and Freeman, Lucy. *The Wandering Husband.* Englewood Cliffs, N. J.: Prentice-Hall, 1964.

Young, Leontine. *The Fractured Family.* New York: McGraw-Hill, 1973.

Chapter 7

Albrecht, Margaret. *Parents and Teen-agers Getting Through to Each Other.* New York: Parents' Magazine Press, 1972.

Bevcar, Raphael J. *Skills for Effective Communication: A Guide to Building Relationships.* New York: John Wiley & Sons, 1974.

Birdwhistle, Ray L. *Kinesics and Content.* Philadelphia: University of Pennsylvania Press, 1970.

Davitz, R. J. *The Communication of Emotional Meaning.* New York: McGraw-Hill, 1964.

Fast, Julius. *Body Language.* Philadelphia: M. Evans and Co., 1970.

Genne, Elizabeth Steel, and Genne, William H. *First of All Persons: A New Look at Men/Women Relationships.* New York: Friendship Press, 1973.

Ginott, Haim G. *Between Parent and Child.* New York: Macmillan, 1965.

Gordon, Thomas. *Parent Effectiveness Training.* New York: Peter H. Wyden, 1970.

Jackson, Don D. *Communication, Family and Marriage, Human Communication,* (Vol. 1), Palo Alto, Calif.: Science and Behavior Books, 1968.

Lehman, Edna. *Talking to Children About Sex.* New York: Harper & Row, 1970.

Nierenberg, Gerald I., and Calero, Henry H. *How to Read a Person Like a Book.* New York: Pocket Book, 1973.

Nirenberg, Jessie. *Getting Through to People.* Englewood Cliffs, N.J.: Prentice-Hall, 1963.

Rosenthal, Robert, and others. "The Language Without Words," *Psychology Today*. September 1974.

Ruesch, Jurgen. *Therapeutic Communication*. New York: W. W. Norton, 1961.

Satir, Virginia. *Peoplemaking*. Palo Alto, Calif.: Science and Behavior Books, 1972.

Smith, Alfred G., ed. *Communication and Culture*. New York: Holt, Rinehart & Winston, 1966.

Smith, Gerald W. *Me and You and Us*. New York: Peter Wyden, 1971.

Chapter 8

Bach, George R., and Goldberg, Herb. *Creative Aggression*. Garden City, N.Y.: Doubleday, 1974.

Bach, George R., and Wyden, Peter. *The Intimate Enemy: How to Fight Fair in Love and Marriage*. New York: William Morrow, 1969.

Back, Kurt W. *Beyond Words: The Story of Sensitivity Training and the Encounter Movement*. New York: Russell Sage Foundation, 1972.

Brightbill, Charles K. *The Challenge of Leisure*. New York: Prentice-Hall, 1960.

Cheavens, Frank. *Creative Parenting: Advantages You Can Give Your Child*. Waco, Tex.: Word Books, 1971.

Chess, Stella. *Your Child Is a Person*. New York: Viking Press, 1965.

Clinebell, Charlotte Holt. *Meet Me in the Middle: On Becoming Human Together*. New York: Harper & Row, 1973.

Davis, Gary, and Scott, Joseph. *Training Creative Thinking*. New York: Holt, Rinehart & Winston, 1970.

Feldman, Fred. *Discover the Real You*. Philadelphia: Dorrance, 1974.

Gustaitis, Rasa. *Turning on Without Drugs*. New York: Macmillan, 1969.

Hein, Lucille E. *Enjoy Your Children*. Nashville, Tenn.: Abingdon Press, 1959.

Lair, Jess. *I Ain't Much, Baby—But I'm All I've Got*. Garden City, N.Y.: Doubleday, 1972.

Lewis, Howard R., and Streitfeld, Harold S. *Growth Games: How to Tune in Yourself, Your Family, Your Friends*. New York: Harcourt, Brace, Jovanovich, 1970.

Mace, David, and Mace, Vera. *We Can Have Better Marriages*. Nashville, Tenn.: Abingdon Press, 1974.

Maslow, Abraham H. *Religion, Values and Peak Experiences*. New York: Viking Press, 1970.

Mooney, Ross Lawler, and Razik, Taher A. (eds.). *Explorations in Creativity*. Chicago: Harper, 1967.

Rogers, Carl R. "The Group Comes of Age," *Psychology Today*. December 1969.

Torrence, Ellis P. *Guiding Creative Talent*. Englewood Cliffs, N.J.: Prentice-Hall, 1962.

Chapter 9

Bosco, Antoinette. *Marriage Encounters: The Recovery of Love.* St. Meinrad, Ind.: Abbey Press, 1972.

Bugental, James F. T. (ed.). *Challenges of Humanistic Psychology.* New York: McGraw-Hill, 1967.

Clinebell, Howard, Jr. *The People Dynamic: Changing Self and Society Through Growth Groups.* New York: Harper & Row, 1972.

Farrell, Warren. *The Liberated Man.* New York: Random House, 1975.

Gillies, Jerry. *My Needs, Your Needs, Our Needs.* Garden City, N.Y.: Doubleday, 1974.

Graves, Henry. "Levels of Existence: An Open System Theory of Values," *Journal of Humanistic Psychology,* Fall 1970 (Vol. 10).

Howard, Jane. *Please Touch: A Guided Tour of the Human Potential Movement.* New York: McGraw-Hill, 1970.

Levy, Ronald. *Self-revelation Through Relations.* Englewood Cliffs, N.J.: Prentice-Hall, 1972.

Lewis, Howard R., and Streitfeld, Harold S. (See Chapter 8, Recommended Readings).

McGinnis, Thomas C., and Finnegan, Dana G. *Open Family and Marriage: A Guide to Personal Growth.* St. Louis: C. V. Mosby Co., 1976.

O'Neill, Nena, and O'Neill, George. *Shifting Gears: Finding Security in a Changing World.* New York: M. Evans & Co., 1974.

Perls, Frederick S. *Gestalt Therapy Verbatim.* New York: Bantam Books, 1969.

Schiller, Patricia. *Creative Approach to Sex Education and Counseling.* New York: Association Press, 1973.

Schutz, William C. *Here Comes Everybody.* Chicago: Harper, 1971.

——— *Joy: Expanding Human Awareness.* New York: Grove Press, 1967.

Solomon, Lawrence N., and Berzon, Betty (eds.). *New Perspectives on Encounter Groups.* San Francisco: Jossey-Bass, 1972.

Strang, Ruth. *Helping Your Child Develop His Potentialities.* New York: E. P. Dutton, 1965.

LISTING OF INTERACTION
EXPERIENCES ───────────────

INDEX

O.F.L.
$8.95

OPEN FAMILY LIVING

DR. THOMAS C. McGINNIS
and John U. Ayres

Is the family a thing of the past? Marriage an out-of-date ritual? No, says the author of this dynamic new guide to family living. Instead of giving up on the family, as many advocate, Dr. McGinnis wants to revitalize it, and in OPEN FAMILY LIVING he explains a new style of living for today which says to every family member: "*I* can be *me*. *You* can be *you*. Together *we* can be *us* in a balanced blend of living for my sake, your sake, our sake, and the sake of others."

OPEN FAMILY LIVING shows you how to make this new kind of family relationship work for you. It provides warm, wise, and practical advice on how to achieve greater openness individually, in a marriage and within a family. The concept of Open Family Living is to encourage and help each person develop his individual potential while, at the same time, contributing to the development of a more open and healthier relationship among fam-

(continued on back flap)